the prodigal son

VERONICA LANCET

before reading

This is the third book in the series. It is **NOT** a standalone.
Note: Rafaelo and Michele are the same age, with only a few months difference between the two of them. For that reason, when a chapter subtitle mentions the age, it is for both of them
This series is dark. It's **VERY** dark. And this book might be the DARKEST.
No one is a good guy.
Some characters may be **irredeemable**.
Please only read if you are comfortable with the following triggers. The books in the series will get progressively darker.

Trigger Warnings:
abuse, attempted rape, blood (gore), blood play, child death, CSA, descriptive rape, descriptive torture, descriptive abuse, death, derogatory terms, death, drugs, guns, graphic violence, graphic sexual situations, depictions of torture, gaslighting, grooming, homophobia, incestuous situations, murder, mental illness, substance abuse, mentions of suicide, mentions of AIDS.

in this series:

1. The Taste of Revenge
2. The Foiled Plan
3. The Prodigal Son
4. The Counterfeit Lover
5. The Sins of Noelle
6. The Moral Dilemma

one

AGE EIGHT

He watched the play of shadows on the wall, swinging his legs on the side of the bed and fidgeting with his hands. He was alone in his salon, everyone having gone home for the day.

He knew this wasn't the norm.

Other kids had their parents with them through the night, too. But that meant they had to care in the first place. Michele knew that his father and stepmother didn't really care for him.

It was only his governess that spent some time with him at the hospital, sometimes bringing his older sister, Gianna, to visit him.

Gianna was six years older than him, but that wasn't old enough to afford her any independence, though she anxiously wished for it. Certainly, she was older than her years, possessing a maturity and wisdom that made Michele look up to her in awe.

For as long as he could remember, she'd been his lifeline.

More of a mother than a sister, though he didn't really understand the concept of motherhood, she'd always looked out for him. While the adults in his life were ok with footing the bill at the hospital, doing the bare minimum to keep him alive, she was the only one who cared enough to cheer him up when he was at his lowest—and that happened more often than not.

Taking the oxygen mask off his face, he tried to inhale on his own, relief flooding him when he did so effortlessly.

It was easier to breathe now. The doctor had told him that the infection had cleared from his lungs and he had every chance of making a full recovery.

But that, too, was ephemeral. Like all the times he'd been given the green light to leave the hospital only to return the next week, or following month.

It was hard to keep up high spirits when his health was in perpetual decline. He didn't understand much about the medical terms the doctors used, but he understood enough to know he wasn't getting any better, and his chances at survival were minimal.

Cancer of the blood.

That's what the doctors had called it.

He'd heard the simplified version of the explanation, and he knew that his blood was defective. It wasn't doing the job it was meant to do. And the only cure for it was a transplant.

It was hard for him to grasp the concept of a transplant, but he'd prayed for one from the moment he'd heard about it.

His family, on the other hand, probably prayed it never came.

Michele might have been too young to understand the complex terminology thrown around by medics and hospital staff, but he was old enough to feel he wasn't wanted—had *never* been wanted.

From birth, his existence had been accursed. His mother had died soon after giving birth to him, and his father had wasted no time in blaming *him* for killing her.

His stepmom, too, had drilled that into his head from the start, so he wasn't under any misconception concerning his desirability.

He was sick. A monster.

That's what she liked to call him.

Because of his illness, he was less than others—certainly less than his brother, Rafaelo.

He supposed it could be true. After all, there must be something seriously wrong with him to be punished like this.

Yet no matter how much he asked himself *what*, he couldn't come up with an answer.

He was only eight. He'd never hurt anyone.

Maybe he'd fought with Rafaelo once or twice over a toy, but even that was rare considering his stepmother didn't want her son to associate with him.

Perhaps it was in his blood. It *was* poisoned, after all.

If his own body was trying to kill him, then maybe something *was* wrong with him after all.

Releasing a big sigh, he opened the drawer next to his bed, taking out a set of pencils and a small notepad.

At the worst of his infection, the drawing set had been taken away from him, the doctors telling him it could pose a danger to his health. He hadn't understood how, precisely, but if the doctor said so, he followed the instructions. Though he had few things to call his own and he loved them more than anything, he also valued his health.

He knew there were a lot of people who didn't care whether he lived or died—some might even wish he did. Call it foolish stubbornness, but the feeling of being unwelcome and unwanted made him even more determined to prove them wrong.

There might not be many things for which to live for, but it was enough for him. There was his sister Gianna, who loved him more than anyone, and on lucky days, there was also his brother Rafaelo.

The two of them would certainly miss him if he disappeared from this earth. And so, regardless of if his stepmom wished he didn't exist, he wasn't going to help her fulfill that particular wish.

Tracing the sharpness of the pencil against the smooth surface of his thumb, he pressed the tip deep into his skin, the pain a welcome reminder that he *was* alive.

Mayhap it was odd.

From a young age, he'd been in and out of hospitals, subjected to tests and trials that had given pain a new meaning to his body.

He'd been taken to the edge, and there had been moments when he thought he was going to cross that invisible boundary —sink into an abyss so full of pain, he'd never manage to get out again.

For all he'd been through, he didn't despise pain. He didn't have an aversion to it.

If anything, it made him feel alive. It let him know that his body was still functioning,

It hadn't let him down.

The room was bathed in darkness, and feeling his way around the wall, he hit a switch, a small light enveloping his tiny corner.

Shuffling through his notepad, the corners of his mouth tipped up as he glanced at a drawing of his sister.

He'd done that particular one before he'd been rushed to the hospital with liquid in his lungs. Even on the brink of suffocation, he hadn't uttered a word as he'd continued to sketch her.

It wasn't normal, but there was something about the art of drawing that enthralled him. Pencil in hand, eyes on paper, there was nothing else around him but the scratchy sound of carbon staining the whiteness of the sheet. It tugged at his senses and wrapped him in a type of happiness he'd never encountered before.

Lines laid down on paper, he became completely lost in his project as he used his thumbs and every surface of his hands to convey the fall of shadows on paper.

Often, he'd end up covered in soot to his elbows in his attempt to give the drawing a realistic feeling—following every natural contour and the way light hit a shape at an angle. But his hazardous manner of indulging in his hobby was not ignored by his family.

Cosima, his stepmother, made no effort to mask her disgust when she saw him dirtied up from having finished a drawing. She wasn't even subtle as she delivered jibe after jibe.

Her favorite appellation was *monster*. But on other days she settled on dirty, disgusting, peasant, or son of a whore, among others.

He supposed monster was better. At least it was constant and he'd learned to ignore it in his own way. But every time she came up with a new derogatory term to call him, he couldn't help but flinch, a look of hurt crossing his face. And *that* was exactly what Cosima wanted.

She wanted him to *feel* her disdain.

And he did.

He felt it on a daily basis, and sometimes it was even more suffocating than a lung infection.

Still, he remained in his weird little world. For all the pain Cosima caused him, there was much more joy to be derived from his hobby.

Bringing his attention back to the drawing, he traced his sister's features with his finger, unable to stop marveling at her beauty.

She was only fourteen, but she was the most beautiful thing

he'd ever seen in his life. Yet, there was a part of him that hurt as the pads of his fingers settled on her hair—light and blonde and so unlike his own. Without realizing, his other hand was already on his head, feeling for the small follicles of hair that were just starting to grow anew.

Both Gianna and Rafaelo had blonde hair. He was the only one with black one. He didn't know why that was the case when both his mother and father had light looks.

It was yet another thing Cosima could cling on to, and her comments never went unnoticed. They had been even worse when his hair had started falling and he'd had to shave all of it to avoid seeing the gradual loss.

In Cosima's words, he was getting punished.

"The sins of the parents always visit the sons," she'd snicker at Michele whenever she'd see him more self-conscious about his look. Her acidic words never failed to put him on the spot, the sins she was referring to most likely those of his mother.

He'd heard enough over the years to shape his perception of the mother he'd never met. She was easy, a whore. He didn't know exactly what that meant, but he was aware it was shameful.

At school, kids made fun of him and his lack of hair, while at home Cosima picked on anything she could, her favorite pastime being making him feel insignificant. In and out of the house, there was always a battle to be fought—one he most often lost.

Cosima rejoiced at that.

And if she was happy making his life a living hell, then his father was all the more happier ignoring it. After all, he was Cosima's puppet.

Michele might have been young, but he was old enough to realize the power his stepmom had over his father—all of it to his disadvantage.

He assumed that was why he was often short with him. He never wanted to hear what Michele had to say, never had time to spend with him.

For a while, seeing all the kids with their parents at the hospital, Michele had thought that being sick meant his father might come too. They might have a reunion that would mark the start of something new.

But it had never happened.

He'd called a few times in the beginning—at his sister's insistence, no doubt. After a while, though, and after too many visits between home and the hospital, he'd forgotten about Michele.

Turning his notebook to an empty sheet, he took one pencil and started tracing shapes. In the beginning, the idea was wholly abstract. He had nothing after which to model his thoughts—nothing tangible. Yet his mind was pushing him towards something.

Was it real?

His small brows furrowed in concentration as he toiled with his lines, wiping at them when the slightest trace of hesitation became evident in the sketch. He drew, then wiped, then drew again until the abstract became the ideal.

The shapes were singing to him, almost as if they were appearing before his eyes and he had only to lay them on the paper, order them around and place them in the right position.

When it was all done, he finally drew in a breath.

Blinking rapidly, he stared at the picture before him, amazing at finding what his fingers had traced.

It was…a family.

To him, the abstract. To others, the norm.

Maybe that's why he was so hung up on the idea of family. To others it seemed to come so easily, yet to him, it was something he didn't even dare hope for—not anymore.

He knew he should be grateful that he at least had his sister who always fussed over him. But she was also a child.

Michele wished he had someone else too. Perhaps it was greedy of him to hope so, but watching all the other kids in his wing with their parents had awakened a certain longing inside of him.

He'd seen the mothers as they embraced their children, holding them to their chests and murmuring sweet words. Something like that was entirely foreign to Michele.

Proclaimed dead soon after giving birth to him, Michele wondered if he'd ever received a hug from his birth mother. Had she held him? Had she also looked upon him and seen a monster, not a human being?

The more he thought about that, the sadder he became. Maybe it was better not knowing. He wasn't sure he could take it if his own mother had despised him too.

Though he had a father, Benedicto wasn't really one.

The fathers he'd seen around the hospital always had a smile on their faces, positive energy emanating from them. They would always go to their kids and offer to play a game, or try to teach them about some sport.

He'd heard all of it. He'd been observing all along.

Yet how could anyone explain to a child of just eight that it wasn't his fault that his parents had not wanted him? Or that his current family didn't care much for him.

It was impossible.

No matter how much Michele looked on from the outside, he knew he'd never experience that. Yet what he didn't know was *why*.

He was too young to comprehend that the sins of the parents were *not*, in fact, visited upon their children. In his young and malleable mind, though he realized something wasn't quite right, his stepmother's poisonous words reached their target, and slowly, they started to fester.

He might have been a bright child. But he was *only* a child. Shaped by his surroundings, he couldn't help but absorb everything around him.

And *that* was the beginning of the end.

He came into the world a blameless child, yet he could never shake people's perceptions of him.

He might not have been a monster from the start, but he was equipped with everything he needed to embark on the journey to become one.

His pencil came to a stop.

Family.

Such an odd concept.

It only required two other parts besides himself. The nurturing of a mother and the attention of a father. Things he would never get, no matter how much he wished for them.

Spurred by an aching sense of hopelessness, he tore at the paper, the faceless people standing next to him in the painting becoming nothing more than bits and pieces of what *would* have been.

He gathered all the pieces in his tiny fist, holding on to them as he let sadness overtake him.

Hopping off the bed, he grabbed his portable IV as he trudged his way to the trash can.

Through the opening of the door, though, he noticed light in the hallway followed by the echo of two voices.

He was about to turn, uninterested in some strangers' idle talk, but then he heard his name.

Frowning, he was careful to move his IV stealthily to not attract attention as he opened the door to his salon only a fraction—enough to get a good look at the two men talking.

One, he recognized as his doctor. The other, he didn't know.

"We've done all we could," the doctor sighed. "I was also thinking the last transplant would be a success. But these things aren't predictable. His immunity is still compromised. Just look at this time. It was only a cold but it devolved into a lung infection. It's not telling what might happen next."

"Are you saying the cancer could come back?"

"No, I am saying the cancer *is* back, and his immunity is thoroughly compromised. I can let him go tomorrow because he can now breathe on his own. But I assure you he'll be back within a month with another infection."

"Sawyer, you *need* to do something about it. I can't let him die. No, under my watch he *won't* die," the strange man said in a vehement tone.

Michele tilted his head as he studied the man. He was wearing a long black coat and an equally black hat that obscured his view of the man's face. Yet there was something compelling about the way he spoke—about the way he seemed to champion for him unlike anyone ever had.

It made Michele curious.

"It's not that simple. Look, I know what he means to you, but we're talking about life and death here. No amount of money is going to buy you that."

"Another transplant then," the man huffed out, displeased by the doctor's grim diagnosis.

"From whom? We've already tried all the family members."

"There is one more."

"One more?" the doctor frowned. "That wasn't in the file."

"It's a new development. I was hoping the last transplant would have worked so I didn't have to resort to this but..." there was a brief pause as the man brought his hand to his face, scrubbing his eyes. "The marrow has been extracted and the cells are frozen. You just need to do the transplant."

"Who is this we're talking about? You know I can't just inject random cells," the doctor's voice rose up a notch.

"It's not random. You have my assurance about that. I wouldn't take risks with his life."

"Nicolo, you don't understand. You can't just bring some random cells into the hospital and demand I do the transplant. We might have been friends in the past, but this is my job we're talking about. I need to know who the donor is. There are forms to be filled out. *Consent* forms..."

"And I'm asking you, as a former friend, to do this for me. There's no one I'd trust with his health more than you."

"This is a reputable hospital, Nicolo. You know I can't do that."

"I'll pay you. Shit, I'll give you whatever you want. Just do the damn procedure!"

The man was getting increasingly more anxious.

Suddenly, he turned around, his fist flying into the wall.

"Nicolo," the doctor hissed. "There are children sleeping. Ill children."

"Just do the damn procedure, Sawyer! What do you have to lose?"

"I don't know? My job? My reputation? Everything? What if the marrow isn't a match? Then I'll have his death on my conscience."

"It's a match," the man answered gruffly. "It's the closest match too."

"But that's impossible unless..."

"Unless it's family. I'm aware."

"What the hell have you gotten yourself into, Nicolo?" the doctor shook his head, pacing around the hallway.

"Nothing I can't handle," he shrugged. "I can take care of myself, Sawyer. And I can take care of that boy too. You know he'll get worse. What if the next time they bring him to you is the last? I can't see him dead."

"Why? What's with the sudden act of sentimentalism? This isn't like you, Nicolo. You didn't even *like* her."

"No, I may not have liked her, but it happened. She wanted to stick it to her husband for cheating on her with that bitch so I indulged her for a night," the man said casually. "That it had consequences, I was pissed too. That doesn't mean this goes away, or that he doesn't exist."

"This will blow in all our faces. What if *he* finds out too? That will mean war, and you know it."

"He won't. He doesn't give a damn anyway. That viper of his wife has already made sure to sever the relationship before it began."

"Does he know?"

"That it's me?" He shook his head. "But he knows he's not his."

"That makes sense then. He's never around," the doctor mentioned.

Michele kept listening, though he couldn't understand anything they were saying. One thing was for sure. They were worried about his health. And that meant he didn't have much time left.

He wasn't entirely certain what death entailed. He understood it had something to do with presence and absence. Every time another child died in his wing, he simply disappeared.

That would probably happen to him too. But whereas the other children had been mourned by the people around, he wasn't sure anyone would feel *his* absence.

"Suggest the transplant. No one will bat an eye, I promise you."

"His stepmom might. That woman," the doctor cursed under his breath. "I've never met a more combative woman. She argued with me about everything. Of course, she tried to make it seem like she was concerned for him, but I already knew from what you'd told me that it wasn't the case."

"Yeah, she can't have a say in this. I'll make the arrangements to have the bone marrow delivered, as well as the compatibility tests we performed. I'm serious about this Sawyer. He needs to live."

"Why?"

The question was simple, and it was one that Michele was curious about as well.

Why would this stranger be so invested in whether he lived or not? Was it that he would feel his absence? But he didn't know the man, so how was it possible to feel the absence if he'd never felt the presence?

"You well know why," the man replied in a grim tone.

Michele continued to listen to the conversation until the men said their goodbyes, the doctor leaving in the opposite direction while the other man lingered around.

Without notice, he turned, his eyes meeting Michele's.

He gasped, taking a step back.

But it was too late.

The man, Nicolo the doctor had called him, walked determinedly towards him.

His big hand connected with the door as he pushed it wide open, his eyes on Michele as he studied him from head to toe.

"Isn't it past your bedtime, boy?" He asked in a stern voice. Yet his warm eyes belied his tone.

Michele blinked, looking at him as if he could not figure him out.

"Who are you?" He asked, bringing his hands to his front as he played with the material of his shirt.

"It doesn't matter. For now, a friend."

Michele tilted his head, squinting to get a better look at the man.

"You have such unusual eyes," he commented, and a blush suffused Michele's cheeks.

"You... You think so?"

"I know so. They are a very rare shade, you know," he continued, dropping to his haunches to be on eye-level with him. Tipping his hat backwards, he invited Michele to take a closer look at his eyes.

"You have them, too," a smile spread over his face as he pointed at the man's eyes. A pool of swirling amber, they teetered between light brown and gray, a shade so light, it was almost translucent.

"I do," the man's lips tipped up in an amused grin.

"My stepmom says they are unnatural," Michele added in a low voice, fidgeting with his hands.

"Your stepmom is jealous. Not everyone has eyes like yours, boy. You should be proud of having something unique."

Michele's ears perked up as he looked in awe at the man in front of him.

Never in his life had anyone told him he was special, or unique. Never before had anyone praised him for *anything*.

"Thank you," he whispered, warmth enveloping his entire being.

The man grunted, still studying him.

Bringing a hand to his head, he rubbed at the bald spot, self-conscious about the man's appraising gaze.

"This will grow back." The man caught his hand, bringing it down. Instead, he brought his own to his head to pat it down, almost as if he was smoothing down unruly strands of hair. "And everything will be over soon."

Michele didn't know how to answer that.

He was rooted to the spot as he let himself enjoy being the

center of attention for once. He'd never had that before—never had an adult shower him with attention and kind words. So he simply nodded, his lips tipped up in a shy smile.

"Here," Nicolo continued, reaching into his coat and pulling out a small box.

Michele's eyes widened as he extended his hand to give him the box. He stared at it for a second, unable to move or reach out for it.

"Take it," the man insisted.

"For me?" He asked carefully, wanting to make sure he was allowed to touch it.

He'd had enough incidents in which he'd touched things that did not belong to him, and he'd always ended up punished for it. But more than being grounded or beaten for it, he was afraid of the words.

In his mind, he always liked to picture that he owned some things—that they were his and only his. He imagined that some faceless stranger would give them specifically to him.

But the words he'd receive when he was chastised dispelled that illusion. They reminded him that they weren't his and would never be his. That *no one* would gift him anything, no matter how small.

He supposed his sister would if she could. But she had no means to buy anything.

"For you," the man nodded.

Michele's eyes sparkled with unshed tears as he took in the small box, his hands slowly darting forward to cup it. He was careful—oh, so careful. He treated the object like it was sacred as he brought it to his chest.

What followed were careful movements marred by small instances of impatience. He was curious, but he was also too afraid to do something wrong. As such, he tried to temper his enthusiasm as he opened the box.

Inside, there was a small replica of a piano. Shiny, mahogany wood complemented the black and white alternation of keys. The more he stared at it, the more he fell in love with it.

"Click here," the man reached with a finger, touching the underside of the piano. Immediately, sound started emanating from the little thing. It wasn't loud. But in the quietness of the night, it was like being seated in the front row of a concert.

Beethoven's Fur Elise started playing and Michele's mouth dropped open in astonishment. He didn't know the piece, but to his ears, in that moment, nothing had sounded more beautiful.

"It's for me?" He asked again, almost as if he could not convince himself that the gift was, indeed, for him.

"Just for you," the older man confirmed, standing up and taking a step back.

"Wait!" Michele called out. "You're leaving?"

"It's not visiting hours, boy."

"But you're here."

"So I am," he narrowed his eyes at him.

It was on the tip of Michele's tongue to ask him *why*. Why was he visiting him or inquiring about his health when his own family couldn't care less about it.

"Thank you," he murmured instead. He didn't want to question the kindness when it was the only one he'd gotten in what felt like forever. He reckoned that if he was grateful and did not make a fuss, the man would come again.

"You'll come again?" He inquired softly, wanting to make sure.

Since young, he'd been slapped in the face enough by life to know not to make false illusions about anything. Yet he couldn't help himself. He couldn't help the optimism that was almost one with him. From the beginning he'd had the unlikeliest of chances. He'd been declared dead more than once. Yet he was still living. He took that as a sign. And so he hoped that this stranger that brought him so much happiness returned. Even if he never brought him gifts again, he would be pleased with his presence alone. With being important enough to someone for them to visit him...

"Maybe," he answered. "Soon, you won't be in the hospital for me to visit, though," he added.

"I know," Michele nodded. "I'll be dead," he said the words without giving them much thought. After all, death around him was talked about plenty of times. Never in actual terms, but it was enough for Michele to become used to the thought of death.

He even wagered it wouldn't be such a bad thing.

Since it was only a matter of absence versus presence, and he knew that his presence was barely tolerated, he guessed his absence wouldn't be felt that much.

Still, it miffed him to give Cosima the satisfaction of his absence. She might be his tormentor, and she might make his life a living hell on a daily basis, but in his little mind, he was aware he was also hurting her with his presence.

And so, he wished to be forever present—a thorn in her side.

"You won't be dead." The vehemence of the words took him by surprise. The stranger's eyes widened at his outburst, and taking his hat off, he threaded his fingers through his dark hair. Releasing a sigh of frustration, he once more set his gaze on Michele.

"You won't die," he reformulated in a gentler tone. "You'll get well soon, and after that we may meet again."

"Promise?" He found the courage to ask.

"Promise," the man regaled him with a smile. One last glance, and he stepped back in the hallway, placing his hat back on and leaving.

Michele watched his retreating figure, his fingers clutching tightly at the little piano.

And as he stepped back, closing the door to the salon, it was to keep replaying the song. Time after time, he stared at his little gift while he memorized the melody.

His first gift.

There was someone out there who cared about him.

And that made him happy.

two

AGE EIGHT

"You can pull your shirt now," the doctor told him, taking a step back. "You've improved significantly and I think it's safe to say you can go home. For now," he raised a brow, emphasizing that it was a temporary situation.

Michele nodded.

He understood what the doctor was trying to tell him.

"I'm scheduling your transplant for next week. But until then, you have to keep taking your medicine. We don't want another infection, ok?"

"Ok," Michele readily agreed.

Due to his weakened immune system, it was imperative he took care of himself until the day of the transplant. And remembering his promise to the strange man, Michele was ready to do whatever it took to ensure he would get through this.

He *wanted* to be healthy—although he didn't really know what that meant.

Since he could remember, he'd been in and out of hospitals, the state of being *un*healthy his normal. He was used to feeling ill, and having no strength. At the same time, though, he was curious about what it meant to be healthy.

Could he run with the other kids? Could he play with them too?

He hadn't been very present at school because he'd taken prolonged breaks from it, so not only his education had suffered but also his social life.

He had no friends outside his home. He didn't even know other boys his age except his brother, Raf. But that was too complicated for him to ponder now.

Raf was...he was his friend. But not a constant one.

There was always Cosima's shadow lurking around, and while Raf did his best to be a good friend to him, more often than not he tried to ignore Michele so as not to incur his mother's wrath.

Because of Michele's illness and his presumed wretched birth conditions, Cosima considered him *impure* and a monster. At times, she'd even yelled at him for poisoning her own son and contaminating him with whatever evil was within him.

He didn't believe that. Neither did Raf. As such, their interactions happened mostly in secrecy. As long as Cosima was out of the picture, they were the best of friends. But the moment she appeared, Michele ceased to exist.

He supposed it was better than nothing. Deep down, though, it bothered him.

After his consultation was done, he was led out of the cabinet to where Gianna, Raf and their governess was waiting for him.

"You're good to go?" Gianna stepped forward, coming towards him.

He barely nodded before her arms came around him, bringing him close to her and smothering him to her chest.

"Yay, you can come home with us," she exclaimed, and he melted against her, absorbing all of her love.

The governess grunted her approval. She wasn't an overly affectionate woman, but she wasn't too bad either. She was merely doing her job looking after them. She wasn't paid to care, too.

After Gianna let go of him, he came face to face with Raf.

Despite being half-brothers, there was nothing similar about them.

His brother was fair—too fair. Golden skin and light blonde hair, he also had their father's blue eyes.

For as long as he could remember, Michele had wished he looked like that too. Maybe then he wouldn't be so unwanted. If only he had Raf's blue eyes instead of his own unusual light ones...

As soon as that thought crossed his mind, though, he threw it aside. He remembered the stranger who'd complimented his eyes and for the first time he felt a modicum of pride at having something *unusual*—unique.

A smile tugged at his lips as he looked at his brother with new eyes—not with envy but with contentment. And as Raf came to hug him too, he wrapped his arms around his ribcage, accepting the gesture.

Despite being a few months younger, Raf was larger in size. He was almost a head taller than Michele, and around ten pounds heavier.

That would have been another reason for him to be jealous, but the doctor had been kind in explaining that his illness had taken a toll on his body. Once he was cured, he would recover and likely catch up to his brother.

He remained optimistic.

Now, he had something to hope for.

He *had* to get well.

Leaving the hospital, Gianna proposed they went to get cake to celebrate Michele's discharge from the hospital.

The governess took a little longer to convince, but eventually she took them to a place close to their house where they all ate to their heart's content.

Gianna chose a strawberry vanilla cake. Raf went for a hazelnut chocolate one, and Michele decided to indulge so he went all in by choosing a chocolate lava cake.

For a few hours, the three siblings ignored the outside world as they talked and joked and spun tales about school, friends and the other shenanigans.

Michele listened attentively. Unable to add any stories of his own, he focused on what Gianna and Raf were saying, storing the information for later when he could use it.

He wasn't very versed in the outside world. For him, his little existence revolved around home and the hospital, rarely able to indulge even in something as small as going for cake in the afternoon.

Compared to his siblings, his life experience was insignificant.

Yet he wasn't beaten down about it. Now that he possessed a new found optimism, he knew that one day, he'd have that too. He'd be able to go to school, make friends and engage in silliness as befitting a child his age. He was convinced that his time would come.

Until then, he allowed himself to live vicariously through Raf's words, imagining a world in which he was be a normal boy, too.

"Mrs. Donovan grounded him for a week," Raf giggled, telling them about the latest mischief that happened at his school. The other two giggled, while their governess rolled her eyes at the silly stories. Still, she didn't interrupt them.

"Dr. Evans said I can go back to school too after my transplant," Michele added eagerly.

"We'll be together," Raf nodded, a big smile on his lips.

"And I'll be there too," Gianna winked.

Though she'd be in a different grade, she'd still be around to watch out for him, and that warmed him even more.

Their time away from home soon came to a stop, and they had to return.

Michele's cheeks were flushed with happiness, and though he knew his arrival would not be seen positively, he kept up his spirits. So many good things had happened to him lately that he wasn't going to let his stepmom mar his mood.

Yet he didn't count on Cosima's vengefulness.

In his innocent mind, he still hoped that one day she would accept him. That everyone would accept him.

The moment they stepped inside the house, Cosima was upon them.

Her arms reached for Raf as she tugged him to her chest, her eyes shooting daggers at the rest of the entourage.

"You," she spat at the governess. "Who allowed you to take my Raf with you?"

"But... I couldn't leave him alone. You were gone and..."

"And you took him to the hospital? To that dreadful place full of...germs," her nose scrunched up in disgust, her gaze landing on Michele as she uttered the last word.

Depositing her son behind her, she moved towards Michele.

Instinctively, his arms went up to shield himself as he squeezed his eyes shut, waiting for the incoming blow.

She didn't strike him.

Nothing touched his skin.

Still, the sound of a slap resounded through the room, the echo holding additional sting as the sound traveled through the great hall.

Opening his eyes, Michele saw his sister standing in front of him.

One hand to her cheek, she stared at Cosima with defiance.

Her arm was up, shielding Michele as she held him near, placing her own body in front of his.

"Don't," he whispered, his small hands tugging on her dress.

"You don't hit my brother. You don't touch him," Gianna raised her voice, not backing down even as Cosima rose to her full height, the look in her eyes promising tenfold retribution.

"The little bitch," she sneered. "You think to order me in my own home?"

Her fingers wrapped around Gianna's arm, she tried to push her aside.

"Stop, *mamma*," Raf flung himself at his mother, hugging her midriff and stopping her from advancing. "Leave them alone, please."

"Raf, how can you talk like that to me?"

Like magic, Cosima's venomous tone turned sweet as she addressed her beloved son. Turning her attention to him, her gaze softened, her grave features relaxing and giving her an unlikely glow.

Michele blinked, unable to believe how she could transform so under his eyes. And as he looked upon her, he had to admit that she *was* beautiful. Too bad that she wasn't *always* beautiful.

"My tummy hurts, *mamma*," Raf complained, clutching his stomach. "I think I ate something bad..." he trailed off. But that sentence was enough to shift Cosima's attention to him.

No longer minding Gianna and Michele, she swept Raf in her arms as she took him with her towards the kitchen. Never mind that he was already a big boy and she could barely lift him up. In that moment, she displayed Herculean strength as she took off with him.

"I'll make you some tea and..." her voice drowned out as she disappeared from sight.

Both Michele and Gianna sighed in relief.

Her cheek was red where she'd been slapped by Cosima, but

she didn't complain. Plastering a joyous smile on her face, she took Michele's hand as she led him upstairs to his room.

For all the benefits of having a mother, at that moment Michele was proud he had a sister. One who loved him and protected him.

He vowed that when the time came, he would return the favor.

"You're very quiet," Gianna noted.

Michele's gaze snapped up, meeting hers. He gave a slight shrug.

"Are you scared about the transplant? You know it's going to be ok," she tried to assure him, coming to sit on the bed next to him.

"What if I die?" He found the courage to ask.

"Michele... You... You're not going to die! How can you say that?"

He tipped his shoulders up, answering her question with silence.

"You don't really think that, do you?" She repeated, grabbing his hand in hers.

The contact warmed him, and for a second he allowed himself to breathe in the fresh scent of the room. After so long in the hospital, it was like a balm for his battered nose—and more than anything for his decaying spirits.

"I don't know," he answered honestly.

"You won't die. I won't allow it."

"You won't be able to do anything, Gigi," he gave her a small smile. "You're not God."

"And you're not a soothsayer, either. You don't know you're going to die."

"Gigi," he took a deep breath as he turned to her. "I'm not that ignorant of my illness. I know the odds," he told her in a gentle tone.

For all his usual calm and optimistic personality, he knew the hard facts. He'd read things on the internet, and though his understanding wasn't as advanced as an adult's, he understood enough. Yet he'd never voiced that particular concern until now for her benefit, and maybe, in the deep recesses of his heart, for his, too.

"You'll beat the odds," she declared with unwavering conviction. "I know you will."

"Thank you for the vote of trust," his mouth pulled up in a smile.

"I'm not going to let anyone take you from me," she cried out before, suddenly, her arms came around him.

He stifled a wince when she hugged him a bit too tightly. His body ached, and his bones felt brittle and about to snap at every moment. While he may have recovered enough to breathe on his own and be able to leave the hospital, his body wasn't fully healed.

That was another reason why he suspected his fight against cancer might not be for much longer.

He'd read case studies, and he'd looked at forums. He knew that one of the prime requirements to successfully withstand a transplant was having a robust immunity. And his was shit.

"Why?" he asked on a whisper. He didn't mean to question her affection. Instead, he sought to understand it. Just like he sought to understand everything around him.

It was one of the reasons why he'd never been quick to judge. Instead, he'd tried to put himself into the other person's shoes and understand *why* they were behaving as they were.

Why was his father distant?

Why did his stepmother hate him so much?

Why was everyone so against him?

Why was Raf given special treatment when *he* was the eldest born?

And *why* was Gianna the only one who accepted him as he was?

The questions had been on his mind for as long as he could remember. And every time he thought he came up with an answer to them, it was to find new data that changed his perspective.

They might consider him slow, or not very bright. He was none of those.

He might not be on top of his school work, having missed a lot of those formative years by being in and out of the hospital. But he wasn't dumb.

He was just more contemplative.

His brother had once called it naïveté. Maybe it was to a certain extent. But more than anything, he preferred to reserve judgment until he'd seen more than *just* one side of the coin.

He'd seen that firsthand with his brother, and his often mercurial moods.

When Cosima was absent, they were best friends. When she was present, he barely acknowledged his presence.

In the beginning he'd been angry about it. He'd been confused and hurt by his brother's disregard. He already had few people to call his own, so when Rafaelo had stepped back so suddenly from his life he'd been flabbergasted.

But then he'd observed.

He'd developed such a keen sense of observation that little escaped him.

And he saw that Rafaelo wasn't ignoring him. No, he was *protecting* him.

Attention from Cosima was always bad news, and both of them knew that. When she was present, Rafaelo would simply direct her attention to himself and try to pretend Michele wasn't even in the room. In turn, this made Cosima forget about him and focus only on her son.

An even more poignant incident had been when he'd come across one of his bullies at school. Because Michele was often absent for long periods of time, when he came back, bald and all skin and bone, the kids would call him all kinds of derogatory terms, making fun of his appearance and lack of strength. Sometimes they straight up behaved as if he was a leper and would infect everyone around.

It didn't matter that he'd explained his illness wasn't infectious. Their minds had already been made.

He was the *other*.

In the beginning, the bullying had gotten to him. His self-esteem had taken a huge blow and he would avoid any mirrors that would show him his defects, thinking himself worse than an ogre.

But everything had changed when he'd come across one of the classmates who had engaged in the bullying.

Huddled in a dark corner in the back of the school, the kid had been trying to hide a discolored patch of skin that had appeared on his arm. He'd known that a visible disability at their age was just a weapon for the others to use against them.

Against all his common sense, Michele had approached him, asking him if he was alright. The look the boy had given him had shocked Michele.

He'd looked trapped.

So thoroughly trapped, tears had appeared at the corners of his eyes.

Yet Michele hadn't given up. Slowly, he'd coaxed an answer from him, finding out he was suffering from a skin condition that had flared unexpectedly. He'd also begrudgingly admitted to him that he was aware this could get him delegated to the same level as Michele—the other. The defective that was, in fact, the misunderstood.

As he'd come across that classmate and his secret, he'd

realized just how the *other* was despised. It wasn't a matter of *him*. It wasn't him that they were ridiculing, or making fun of. It was the idea of him—of something outside the norm for them.

He wasn't the target of the insults, any more than he was the target of the cancer. Both had found a weakness in him and they were exploiting it.

From then on, Michele had started to be more temperate in how he viewed the world, trying to understand it from both sides instead of basing everything off his immediate anger.

"You're my brother, Michele," Gianna leaned back, softly stroking his cheek as he regarded him with a gentle look in his eyes. "I love you because you're my brother."

"And if I weren't?" he asked, tilting his head to study her.

"I'd still love you," she smiled.

"Why?" he continued with his line of questioning. All in an effort to elucidate the mystery of this so-called love.

His only notion of it was through *her,* and so he thought she could give him the keys to enter this entirely new realm of love.

Maybe then, he'd be worthy of even more love and he'd attract other people who would love him too. He didn't know if things worked that way—doubted it, mostly—but he still wanted to try. Anything to alleviate the loneliness that he sometimes felt—that deep, soul wrenching sense of not belonging, of not being, of barely existing.

He had her, that was true. But he was greedy, because he wanted someone else to love him too. Someone who didn't do it just because of a familial connection, though God knows that wasn't a prerequisite.

"Because you have a kind, kind soul," she answered.

He frowned.

"A kind soul?"

"It's why I try to always be there for you. Because I know

how hard things must be for you, and yet you're still..." her lips tipped up, "*you*."

He blinked, taken aback by her words.

"And I never want you to change."

"I won't," he nodded in a solemn promise. "I won't," he repeated as he brought his hand to her cheek and swiped a little bit of moisture from under her eye. "Do you think mother loved me too?" he asked in a small voice.

He'd never voiced that question before; never brought up their mother because he knew it caused Gianna unspeakable pain. Whereas he'd been a baby when she'd died, she'd already been five. She remembered her. He only remembered what people thought of her—and it was rarely good.

"She did. She used to sing to you when she was pregnant. She said you'd respond to the melody," Gianna reminisced fondly, eliciting a small smile from Michele too.

"Tell me more."

And she did.

She told him how their mother would always take Gianna with her everywhere they went. She already had big plans for when Michele would be born, and she was excited about meeting him.

"She loved you before she even met you. I am sure of that."

Michele nodded.

"Is it true what they say about her then? That she was a wh- whore?" he felt his cheeks heat as he uttered the forbidden word.

"No," Gianna stated vehemently. "That's just Cosima speaking from her high horse. She wants people to hate *mamma* and love her instead. She wants to forget she's just the second wife."

"I see..."

"Don't let her poison your mind with her lies. She only wants to make you feel bad."

"I won't," he promised. "After all, I have you. That's enough," the small lie slipped through his lips, but he couldn't regret it when her smile brightened the entire room.

For now it was enough. He could only hope that in the future he'd find someone else to love him, too.

Someone who didn't see him as the *other*.

three

AGE TEN

The sound of pouring water startled him back to reality. He blinked as he stared at the mirror. He raked his gaze over his pale, almost translucent skin, following the curve of one blue vein as it protruded around his temple. It was the same color of his eyes. The same *icy* color as his eyes.

He felt *cold*.

His body was warm, yet the coldness seeped into his pores, not external but internal. It was coming from an ineffable place, and it had nothing to do with his surroundings.

"Raf? We're leaving," Mark, his classmate, called out, beckoning him towards the door.

He gave a brisk nod, turning the faucet off and rolling his sleeves back on.

He could do it.

One more day.

But it wasn't *just* one more day. It was day after day. The clamoring noise inside him increased in volume, ever so slowly, it was becoming deafening.

He told himself he just needed to get through that day. Then he could breathe out relieved.

But that was only the optimist in him talking. That idealist part of him that had already mapped every potential outcome—everything ending on a positive note.

Yet there was another side of him. One he wanted to squash down and keep at bay. It was that *bad* part of him that wanted to end everything.

Stop pretending to be a good boy.

Stop pretending to be a good student.

And...stop pretending to be a good son.

It was there, right there. On the tip of his tongue. He wanted to get out in the hallway of the school and yell at top of his lungs.

This isn't me!

And it wasn't. Not really. But years of conditioning, and even more years to come, eroded that side of him—the rebellious, *not* good side. Soon, he would lose every single unruly bone in his body. Because once you started pretending to be something, you ended up believing it.

But he wasn't quite gone. At least not yet.

He still held onto that small flame inside of him—the one spark that told him it was alright not to like certain things. That it was completely fine not to like *everyone* or try to please everyone. And more than anything, that it was ok to disappoint his mother. She might be upset in the beginning, but she would eventually forgive him.

Not doing that, though, could have far reaching consequences.

But he didn't know yet. He didn't know how his one weakness would influence the rest of his life.

He was still fighting with his own self—with that half of his being that wanted to be set free.

Even young as he was, he was clever enough to read the world around himself for what it was. His independence of thought gave him an edge when interacting with his peers and his easy going personality made him the most popular kid in the room. But that intelligence also whispered things in his ears. Things no child should know or think about.

He saw the ugliness of the world, and he knew that there was nothing he could do about it. Maybe that's where his obsession with the meaning of *good* started. When he realized that the world was *rarely* good. That his façade was merely that—pretending for the benefit of others.

He saw injustices at every step, and while he sought to be the good boy he was raised to be and help correct them, he was also wise enough to realize he could never help *everyone*.

Walking towards his classroom, his stance was the model of decorum. It was the result of years of harsh yet loving discipline at the hands of his mother.

She was a perfectionist in everything she did, and God forbid her son had *any* imperfections.

From his manners, to the way he behaved and dressed, everything was carefully curated to present the perfect image—the golden boy. Only then could she brag about her son in her social circles, praising his conduit and his stellar grades. Most of all, she boasted about his already planned out future. Because he wouldn't have been her son if his future had not been decided from the moment he was born.

He was to do as he was told, behave without reproach and bring honor to the family name. At the same time, he was also supposed to follow a narrow path in life.

His schools had all been decided. Only the very best for a future leader in the making. His high school and college were already singled out, both of them legacies. His father had attended those, so it befell to him to attend as well. His course of study, of course, had been chosen from the start too. After all, the family needed someone with a keen brain for numbers and law. For while there was always someone to hire to perform those functions for the family, the head should always be able to interpret his reports carefully.

In the cutthroat business of blood money, hunger was insatiable. Nothing was fair, and because of that, the greed to take more and more became the one impetus to succeed.

And as Rafaelo had been told since he was a little boy, *he* was the next leader.

This wasn't just a passing fancy for his mother—the expensive lessons, the extracurricular activities or the skills he was forced to learn. No, these were all the keys to success for the future.

He would be the *don*, and he would rule with a fist of iron and a clear mind.

That had been her decree from the beginning.

It didn't matter that Rafaelo was the second son, or that the position was meant for his brother, Michele. It didn't matter that Italians valued tradition above all else and the eldest son was the *only* one who could inherit.

It mattered not at all that Rafaelo himself did not want this.

Because his mother wanted it. And what she wanted, she got.

"I didn't work hard for you to throw this opportunity away, Raf," she'd chide gently, but her voice would hold a steely quality to it that told Raf that it was her way or none at all.

"You don't know what it was like. The poverty. The hunger. We went through that," she'd sigh, her gaze distant as she'd tug him to her chest. "We went through that and worse. All because we came to this country with only hopes to keep us warm. And it doesn't work like that. Hope can help you succeed. But it doesn't put food on your plate."

Rafaelo, being his mother's child, and having a peculiar affinity to her, had placed his head on her shoulder as he'd asked.

"Was it very hard, *mamma*?"

She'd teared up then. One of the few times in his life when he'd seen her cry.

Dabbing at her lashes, she'd tried her hardest to hide the sorrow from her gaze or the pain that laced her voice.

"Remember one thing, my darling boy," she'd looked at him then. But instead of telling him more of her past, or the struggles of her family, she'd imparted one piece of advice. One that he'd remember for the rest of his life. "No matter how hard things get, there's always something worse. When you're free falling, the abyss embraces you, swallowing you up and eating you alive. There's always more darkness. More pain. More suffering. But that doesn't mean you should give up. Because where there's darkness there's light. Aim for the light. With everything you've got in you, aim for that light," a sad smile had crossed her face. "I found mine when I met your father. He pulled me out of my abyss. But if *I* hadn't taken the necessary steps to propel myself forward, he would have never been able to reach me."

The lesson was obvious. He should not let himself depend on anyone.

In fact, that one tidbit had been drilled in his head since he was but a baby.

Be the best. Get to the top so that *no* one can tear you down.

And he'd put it into practice.

Yet for someone who was taught co-dependence was the root of all evil—that only *you* can make your own happiness, his mother was awfully reliant on him.

He was her happiness. Because he was the physical proof that she had made it. He was the reason she was now at the top.

Taking a seat at the front of the classroom, he straightened his back as he placed his notebook and textbook on the desk. One glance to the side, though, and he noticed his brother, Michele.

His lip was split, his pale face marred by bruises. Thick, black curls hung low on his face, hiding some of the worst injuries.

He'd gotten bullied again.

Rafaelo sighed, taking a deep breath as he brought his hands to his temples, massaging them.

He knew Michele was getting bullied, and more often than not, he would step in to help him. Yet he couldn't do that forever, could he?

They were the same age, but Michele had always been the more frail one. Even now, a couple of years after his cancer had gone into remission, he was still slender and a little shorter than the other kids in the class.

That and his delicate, almost doll-like appearance made him the butt of jokes.

Kids their age could be cruel, especially with things they did not properly understand or would only gather through hearsay.

Such was the case for Michele.

His face held a special appeal, his features soft and feminine. To the trained eye, he was a breathtaking man in the making. To the eye of the kids, he was a freak.

They called him everything in the book—gay, sissy, girly, and so on.

He took everything in stride, but Rafaelo knew it always got to him.

Because of that name-calling, he'd tried to act tougher and prove everyone wrong. But he wasn't made for that. Not when he would fall at the slightest push, or when he couldn't defend himself even against the weakest boy in the class.

He was weak. That was the truth. And everyone took advantage of it.

Just last week, Rafaelo had helped him against a band of hooligans, getting hurt in the process too. He didn't mind the pain. That was transient and hardly mattered. But he did mind the blow to his *perfect* reputation and the fact that people were starting to lump him together with Michele.

It was even worse that rumors had started that Michele had only advanced grades as fast as he had because their father had paid the board to *help* him.

And the last thing Rafaelo wanted was for his hard work to go to waste and be branded as *privilege*.

It might have been a privilege that he could attend that prestigious academy in the first place, but each grade he got, he earned.

He was first in his class, but *no* one had paid for those results.

They were simply the result of his hard work.

But even so, if one took his own preoccupations out of the equation, there was still the matter that Michele would never stand on his own two feet if Rafaelo continued to help him time and time again.

Though Michele was the older sibling, Rafaelo had always been the one to protect his brother. Time and time again, he'd been his shield. At home, serving as a buffer between Michele and their parents, specifically his mother, but also at school, trying to stop the bullying.

For as long as they've been together at school, he'd stepped up when the situation had gotten out of hand. As such, Rafaelo was the only thing that kept Michele afloat. Proof being that he'd missed school for a couple of days since he'd been nominated for a regional rhetoric competition. In that time, Michele had accumulated bruises all over his face and body. It was even worse that no one at home cared about his injuries. Anyone could abuse him and no one would jump to his defense.

This pissed Rafaelo, but it also made him angry.

Why couldn't his brother hold his own? Why couldn't he try harder?

But that was just the issue. Michele was not cut for that type of behavior. He didn't have a mean bone in his body. For everything that had happened to him, he was still optimistic about the world. He had a gentle and forgiving soul and somehow he *never* got mad.

No matter how much people hit or cursed him, he never reciprocated in kind.

One time, Rafaelo had asked him why. He couldn't understand how Michele could withstand everything and not break. Michele had nodded thoughtfully when he'd voiced his concern, the only words coming out of his mouth being, "They don't know better."

It had stunned him.

Rafaelo had always thought himself smarter, more capable and more hardworking than the rest. After all, his aim was to be the golden boy. He was supposed to be *good*—at everything. Yet those few words had proved to him that he was just a farce.

Whereas inside of Rafaelo there was a storm waiting to be unleashed, a fire stifled by the tight confines of the expectations placed upon him, inside Michele there was a calm breeze that sought to extend to the outside. He was not bothered by what people thought of him, embracing everything with an ease that made him the *epitome* of good.

What Rafaelo strived for, Michele had been blessed with.

And he couldn't help the tiny tendrils of jealousy that enveloped him.

Michele had a freedom that Rafaelo could not afford. He had people relying on him and expectations placed upon him. Michele had none.

Though he was close to an outcast both at home and at school, wasn't there a degree of freedom to that?

Sometimes, when everything was too much, Rafaelo wished they could switch places. He would easily give up his position of privilege for one day where he didn't need to pretend to be something he wasn't—where he didn't have to care about anyone and anything.

He wanted to be free.

Free like his brother.

More than anything, he wanted to share Michele's outlook on life. No matter how wrong things turned out for him, he always saw the full half of the glass.

It might be due to his social segregation, since he'd missed years of school and having friends—he'd missed on experiencing the world. And so there was an unspoiled innocence to him that persisted.

Whereas Rafaelo was growing too fast, seeing and learning things no child his age should, Michele remained in blissful ignorance.

And sometimes that grated on his nerves.

Because Benedicto, their father, considered Michele defective—likely always would—he'd taken it upon himself to initiate Rafaelo into their lifestyle. While he hadn't exactly spelled out that Rafaelo would be the heir, and thus fulfill all his mother's fantasies, he had done everything to hint at it.

And so Rafaelo's heart further split.

He was happy to make his *mother* happy. But he was also angry at having to take a position that wasn't his. Because being a *don* was far from being a sunshine and rainbows position. His father had made that clear the day he'd turned nine.

He'd taken Rafaelo to a secret location and he'd made him watch while a few of his soldiers tortured an unassuming man.

The test had been just watching—unflinchingly stare at the blood pooling at the man's feet, at the mangled flesh caused by fists and kicks and other devices of torture.

That was the moment his *innocence* had died.

Late at night, he could still hear the groans of pain, the shrills and the screams. He could see the man as he'd looked at *him*, pleading with his eyes to help him.

And he'd wanted to. But he wasn't supposed to.

That day, a conundrum had taken shape within Rafaelo.

How could he be good, and accept that? How could he be good without being good?

And so his jealousy of his brother increased. A little bit each time he saw the ignorance and infantile innocence still residing in Michele's eyes.

It was *his* place there, by their father's side. Not Rafaelo's.

The excursions continued. His father took him everywhere with him when the task demanded. He saw things no ten-year-old should ever see.

And yet, it was expected of him.

Most of all, it was expected of him to keep everything inside.

To be good.

The teacher, Mrs. Anne, strode in, dumping a stack of papers on the desk as she took in his class.

Everyone straightened their backs, their attention suddenly to her.

Only Michele was still in his own world.

From the corner of his eye, Rafaelo could see his brother bent over his desk, pencil in hand as he continued to doodle on his paper.

Truth to be told, Michele did possess an unusual talent for drawing, but he knew that it would never be appreciated in their world. Already, their father expected Rafaelo to not blink at blood and murder. He didn't want to think what he would do if he found out his other son's preoccupations were strictly artistic.

"I've marked your tests," the teacher said. Moans of despair resounded in the room. Rafaelo's eyes glinted in excitement.

He'd studied hard for this test, and he knew he would get a good, if not perfect score.

"I'll pass them around so you can have a look and then we'll have a short conversation about my expectations."

Rafaelo tapped his foot restlessly as he awaited his result. The teacher walked around the desks, laying their tests face down so no one could peer at their scores. And when she finally reached Rafaelo's desk, he could barely hold himself from turning the entire thing over. Instead, he maintained a calm that belied the storm raging inside of him as he carefully folded a corner to reveal his result.

99 percent.

An almost perfect score.

He was sure his mother would make a backhanded comment about it not being a *perfect* one, but he was more than pleased with himself.

Between the excursions with his father and the other activities his mother made him attend, it was a wonder he'd manage to sneak in some hours to study for the test.

A soft smile on his lips, he sneaked a glance at Michele only to find him still doodling away. His test was on the edge of the desk, unturned, and he didn't seem remotely curious about how he'd done.

He wanted to reach out to ask, but then thought better of it.

Michele wasn't a great student. He didn't apply himself, but there was also the tricky part of him missing most of his schooling years due to his illness.

Their parents hadn't cared that he was too behind others his age. They had insisted he be placed in the same class as Rafaelo to save face.

After all, that was the most important aspect of their lives.

Saving face.

And so they had paid their way to enroll Michele in his class, not caring that he might struggle compared to the other kids. He barely had any basics of math, or science, or even English.

He spoke it well, but Rafaelo doubted Michele could write it just as well.

It was simply impossible with how much time he'd missed from school.

But given that this test had been on science and math, he knew he must have done poorly.

As he watched, though, he saw something change.

Just like him, Michele tried to look unbothered as he raised the corner of his paper slightly, the ghost of a smile on his lips as he took in his result.

He must have done better than expected, Rafaelo thought.

But how good would that be? Good enough for him to pass?

"There was one perfect score in the class," the teacher said and Rafaelo's ears perked up. He frowned as he stole another glance at his score, unable to understand what the teacher was talking about.

It was common knowledge that he was always the top of the class, so what was he talking about?

"It's Rafaelo, isn't it?" someone laughed from the back.

"No, it's not," the teacher looked at him for a moment before his gaze slid to Michele. "It's his brother, Michele."

At the sound of that, Michele finally lifted his head to engage with the class, his attention on the professor as his lips tipped up in a small smile.

"Michele?" the shushed voices began.

"No way," another declared.

"Yeah, no way. He barely gets a fifty, but a perfect score?"

Their classmates continued to question the teacher's words,

some of them genuinely concerned it was a mistake while some just took it as an opportunity to make fun of Michele.

Through all the chatter, his brother didn't flinch. Not when he heard the name calling, or when some called him an idiot. He continued to gaze at the professor, probably waiting for the praise.

Rafaelo didn't know how to react.

Michele getting a perfect score? *How?*

He was quiet as he waited to see what would happen, but on the inside the scenarios were already building in his head.

His mother would be angry. No, angry was an understatement. His mother would be furious about it.

If it had been anyone but Michele, maybe she would have forgotten it soon after. But because it was Michele who got that one extra point more than him, he knew she would go crazy.

Would she punish him? Likely.

She wouldn't beat him. She never touched a hair on his body, her adoration not allowing her to do him any real harm. But she would ground him and hurt him, nonetheless. With her disappointment. With the guilt she'd wreck on him. Because that's what she did best. She hung onto an issue far longer than it was worth it, and she held it over his head as she murmured how disappointed she was in her son.

"You'll be the death of me, Raf," she'd sigh dramatically when Rafaelo would do something she did not approve of. "Is that what you want? To send your mother to an early grave?"

The guilt tripping would continue forever. But more than that, he didn't want to imagine what she'd do to Michele.

"Silence everyone," the teacher intervened. "I want to make it clear that there is a zero tolerance policy against cheating and we will take the appropriate measures in this case."

Cheating?

Rafaelo turned to his brother, finding the same question written on his face as it was on his.

Michele blinked, his brows scrunched together in confusion.

"I...I didn't cheat," he found his voice to say.

"Yes, you did," the teacher countered in a calm tone.

"I didn't," Michele shook his head vehemently, before gazing at Rafaelo, almost as if he waited for his brother to defend him.

"Michele," the teacher started in an exasperated tone. "If you didn't cheat, can you tell me how come you got a perfect score when you've been getting nothing but barely passing marks?"

Michele shrugged.

"I studied."

"You're telling me you studied an entire year worth of science in a few weeks and got a perfect score? When not even your brother could manage that?"

Rafaelo felt his cheeks heat at the comparison and he dropped his eyes to his desk, not wanting to look at either his brother or the teacher.

"You may think you can get away with this because your father donated a library to get you into this class, but I'm here to tell you that you can't."

"But I didn't cheat. I swear I didn't."

"Prove it," Mrs. Anne challenged. "Let's see. Go to the board and solve a problem."

Michele swallowed hard. Any moment now he would accept his blame and move on. Rafaelo was sure of that.

But he amazed everyone as he stood up, shoulders slouched down, his gaze on the floor. His body language didn't scream the confidence he displayed as he stopped in front of the board, pen in hand as he awaited further instructions.

His fingers were trembling on the pen but he stood his ground.

Rafaelo was shocked by this side of his brother. Michele usually avoided conflicts. If he could, he didn't get into arguments, sometimes preferring to let people believe the worst of him instead of stepping in and telling his truth.

It was one of the things that had always bothered Rafaelo, and why Michele would never stop getting picked on. As long as he allowed everything, the bullies would keep going—seeing him weak and pathetic.

But this was different.

What had changed?

What had prompted his brother to put himself out there? To defend himself when he hadn't done that before?

Mrs. Anne started dictating the problem, and reluctantly, Michele begun typing on the board.

Something was wrong. As the teacher continued to speak, Rafaelo realized this wasn't a problem from their textbook.

For the test, every question had been based on a random problem from the textbook—and there were plenty to choose from.

Rafaelo himself had practiced solving all of them to be as prepared as possible for the test. But even he hadn't managed to get every answer right. He'd missed one.

Had Michele really cheated?

It was possible. After all, if he'd had access to every solution during the test, he could have very well done that.

Rafaelo didn't know what to think. On the one hand, his brother had never been invested in school work. He'd never tried to get better grades, always being satisfied with just passing. Yet now? Suddenly a perfect score? Something was amiss.

The teacher stopped, leaving Michele to solve the problem.

Seconds passed. Then minutes.

Michele was holding tightly onto the pen, staring at the board. Yet he wasn't solving anything.

"Could... Could I get a problem from the textbook?" He asked, turning to face the teacher.

"No. If you really solved everything by yourself, then you'll know how to solve this one too. It's very similar to the last problem. Just a couple of things changed," she said smugly.

More time passed and Michele still couldn't solve it.

"Are you willing to confess that you cheated?"

He shook his head.

"I didn't cheat."

"Really?" she laughed drily. "And how did you get 100 then?" she raised an eyebrow as she watched him intently.

"I...I memorized them," he answered in a soft voice, his gaze not daring to meet that of his teacher's.

"You *memorized* them?"

He nodded.

"Unbelievable. That's your excuse? How would you even know which to memorize?"

"I memorized them all," he suddenly said.

Silence descended upon the classroom as everyone stared unblinkingly at him.

"All?" The teacher repeated, a hint of disbelief in her voice.

"Yes," Michele continued to nod, his expression innocent.

"There are over one thousand problems in the textbook, Michele. How could you have memorized all?"

"I simply did," he shrugged. "I didn't cheat."

"Rafaelo," Mrs. Anne called out. "Did you know about this? That your brother apparently has a super memory?"

Rafaelo felt caught between the two. He dragged his gaze from Mrs. Anne to Michele, only to find him looking back with a hopeful expression on his face.

He wanted Rafaelo to take his side.

But how could he when this was the first time he'd heard

such a thing? He'd never known Michele to display any such characteristics.

He was caught...truly caught.

There were only two options. He could tell Mrs. Anne that he knew, protecting his brother once more. But that would be a lie. Or he could admit the truth.

He didn't like to lie.

Yet he didn't want to betray his brother either.

"No," he answered in a small voice. "I didn't know."

Michele's face fell at his words, and he swiftly looked away from him.

"I can prove it. Just ask me any problem from the textbook," Michele pleaded.

Why was he so invested in his grade? And why this time?

"I can't do that, Michele. I gave you a chance and you didn't know how to solve the problem. Let's say you memorized the entire textbook," she rolled her eyes at him. "Isn't that the same as cheating? You *don't* in fact know how to solve them."

"But..." Michele tried to argue.

"No buts. This is final. You'll get a 0 for the test."

Grabbing the sheet off his desk, she took a red pen and crossed the 100 and wrote a big 0 at the top of the sheet of paper. Then she handed it back to Michele, inviting him to take a seat again.

He did as told, looking dejected as he stared at the 0 on the paper.

The lesson continued, but Rafaelo found he could not pay attention. Not when his brother appeared so upset by the score when he regularly didn't care what he got.

When the day ended, and they were on their way back home, he finally got to ask him why.

"Because father promised me. If I got a perfect score, he

would spend a day with me," he told Rafaelo in a sad voice. "But it's ok. I'll find another way," he strained a smile.

The disappointment was visible, and Rafaelo felt like the biggest idiot for not standing up to his brother.

"I'm sorry. I really didn't know you memorized that," he apologized.

"It's fine," Michele shrugged.

But why did Rafaelo have a feeling it wasn't fine? That he should have done more? Stood up for him more?

The only positive was that Michele had no idea what their father would have subjected him to if he had agreed to spend a day with him. He knew that very well, since he often tagged along.

Michele was too sensitive for that side of their father—or of the family. He was too frail and innocent to withstand that ugliness. And so he told himself it was all for the better.

But while Rafaelo struggled with his own demons, the weight of his parents' expectations and his own conflicting feelings, Michele was slowly losing himself.

For all the closeness they both proclaimed, neither truly knew the other, or what the other was going through.

The intention was there, and although sometimes he felt stifled by his position, Rafaelo did want what was better for his brother. Yet that desire was in conflict with everything else. Everything that dictated he only cared for himself.

They were brothers. They were friends. But at the end of the day they were two strangers.

four

AGE TEN

The night breeze brushed against his face as he tipped his head back, enjoying the feeling of solitude he'd always find up there.

The day had been eventful.

Was there any day that wasn't?

Sometimes he was tired of it all. Why did everyone count on him as if he were some robot able to withstand it all? He was sure that at times, both his mother and his father didn't see him as *human*, more like a machine that took orders and behaved accordingly.

He'd never defied them. How could he, when his entire identity was wrapped around being the *perfect* son?

At only ten, he was already exhausted. He didn't want to imagine how things would be when he grew up. When the responsibilities increased.

Letting out a soft sigh, he closed his eyes as he let himself relax for the first time that day.

"You're here early," Michele's voice startled him from his thoughts.

On his knees, he made his way to where Raf was sitting,

gathering his legs under him and fitting himself in the tiny space on the ledge of the roof.

"I needed out," Rafaelo nodded, his gaze distant.

"She'll come around. You know she will," Michele tried to assure him.

"She seemed pretty upset this time."

"Only because she doesn't like you to get hurt," Michele told him, surprising him with his words.

After a fight gone wrong at school, where Rafaelo had jumped in to help Michele out, Cosima had been called for an urgent meeting with all the parents of the other kids involved.

As usual, the blame had been placed strictly on Michele.

The other parents refused to believe their children had been the perpetrators of such a heinous act, and they had immediately reached the conclusion that Michele must have done something to taunt them and cause them to behave so uncharacteristically violently.

And since his brother had no one in his corner to champion for him, the parents had unanimously decided he should be the one held accountable for the fight.

None of the teachers had intervened.

No one had said anything.

In fact, from what they'd heard while eavesdropping on the meeting, Cosima had been quick to point fingers, suggesting that it was Michele's pastime to instigate trouble, and would always inadvertently draw his brother in the midst of it.

Rafaelo had seen the look on his brother's face when he'd heard that. It had been a mix of resignation and pain. His already battered face had looked worse than before—if that was possible.

Even now, as he sneaked a glance at him, it was to see his split lip, the blood crusted around the area.

"You're the one who got hurt," Rafaelo pointedly replied.

Michele shrugged.

"It doesn't hurt."

"You should get Gianna to clean up the wound," he advised gently.

Their sister was always fussing over Michele. He might not have a mother, or the attention of their father, but he had her. And in Rafaelo's mind, that was a whole lot to be proud of.

Gianna was a warrior. And she'd been Michele's biggest champion since birth.

Retrospectively, he didn't think his brother would have survived without Gianna's protection. She was like a mother hen for her baby brother, and sometimes Rafaelo felt left out.

They had their own duo, and they rarely included him in.

He knew he shouldn't feel jealous for that. After all, how many things did he have that his brother lacked?

"I don't want to worry her too much," Michele answered in a small voice.

"She wouldn't mind."

"No, but I would."

Silence descended as they both looked ahead. Michele lifted his hand to trace the horizon line with his finger, and Rafaelo couldn't hold it in anymore.

"Do you hate me?" He asked, turning slightly to gauge his expression.

"Hate you? Why would I?"

"Because I have everything. And you..."

"I have nothing," Michele completed the sentence with a nod.

Oddly enough, he didn't look offended by Rafaelo's words. His features tightened in contemplation for a bit before he answered his question.

"I don't hate you. You're my brother and I love you," he simply stated.

Without warning, Michele turned, his gaze meeting Rafaelo's. His light eyes glinted in the moonlight, and even under all those bruises, his beauty was unmistakable.

Although the kids at school were right that his face had a certain femininity to it, it only lent to his androgynous beauty. And there was nothing wrong with it. In fact, it made him special. Certainly, his unusual features held more appeal than Rafaelo's own tepid ones. He knew he was a handsome boy, with his blonde hair and blue eyes. But he was one of a bunch. Michele was more than that. He was unusually beautiful.

"But..." Rafaelo made to object, but Michele interrupted him.

"You might have more toys, more attention...more love," he tilted his head as he studied his brother. "But it's not for free, is it? Nothing is for free?"

Rafaelo blinked in surprise.

"What... What do you mean?"

"I can see how from the outside we're like the prince and the pauper," Michele chuckled, "yet even though you have all these things, why have I never seen you happy?"

"I am happy," Rafaelo swallowed, feeling compelled to defend himself.

"Are you? It's ok if you're not. Most times, I'm not either," Michele shrugged, the words so matter-of-factly, Rafaelo had to do a double take at his brother.

"How do you know? If you're happy or not?"

"That's a good question," Michele nodded appreciatively, pondering over those words. "I don't know if it's the same for everyone, but for me, happiness is when the thoughts are quiet."

"Thoughts?"

"Worries, fears, concerns," Michele explained. "Things that won't let me be. It's so rare that I get a moment of quietness that I've come to associate it with happiness."

Rafaelo stared in awe at his brother. His words touched something deep within him because he knew exactly what he was talking about. He'd been feeling that way his entire life.

All he'd ever wanted had been for his thoughts to quiet. For time to freeze and give him a respite.

He already felt so old for his young years.

His inner voice had already split into three—his, his mother's and his father's.

Recently, though, his had begun to be but an echo. There was only his parents' voice.

His father had always told him to be strong—to be a man. That he had to learn the ropes of the organization from a young age so he didn't make the same mistakes as him. All his lessons had involved shedding his innocence and learning how to stifle his emotions. Because men couldn't be vulnerable. No, they had to be *men*.

He didn't agree with his father, but that didn't mean he wasn't right. At least when it came to the feelings aspect. Since the moment he'd seen a dead body for the first time, a man killed by his father's people, he'd learned to rein in his emotions.

It wasn't a matter of being strong. It was just a matter of surviving. Now, that was the only way he could move forward. By muting everything out. Seeing, but not really seeing. Hearing, but pretending to be deaf. It was his curse, and he would have to bear it for the rest of his life.

Then there was his mother. And her voice was perhaps the loudest in his brain. The voice of failure. Of not living up to expectations.

The voice blaming *him* for her suffering.

He loved his mother too much to make her sad, and he never wanted for that to happen. But even in his young mind he realized that she was taking advantage of that side of him that valued her opinion above all. She was manipulating him with her feelings, extorting him to do what she wanted and then blaming him when he didn't.

He may be young, but he wasn't stupid. And though to a certain extent he knew what his mother was doing, he couldn't stop.

He wasn't strong enough...

Maybe his emotions were not completely muted, because she was his weakness. And she knew exactly which buttons to push in order to bend him to her will.

"Quietness," Rafaelo nodded. "I think you're onto something," he gave his brother a tentative smile.

Michele returned it with one of his own before setting his gaze once more on the horizon line.

"With all the things you have, sometimes I wonder if your mind is quieter than mine," he mused.

"I reckon it is," Rafaelo replied, thinking back to everything Michele had gone through. He'd had to battle death itself, and for that, he didn't think he deserved a place at the same table as his brother.

"I admire you, you know," he confessed to Michele. "So many things happened to you, *still* happen, and I've never seen you complain about anything."

Admiration was an understatement. He looked up to Michele for his unwavering strength, both with respect and a little bit of envy. There was nothing more that Rafaelo wished for than to share his brother's strength of character.

For all his frail appearance, he was staunch, like a tree in a storm. No matter how the winds sought to batter and uproot it, he still stayed strong.

"There's no point in complaining," he shrugged, a bittersweet smile on his face. "It won't last forever. Once I grow up I'll be on my own and I won't have to depend on anyone. They can't pick on me forever."

"You're right. Once we're old, we should be able to do anything we like." Rafaelo smiled.

Michele didn't reply, and they both settled against the ledge as they looked at the sundown.

Deep down, they both knew that things wouldn't change much even as they grew. Their father's organization was already primed to accept Rafaelo as the official heir instead of Michele. They already knew all the details of the boys' childhoods, and had concluded that Michele was simply too weak to rule.

Benedicto Guerra was proud of that fact, since he'd never planned on having Michele step in his shoes. In fact, he'd done everything he could to ensure he would never become the *don*.

Still, the brothers chose to hope.

In that shared moment, they still had hope.

five

AGE TWELVE

Tiptoeing down the stairs, he was careful to avoid detection as he put one foot in front of another. His ears were attuned to the heavenly sound coming from the dayroom, the melody lulling him in and making his chest constrict with wistfulness.

He knew what it was.

He knew how forbidden it was.

And most of it, he knew he shouldn't like it.

But how could he reconcile the artist with the art? How could he hate on the hands that brought to life that divine melody, even if they were hands that hurt him?

Michele was courting danger just by daring to go closer to the source of the sound. But by some unexpected twist of fate, he couldn't stop himself. He could not help the way the music served as therapy—as a slow healing of the soul.

Maybe her touch was bruising, but those notes that reverberated through the air had the power to put him back together.

Perhaps it was all a huge cosmic joke. Yet he didn't want to believe that. He didn't want to dwell too much on the significance of this, merely wishing to enjoy the music in peace.

Since the strange man had gifted him the singing piano, years ago, he'd found an inexplicable comfort in the sound of music—the sound of the subliminal and everything that *wordlessly* spoke about human experience. There was pain, and there wasn't. Everything was feeling. Everything was sensation.

From a young age he'd been faced with the immense power of words—how they could hurt and scar, and in some rare cases, soothe and calm. He'd learned the hard way how once spoken, words could never be taken back.

He'd been cursed, beaten with harsh words, and those wounds were sometimes more painful than actual corporeal punishments.

He'd learned that, and he'd put it into action. He rarely spoke, unless there was something he wanted to get across, preferring to interact with neutral silence.

Words had damned him. He wasn't going to use them to damn someone else. As a rule, he usually weighed his words and spoke in a calm and composed manner. Michele wasn't one to give in to impulsiveness. Not unless his regular state was altered —rattled by incessant noise that awoke the little something that simmered inside of him.

He wasn't perfect, just like no one was. But he was better than most at hiding his imperfections because he knew he'd be punished for them. And so, he'd selectively altered his personality when interacting with others, displaying a serene façade.

But music was different. Music—wordless melodies—affected him in a strange and elusive way. Music had the power to convey ineffable feelings. But more than anything, it had the courage to convey them.

Rounding the corner, he slowed his steps as he headed towards the entrance of the dayroom.

The music boomed through the hall, the sound louder and louder. He stretched his arm forward, grabbing on to the wood of the door frame as he sneaked a glance inside.

"Again," Raf chuckled as he looked up to his mother, his expression happy and carefree.

"What should I play next?" Cosima asked, her voice soft and warm. It was unlike the voice she used with Michele. In fact, he'd never heard her speak that way, and if he wasn't looking straight at them, he wouldn't have ever believed she was capable of it.

"Play that one..." Rafaelo paused, deep in thought. "The one you said was very simple to learn. I want to watch your hands," he pointed to the keys.

Cosima's face erupted in a huge smile as she nodded at her son. Before playing, though, her arm sneaked around his shoulders, tugging him closer to her on the bench and wrapping him in a big hug.

"I'm so happy we get to spend some time like this," she said as she kissed his forehead. "You've been so busy with school and with your father lately..." she sighed audibly. "Maybe I'm a greedy old lady, but I love what time we can spend together."

Instinctively, Michele brought his hand to his forehead, the pads of his fingers tracing that spot in the middle that Cosima had kissed on Rafaelo's forehead. He wondered what that would feel like.

His sister would give him gentle kisses on the cheeks, and he greatly enjoyed those. Still, he couldn't help but wonder if a mother's kiss was different. If that kind of love felt differently.

Catching his thoughts, he mentally chastised himself.

What was wrong with him?

This was Cosima, the woman who hated him more than anything and who wished he'd died years ago.

But it wasn't *her* specifically that awoke this emotion inside of him. It was what she represented—what Michele had never experienced, and never would.

He was torn.

On the one hand, he told himself it was alright. That he was fine in spite of not having a mother—in spite of not having parents at all. But there was also that side of him that couldn't help but yearn for it, especially knowing it would never happen.

He continued to watch Cosima's interactions with her son, unable to believe she was the same woman who hated his guts and cursed him out every time she saw him. She was so gentle, so soft, almost as if she'd had a personality transplant.

There weren't many things that made him jealous of Rafaelo, mostly because he knew that he was being exploited by everyone around, the expectations placed upon him continually increasing. Yet *this* was the only thing that made him a little envious of him.

Love.

Rafaelo had too much of it, while Michele had none.

He supposed he couldn't help it if people loved him or not, but sometimes he wished he were a little more lovable. Just a little more...

The music started anew, and Michele closed his eyes, simply enjoying the melody. He stood there for the longest time, unmoving and simply locked inside his mind, the music the only outside stimuli.

His feet tapped quietly to the rhythm, and he thought he felt that piece to his soul, a magnitude of feeling that left him reeling.

The spell was broken, however, when the front door suddenly opened.

Michele blinked, suddenly trapped.

There was a direct connection from the front door to the entrance of the dayroom, and whoever would enter the house would be able to see him standing in the doorway.

His body moved before his mind registered it, his feet carrying him up the stairs as he dashed to his room.

Breathing harshly, he kept his body fitted to the door as he attempted to regulate his heartbeats. He couldn't be caught snooping or eavesdropping. That would mean he'd be punished, and if Cosima thought he was spying on *her*, he knew only hell awaited him.

More sounds erupted from downstairs and as he kept his ear to the door, he could make out some words—enough to realize his father had likely arrived home.

More reason to stay locked in his room.

He could feel a sense of disappointment enveloping him, but he didn't want to let himself become a slave to his emotions. And in his fashion, a trained and rehearsed ritual, he stepped forward, stretching his limbs and doing some breathing exercises.

He'd been taught these techniques in the hospital. There had been mental health professionals who would occasionally come by and tend to the patients, helping them cope with the mental toll of illness. It had been imperative to have such a professional in the kids' wing, since repressed feelings could catch up with them into adulthood and transform into trauma.

Michele was aware of all this, as he'd listened to all the talks given at the hospital. But more than anything, he was aware of the danger within him as well.

He'd repressed a great deal of his feelings over the years, preferring to continue being his calm and composed self, even while knowing that there was something lurking beneath the surface. A compilation of all his unfulfilled emotions and unrequited feelings. Because how could any person grow up so reviled and so deprived of affection and still function as a normal human being?

Still, Michele tried.

He knew the perils of his own mind even at such a young age.

His progressive introspection was a product of his inherently analytical mind, and it had slowly revealed to him that everything that had happened from his childhood until then had had an effect on his psyche. He wasn't as unaffected as he'd like to be.

He pretended. Yet he still felt the lack of love—yearned for that elusive feeling.

Instead of dwelling on those emotions that threatened to burst to the surface, he quieted all his thoughts as he emptied his mind and heart.

Calm.

He sought the calmness.

His breathing became sparse, and he regulated each point of inhale or exhale. Soon, he felt his pulse slow down, his erratic heart going back to its status quo.

And when he finally felt fully in control of himself, he opened his eyes.

His room was bare. Save for the strict necessities—some stationaries for school and a few changes of clothes—there wasn't much to see. But he was ok with that—he had to be.

There were no toys. No computers. Nothing a regular boy of his age would usually own.

Yet that didn't matter for Michele. Not when he had his most prized possessions.

Under the bed, his little piano was hidden from sight. He was still so enamored of the little gift that he'd kept it away and for his eyes only. It was, perhaps, the only thing that had always truly belonged to him, and he didn't want that to change.

But then there was also his pencil case, which contained all the tools he needed for his drawings.

Yet things had changed in that regard too.

His father had somehow gotten wind of his hobby and had confronted him about it. Michele had lied that it wasn't true, that he didn't spend his time drawing—for that would have not been an activity befitting his father's first born. By some stroke of luck, he'd managed to convince him that it was just an unfounded rumor. But since then he'd had to either hide his drawings exceedingly well, or destroy them himself to not risk exposure.

Every drawing he tore apart or burned hurt him as if he was physically hurting himself. He couldn't help it. Tears gathered at the corners of his eyes every time he put his hands on a piece of paper with the purpose to destroy it, and he felt the rip in his own soul.

Yet every time, his resolve grew stronger.

Because when he was older, he would be able to do things without seeking approval, or without anyone looking down at him.

On his desk, there was a little calendar that covered a ten-year range. He was already counting down the years until his majority when he'd be able to shout at the top of his lungs that he was an artist, and that was all he'd ever be, for he didn't want anything else. He'd stand proudly with his sketches, and he wouldn't give a damn about what *anyone* said about him.

Six more years.

But that was six more years of hiding and avoiding his father's and stepmother's wrath. He was convinced he could do it, but he was still worried he might not get out unscathed.

Making sure his door was locked, he headed to his bed. Pulling on the mattress, he took out the only drawing pad he still kept. It had his most beautiful drawings and the ones he was most proud of. Still, he knew that the moment the pad was full, he'd have to give up on it to be able to get a new one. It was a routine he hated, but it was one he needed to continue if he wanted to keep everything hidden.

Flipping to one of the empty pages, he got an appropriate pencil as he took a seat on the floor, his hands already at work.

The little he'd manage to hear of the piano music had given him some inspiration for his next piece.

Holding lightly on to the pencil, he started to sketch, slowly losing himself in his art.

Bit by bit, the drawing took shape, a man standing tall and proud in the center of the paper. With skilled movements, Michele added the shadows and indentations to the drawing so it had a realistic feel to it. Only when he was done with the foundation did he add his little flourishes. Because this wasn't *just* any man. No, this was someone he called Lasso, and he was a protector—a superhero.

In his mind, Lasso was already a real character. He had a name, personality traits and a goal—punish those who hurt children and stole their dreams.

It had all started with the seed of an idea when Michele had seen a cowboy movie and the cowboys had been skilled in using a rope to catch cattle, or even bad guys. From there on, the rope —a lasso—had become the central piece of his work. It had the power to stop movement, but also to restrain the enemy.

An avid fan of superhero movies, he'd always wanted to have his own. His personal protector that would save him from his unfortunate existence and would guard his dreams and help him foster them. And if he couldn't have one, then he'd create one.

So Lasso had taken shape.

He'd made sure to pay attention to each detail, giving him muscles and strength to defeat all obstacles as well as some super powers to help him in the fight against evil.

A smile pulled at Michele's lips as he continued to contour Lasso's pose, making him ready to strike against his opponent.

He'd spent so much time with him, that he was convinced that his purpose was to give him life beyond that sheet of paper, and beyond the four walls the pad was hidden in. Lasso needed to be known by a wider audience. As such, slowly, his dreams had taken shape.

Just like that approaching date when he'd be free of his parents, he could also see the beginning of a new kind of life for him.

He wanted to set his creations free, and he wanted people to see them and enjoy them too. Just like he'd needed a superhero in his own childhood as he'd stared at the bleak hospital walls, so he wished other kids would take refuge in Lasso and his superpowers. That he would give them the support and confidence they needed to survive.

In the future, he hoped to do just that—create comic books and stories with Lasso for everyone to meet him.

He didn't know how he'd succeed in doing that. He had nothing aside from his talent and imagination, yet his conviction was strong.

If there was a will, there would be a way.

Six more years.

Enough time to perfect his art and make sure he had something to give to the world.

Yet in his still young mind, he wasn't very versed in how the *real* world worked. He had no idea that he needed money to survive on his own, and that art rarely paid off in the manner in which he envisioned.

He only had his dream. Nothing else.

So focused he was on his drawing that he barely heard the lock turn on the door. Only when the sound of the rusty hinges penetrated his attention did he realize what was happening. He quickly shoved the drawing pad under the bed, hiding everything as he could before assuming an innocent position as he'd learned to do—time and time again.

His father's boots were the first thing he saw. The shiny

leather glinted in the dimly lit room, and he barely dared to raise his gaze to meet his father's.

"Father," he said, managing to keep his voice from trembling.

"Mara tells me you were spying on Rafaelo with his mother?" he asked in a stern voice.

Michele's eyes widened. He'd been seen. And Mara had told on him. Not that he didn't expect that since she was his stepmother's most faithful employee. Yet he hadn't seen her, and *that* was on him.

"I wasn't," he answered in a soft voice. If he raised his voice at his father, there would be hell to pay and he was well aware of that. "I was just going to the kitchen when I heard Cosima play. She plays really well," Michele continued, thinking that praising her could help him get out of this unscathed.

His father grunted, and at that moment, Michele dared to lift his gaze.

Benedicto was surveying the room with sharp eyes, and a shiver went down Michele's back at that perusal.

Please, don't let him see anything wrong with my room...

He was twelve, already a big boy. But when he was in the same room with his father he felt insignificant. Maybe it was the way Benedicto had always behaved with Michele—with distance and coldness. Or maybe, there was also the fact that Michele could feel his father bore him no love—no affection. And that hurt.

He could understand why Cosima didn't like him, she wasn't related to him. But his father? The fact that his own sire had no lost love for him made him feel like the ultimate fool.

Was there something really wrong with him?

Monster.

Cosima didn't shy from calling him a monster. But did they see something in him that he, himself, did not?

"Don't do it again. You know your stepmother doesn't like it when you loiter around," he warned in a gruff voice.

Michele nodded.

"Of course. I'm sorry," he immediately apologized, hoping his father would leave him alone. The more time he spent in his room, the more chances of discovery there were. And his father would *not* take kindly to seeing his artistic hobby.

There had been one time, years ago, when he'd caught him. He'd confiscated everything and torn all his pieces. Then he'd beat and cursed him, telling him he was prohibited from ever thinking about art.

"No Guerra will be seen doing something so undignified."

Since then, he'd always taken extra measures to ensure no one caught him.

"Good," Benedicto finally said, turning around and ready to leave.

Just as Michele was ready to breathe out in relief, Benedicto stopped.

"What's that?"

He stilled.

That voice. It was the voice that signaled he was in trouble.

Before he could order his limbs to obey him, his father was already on him, kicking him aside to reach under the bed.

Michele yelped both in pain and in surprise as he saw his father crouched on the floor, his searching hand bumping into something under the bed.

His eyes went wide with disbelief as he saw him remove his pad from under the bed, as well as a couple of pencils that he'd hidden there.

"Father... That..." Michele stammered, his heart beating loudly in his chest.

He could only watch, helplessly as Benedicto's fingers tightened over the pad. He sifted through its pages, his features drawn up in anger as he took in drawing after drawing.

"She told me you were still doing this," he finally spoke, his voice grave. "But I assured her you'd learned your lesson." *Her.* He assumed it was Cosima who Benedicto was talking about. Of course she'd try to throw Michele again and again under the bus.

"I... It's for school."

"Really? This?" He lifted the pad, aggressively pointing towards one of the pictures with one finger. It was an incipient draft of Lasso. "Or this?" Benedicto tore the page as he pointed to the next one. "Or this?" He continued like this? Tearing each page before asking about the next drawing, getting increasingly angrier at Michele's silence.

"You didn't learn your lesson, did you, Michele? You learned nothing!" Benedicto declared, flinging the pad on the floor and away from him.

"Please," Michele whimpered as he assumed a subservient position, going to his knees and rubbing his palms together as if he were praying. "No one knows. And I'm not hurting anyone," he continued to plead with his father, tears already coating his lashes as he glanced at his torn drawings—at the torn parts of his soul.

"You're not hurting anyone?" Benedicto lifted a brow as he took a step closer. His features were stern, his voice dangerously low.

Michele startled at the approach. Especially as his father kicked the door closed with one foot, all the while focusing his attention on him.

"You're fucking embarrassing me, that's what you're doing! What do you think people will think of me, or of our family when they find out my first born son is a fucking artist?"

"But... It's not a bad thing...."

"It is a fucking bad thing, Michele. It's a coward's thing. And it's a fucking female activity. Are you telling me you're a little girl?"

"No, sir, no..."

"Are you fucking telling me my son is actually a little girl?" He asked again, his voice more punctured as he grabbed Michele's lapels with both hands, lifting him off the floor.

"It's just a hobby," he whispered, wincing as he felt his father's hand around his throat.

"Next you're going to tell me you're taking it up your ass because it's just a hobby, ain't that right, boy?"

"Wha-what?" Michele blinked, unable to understand what his father was saying.

"I won't have a fucking pansy for a son, you hear me?" He growled as he shoved Michele backwards.

His back hit the wooden frame of his desk, his frail bones colliding directly with the hard surface. He couldn't help the tears that leaked out of his eyes. The pain radiated from his back and to his entire body.

"Please..."

"I'm going to teach you a lesson boy. And this time, you better pay attention," his father said before his palm made contact with Michele's cheek. The strength of it was so great, it made his head reel to the side.

Before he could even react, though, his father had his belt off. Folding it around the middle, he took hold of the lower end before flinging the other one with his entire force towards Michele.

He barely had time to raise his arms or defend himself.

The entire length and width of the belt connected with his body, the stinging pain making him howl in pain. Still, that didn't stop his father. It only enraged him.

In between the harsh blows, Michele managed to curl around himself like a hedgehog in danger. Though his front was guarded, his back was not. Blow after blow, and the pain was becoming overwhelming. His face was red, his breathing harsh.

"Please..." he whimpered in pain, but Benedicto did not stop.

Only when he was tired and sweaty did he tuck away his belt.

"You're grounded. You're forbidden to leave your room for the foreseeable future. And you'd better forget all about your stupid art, boy. It's worthless anyway," Benedicto sneered at him.

Michele lay on the floor, barely moving. Out of everything his father had told him, the fact that he'd called his art worthless rang in his ears. Moans of pain erupted from his mouth before they turned into wails of pain—both physical and spiritual.

Six more years.

But he didn't think he could make it.

Six

AGE TWELVE

Stifling a groan, he lifted his shirt as he looked in the mirror. His entire back and side were red, deep welts marring his skin. He wondered if they would blister. Usually they did, so he wouldn't be surprised if he had to deal with even more pain when that happened.

His father had never shied away from the corporal punishments. Michele was used to it, but that didn't mean it ever got easier. Especially since he'd never had a strong body, the beatings would take an even greater toll on his body.

He did the best he could, applying some soothing gel to his back before steeling his resolve.

This couldn't go on.

His art wasn't worthless.

He wasn't worthless.

And he needed out.

Somewhere between the slapping sound the belt made when it hit his flesh and the time it took for the body to register the pain, his decision had been made.

He couldn't go on like this. And he couldn't wait six more years.

With little enough belongings as it was, he only needed his school backpack to stuff inside anything that might have been of value.

He put the little piano, a sandwich for later, and a change of clothes.

Maybe he didn't know where he was going, but one thing was for sure. He'd work, and he'd do whatever he could to earn his existence as long as that meant he would be far away from the house and from the family that clearly didn't want him.

It was past three in the morning when he tiptoed his way around the back of the house, using the staff exit to get out. For a moment, a very brief moment, he felt guilty for abandoning his brother and sister. But then he remembered that they had people who cared for them.

Gianna was Benedicto's favorite, and Rafaelo had Cosima. He...well, he had his siblings, but he also had the hate of the rest.

It would be better for everyone if he simply disappeared.

He took a few steps away from the house before starting into a sprint, going out back and avoiding any of the guards he knew would patrol at night. It was almost like a hide and seek game as he avoided any detection before leaving his family's land and making it to the highway.

After that, though, he was a little lost.

He removed a small school notebook from his backpack, and with a tiny lighter he looked over the map of the state that was drawn on the first pages. It wasn't detailed enough for him to get any sense of where to go, but he wagered he was about an hour away from the city on foot. After all, by car, it took only about twenty minutes to reach his school. A few calculations later, and he was convinced he could do it.

And if he could find someone to take him to the city, even better.

It was minutes later that he kept on walking by the side of the highway. His back was killing him, the added weight of the bag making his wounds chafe against his clothing. He was tired and in pain. Still, his resolve was ever so strong.

Once he got to the city, and during daylight, he'd try to earn an honest wage by drawing people on the streets. He'd seen that before and knew it was possible.

He had maybe ten dollars on him, but if he rationed it well, he could buy some paper and draw with the pencils he still had left over.

In his optimistic mind, the plan was bound to work. And once people on the streets saw his talent they might help him achieve his dream of becoming a professional comic book artist.

And so, despite the pain, Michele had a huge smile on his face as he imagined himself at book signings, drawing for people and making children feel happy with his superhero, Lasso.

Not too much time later, a car pulled up on the road, the driver looking Michele up and down and frowning at him.

"What are you doing here at this hour?" He asked him skeptically.

An older man of about fifty, he had a fatherly look about him as he inquired about Michele's wellbeing.

A little ashamed to lie, but knowing it wouldn't work otherwise, Michele told him he needed to get to the city to the hospital since his mother was there.

"What hospital," the man continued to ask, not believing Michele's answer.

"Mount Sinai on the Upper West Side," he replied glibly, being all too familiar with the hospitals in the city.

Eventually the man grunted, inviting him in the passenger seat and proceeding to ask him a bunch of other questions—

what was wrong with his mother, where was his father, and why he was going alone. Possessing a shrewd mind and an unusual attention to detail, Michele managed to answer all the man's questions in a believable fashion.

And not half an hour later, he was dropped in front of Mt. Sinai with a five dollar bill to grab a sandwich and a message wishing him luck in the future.

The little interaction might have been harmless for the old man, but for Michele it was priceless in one aspect—it restored his faith in humanity.

The man had helped him without expecting anything in return, and he'd even given him five dollars, which Michele had been a little reluctant to accept despite his poor financial situation. Everything had shown him that there *are* good people in the world, and so he had renewed hope for the future.

A smile on his face, he started wandering on the streets. The city was still alive with color, lights coming off from every building.

"This is it," he whispered to himself. "I can finally be myself."

If no one knew his past, then they wouldn't judge him the same.

He spent minutes on end walking around aimlessly. Though the pain in his back was ever present, the excitement he felt drowned it out. Everything was possible now, and a little pain would surely not stop him from enjoying himself.

Soon, though, he realized he'd ventured off the beaten path. The lights weren't so strong in that part, and the streets seemed smaller and smaller.

Frowning, he stopped, orienting himself around and trying to think which way to go. He had no destination in mind, but he knew he needed to get *somewhere*.

"A little late to be wandering about, boy," a thick voice whispered from behind.

He pivoted on his heels, his brows drawn in consternation as he took in his surroundings.

A figure emerged from the shadows, slowly moving towards him.

The man was disheveled, his clothes hanging off him as if they didn't fit him properly, the hem of his shirt a little torn, while his pants were folded at the ankles.

As he neared Michele, he could see his face better.

He had a thick beard that seemed to hide his entire face. But the moment he came closer, he could feel the smell emanating from him.

His nostrils flared, and he instinctively took a step back.

"Where are your parents, boy?" He asked, his breath almost on Michele's face.

Though he hadn't encountered such a person before, instinctively, Michele knew he was in over his head. *This* was danger. Something inside of him told him to run.

Backing away, he schooled his features to mask the disgust he was feeling. Any moment now he would start running.

But just as he was about to make a dash, the man's arm darted out, grabbing him roughly by his bag and dragging him further into the shadowy area.

Michele started squirming, kicking and yelling for the man to let go. The position he got him into didn't help either as it put more pressure on his wounded back, the pain so biting he was finding it hard to find the strength to fight the man.

Out of nowhere, a punch connected with his face, the man's knuckles grazing his cheekbone. A horrified gasp escaped Michele, unable to believe what was happening to him. Another fist followed, that one catching him in the eye. The pain was unlike anything he'd ever felt, the wounds on his back nothing compared with the way his eyes rolled in the back of his head.

"Let me go," he yelled. "Please, let me go."

The bad smell was getting worse as the man dragged him in the darkened alley. It wafted to his nostrils and it made his stomach lurch in protest.

"You knew what you were doin' out at this hour, boy," the man chuckled, his words almost stilted.

Michele was teetering between a state of being and not being, his brain foggy, his mind slipping from him.

He felt his knees give out. Or maybe it was the man who pushed him down, as his dirty hands were suddenly holding him down.

The hard asphalt was riddled with small pebbles, all digging into his skin. Pain was coming from all directions and he didn't know how to withstand it all.

"I'm sorry, please... Just let me go," Michele tried again, his voice broken.

"Behave yo'self and I just might," the man chuckled and before he knew it, Michele felt a blade at his throat.

"What... Please..." He kept pleading, but it was all in vain.

One of the man's hands was in his hair, tugging so hard he felt his scalp burn. The other was struggling with the fastening of his pants.

Michele had no idea what was happening. His teeth was clattering, his heart was hammering in his chest. Pain pulsated from everywhere, and his eye was starting to fail him, slowly closing itself shut. He knew it was going to get swollen—it had happened before.

But right now, he needed all his strength. He needed... he didn't know what he needed, but he knew he had to get out of there. He had to fight.

"Suck me off nicely, boy, and I'll let ya go," the man told him in a gruff voice.

It took Michele a moment to realize what he meant, and by then, his pants had snapped open, a putrid smell wafting towards him and making him sick.

He barely swallowed back the vomit rising in his throat.

It was the stink of piss, of uncleanliness and death... It was so nasty, his stomach rolled, another wave of nausea hitting him.

The old man brought his head closer to his crotch, the smell terribly unbearable. Michele yelped in protest, his voice resounding loud and clear even in the isolated space.

Suddenly, he sensed something close to his face, and with a whimper of disbelief, he closed his eyes.

The man grabbed him better by his hair, tugging his head down so he could angle his mouth to his dick.

The moment stretched forever as Michele felt trapped inside his own body, the situation a nightmare he'd never thought he'd find himself in.

But just as the man was about to force his mouth open, a loud shot resounded in the air.

One more. And another.

That's when the man's hold loosened, and a few seconds later he dropped to the ground.

Michele felt a warm liquid splatter on his face, yet he didn't dare open his eyes.

He just lay there, trembling, shock and pain accumulating to such a powerful crescendo he didn't think he had it in him to react.

"Michele?" A voice called out his name. "Michele, open your eyes," it was a man's voice. And in the deep recesses of his mind, he recognized it.

Lulled by a sense of security he did not know existed, he

squinted with his uninjured eye, making out the shape of a big man standing in front of him.

"Are you ok, son?" The man asked him, and slowly, his face came into sight.

Losing his equilibrium, Michele fell on his ass, blinking rapidly as he recognized the man in front of him. It was *him*. The stranger from the hospital.

"I... I know you," he uttered the words softly.

"I'm happy you remember me," Nicolo smiled stiffly. " But we need to get out of here. Are you good to go?" His voice went down a notch, as if he was trying to address him in a gentle tone so as not to scare him more than he already was.

Michele gave a numb nod, and as Nicolo extended his hand for help, he took it.

Helping him to his feet, Nicolo patted him on the back, urging him to let go of his bag. Michele obeyed, happy to have that weight lifted from his shoulders. But as he regained some control over himself, he glanced to the side, his eyes widening as he took in the old man on the ground, blood pouring from his body.

Almost like a robot, he lifted his hands to his own face, feeling for the liquid he'd been stained with, shocked to see red coming off on his fingers.

"He..."

"He's dead," Nicolo stated. "As he should be for messing with a kid. With *you*."

"How... How did you know I was here?" He stammered, looking between the dead body and the man by his side.

"I've been watching you, Michele," he simply said. "Shall we? We can talk about that later."

Michele found that he couldn't tear his gaze away from the dead man, or the fact that Nicolo had killed him so easily. Was that to be his fate too? But he didn't think so. He wouldn't have saved him just to kill him. More than anything, Nicolo had only done him favors until now.

"Ok," Michele eventually nodded.

In his mind, he went over everything that happened, the residual shock still clouding his mind. Still, he was able to see Nicolo for what he was—his protector.

He walked carefully to the car, his wounds making him wince with every slight movement. And though he'd been beaten and almost abused by the old man, a part of Michele couldn't help but feel bad about his death.

The family's business had been in the open for as long as he could remember, so violence wasn't something Michele was unfamiliar with, especially since it was doled out by his own guardians. But this was the first time he'd seen someone die, especially because of him.

And he didn't know how that made him feel.

The car started, moving slowly out of that alleyway and on to the main street.

He still looked back to the place where the old man had died, his feelings mixed, his heart heavy.

"Don't," Nicolo said. "Don't feel sorry for him. Do you think you're the first one he tried to rape?"

His question made Michele pause, and with a slow shake of his head, he pursed his lips whispering a soft *no*.

"And you wouldn't have been the last either. These people," Nicolo shook his head. "Don't worry about it. Ok, son?"

Son.

He'd never heard that term from his father, and hearing it from Nicolo made him feel...good.

"Ok," he gave a brisk nod.

For a while, Michele was worried Nicolo would take him back to his home. He didn't want to know what would happen if his father knew he'd run away from home. The beating he'd gotten before would be a fluke compared to what he'd do to him if he found out Michele had expressly disobeyed him. But he didn't. Instead, he instructed the car to take them to a certain location he called the *ground*.

"You're not taking me home," Michele observed in his quiet manner.

"Not yet," Nicolo answered. He was seated across from Michele, and this time he could analyze his features better.

Their eyes were the same, but that was where the similarities ended. Whereas Michele had a soft and delicate face, his features small and dainty, Nicolo's were harsher. Age lines marred his forehead, and his skin was roughened by carelessness and years in the sun. His lips were thin and barely visible, his jaw peppered with the dark shadows of an incipient beard. He wasn't a bad-looking man, but there was a scary aura that surrounded him and made Michele tread carefully around him.

"Why did you leave?" He suddenly asked, and Michele noted he hadn't asked him how he got to the city or where he planned to go. No, the question was put in such a way that Michele had to wonder how Nicolo had known to find him.

"I want to be independent. On my own," he shrugged.

"Independent? How old are you, son?"

"Twelve..." Michele lowered his gaze, feeling a little silly at his proclamation.

"Twelve, and you want to be independent? How does that work?"

"I don't like it at home. And it doesn't like me either," he stated vaguely, though Nicolo could very well understand what he meant.

"You're hurt," he simply stated.

Michele shrugged.

"Show me."

"No, I'm fine."

"You're not, and you know it. Your eye is already swelling, and your entire face is full of bruises. Now, I wager there are more..."

"No," Michele shook his head.

He didn't know why he was so hesitant to tell Nicolo about the beating he'd taken from his father, but he supposed he was ashamed. He wasn't a good son, he'd never been. First, he'd been sick his entire childhood, and now he was small and weak, with interests that only embarrassed the family.

"Tell me," Nicolo demanded in a sharp tone, and Michele's eyes widened at him.

It wasn't long before Nicolo coaxed the truth out of him, and Michele blinked back tears as he expected him to judge him for his interests too.

"So you're saying you like to draw," Nicolo nodded to himself. "Show me," he flung his backpack towards him.

A little put on the spot, Michele complied, taking out a sheet of paper from his bag and a pencil before doing a quick sketch of Nicolo.

His eye didn't miss a thing, and he captured Nicolo's stern expressions as well as the tic in his jaw as he held his anger at bay. So when Michele presented him his work, he couldn't help but raise a brow in surprise.

For the longest time, he didn't say anything, keeping Michele on edge. He simply analyzed the sketch attentively.

"And you want to make a career out of this?"

Michele nodded.

"Tell me more," Nicolo prompted, without commenting on the drawing.

Michele was reluctant to share with him his dreams, but he found that he didn't want to hide them either. Not when Nicolo's gift had been such a godsend for him and had kept the demons at bay when the times had gotten too hard.

He supposed it was only his appearance that was harsh and unyielding, while the inside was softer—otherwise he couldn't reconcile that with his savior.

"I want to draw comic books," he lifted his head high, confidently proclaiming his ambition. "I want to draw comic books about superheroes," he reiterated.

Nicolo leaned back in his seat, regarding him with interest.

"Superheroes? How come?"

And so Michele told him. Once he started explaining, he couldn't stop his enthusiasm from coming to the surface, and he ended up telling Nicolo everything about the fictional character he'd invented—Lasso—and how he would keep the world a safe place from bullies and mean people.

"So you want to save the world?" Nicolo chuckled.

Michele didn't know what was so amusing about it so he just nodded.

"I want to make it a better place. I may not be able to save it —who can? But I can make it easier to live in," he gave a tremulous smile.

"Ambitious. I like that. But you can't save anything if you're not strong, son. That's the first rule in this world," his jaw clicked as he stared at Michele intently. "It's not enough for Lasso to be strong for you. *You* need to be strong too. And seeing...." His eyes roved over Michele's battered body. "That doesn't seem to be the case."

"I am strong," Michele blinked, confused, before frowning. "Well, maybe I'm not physically strong, but I *am* strong."

"You told me about bullies. Do you think bullies care about the strength of your character?" Nicolo laughed. "They only care about what they can do with their fists. And when they see you down, it doesn't matter that you can still stand up at the end of the day. For them, that's a won fight."

"But not a won war. I'd rather lose one battle at a time,

showing them their wrong ways and winning the war by default," Michele burst into a blinding smile, satisfied with his logic.

Nicolo crossed his legs, an amused expression on his face. Shaking his head at Michele, he started laughing.

"Let me get this straight, son," he said between chuckles, "you want to save the world with your preaching?"

"It's not preaching. It's the truth. Fists can only take you so far."

"I'd argue otherwise. Looking at you, fists can definitely take you a *long* way."

"But beyond that?" Michele asked, genuinely curious. "They can beat me however many times they want. That won't change my mind. And if it won't change my mind, have they really won?"

There was a brief pause as Nicolo narrowed his eyes at him.

"If you're dead, then yes. They've won."

The car came to a sudden stop.

"Let me show you something," Nicolo said as he motioned Michele to get out of the car.

A worn warehouse stretched before them, and the moment they approached, the doors opened wide to receive them. Once inside, Michele could see a different side of the world—one he'd never witnessed before.

There was a massive fighting ring in the middle of the room, and all around there were chairs laid out like those inside an arena. The only similar thing Michele had ever seen had been inside of a movie, or a comic book.

A few people walked around, all stopping to show their respect to Nicolo.

Michele followed behind, in awe of the older man and the respect he commanded around him.

"What are we doing here?"

The question was ignored as Nicolo led him to an area in the back.

With his bag on his back, Michele barely kept himself straight. Some areas of his body were numb, while others continued to hurt him like hell.

"Nico," a woman's voice resounded in the arena. "You're back!"

Michele watched in wonder how a slender lady around Cosima's age dashed towards Nicolo, jumping on him. She held a cigarette in her perfectly manicured hand that she lifted in the air as she hugged him.

"And who is this?" she blinked when she saw Michele behind Nicolo.

"Nico, don't tell me... it's him?"

"Yes. It's him," Nicolo simply nodded, continuing on until he reached a small room. He took off his coat and made himself comfortable.

The woman was still watching Michele with a peculiar look on her face, almost as if he was scrutinizing him inside out.

"I'm Camilla, darlin'," she said in a soft voice. One that made Michele blink in surprise. "But call me Cami, will ya?"

"I'm Michele," he scrubbed one hand on the outer leg of his pants before extending it towards the lady. "Nice to meet you."

"Gosh, look at ya, so well behaved," she exclaimed, and instead of taking his hand, she opened her arms and swallowed him in a big hug.

The gesture was entirely foreign to Michele and he didn't know what to do. At the same time, while his back was killing him, he didn't have it in him to protest when it was the first time someone had greeted him so positively before.

"Come, let me help you make yourself comfortable." She said as she took his hand, leading him to the same room where Nicolo was currently deep in conversation with a few men.

Not wanting to interrupt, he allowed Cami to show him around.

"Here, sit and I'll make you some hot chocolate, how does that sound?"

He nodded, taking the time to study her better.

She had black hair, rolled up in some kind of bun. A few loose strands were on her forehead, shielding her skin like a curtain. Black eyes and tanned skin, she had two permanent laugh lines around the corners that crinkled when she spoke. And when she smiled, two more dimples appeared. She had a fresh and happy face, something Michele wasn't very familiar with.

Moving around with natural grace, she put some water in a kettle before getting some sort of packet from a drawer. Removing a mug as well, she placed it in front of him with a smile, dumping the brown contents of the packet inside before adding the hot water.

"Wait a moment until it cools, all right?"

Again, he only nodded.

Cami frowned at his lack of answer, and she squinted at him.

"Love, I don't have my glasses but are those bruises?" she asked, genuine concern dripping from her tone.

Before Michele could answer, she was already yelling for Nicolo.

"Nico, what the fuck happened to the boy? Did you hit him? Did you fucking hit him?" The aggression with which she demanded an answer to that question amazed Michele. She was small, but once she was determined to get something, she really did.

He put his hands on the warm cup, bringing it closer to him as he let his eyes roam about the room.

"Of course not, Cami. Who do you think I am? I don't fucking hit kids."

"You better, or your ass would be on the line."

"Since when are you so involved in this?" Another man chuckled. "Didn't you just meet the boy?"

"So? Look how cute and frail he is. The poor dear has marks all over. So if it wasn't you, then who the hell did it?"

"Dead. He's dead," Nicolo rolled his eyes at her.

Cami pursed her lips before slowly nodding. "Good, good."

"Thank you," Michele finally found his voice, addressing the kind woman who'd taken his side without even knowing him. For him, that already put her in the *best people* category, not that there were many people there.

"Oh, bother," she waved her hand. "You're home here, darlin', ok? This is your home," she gave him a sweet smile.

And just as Michele didn't think things could get better, she got some medicine from the same cabinet she'd been searching earlier, and she started dabbing it on his face, to the places he'd taken the most painful hits.

Her touch was gentle and precise, and though the medicine stung at his skin where it met open wounds, he didn't dare make a word. He endured all her ministrations, happiness blooming in his chest at being the object of someone's care for once.

"Is he done?" Nicolo asked after a while, and Cami hollered a quick yes.

"Come here, son," he called to Michele.

Looking at the older man, he was surprised to see he'd changed. No longer in the gray suit he'd been wearing when he picked him off the streets, he was now sporting a pair of shorts and a white shirt.

"I'll show you what strength means," he commented as he tugged Michele to his feet, taking him out of the small room and towards the arena.

"Behave, boys," Cami called from behind, sending them air kisses.

"Is she your wife?" Michele asked once they were a few feet away and out of hearing distance.

"Wife?" Nicolo guffawed. "I'm not married, son. What, you like her? A little too old for you, but I'm not one to judge."

"No, no. You misunderstood me." Michele was quick to defend himself, a blush suffusing his cheeks. "She was very kind to me."

"She's a very kind woman. To all of us," Nicolo grunted, but he didn't offer much else.

For Michele it didn't matter. Not when she'd been so kind to her without expecting something in return. It was a first for him, and something he'd cherish.

"What are we doing here?" he inquired when Nicolo asked him to sit on a bench right outside the ring.

"You're going to see how a real man behaves. This is a lesson, son," Nicolo explained. "You might have those ideas in your brain that preaching can solve world peace or whatever nonsense you were talking about. But this is the real world, and in *my* real world, we solve problems with our fists. The strongest is the strongest, not because he has a big brain, though that can help sometimes, but because he holds others accountable."

Taking a roll of gauze from the bench, he wrapped the material around his knuckles.

Michele watched attentively, and in that moment he found Nicolo very cool. He was so self-assured and confident, almost as if he knew he would win in any situation. And *that* made Michele watch him with admiration.

"Now sit there and watch. This is what strength is," Nicolo grunted before he sneaked behind the boundary of the ring.

"Who wants their ass kicked today?" he yelled.

Michele's eyes widened. He didn't think anyone would be dumb enough to give himself over to Nicolo. Not when he was clearly a strong opponent.

But he was wrong.

Just as Nicolo asked for a challenger, a line of men appeared on the other side of the ring. Even more people started filling the seats around the arena, and soon, the entire building was full of noise as people were placing bets on who would win.

The first man stepped inside the ring, his cocky attitude evident in the way he was smirking at Nicolo, goading him into starting the fight. But he didn't mind it. He was as calm as ever as he surveyed his opponent.

And when the man charged, Nicolo merely stepped aside, tripping him before grabbing him in a chokehold, using so much strength that the man soon tapped out.

The next opponent was a bit rougher, and there was a flurry of punches—right and left—before Nicolo was once more proclaimed the winner.

And so it continued. None of the men who were challenging him had anything on Nicolo, and he knew it. Still, there wasn't cockiness that he exuded. It was self-assurance.

Michele was in awe as he studied the fights, not for their movements or for their bloodiness, but for the body language—the only thing he was an expert on.

So lost he was in what was happening on the ring, that he barely realized when Nicolo slid next to him, bloody and sweaty and grinning sheepishly at Michele.

"See what I mean, son? They're brave until you subdue them. Until you crush them," he nodded towards the area where the defeated men had gathered, all complaining of pains but begrudgingly admitting Nicolo had bested them in a fair manner.

"I disagree." Michele said quietly, his eyes on the men.

"Hm?" Nicolo huffed in surprise. "What do you mean you disagree?"

"Fighting doesn't make you strong," he started. "Strength is when you know your ability, and others know it too. That way, you don't have to use your physical strength."

"Is that right," Nicolo narrowed his eyes skeptically at Michele.

"Did you see the line from the beginning? I think there were twenty people or so. Out of those, how many did you actually fight?"

Nicolo didn't answer, waiting for Michele to continue.

"Once you defeated a few of them, the rest realized it was useless to continue."

"Yes, but first I had to fight them."

"Not necessarily. When you first stepped into the ring, you were so confident in your skills that at least five people left the queue before the first fight begun."

There was a brief pause before Nicolo started to laugh.

"A little strategist, aren't you?"

Michele frowned.

"You're right and you're wrong," Nicolo smiled sadly. "There comes a time when every man has to throw away his principles and fight—dirty. Your ideas *can* help you get far in life. But they won't *always* help. Trust me. Been there, done that. The best course of action is to learn *both* ways. Keep your principles to yourself. Abide by them. Treasure them. But when the fight of your life comes, throw that fucking punch."

"I hope it never comes," Michele whispered in a low voice.

"I hope so, too, son. I hope so, too."

* * *

At the crack of dawn, Michele was returned to his home. Nicolo left him with one piece of advice.

"Your time will come, son. Just bear with it for now. The time will come when you'll have everything."

Michele didn't know what to think of his words, but he took them as encouragement and Nicolo's way of telling him to show strength. Because only by withstanding the hell that was his home situation could he truly show what he was made of—the fact that his inner strength did not have to be supplied by physical one.

Stealthily, he made his way to his room, but before he could go inside quietly, his brother was on him.

"Michele," he raised his voice as he took in the many injuries Michele was sporting on his face.

"Shh," he brought his finger to his lips, beckoning him inside his room. "They'll hear you," he said as he closed the door behind Rafaelo.

"What happened to you?" His eyes were wide as he took in Michele's appearance and the many wounds marring his face.

"Just a little scuffle," Michele shrugged. "I'm fine."

"You don't look fine," Rafaelo pursed his lips. "You didn't fight back, did you?"

Michele's lips tugged up in a guilty smile as he shied away from his brother, afraid he'd tackle him to the ground or touch his body where his flesh was most tender. He could lie about his face, but he never wanted him to know about what lay beneath his clothes.

"Wait here," Rafaelo said, and he dashed out of the room.

Michele had no time to blink before he was back, though, and with him he'd brought some medicine as well.

"Why do you have that?" He frowned as he pointed to the ointments and the bandages that he could make out in Rafaelo's little pouch.

"Silly, for you of course. I need to tend to you when you get hurt," he chuckled. "If you're not going to fight back, I might as well *do* something else."

"For me?" He blinked, taken aback.

"Of course it's not for me. When do I ever get hurt?" Rafaelo huffed as he took out the healing gel he'd bought for his brother.

"On the bed," he instructed Michele, coming closer to him to examine the state of his eye and the many scrapes littering his cheeks. "Let's hope none of these will scar," he whispered as he took a bit of gel and applied it to the battered region. "We wouldn't want your pretty face to get ruined, would we?"

His easy going banter made Michele smile, and he gave a small shake of his head.

"And let *you* be the most handsome brother? No can do," he joked.

"Exactly. You are the good-looking one," he giggled

"Then which one are you?" Michele asked, curious.

"Me? I'm the resilient one."

"Resilient?" Michele frowned.

"I'm that stone that never moves," Rafaelo explained, but his eyes were on his face as he worked his magic. He wasn't looking into Michele's eyes, and Michele wagered he didn't want to. "The one that slowly gets eroded by time and everything around. But still, it never moves."

"You're moving just fine," Michele retorted, rolling his eyes in an attempt to bring the conversation back to a playful vibe.

He knew his brother didn't have it great either, for all the glory that was to be gleaned from the outside. He knew he was just as empty as Michele, or maybe even worse.

Because he had things, but he could never enjoy them.

On the other hand, Michele never had them, and he didn't know *how* to enjoy them.

Their situations were different. One was the favored son, the other was the invisible one. But that didn't mean either was happy. That didn't mean Rafaelo was any happier than him.

"Maybe," Rafaelo smiled. "Maybe I'll finally move if there's a powerful enough force to push me."

"Maybe," Michele agreed. "But when it does, be careful where you land."

"Anywhere but here," Rafaelo whispered. "Anywhere."

"Wouldn't that be great..." Michele mused.

Rafaelo finished tending to his wounds and he applied a few band-aids to the deeper cuts, instructing Michele to be careful to always keep them clean.

But as the hour became late, he needed to leave the room and return to his.

"Thank you, Raf," Michele's hand darted out as he stopped his brother before he left. "You're the best," he gave him a smile as he lifted both his thumbs up.

"Any time," Rafaelo chuckled, shaking his head as he brought his palm over Michele's head, ruffling his hair in a playful gesture.

Then he was gone.

Michele's smile was still on his face as he stared at the closed door.

Did he have it really that bad? Maybe in those times when he felt hopeless he truly thought so. But now, witnessing both Nicolo and Rafaelo's gestures of thoughtfulness and goodwill, he realized he had a lot more than most.

He had a home. He had food. Maybe sometimes there was added pain. But he *did* have people who loved and cherished him. Maybe they weren't his parents, but they were his brother, his sister, and now his friend.

And for the moment, he truly believed it was enough.

SEVEN

AGE THIRTEEN

"Do I have to come, too?" He rolled his eyes at his mother.

"Of course, dear. It's our wedding anniversary and you're part of the package," she winked at him before returning her attention to the mirror. Bringing her red rouge to her lips, she dabbed it gently all over for a smooth effect.

His mother was a beautiful woman. Light auburn hair that went just below her shoulder blades, she had a flawless complexion and a pair of light gray, soulful eyes. She also possessed an impeccable sense of style and was often envied for her fashion and poise in their circle.

"But it's your time with *papa*. I don't want to intrude," he tried to convince her.

"Of course you're not intruding. Why, we're going to that place downtown, the one with the jazz band?" She continued, ignoring his plea. "I have a little surprise for you too."

"A surprise?"

She merely smiled, rummaging through her bag and waving two sheets of paper in the air. Narrowing his eyes at them, Rafaelo realized they were music sheets.

"I might have come up with a song or two," she smiled sheepishly.

"*Mamma*," Rafaelo groaned. Yet he wasn't annoyed. If anything, this changed things, since he was now too curious about her new composition to argue about *not* going to the restaurant.

Rafaelo and his mother had an established routine going on. She would always experiment with sounds on the piano to test and play with his brain and its perception of sound.

Since young he'd discovered he had an odd ability to distinguish sounds by taste. But it went beyond that. His brain worked in such a way that all of his senses sometimes mingled together, everything channeling down on taste. In addition to sound, even sights and smells could end up on his tongue, allowing him to experience the world in a novel way.

In the beginning, he'd thought everyone could feel what he was feeling. He'd had no idea that it was a rare condition called synesthesia that was causing it. When he'd remarked to his mother that one of her pieces tasted like mint ice cream, she'd been befuddled, asking him to tell her what he'd meant. Slowly, she'd coaxed out of him all of the details pertaining to his condition, and instead of seeing him as odd, she'd made it her mission to find as much as possible on the topic of synesthesia and help Rafaelo use his new found ability to the fullest.

And so an interesting routine had started between them. Since piano was her specialty, she would often compose short pieces in order to elicit certain tastes and reactions from him. She'd play it for him and then would wait excitedly to see if her perception of what her music would taste like aligned with his.

It was silly, really, but it made them feel closer in a time where he didn't get to spend too much time with her.

For the last couple of years, their family had been going through a rough patch financially. Though just a kid, he hadn't been spared of the information or the fact that his parents had high hopes for him to, simply put, get them out of that mess when he grew up.

Benedicto, his father, had grand dreams of mingling with the New York elite and rubbing elbows with the richest of the rich, slowly putting behind his criminal background.

Easier said than done.

Benedicto didn't have much financial acumen, and whenever he managed to turn a business around, it was purely luck, not skill. As such, though his dreams remained big, reality and circumstances made him continue with his criminal activities.

Legal business could always fail. Illegal ones, not so much when you had the name to back you up. And the Guerra name was enough to give Benedicto a seat at the discussion table of the underground work. He might not be the most agreeable man around, but he was received. And he took advantage of that.

That didn't mean that the expectations placed on Rafaelo didn't exponentially increase as time went by. His father placed all his trust in him to one day be smart enough to make wise financial decisions, all the while teaching him the ropes to becoming a veritable mafioso.

"Shall we?"

Rafaelo reluctantly nodded, curious about the piece she'd prepared for him, but also wishing to make her happy on such an important day.

As they went downstairs, his father was waiting at the entrance, his eyes sparkling as he took in his mother.

"*Bellissima,* as always," he told Cosima in a charming voice as he took her hand, laying a kiss on her knuckles before tucking her hand in the crook of his arm.

"You look quite dashing yourself, Signor Guerra," she batted her lashes at him, blushing profusely from the way he was eating her up with his gaze.

Thirteen years. They'd officially been married thirteen years. Yet they still looked very much in love.

Since Benedicto had taken Rafaelo under his wing, bringing him in the middle of the *famiglia* and explaining its workings, he'd been able to observe the men around him more. He knew how they were—fond of women and alcohol, but with a cross always nestled beneath their collars, since God Forbid that Virgin Mary went unpraised for a day.

It was a ubiquitous phenomenon. They all praised the Lord, yet they all took His name in derision. His father notwithstanding.

But for all the whoring he'd seen around, he'd yet to witness his father step out on his marriage vows.

Now, Rafaelo was old enough to understand certain nuances to be found in conversations or in adult interactions. He was also smart enough to observe quietly and make his own opinion.

And while most of the men his father surrounded himself with had mistresses, he didn't think Benedicto had one.

Not with how besotted he was with Cosima.

He knew from hearing men talk that at least half of them never returned for the night to their wives, preferring to spend the time at clubs or brothels—those who preferred to have a varied selection. The others had separate families with their mistresses, whom they always preferred more than their wives.

Maybe it was because Cosima had *been* that mistress that the situation was different.

He knew the entire story, as some of the older members in the *famiglia* had delighted in telling him.

Benedicto had been married to Michele and Gianna's mother first in an arranged marriage. Theirs had been a business arrangement as well as a contract to abide by tradition. Their union hadn't been happy, and after Gianna's birth, Benedicto had been gone from home most of the time—whoring as it was expected of him.

Not long after though, Benedicto had been on a business trip in the Bronx, and he'd caught sight of Cosima helping out with her family's restaurant. He'd been instantly smitten.

A second generation Italian girl who still followed tradition closely, she was also more open-minded than most of that time. She had dreams and aspirations, and she wished to become an actress. She'd played in a few commercials and small gigs, but never anything big. And as the story went, she'd taken one look at Benedicto and she'd fallen madly in love.

She'd been just nineteen at the time, and while she often used to tell Rafaelo that it had been love at first sight, she'd also made him work for it.

"Men like that, they don't like easy prey. I was never available when he'd call, and then he'd call again and again, until I was. Your father liked the chase, so I gave him a marathon," she'd cheekily told Rafaelo one time.

Maybe it was due to that marathon that Benedicto had decided to become completely devoted to her, even at the expense of his own wife.

He'd installed Cosima as his mistress, and he'd moved in with her. On the rare occasion he would go home to his real family, he would do so to see his in-laws during their visits or to meet with Gianna.

Rafaelo hated how the entire situation had come about, because in a fit of jealousy, Benedicto's wife had gone into labor, delivering Michele early. As her body and mind had continued to steadily deteriorate, she'd eventually succumbed to her death not long after giving birth.

Soon after, Benedicto had shocked everyone by marrying Cosima, not even observing the necessary mourning period. Of course, at the time Cosima was pregnant with Rafaelo, and Benedicto was pressed for time to make sure his son would be legitimate. Still, the entire affair had cast a shadow on their family and had made a lot of people point fingers at Benedicto—most of all from his former in-laws.

Though his mother had been a mistress first, and Rafaelo himself was the product of cheating, he didn't think his father had ever stepped out on Cosima.

He was never absent from home for prolonged periods of time, and he always maintained tight communication with Cosima. To that end, if Benedicto ever thought to have another mistress, Rafaelo didn't doubt his mother would know.

And so despite the unfortunate way through which they'd gotten together, Rafaelo couldn't deny that there was something hypnotic about the way his parents loved each other.

It was something he knew to be rare in their world—but more than that, he knew it to be rare *everywhere*. It made him want to achieve something like that too.

That was the only time he wished he were like his father. He wanted to fall in love with someone at first sight too, but more than anything he wanted to *love*. The pure, boundless and abundant love his parents had for each other.

He wanted that too.

And knowing it existed made him all the more inclined to wait for it.

The place his parents had chosen was a classy upscale restaurant, and after they were led to their seats, Benedicto and Cosima wasted no time in making eternal avowals of love to one another.

Rafaelo made himself small in his seat, maintaining it had been a mistake to get him to come too. He was the third wheel, and he felt like he was intruding on a very intimate moment.

Not to mention the fact that some of the language his mother and father were using made him uncomfortable.

He knew about sex. He'd seen movies with sex in them, and had heard enough talk about it to last him a lifetime. But he did *not* want to imagine his parents having sex. Yes, it was clear they were very much still going at it. But it was a detail Rafaelo didn't want to be privy too. It was too...disturbing.

His face scrunched up in distaste as they started kissing each other and murmuring sweet words. It was romantic, he couldn't deny it.

But they were his parents.

He didn't want to see them like that!

It felt like time passed by increasingly slow, and while he attempted to pretend he was enjoying himself, he wasn't.

He realized his presence was all for show, and it was his mother's way of ensuring everyone would see them together—that they would see them as the nucleus of the family while forgetting about his siblings, Cosima's *non*-biological children.

Rafaelo loved his mother. He adored her. But he also knew her to be a cunning woman and an excellent actress. Yet more than anything, she was a true strategist. She knew how to comport herself, when to strike and when to retreat. It wasn't a fluke she'd landed his father. Maybe it had been careful planning from the beginning. He certainly hoped that the woman who'd catch his eye would not be like that. He appreciated his mother, but he also liked honesty and integrity.

He wanted someone with his mother's fortitude. But he also wanted someone soft. Someone who nurtured rather than schemed. He wanted real warmth, not calculating coldness. And he certainly didn't want to be *trapped*.

In a way, even in his young mind he could see the appeal of the chase, and in a manner that he could still not understand, it made him feel oddly intrigued by it. But he disliked the way his mother had put it—a marathon to keep his father's interest. Why the artifice?

Slowly, by combining the attributes he loved from his mother with those he cared less for, he started to form an idea of the woman he'd like by his side.

Strength and honesty. Those were the core values he looked for.

Yet as his thoughts went in that direction, he realized he needed to bring something to the table too. He couldn't demand that his future partner be perfect if he wasn't either.

And so while his parents were caught up in saccharine exchanges, Rafaelo's mind slowly worked at understanding his trajectory and what he'd need to do in order to get to where he wanted.

There was also the slight issue that his father might impose on him with an arranged marriage, as dictated by tradition. And seeing that he preferred Rafaelo to Michele when it came to the dark aspects of the underground world, he assumed the same would stand for its obligations.

He didn't know how, but he would convince his father to see reason. If Benedicto could have such a great love story with Cosima, why couldn't Rafaelo be given the opportunity, too?

The evening came to an end with his mother's performance at the piano, and he listened attentively to what she was playing, a happy smile on his face at the little piece she'd come up for him.

"So, what's the guess?" She asked a while later as they made their way back home.

"Almond. There was a bitterness to it," Rafaelo answered thoughtfully.

Cosima frowned.

"Bitterness? Odd."

"What was it?"

"Well, I wrote it hoping it would be sweet. Yet it ended up bitter," she sighed. "Next time," she winked at him.

As they reached their house, his parents retired for the night, the loud noises from their kisses giving Rafaelo enough of a hint of what they were up to.

Shaking his head in amusement, he took off his jacket, handing it off to one of their staff.

It was February, and the weather was still chilly. Yet as he felt himself shiver, it wasn't the cold weather that was freezing him to the spot. It was his sister's look as their gazes clashed.

She was wearing a long dress cinched at the waist that emphasized the perfect shape of her body. Long blonde hair, pale skin and honey brown eyes, Gianna Guerra was absolutely breathtaking to everyone who met her.

All his friends at school were obsessed with her, and though he'd tried to put a stop to the rumors going around, he knew that all boys of puberty age were using her as their personal fantasy. The mere idea disgusted him, but he'd long realized there was little he could do.

As Gianna had started high school, she'd enrolled in a fancy lyceum right in the heart of Manhattan. It had been their father's plan to use her charms to slowly ingratiate himself in the high society circles of New York. And to a degree, he'd managed. Gianna was ever so popular, and her invitations usually extended to the entire family. He didn't doubt that she'd saved Benedicto quite a few times from financial troubles he'd gotten himself in.

She was smart, beautiful and driven. Supposedly, she had everything. Yet the truth was from that. He only knew what people were saying of her because the rumors had taken the city by storm just like her beauty had. He knew they were the product of jealous people who tried to put his sister down. At the same time, he didn't want to imagine what it was like for

Gianna to see the accusations' on everyone's faces, or to meet with undeserved disdain from people who didn't even know her.

Still, she always displayed strength and wisdom far beyond her wisdom as she vanquished everything that came her way. Lately, he had also noticed a never before seen tranquility on her face. Mostly since Benedicto had hired a new bodyguard for her. One that Gianna seemed a little *too* partial to.

"Gianna," Rafaelo strained a smile.

"You went out with them," she simply commented, nodding while condemning him with her gaze.

"They wanted me there," he shrugged.

"There will come a day, Raf," she started, coming closer to him, "when you'll have to choose."

"What do you mean?" He frowned.

"Your mother, or us," she fixed him with her eyes.

"No," he shook his head. "I won't do that."

"You may not want to. But you'll have to," she blinked, and her initial accusatory look shifted to a gentler one. "With Cosima, there is no place for anyone else. She'll see you at the top, and everyone else at the bottom."

"I know," he reluctantly said. "And I'll do my best to prevent that. But I can't just discard my own mother."

"I understand that," the corners of her mouth tipped in a sad smile. "I know you have divided loyalties. I'm just telling you to be ready, and I'm not referring to myself. Cosima and I may not stand each other, but I'm not a real danger to her. Michele *is*."

"What are you trying to say?" He narrowed his eyes at her.

"Michele is in her way. You know the tradition, don't you? It's his right to be father's heir, but your mother won't allow that."

"But can she really do anything?" Rafaelo asked. "It's not her who will have a say in it. It's the *famiglia*. They will be the one to reinforce the values and father will have no choice but name

Michele his successor," he explained. At least that's how he hoped things would turn out.

For years now, his father had tried to introduce Rafaelo to the family's way of life, but he'd realized early on he didn't have what it took to be a mafioso. He didn't want to be the next in line. He didn't want to have anything to do with that facet of their family history. He would go to college, earn a decent degree and would forge his own way into the world in a *legal* way. So if Michele was to be his father's heir, then he was welcome to the position.

"You don't get it, do you?"

"What do you mean?"

"There won't be a discussion about it if Michele is dead..."

"What are you talking about? Dead?" Rafaelo frowned at his sister. "You're not implying that my mother..."

"I'm not implying anything, Raf. I'm stating it. Cosima will sooner *kill* Michele than allow him to become Benedicto's heir."

"You're wrong. My mother would never..."

"Oh, Raf," her lips tightened in a flat line. "You know she's capable of it. You just don't want to accept it."

"My mother would never," he continued to shake his head.

Gianna came closer to him, her palm on his shoulder as she patted him affectionately.

"I'm sorry, Raf, but she would. She would kill Michele, *will* kill him."

His mouth opened as he prepared to defend his mother, yet he found that no words would come out. He knew his mother wasn't a saint, yet he could never see her commit murder —never.

"Do you know how my mother died?" Gianna suddenly asked, and Rafaelo whipped his head up, his eyes widening at the mention of Gianna's mother.

"An infection after Michele's birth," he answered, repeating what he'd been told since young.

Gianna didn't contradict him. For a moment she just smiles sadly at him, her fingers tightening on his shoulder.

"I remember it. It happened here, in this house," she pursed her lips. "She wasn't doing great after the birth, it's true. But she was well enough to talk and move around the house. Until one morning. I came to get her because Michele was crying and couldn't be placated. That's when I found her," she whispered. "She was gray, her mouth wide open, lifeless..." Gianna trailed off, and one hand went up to wipe a tear from her right eye.

"I eavesdropped when my father was talking with the family doctor, and it was no infection that killed her. Someone had suffocated her to death."

"What are you trying to say?" Rafaelo barely found his words, afraid to hear the direct confirmation.

"She didn't die of natural causes, Raf. She didn't die of an infection. She was *killed*."

He blinked, the accusation clear.

"You can't be sure my mother..."

Gianna gave a dry laugh.

"Yes, I can't be sure it was your mother. And if it wasn't her, then the only other suspect is our father. One of them is a murderer, Raf."

He bit his lip in apprehension, the new information overwhelming him in a way he was not accustomed to.

"One day, you'll have to make a choice. I just hope to God it will be the right one," she told him gently, leaning in to kiss his cheek before leaving him alone.

For days after, Gianna's claims continued to plague his mind. He wasn't blind where it concerned his mother, but he did not believe her capable of going that far. She might not be the kindest person to Michele, but to think she would resort to murder was unimaginable.

eight

AGE THIRTEEN

One afternoon, as he was returning home with his mother after an entire day spent shopping, he dared to approach the subject with her. All the while, he prayed he would just dismiss his concerns, not prove Gianna's suspicions.

"*Mamma?*"

"Yes, dear," she smiled at him. Her smile was always warm when it was directed to him, and he knew she loved him beyond reason. If he only erased everything else, she *was* the perfect mother.

"Do you know how Laura died?"

Her expression didn't change at hearing the name of Benedicto's wife, yet the atmosphere in the car got considerably colder.

"What brought this on, dear?"

He shrugged.

"She died around this time, didn't she?" He said carelessly, belatedly realizing his faux-pas.

Because if she'd died around this time, it meant she died mere days or weeks before Benedicto would marry again—before he'd marry Cosima.

Her eyes flared, but she controlled herself.

"She did. Poor thing," she sighed. "Such a shame. Gianna must be having a hard time, no?"

He nodded.

"I heard she was killed," he simply stated, his eyes studying his mother's micro-expressions.

She didn't give anything away.

Instead, she merely frowned.

"Let me guess," she rolled her eyes. "Gianna told you that, didn't she? Did she also say I killed her?"

"She didn't."

"I'm surprised," she huffed. "She's been accusing me of killing Laura for as long as I can remember."

"Is it true?" He dared to ask.

"Of course not. She wasn't killed. She killed herself."

"But Gianna said she heard the doctor say she had been suffocated by someone."

"Raf," Cosima pursed her lips. "First of all, you know Gianna has started a crusade against me, and she wants to discredit me in front of everyone. It's no wonder she'd point fingers. But I can see why she'd think that. After Laura died, Benedicto didn't want anyone to know she killed herself. You know how frowned upon that is," she waved her hand.

And it was. Those who committed suicide could not be buried on hallowed ground. Their family was staunchly Catholic, as were most of their acquaintances. He could see how people knowing Laura had committed suicide would be a bad thing.

"Then why did Gianna hear that?"

"Because they were debating what to write on her death certificate."

They soon reached their house, and Cosima wasted no time in asking him to follow her to his father's office.

"Are we allowed here?" He asked in a small voice, knowing

Benedicto did not like people meandering into his personal space.

"Your father and I have no secrets," she stated, getting her wallet and slipping out a key from it. Placing it inside, it clicked into the lock, the door soon opening.

"Come," she said, pointing to the large safe at the back of the room.

With obvious ease, Cosima plugged in the combination to the safe, opening it. Behind her, Rafaelo peeked, noticing money, gold, and other valuables. But Cosima wasn't looking for that. She stooped low to dislodge a stack of papers, quickly skimming the contents before removing a folder and handing it to Raf.

"This is her autopsy report," Cosima told him.

"It's ok, *mamma*. I believe you," Rafaelo was quick to say, seeing the extent Cosima would go to prove her innocence.

"No. Please look. I don't want any doubts between us."

The sincerity in her tone was his undoing, and he nodded, opening the folder and scanning the contents of the files.

Eventually, he found the original death certificate, and reading attentively, he came to the cause.

Overdose. Ruled a suicide.

There were a few other notes to accompany the cause of death too. She'd had postpartum depression, and it hadn't been the first time she'd exhibited signs of wanting to end her life.

"I know you think I have something with your brother and sister because they were Laura's children. And yes, it's true. I don't love them. I never have. You are my only son, and the only one I love. At the same time, I don't wish them ill. I know I was your father's mistress before Laura's death, and that in itself speaks badly of me, undoubtedly making me the prime suspect in this conspiracy theory. But if anything, I felt pity for her. I had Benedicto's love. She didn't."

"Thank you for showing me this," Rafaelo told her. Seeing everything first-hand, he realized that his mother was speaking the truth. Laura had taken her own life, and there had been no trace of foul play.

"I can stand having everyone pointing fingers at me. But never you, Raf. Never you," she said emphatically. "You're my only reason for living, you know that, don't you?"

He nodded, a small smile on his lips.

"I love you, *mamma*."

"Oh, dear boy," she cried out, her arms coming around him as she hugged him to her chest. "I love you. Always."

He returned the hug, a deep sense of shame enveloping him. He shouldn't have even entertained the thought that his mother would be capable of something like that. But he couldn't deny that holding the evidence in his hands did make him feel better, a calm settling over him.

He'd been right.

His mother might be many things, but a murderer she was not.

And he'd never doubt her again.

* * *

May quickly arrived and the tensions in the house were higher than ever. Everyone was getting ready for Gianna's engagement party, yet no one was celebrating it—no one but Benedicto, the only one who'd benefit for the alliance.

Waking up after an entire day of festivities, Rafaelo went downstairs to find his father waiting for him.

Benedicto assessed him with narrowed eyes, looking him up and down before nodding appreciatively.

"You're a man, now, Raf," he said in a clipped tone, but the pride beneath the words was unmistakable.

Although Rafaelo didn't think himself a man yet, he appreciated his father's praise. Trapped in a limbo, he'd just recently had a growth spurt that made him almost as tall as his father. For a kid of thirteen, that was indeed a feat. But everything else was off. His limbs were disproportionate in size, almost as if they'd forgotten to grow alongside his body. His weight was also fickle, sometimes favoring one side, sometimes the other. He might be the size of a *man*—though debatable—but he did *not* feel like one.

He certainly didn't want to feel like one.

If *now* he felt he had the world's weight on his shoulders, he didn't want to imagine what it would be like when that weight started pushing him down to his knees.

"Happy birthday, son," he continued as Rafaelo approached, patting him slowly on the back in a fatherly gesture. His father was a man of few words, and aside from Cosima, he largely kept himself aloof, not putting his feelings on display. It was a quality Rafaelo respected, as he'd seen many people ruled by their mouths.

"Thank you," he nodded, his lips tugging up in a smile.

"I have something prepared for you today," Benedicto continued, his hand on Rafaelo's back as he led him out of the house. "It's a very special occasion and must be celebrated accordingly."

"What do you mean?" Rafaelo's brows shot up, looking at his father with question in his eyes.

"We'll follow tradition," was all his father revealed. "Just like I did before you, and my own father before. It's time you fully embraced your fate and became a man."

Benedicto's words were vague, but Rafaelo had a feeling he wasn't going to like the entire *becoming a man* business. He knew exactly the things his father and his associates prized as being *manly*, and he wouldn't like to partake in anything.

Still, he was thirteen. That gave him some hope that the celebration his father was talking about wouldn't be something too outrageous.

It was early in the morning as they exited the house, heading for one of the cars waiting in front of the house.

Everyone was already out of the house by the time they emerged.

Gianna had left shopping at the first crack of dawn, taking Michele and her bodyguard with her and promising their father she would buy a worthy trousseau. With her engagement fast approaching, the preparations were speeding up just as the stress was mounting. Not in the least, their father was watching everything with a hawk's eye, wanting to ensure his business deal would go through.

Rafaelo was getting increasingly more worried about her. He didn't like how their father was forcing the issue of the marriage, or the fact that the groom was a creep. He supposed Gianna liked that even less, as she tried to find excuses to be out of the house every time he was visiting. And after her little stunt at the emergency room, he couldn't help but think that Benedicto was sending Gianna to her death. If she'd tried once before to take her own life at the prospect of marrying Clark Goode, what was to stop her from attempting it again once they were married. The entire situation was bleak.

He'd tried to bring the issue to his father, but Benedicto hadn't budged. If anything, he'd prohibited Rafaelo from speaking on the issue, assuring him that his sister was on good hands and that everything would happen as it was supposed to.

Well, that was the issue.

This *wasn't* supposed to happen. How could anyone agree

that it was Gianna's fate to marry a middle-aged man just to fill her father's empty coffers?

But the more he saw his father's insistence that the wedding preparations continue, the more he finally realized that when the time came, he'd be put in the exact position.

He could already see both his father and mother talking him into agreeing to some random wedding match, hounding and emotionally blackmailing him until he agreed to it. And he knew he would, though he detested the thought of marrying someone he didn't love. If his mother set her mind to it, she could wear him down very easily. After all, she *was* his biggest weakness. And she knew it very well.

The entire situation was doomed. Their futures were up in the air, to be decided by the elders who would *not* be living that life, yet they would easily condemn someone else to it.

He was a good son. Yet there were times when he resented his parents. He begrudged the fact that they were treating him like a puppet whose express purpose was to please them. He loved them but he resented them and the life they were forcing him into.

Though he was curious what his father had in plan for him, he wasn't looking forward to finding out lest it be something he wouldn't be on board with. Because whether he liked it or not, his father would make him do it. After all, he couldn't show a weakness with his son—especially his *chosen* one.

From the time he could understand what was going on in their world, slowly learning the ropes of the *famiglia* and the honor that came with being part of such an organization, he'd known that the worst one could do was show weakness. The *famiglia* was strong because it was together. But more than anything it was strong because of each individual—the sum of all its parts. He already had the disadvantage of being the second-born, which naturally relegated him to the shadows. Thus, he needed to show an even harder exterior, taking everything sent his way without complaining. And that was the issue. The options were unlimited. Yet he didn't know how much he could withstand.

He didn't like the lifestyle. He didn't like the people.

He *hated* it.

Benedicto talked away as the car drove out of their property, taking the highway leading to the city.

"Is it a celebration with the family?" Rafaelo asked, hoping from the bottom of his heart it was just a normal party.

"Of course. Your uncle can't wait to see you. Marco, too. I think Fabio came straight from L.A. to wish you happy birthday," his father chuckled as he went on to enumerate all the people who were to be in attendance.

His uncle, Franco, was his father's right hand—the consigliere. Though the position usually implied a degree of wisdom, things were done a little differently within the Guerra hold. Franco was the one doing the dirty work while Benedicto maintained a façade of normality to the outside world. Fabio was one of Benedicto's underbosses, and he also served as liaison to other syndicates on the West Coast, which explained his many trips to LA.

Marco, too, was one of the higher ranked members of the famiglia. A distant cousin on his father's side, he was a kid from Messina who'd come to America when he'd been younger than Rafaelo, hoping to get ahead in life and provide for his family back home. His total dedication to the *famiglia* had ensured he climbed ranks fast, while his last name put him in line for an important position in the future—maybe an underboss or caporegime.

There were many with similar situations to Marco within the *famiglia*, distant relatives living in abysmal poverty that decided to try their luck with a life of crime—not that Rafaelo could blame them. He knew the situation in certain regions of Italy, and he imagined he would have done the same if one day he woke up not being able to provide for his loved ones.

Their loose connection to the Guerra name afforded them a small advantage, yet they still had to prove themselves, starting from the bottom and working their way up. On the other hand, that small connection they had to the nucleus could help propagate them further, into titled positions, as was the case for Marco.

But then there were the other people. Those who had no Italian ancestry and could not invoke any relation to the Guerra name. Usually people already steeped in a life of crime, they eventually took a vow to work for the family. Even so, because they were considered outsiders, they would never be anything but low-ranking associates. It was rare that any outsider made it to the rank of soldier, and never heard of anything higher than that.

Winding down the streets of New York City, they soon drew to a stop in front of a nondescript building. Though from the outside it looked like any other edifice in the area, it was in fact the Guerra headquarters for anything off-the-books.

The car parked, Rafaelo trailed after his father as Benedicto led him inside.

The building was equipped with offices, as well as living quarters and other rooms designed to facilitate the workings of the organization.

On the first floor was the main entertainment room, and as soon as they stepped inside Rafaelo recognized it was going to be a *long* day.

Everyone was gathered around. Music was blasting loudly from speakers situated on each corner of the room. Alcohol was also freely flowing, and one gaze to the center of the room and

Rafaelo could see an ice freezer full with bottles of beer, wine, champagne as well as hard liquor.

And when they came into sight, everyone suddenly stood up.

"There he is," someone said.

"Rafaelo is finally a man."

"Happy birthday, big boy," another chuckled.

The entire atmosphere was playful, and straining his cheeks into a fake smile, Rafaelo tried to relax.

Maybe it was just a party. Nothing to worry about.

People nodded their heads at Benedicto, inviting the duo to take a seat on the couches spread around.

Keeping to himself, Rafaelo was quiet as he sat down, letting his eyes roam around the room and documenting everything in sight.

"Man, when I was your age," Marco whistled, coming around and draping his arm over Rafaelo's shoulder. His breath stunk of alcohol, but it wasn't surprising with a bottle of straight gin in his hand. Lifting it in the air, he tilted his head as he regarded Rafaelo.

"Say, Signore," Mateo raised his gaze to Benedicto. "Has he had alcohol yet?"

Rafaelo thought his father would say no and advise him to not put any strange ideas in his head. Yet he did not.

Benedicto chuckled, turning to Rafaelo and smiling at him indulgently.

"There's a first for everything, right?"

Rafaelo blinked.

He had to admit he was curious about alcohol since he'd seen everyone around him imbibe some. Even his mother would have a nightly glass of wine to accompany her dinner, and she did *not* usually drink. That raised some questions for Rafaelo. Yet as much as he'd always been curious about why so many people would fall prey to this vice, and if there was anything special about it, he'd never expressly disobeyed his parents by stealing into their liquor cabinet or swiping a swig while one wasn't looking.

That was just his personality.

He might want something—might burst of want. But he obeyed. The rules always came first, before his wants, before his desires.

He supposed that was why he'd end up a slave to his parents' wishes. Because he did not have it in him to tell them no.

It was like it had been coded in his very DNA to be an obedient child—to observe his parents' will even at the expense of his own. In another life, maybe this could have been a virtue. In the life he found himself, it was a weakness. And it was paving the way for his destruction.

In no time, everyone gathered around, watching with curious eyes, some chanting, some whistling at Rafaelo. All wanted to witness the moment the presumed heir to the Guerra name would have his first sip of alcohol, the first of many firsts planned for the day.

Mateo grinned from ear to ear as he took a shot glass, slamming it in front of Rafaelo before filling it up to the brim.

He regarded the glass carefully, but the men's eyes were all on him as they cheered him on, inviting him to take his first sip of alcohol.

"Drink! Drink! Drink!"

Rafaelo sneaked a glance to his father, wondering why he wasn't putting a stop to this. He was aware that in Europe underage drinking was much more normalized. He'd been to the Continent a number of times and had witnessed his teenage cousins drinking alongside the adults. Still, he couldn't fathom his father agreeing to this.

He was still thirteen. Not fifteen, or sixteen, or seventeen.

"Go ahead son," Benedicto nodded at him. His tone was encouraging, almost as if he was saying *make me proud, son.*

Rafaelo eyed the glass, slowly wrapping his fingers around it and lifting it up.

Everyone was nodding it him, almost on the edge as they followed every little movement of his hand, wanting to catch the exact moment the alcohol hit his lips.

Steeling himself, he opened his mouth, his eyes on Marco as he tipped the glass up.

The fiery liquid met his tongue, a stinging sensation filling his mouth, only intensifying as it went down his throat.

He pushed everything down.

Knowing he was the center of attention, he stifled a cough, swallowing deeply regardless of the need to barf at the taste and the bite of the liquid.

"He's a man!" Someone yelled, and soon everyone joined in a choir of congratulations.

But just as he thought he was done with this silly demonstration of *manliness*, Marco poured him another glass. This time, instead of waiting for him to drink, all the men aligned with their own full glasses, ready to toast against his own. One by one, each came forward to toast with him, wishing him a happy birthday and kissing his cheeks.

The second glass was not as bad. Still, the taste made him cringe. His curiosity was now assuaged, and he did not know why people succumbed to the bottle. Not when it tasted so vile.

Music was blasting away, the entire room shrouded in smoke. The alcohol wasn't enough, though. Rafaelo still had more *manly* things to get done. That's how he found himself with a cigarette in his mouth, his father's hand extended in front of him as he held on to a lighter, the flame touching the tip of the cigarette in a red spark.

"Inhale, boy," his father advised, which he did.

Bad idea.

This time, the cough came unbidden. He couldn't help it when he felt his lungs on fire. If the sting of the alcohol had been bad, the combined taste and clogging feel of the cigarette smoke made him gag.

No one helped though.

Everyone laughed by the side, each telling their own stories of their first cigarette, or their first glass of alcohol. And that's exactly how the day continued. The anecdotes poured out of the men as they recounted times they'd been so drunk they'd passed out in the middle of nowhere, without phone or cash to get back home. People found that funny, and Rafaelo, too, pretended to understand the joke behind it. Mentally, though, he could not believe why they would feel so proud of such an achievement.

Putting the cigarette out, he barely stifled a cringe. Yeah, that was decidedly *not* for him.

The boisterous talk continued, and Rafaelo tried to keep up with everyone around him.

It was a while later that his uncle, Franco, made his appearance too.

He was a stern looking man, and Rafaelo had never quite liked him. He seemed the type to fawn over people for personal gain. He didn't know why his father trusted him so much. Yeah, he was his father, but he had never done anything note-worthy as *consigliere*. If anything, he complemented Benedicto's ineptitude at business perfectly. They went from one idea to the next without gaining any experience, lessons, or money. They just tried everything they could, most often than not making an even bigger mess than before.

To think they were still afloat and not already insolvent was a miracle.

But Rafaelo guessed that was a cumulative effort. If it had been only his father and his uncle there would have been no

Guerra family so to speak—and nothing for him to ultimately inherit.

As Franco trudged his way in, everyone went quiet.

Benedicto was watching his brother through narrowed eyes, giving him a brisk nod before pouring himself more alcohol. He leaned back in his seat and just watched.

Having received his signal, Franco took off his jacket, draping it on a chair and folding the cuffs of his white shirt before moving back.

A minute later, distressed sounds resounded through the big room, the echo startling Rafaelo and making him pay more attention to what was going beyond the main area. But he didn't have to wonder for long.

Franco strode back in, dragging after him a bloody man who was struggling against his bounds. He was gagged, but he still wailed against the cloth strapped across his mouth, his eyes searching the entire room and pleading for help with each of the men present.

Everyone was quiet as Franco dropped him in the middle of the floor, wiping his hands on his trousers before spitting on the man on the ground.

"All yours, Ben," Franco sneered, his eyes still on the floor.

"Your job is done, brother. Stand down." Benedicto declared, rising from his seat.

A big, brown cigar in one hand, a glass of scotch in the other, he walked languidly towards the man writhing on the floor.

"So what's it going to be now, Micky boy? You think I haven't gotten a full report of your latest shenanigans?"

Rafaelo blinked when he heard the name.

Micky was one of his father's soldiers. He knew him from the times he'd come to the headquarters in the past. Yet he hadn't been able to recognize him as he was, his face swollen and stained with red. Whatever he'd done, it had been bad enough that he was going to be exposed to the entire *famiglia*.

Micky cried out against his gag, trying to speak in his defense, but no one was interested in what he had to say. He'd already been tried and judged in everyone's minds because the boss had said so.

It was only Rafaelo who stood up, slowly approaching his father and uttering out loud what no one had the courage to ask.

"What has he done, father?"

Benedicto pivoted, facing Rafaelo with an expression of disbelief.

"I know Micky, and he's always been loyal to you," Rafaelo continued, seemingly not knowing when to shut up. But while everyone thought him foolish for intervening like this, he knew that it was the only way to stop his father from doing something he might later regret. With everyone gathered for *his* celebration, it was less likely his father was going to punish him in front of everyone. No, that would only discourage people from taking to Rafaelo, and that was not what Benedicto wanted. Since he was looking to gain acceptance for his second son instead of his first, he knew he had to tread carefully.

It was a double edged sword.

Benedicto didn't want to come across as weak in front of his men by answering to his thirteen year old son, yet at the same time he didn't want to undermine Raf's authority since first impressions were all that mattered. And if his people saw Rafaelo as strong from the beginning, then the road to making him his official heir would be much smoother.

His father grunted, righting his back as he positioned himself in front of everyone.

"Who can tell me what Micky boy did?"

Franco scrunched his nose in disgust as he removed a knife, stooping low and trailing the blade all over Micky's face.

"He sold us out to Lastra, didn't you Micky? We were supposed to close a big deal on Friday but it never happened, because Lastra closed it the day before. Isn't that right?" His uncle asked in a chilling voice as he dug the knife into his skin. The gag prevented him from screaming out loud but his eyes widened, tears flowing down his cheeks and mingling with the blood leaking from his wounds.

"Do you know for sure it was him?" Rafaelo asked for confirmation, unable to believe the Micky he knew, the one who'd always smiled pleasantly at him and ask him how his day had been, would be capable of such a thing.

"We have footage of him meeting with one of Killian's men. It's for sure."

Though they all seemed so certain of his guilt, Rafaelo felt reluctant to agree with the verdict. Why would he have done something like this?

At the same time, loyalty was everything in the *famiglia*. The circumstances didn't matter. You were your word. Period.

And so he knew he could not argue further. Not when Micky's fate had been decided the minute he'd sold out the *famiglia*.

He took a step back, nodding to his father. He was already ready to leave, not wanting to see how Micky would meet his end. And meet he would, since only a special type of punishment was reserved for traitors.

"Not so fast, son. This is perfect," his father called out when he was about to return to his seat.

Turning to face his father, Rafaelo frowned.

"You're a man now. It's time you took your place too."

"What do you mean?"

"Why do you think I brought you here?"

Rafaelo didn't answer.

"My father initiated me when I was your age. Most of the

people in this room began their journey in the same way. And if you hope to one day stand where I'm standing, then you need to be committed."

"Committed?"

"You need to take your oath."

Presently, the organization had a little bit of everything. It resembled a secret society in its secrecy and they way members interacted with information, yet it was also mainly genealogical, with most resources focused on descendants on one line.

The tradition was ever present in people's minds, but the *famiglia* had evolved once with the times. They'd learned and adapted, and while they still obeyed some of the old laws, they'd had to make space for new ones, too.

The initiation was still part of the old order. It was how someone officially became a member, swearing fealty to the don and assuming the secrecy imposed by the organization.

Even though Rafaelo was the son of the don, he still had to take the same oath. For a moment, he had to wonder if his father was ever going to try to make Michele do it too. But his brother was too frail. He was too sensitive to ever dive deep in the underground. Rafaelo could bet he could not withstand one day in the presence of seasoned criminals—no matter that they were family.

As much as he knew that the oath was a necessity, he had no further notion about what it entailed. He'd heard about some trials, and a sacred ceremony. But to that end, each *famiglia* put their personal touch to the initiation. Not one was the same as the other though the end goals were identical. And so Rafaelo found himself at a loss of words.

Staring down into Micky's anguished face, he could wager a guess to what his initiation would entail. Yet he couldn't back down. Not only he did not have it in himself to give up and show such weakness, he knew he could not disappoint his parents.

Briefly, a flashback to the night before appeared before his eyes. Right as he'd wrapped up his party with all his classmates, his mother had lingered behind, smiling softly at him as she'd talked about honor and courage.

"Do you know what makes a man, dear boy?" She'd asked.

The two of them were in the kitchen as she cut another piece of cake for him. The subject had seemed out of place at the time, but now, realizing what both his mother had planned all along, he knew it had been on purpose.

"What makes a man?" He'd frowned at his mother's strange question.

A man was a man because he was born so. And that's exactly what he'd replied to his mother.

The corners of her mouth tipped up, she'd giggled softly.

"That's just your assigned sex at birth, Raf. You don't become a man just because you're born one. You need to earn it."

"I don't understand."

Still smiling pleasantly, she'd taken a seat at the table, pushing the plate of cake in front of him and proceeding to watch him eat.

"A man has three core qualities. Honor," she raised one finger, "courage," she paused, the second finger joining the first. "And he protects those he loves." She wiggled her three fingers.

"Honor is what you foster inside your heart. How you decide to live your life both for your own sake, but also for those around you. Courage is when you're willing to risk your life, and well..." she'd smiled. "I think you can see how both connect with the third."

"I think I understand what you mean, *mamma*," Raf had noted, his expression pensive. Though his mother had tried to prepare him mentally for the following day, she'd also given him food for thought. "This is all about having the strength to be there for those we love, isn't it?"

"Indeed," she'd winked at him.

Now, looking into his father's eyes, his mother's words echoed in his ears.

"I'm ready," he told his father.

And he was. Because this wasn't just making his parents happy. This was also the first step in protecting them—protecting those he loved.

Benedicto grinned, looking around and meeting each of his men's eyes.

"That's my son," he boasted.

nine

AGE THIRTEEN

Two soldiers rose from the table, grabbing Micky and pinning him to a chair in the middle of the room.

"Rafaelo," Benedicto started in a stern voice. "As you know, we value loyalty the most. The initiation isn't something bad. It's an exchange. We exchange *your* secrets for ours."

Rafaelo frowned.

"I see you're confused," he smiled. "There is one thing that binds every man in this room. Something they *all* share."

He paused, and the room was suddenly quiet.

"Everyone has blood on their hands."

Rafaelo refrained from showing any emotion on his face, though the pronouncement hit him deep in his heart. He couldn't say he hadn't imagined that one day he'd be forced to take a human life. But now....?

"The process is simple. You kill Micky in front of everyone, thus bestowing *your* secret to them. In exchange, you will receive everyone's secrets. This is a blood oath, my son, and it will be sealed with blood."

Rafaelo slowly nodded.

"I understand," he stated, not betraying any weakness.

Inside, he was boiling with anxiety. But he didn't dare show that. He couldn't.

Putting on a smile, he looked his father in the eye.

"Good. That's my boy," Benedicto chuckled. "Now a man."

"How..." He swallowed hard. "How do I do this?"

"However you want son. The stage is yours," his father stepped aside, pointing towards Micky.

Although unspoken, Rafaelo understood what his father meant. It was all up to him, but at the same time, everyone would be silently judging his choice in dispatching the traitor.

He couldn't show himself too brash—there had been whispers of such men in the *famiglia* and it was often frowned upon. No one wanted someone they couldn't control. But he couldn't be too soft either. That would speak ill of his future as his father's heir.

He needed to keep himself in check and proceed in an almost clinical fashion.

Traitor. Micky was a traitor. He wasn't the man with the easy smile. And Rafaelo needed to bear that in mind.

Nodding to everyone on the sidelines, he headed straight for Marco. Before the older man could react, Rafaelo withdrew the knife Marco had stashed against his belt.

Someone whistled behind. He couldn't be sure.

Not when he was so focused on not sweating. On not making a sudden move or showing weakness. He needed to perform this perfectly. And that's what it was—a performance.

In that moment, Rafaelo did not internalize the fact that he was about to take a human life—that he would commit murder. He only knew he needed to give the men a show and prove himself worthy of his father and the Guerra name.

He needed to be christened in blood. And if that was required of him, then so be it.

His face was grave, his eyes an icy blue as he took three large strides towards Micky.

Firmly planting himself in front of the bleeding man, he took a moment to assess him.

He'd taken biology courses and he'd also seen other soldiers torture and maim before. As such, he wasn't entirely unfamiliar with blood and pain. And he would do with this moment what he did with the others too—he would look at it as a necessity. It wasn't him who did it, it was the *him* he needed to be.

Paradoxical though that was, it was his only coping mechanism. He could separate himself into two beings—the Rafaelo he knew himself to be deep down, the one who yearned to come to the surface, as well as the Rafaelo who everyone else wanted him to be.

And so he shut everything down.

Closing his eyes, he took a deep breath. And when he opened them again, the switch was immediate.

Wielding his knife wish assured movements, he brought the blade to the man's sternum. The tip of the sharp knife dug into the area just below his Adam's apple.

Everyone was quietly watching.

His mouth tipped ever so slightly as he observed from the corner of his eyes.

Then it was on.

He pushed, wiggling the tip of the knife around until he made a gash in the man's trachea. Painful, but not enough to be deadly.

Keeping himself still, he exuded unusual calmness as he took out the knife, tilting his head to the side so the jet of blood did not hit him in the face.

Sharp intakes of breath came from behind, the other soldiers watching in awe how he handled himself.

This was a show. *Just* a show.

Continuing downward, he popped his shirt open, cutting through the material to get access to his chest. Once in sight, he simply dug the blade into Micky's skin, tracing two lines to form the letter T. And as he was done, he stepped aside for a moment, letting everyone see.

"He was a traitor," Rafaelo said, his voice not his own. "And he dies a traitor's death," he continued. Positioning himself behind Micky, he brought the blade to the man's throat, making a clean line across his neck until blood started oozing everywhere.

He was still calm, knowing he couldn't afford to be anything but.

The blood stained his hands, the sticky, red substance the perpetual reminder of what he was doing.

He swallowed. Closed his eyes. And then he was back.

Straightening his back, he met everyone's gaze squarely.

And as Micky gave his last breath, silence descended upon the room.

People were staring at them. He didn't let that faze him. His father was staring from the side. He ignored it.

He ignored everything but the beat of his heart. It drummed against his ribcage, the sound so loud he could hear it in his ears. It was such a screeching noise, he felt his eardrums weeping in pain. Yet he did not move. He made no sound. He just stared back.

A second passed before everyone suddenly clapped. Cheers and loud screams of joys suffused the room. One moment he was standing behind the now dead Mickey, the next he was being carried around by ten men, all singing him praises and congratulating him on his execution.

Now it was time to shift.

He let the other Rafaelo take the back seat as he slowly

returned back to himself—to the person who could, in fact, enjoy such a celebration. The person who hadn't just murdered a man in cold blood. The Rafaelo he still was, somewhere, deep down.

He smiled.

When everything quieted, it was time for the oath to be taken—now literally.

Franco handed Rafaelo a small knife, settling it against his plan and nodding towards where Benedicto was sitting—now on a high chair at the end of the room.

With assured steps, he knelt before his father, presenting his right hand and bringing the blade against his palm. He winced at the pain, but he held it down.

"I promise to serve and obey..." the words flowed out of him, and once his promise was given, his life was not his own anymore—had it ever been his?

He kissed his father's hand, promising to serve the interests of the *famiglia* for as long as he lived, putting everyone's lives ahead of his own. More than anything, he vowed to bring the Guerra name back to its previous glory, fact that greatly pleased his father.

When everything was done, he didn't feel particularly different. Maybe it was the alcohol in him that had made everything so easy. Maybe.

He continued to smile, laugh and drink with the others, enjoying the celebrations and trying to think about making his parents proud—this was, after all, his goal.

But everything changed when his father interrupted the party once more.

"Now that you're a new member, there's only one more step, Rafaelo." Benedicto grunted.

Immediately, Rafaelo noticed he didn't address him as *son* anymore. No, now he was a member of the organization.

Though he was the don's son and would one day be the don himself, he was still *just* a member.

He nodded.

"It's time to become an *actual* man." His father declared gleefully.

Rafaelo had no time to protest as he was led by a few drunk men towards the back of the building where some of the lodging rooms were situated. He barely had time to realize what was happening until he found himself thrust into a room. The men all winked at him, whistling suggestive comments and making lewd jokes. Still, their easygoing attitude didn't stop them from locking Rafaelo in said room.

He was still reeling from having killed his first man—had barely managed to swallow down the lump that had appeared in his throat. Micky's blood was still fresh on his skin and clothes. How could he move on so quickly?

Yet as he slowly turned around, it was to see a naked woman on a bed, her eyes roving over his body as she bit seductively on her lip.

She was older than him—of that he was sure. She was also most definitely paid to do this—another thing he was certain of.

And as she rose up, untying the small string that held her robe together and letting it fall, Rafaelo had the definite realization of what *becoming a man* truly meant.

He didn't like it. He didn't like it one bit.

The woman approached him slowly, undulating her body in a way she hoped would arouse him. Though he wasn't a bad looking lad, this was her job, and she always wanted to get it over as fast as she could. Knowing he was a fresh one, she didn't think he'd last too long.

Rafaelo gulped down uncomfortably as he averted his eyes from the woman's body, embarrassed to be put in such a position. On the other hand, quick thinking and natural instincts told him he needed to tread carefully.

Getting over his initial bout of shyness, the red of his blush still lingering on his cheeks, he moved one step back, molding his ear to the door and listening. The woman was quiet, and that in itself allowed him to hear the small noises from the other side of the door, confirming that the men had not left. They were likely listening closely for proof that Rafaelo had become, indeed, a man.

He gritted his teeth, suddenly annoyed with the matter at hand.

And though he'd initially been bashful at seeing the naked woman, he quickly got over it, his brain taking the central stage.

Just as the woman got closer to him, he pivoted. Grabbing her hand, he tugged her to the far end of the room, putting some distance between them and the bed.

"I'll give you my watch." he raised his eyes to meet hers. He hadn't even looked lower, hadn't wanted to sneak a peek at her body, and that immediately commanded her attention. "In exchange, I want you to pretend you're doing what you're supposed to do," he nodded at her.

Her brows pinched together, she regarded him thoughtfully.

"You don't want me," she stated. He didn't comment.

"You have yourself a deal," she said as she swiped the watch from his hands, moving it around as she tried to gauge its value. "I'll give them a good performance," she said before stooping down to grab her robe, pulling it around her body.

"What's your name?"

"Rafaelo," he answered.

"Good," she winked before settling on the bed.

Rafaelo, too, took a seat on an adjoining chair, curious to see what would happen next.

The woman, though, surprised him as she started moaning and screaming, calling out his name for everyone to hear.

His eyes closed, a groan of frustration escaping his lips. That's what she'd meant by a good show... Well, at least that should erase any type of doubt about what happened in the room—that Rafaelo was now a man.

And so he released a sigh of relief.

He was well aware how men in the *famiglia* regarded sex and women. They were equal parts currency *and* a sign of status. Most often than not, while they had wives at home, they still bought sex—just because they could.

Rafaelo didn't understand that. He knew the mechanics of sex, but he also saw it as something too intimate act to share with a stranger. Not only that, but the act of *paying* for it was thoroughly distasteful to him.

Growing up with the indomitable force that was his mother helped put things into perspective. It made him respect women and treat them as human beings, not *some* beings. He knew it wasn't a view shared by everyone in their culture, but it was one that had been instilled in him since young.

More than anything, though, he was a dreamer. He didn't want a meaningless affair. He didn't want sex for the sake of sex, since he'd seen how easy that was to obtain. He wanted it to mean something—for it to be the culmination of *something*. And until he found that, he would simply hold out for it.

The performance was soon over, and as he rumpled his clothes a little, he finally exited the room, coming face to face with *everyone*.

They took one good look at him and started shouting and praising him, thereby allowing the celebrations to continue.

They partied the entire day. Drinking. Smoking. Whoring.

Rafaelo put on a pleasant smile as he kept to the sidelines, interacting when it was required of him.

"I'm proud of you, son," his father declared later that night. "And this is just the beginning..."

Rafaelo nodded dutifully, happy to make his father proud but sad at the prospect of pretending once more. It was what he'd been doing his entire life. Now, he just added another mask to his collection.

* * *

He took a deep breath, the clean, cold air of the night rejuvenating him. Everyone was asleep, or so he hoped. After they'd returned from the celebration, his mother had congratulated him on his new identity, but she had not inquired exactly what had happened while he'd been away. Benedicto had given her a wink, and she'd seemed to understand the situation. That in itself had hurt Rafaelo more than anything else that had occurred that day.

His mother had approved everything. She *knew*. And she hadn't tried to intervene or do anything. In fact, looking back on their *talk*, he realized she'd tried to prime him for everything.

He sighed. That was to be his life from now on. It wasn't as if he'd had much control over it before. Now, it was fully within his parents' grasp. There was little consolation that he'd managed to refuse the prostitute when he knew he'd be forced to do much worse in the future. He still had control over his body, but what was the point if his spirit was owned by others?

"You don't look too good," a gruff voice said. Rafaelo startled, jumping from his position on the porch and looking back.

Bass, his sister's bodyguard was leaning against the back entrance, his eyes narrowed as he regarded him.

"I'm fine," Rafaelo shrugged.

Bass was a nice man, but they hadn't interacted much. He

was always accompanying his sister everywhere, and on the off-chance, Michele would join them. Rafaelo had never been *that* close to them to be invited on their outings, but he knew that was mainly because of his sister. She had a soft spot for Michele, always preferring him to Rafaelo. Sure, she loved him too, but Michele was the weaker one—the more frail one. As such, he was the center of her world.

Sometimes Rafaelo wondered if she forgot he was also her brother.

"You don't seem fine," Bass grunted, taking a seat behind him.

Rafaelo kept his head down, thinking that if he ignored him, he'd go away. He didn't want to talk to anyone at the moment. For once, he wanted to be alone with his thoughts. There was such clamoring noise inside his head, he needed to sort things out.

Usually, he was good at compartmentalizing, pushing things out and focusing on what was important instead of what was detrimental. But today he found it particularly hard.

His routine was simple. He zoned in on the person he *needed* to be, instead of the one he was. After so many years, he knew what was expected of him and what was frowned upon.

Yet today, the simple action of switching gears, of burying his real self to the benefit of his other self was agonizing.

His soul was weeping blood. Maybe it was the blood he'd shed. Maybe it was something different.

Though he was quiet and didn't show it on the outside, his mind was a battlefield.

"I don't think so," he measured his words as he replied to Bass.

He didn't want to talk about his *feelings* with anyone. He certainly didn't want to lay himself bare for another to take advantage. He knew what the deal was in their world. Men had to be men, and he'd just started on that journey. That alone meant he could show nothing—no fear, nor regret.

Nothing.

"Here," Bass' finger reached out, swiping something from his temple.

"What..." Rafaelo swiveled, his eyes widening as he saw traces of blood.

"You missed a spot," Bass drawled, and shame traveled up his cheeks, staining them with a deep red to rival the color of the blood.

"You don't have to hold it in, you know."

"What do you know about it?" Rafaelo mumbled.

"More than you think," Bass smirked, leaning back and regarding Rafaelo expectantly.

This was the moment. He could choose to walk away and ignore Bass, or he could open his mouth and talk. He didn't need to tell him everything. Just enough to empty *some* of the burden that was weighing him down.

"Does it get easier?" Rafaelo asked, his question vague.

"Hmm, good question. Not necessarily. But it depends on what you do it *for*," Bass replied, and he seemed to know exactly what Rafaelo was going through.

"Doesn't it make me a bad person?"

"Things are never black or white, Raf. Just like spilling blood doesn't make you a bad person. You're still young, but you'll learn. Taken out of context, actions will always be crucified. Killing is bad while saving someone is good, that's what we're taught."

Rafaelo frowned. Bass, seeing his expression of consternation, explained further.

"It's when you look closer, at the *motive* that things become muddled. Say, for example, that you killed someone to *save* someone. Is that still as bad?" Rafaelo shook his head. "Then consider this. What if you saved someone just for them to end up with a handicap for the rest of their lives?" Bass asked, putting forward an odd scenario in which someone was struggling between life and death. "If you continue to perform CPR until you've got a pulse, then congratulations, you've brought him back to life. But there's a catch. The person is alive, but brain dead."

He blinked, taken aback by the example Bass gave him.

"Even something as certain as *saving* someone can become controversial."

"But killing is killing..."

"Killing is killing when you do it for the wrong reasons. If you do it for someone you love, then it becomes an imperative."

"I see..." Rafaelo answered slowly, though he did not see it.

He understood the reasoning behind it, and he could comprehend the ethical implications to a certain degree. At the same time, he also knew himself and his muted sense of being. After so long stifling his true self—the impulsive, reckless and *alive*—he didn't think the *him* that was now present would ever meet that imperative.

He'd kill because it was expected of him. And *that* made it all the worse.

He had no personal stakes in it other than keeping his parents happy. And he guessed that Bass didn't mean *them* when he said killing for someone he loved.

"You have your whole life ahead of you to weigh these issues carefully. But a piece of friendly advice? If I may."

"Please," Rafaelo nodded.

"Don't let it eat you on the inside. These...things... They have the power to haunt a man, if he's not strong enough."

"I don't know if I'm strong enough," Rafaelo admitted for the first time. And he didn't think he was. He was holding on. But for how long?

"No one is born strong enough, Raf," Bass chuckled. "You become a little stronger every time you defeat your demons. So..."

"As long as I defeat my demons each and every time I can become stronger."

"Right," he smiled, his scar stretching across his cheek.

Bass was a scary man. His appearance made him every man's nightmare. He was big and strong, the scar that marred his face only increasing that horrifying allure he held.

"You're in love with my sister, aren't you?"

Bass watched him with a dangerous glint in his eye.

"And if I am? Any problem?" The tone was suddenly

"Can you make her happy?"

"I can," he grunted.

"Then please do," he told Bass. "As long as you can make sure she doesn't have to..." he trailed off.

"Don't worry. I know what I have to do." Bass assured him.

"Good," Rafaelo smiled ruefully.

At least someone should get a happy ending.

ten

AGE THIRTEEN

Michele tugged at his tie in an attempt to loosen it around his neck. He'd donned one of his finer suits as Nicolo had requested of him, and he hoped he would not embarrass his good friend. Staring into the mirror, he attempted a small smile, watching his reflection and scowling at the sight that greeted him. Sometimes he wished he looked more...normal. Maybe then people wouldn't be so against him from the beginning.

From a young age, he'd noticed how some would take one look at him and their entire countenance would change, their eyes leery, sneers painted on their faces. The bullying would commence soon after, calling him all sorts of names for the simple fact that he had more feminine features than the rest of the boys.

Pretty boy.

He supposed someone else might see that as a compliment. For Michele? That had been his burden to carry since his hair had grown back. And with the pejorative that the kids used came the regular implications—that he was girly, never manly enough. The amount of beatings he'd gotten for being just a little different...

He took a deep breath, straightening his back and puffing out his chest. He couldn't dwell on that now.

For the first time in his life things were better. Maybe he was still being picked on at school here and there, but he was doing fine outside of it. He had a loving sister and a loyal brother—even though their meetings usually had to be secretive. And now? He also had a good friend in Nicolo, who'd taken it upon himself to serve as the father figure Michele desperately needed.

Maybe they didn't see eye to eye on all issues, more often than not debating their respective sides tirelessly. But that was exactly what Michele treasured about their relationship. They both had their opinions, but Nicolo never attacked Michele for his vastly different one. Instead, he listened and they exchanged points, pondering on the quality of arguments and the validity of those ideas instead of caring about *right* or *wrong*.

And that...made him happy. Finally he had someone who he could be himself with, and with whom he could express himself honestly—not holding back because it wasn't the right thing to say.

That's where most people went wrong with Michele.

They saw his frail appearance and effeminate features and declared him weak when he was anything but. His greatest quality, though he hadn't spent enough time to reach that conclusion for himself, was in the staunchness of his beliefs. He would calmly argue someone to the ground to defend his ideals, and with the people he was comfortable with, he did just that.

Though *idealistic*, he was both a dreamer and a realist, but not in a way the two would cancel each other out. While he had an optimistic outlook on life and humans, he liked to root himself in facts before reaching a conclusion. Sometimes he wondered if that wasn't a side effect of all the time he'd spent studying facts and figures to please his father, and if that, at some point, might not have seeped into his inherently creative nature. He liked the logic well-researched problems yielded, but he also liked the freedom afforded to him by his imagination. And in that respect, he was a walking paradox.

Satisfied with his appearance, he shrugged on a small backpack and he exited his room. The house was eerily quiet, everyone gone for the day. As such, no one would care if Michele was going anywhere.

Heading to the back entrance, he folded the sleeve of his suit so he could take a look at his watch. He was on time.

Nodding to himself, he crossed the expanse of lawn around the house before he got to the main highway. Already, Nicolo's car was there waiting for him.

"You look good, son," he praised as Michele got into the car.

Nicolo was wearing a black suit that was custom tailored to his muscular frame, not at all like the lanky one Michele was wearing. Still, Michele was happy he'd thought of him when he'd invited him to the event. Because if one had to dress up, then it must be important, no?

"Where are we going, sir?" he asked in his usual smile as he regarded the older man.

Sitting across from Michele, Nicolo was sprawled on the seat, one leg over his knee as he sported a bored expression on his face. That didn't fool Michele, however. Not when he'd gotten to know Nicolo quite thoroughly over the years. There was a smug quality to the way he held himself, and that made Michele all the more curious about their destination.

"We're going to a funeral," he simply said.

Michele's eyes widened.

"A funeral? Whose?"

"My brother's."

"I'm so sorry for your loss," he was quick to say, his expression going from excited to somber in the span of a second.

"Bah, it was no loss," Nicolo waved a dismissive hand. "I'm

going there to make my presence known. This isn't an exhibition of sadness, son. It's a show of strength," he said and Michele frowned.

"What do you mean?"

"His spineless son inherited his position," Nicolo shook his head, not directly replying. "I need to be there to not let him forget that as easy as he got it, it can be gone."

Michele was quiet, simply studying Nicolo and his perceived objective.

He now knew he was part of the *life* too, belonging to another family that had business interests in New York. And though the information had startled him in the beginning, making him wonder if there wasn't perhaps a conflict of interests in their acquaintance, with time he'd realized he *could* trust Nicolo. He didn't know why he was so kind to him, or why he'd want to associate himself with a kid his age in the first place. But Michele was sorely lacking in friendships, so he was not going to refuse any offers.

With time, he's considered that maybe Nicolo saw him as the son he never had, or, maybe, as Michele had let his imagination soar, he reminded him of *someone* dear. Otherwise he wouldn't have behaved so nicely to him when no one else had bothered in the past—not even those related to him.

Michele nodded thoughtfully as Nicolo continued to complain about his nephew and the fact that the position went to him when Nicolo would have been the better choice.

Suddenly, he had to ask.

"Why are you taking me with you?"

It was a family matter, and one that Michele had no business involving himself into.

"It's a lesson, son," Nicolo grunted.

"I don't understand."

"It's a lesson in strength. You have those pesky ideals of

yours, well, I have concrete reality. And I want to show you exactly how the world works."

"I'm still not following." Michele frowned, fidgeting in his chair as he regarded his friend suspiciously.

Nicolo always sought to *teach* him things—about the world and about people. It was one of their main contentions—the fact that Michele still held on to a rather utopian view of the world while Nicolo fully embraced a cynic one.

"My nephew may have inherited the position, but that doesn't mean that power belongs to him," he continued, his eyes settling on Michele with a chilling intensity. "A position is just that, if you can't match up to it, a position. In history, they were called puppet monarchs. Those who legitimately came into power but could not measure up to it."

It slowly dawned on Michele where Nicolo was heading with his argument.

"Sometimes it's easier that way since people naturally want to be led. They don't want strife, or chaos. They want the stability that a form of government provides. A contract, if you will, between the people and the ruler. The people promise to obey while the ruler promises to lead. All for the well-being of *everyone*, of course. They don't care who pulls the strings as long as strings are pulled."

"You mean people don't care who is in the shadows as long as there is someone in the light."

A smile tugged at Nicolo's lips.

"Precisely. And this funeral is the opportunity to remind Valentino, my nephew, exactly that. He may be the appointed leader, but he cannot do it by himself. His father could not before him, who is to say *he* could?"

"He might surprise you," Michele offered.

"Surprise me?" Nicolo threw his head back and laughed. "That boy could never surprise me. I've known him since he was a babe, and he's never been anything but a weak man. A *led* man. And such men *always* require someone to lead them."

"Someone like you."

"Yes. Someone like me."

'But do you like that? Leading from the shadows? Where is the satisfaction?" Michele asked, seriously pondering the question.

He'd done his fair share of reading in school, and he was very familiar with history and politics—probably because he'd never had access to any children's shows. Instead, he'd resigned himself to watching documentaries—some of them were even animated.

In the beginning, it had been nothing more than a story. But as he'd grown, his thinking had started to mature too, and he'd realized those stories were not *just* stories. Rather, they were lessons to be learned, parables to be listened to and mistakes to avoid.

"The satisfaction is in knowing I could end him in one second if I wished. That I'm like a shadow watching over, the reaper waiting with his scythe raised," Nicolo grunted proudly.

"You like to see people squirm," Michele observed, eliciting a smile from his friend.

"Indeed. Because what says power more than power over feelings? When you can dictate how others feel, *that* is the ultimate form of power. The rest is all a by-product of that."

"I see," Michele acquiesced, able to see Nicolo's perspective. "But that means you'd never be credited for your work," he continued.

For himself, he didn't know what he'd rather—work from the shadows and gain control over everyone, or be in the light, where *everyone* knew who he was.

His logical side told him the former was the better choice, Nicolo being right about the ultimate expression of power. But there was also that part of him, deep down, that wished his abilities would be recognized for once. He'd always been in the shadows—powerless and in the shadows. He *only* knew that, and so he wished to experience the opposite too.

Maybe it was vain of him to desire something like that, but he was tired of hiding—tired of pushing down his real self and what he considered to be his qualities in order to please others.

And in the ideal, utopian world that Michele dreamed of, people recognized his strengths and praised him for them instead of trying to tear him down.

"Only fools need someone else's validation," Nicolo said with astounding certainty. So much so that it made Michele reel, his previous thoughts at direct odds with this line of thinking.

"True strength requires only *your* confidence. Everyone else can go fuck themselves," he cursed low.

Michele's mouth was hanging open as he blinked repeatedly. A small blush went up his cheeks as it dawned on him *he* was one of those fools who needed validation. But did he need it, or did he merely *want* it. He wasn't sure of the difference.

He only knew that he wanted to be in the light, never in the shadows again.

Maybe to Nicolo that was weak—foolish. But to Michele, it was the culmination of all his childhood dreams. Of everything he'd seen himself being but never quite managing to be.

Once more, his goal of being a comic book writer came to mind. Then he *would* be in the spotlight, because everyone would know it was *him* who created Lasso—his name being on the front cover of the comic. Then, he would be front and center for once. More than anything, he would bring something to people, he would be *special* to someone—something he'd yearned all his life but had never happened.

The rest of the journey continued as they engaged in a comfortable banter. Michele didn't contradict Nicolo on his idea —maybe because he knew it was the right one but couldn't bring himself to fully acknowledge it. Or maybe, because he wanted to hold on to his dreams of being special to someone for a little longer.

The car pulled into a parking lot, and Nicolo signaled Michele to follow him. Hopping off as he adjusted his bag on his shoulder, it was to see a massive cemetery. And in the distance, he spotted a crowd of people gathered in one place, around an open hole.

"Let's go. And the lesson today," Nicolo paused, watching the people intently, "is body language. Watch *how* they squirm," he chuckled.

They walked forward, following a beaten path as they passed by countless tombstones. Michele looked right and left, this being his first time in a cemetery and attending a funeral.

The sky was gloomy, the entire atmosphere morose and accented even more by everyone wearing black.

So much black.

There were at least fifty people. Some women were crying in a corner. Some were bringing their left hands to their front in the sign of the cross.

A closed casket was in the middle of the crowd, a priest nearby that dealt with the grieving people.

Michele didn't want to be near the dead person.

He thought the day miserable enough without the sight of a corpse—a real life corpse. He shuddered just thinking about it.

But the change as they arrived in the midst of the people was unmistakable, just as Nicolo had said.

Almost like a sudden intake of breath, it felt like everyone stilled for a moment as they spotted Nicolo. Their expressions were unguarded, and Michele finally saw it.

The squirming.

But more than anything, he spotted the disgust, the fear, and the apprehension. His friend wasn't the benevolent type of power—no, he was the type that instilled dread in people. And that gave him pause as he sought to reconcile the version of Nicolo that *he* knew with the one these people did.

A couple was by the casket, the man with his arm around the woman as he cradled her head to his chest. When his eyes made contact with Nicolo's, he stiffened. And with a quick word to his companion, he strode forward.

"Uncle," he spoke, his eyes narrowed on Nicolo.

"Valentino," Nicolo greeted with a fake smile.

Michele looked up between the two men, and in his mind, he didn't see Valentino as weak—not when he was holding his ground, staring at Nicolo as an equal, not as someone who was used to puppet strings.

Nicolo had mentioned body language. But as far as Michele was concerned, Valentino didn't seem to squirm too much.

"Good of you to come. The ceremony is about to start," the man nodded tensely, his gaze sliding down to Michele. "And who might this be?"

"My mentee," Nicolo added with an amused smirk. "He follows me everywhere," he said as if it wasn't a big deal.

Valentino regarded Michele for a little longer, almost as if he were a puzzle he couldn't solve. At last, he nodded.

"You should take your seat. I'm not looking for trouble today, Nicolo," Valentino mentioned in a silent warning.

"If I were looking for trouble, Tino, I wouldn't have brought a child with me," Nicolo chuckled. "You're safe from me…for now," he winked, making light of the situation.

Valentino frowned, almost as if he didn't know what to make of Nicolo and his intentions.

Michele, too, looked between the two men and finally saw what Nicolo had meant by *squirming*. Yes, he did make the others uncomfortable and there were expressions filled with fear as they looked at Nicolo. But with Valentino it was an entirely different matter.

Confusion.

He was making him squirm in confusion.

Valentino scoffed, turning back and returning to his woman's side.

It was then that Michele noticed another thing. Almost everyone was married—everyone but Nicolo.

He'd wondered about that before, especially since he'd met Cami and some of the girls that frequented the gym. He knew that in the *famiglia* the custom was to be married in your early twenties, more often than not to someone that was beneficial for the organization.

Valentino himself looked to be just slightly younger than Nicolo and he had a woman.

As they took their positions by the sidelines, Michele couldn't help himself from asking.

"Why aren't you married?"

The question took his friend by surprise, and for the first time, Michele witnessed something akin to genuine emotion on his face.

"Never had the taste for it," he quickly masked his feelings, choosing to go with a mocking reply.

"But didn't you *have* to?" he continued.

"Maybe. But I've never been one to do what I'm told," he smirked, his eyes on the casket.

But soon, the amusement left his face as a shadow descended over it.

"Some people marry out of necessity. Others marry because it's what's expected of them. And some... Some marry for love."

"I guess you were none of those?" Michele attempted a chuckle.

"Oh, I was," Nicolo answered bitterly—and surprisingly

earnestly. "I would have married her, if she didn't marry out of necessity first."

Michele blinked, a little confused.

Nicolo looked down on him, his mouth set in a grim line.

"I might have married for love," he shrugged. "But that was probably a youthful ideal. Love," he shook his head, smiling sadly.

"Why would it be a youthful ideal?"

"Because love is the last of your concern in this world. Because, in the order I told you, love always scores last," he sighed.

"Then why not marry for the other two?" Michele probed.

Nicolo froze for a moment.

"Why not indeed," he mused to himself. "Maybe we're not all that different after all, son. Maybe I'm a little idealistic, too."

He didn't continue. He let the conversation die, his expression one of consternation and...sorrow.

Michele realized that for all his tough exterior, his friend might have a heart—a strong beating heart that had been hurt in the past. And that made him sad.

Taking it as his time to be quiet, he observed the beginning of the funeral as the priest started talking. Yet as the ceremony kicked in, he grew increasingly restless and tired of listening to all the morbid talk. Slowly, he retreated, spotting a row of benches a short distance over.

Sinking down on the cold wood, he released a sigh.

Grabbing his backpack, he took out a small notepad and a pen, the only ones he could get away with these days. And raising his gaze towards the funeral procession, he started drawing.

He didn't know why he needed to capture that moment in time. He'd heard that Nicolo's brother wasn't going to be missed. Even at his own funeral, the nice words were far in between, despite the priest's urgings.

Still, the desolate scenery stole him away.

Pencil to paper, he started tracing light lines.

"What are you doing?" a small voice asked, barely penetrating his ironclad focus.

He blinked, the tip of his pencil stopping in place as he lowered his notepad to look in front of him. A child of about five stood in front of him, studying him with curious eyes.

Eleven

AGE THIRTEEN

The first thing he noticed about her was the rich mane of auburn hair framing her porcelain skin stained with bits of mud. Her hair was streaked with dirt as well. And as he looked lower, he realized her clothes were dirty, too, the black dress she was wearing completely soiled.

She was a pretty child, her face resembling that of a doll. But she was a *very* dirty child.

"I'm drawing," he answered in a soft voice, especially as she turned her big eyes towards him and regaled him with a wide smile.

"Can I see?" she squeaked, coming closer.

For a moment, he wondered what she was doing all by herself over here. She was too young to be left to her own devices, and given the condition of her clothes, he suspected she needed constant supervision.

"Only if you tell me where your parents are," he said playfully. He didn't like the thought of her wandering around by herself.

Immediately, the smile died on her lips as she took a deep

breath in, turning slightly and pointing her finger towards the crowd of people.

"There," she said with a small shrug.

"Why don't we go find them?" Michele suggested.

"No," she shook her head. "There," she pointed again, this time towards the casket.

"That's your father?"

She nodded, but didn't seem particularly sad.

Odd.

"What about your mother?"

Another shrug.

"She left me. Loooong time ago," she said in a high pitched voice, but there wasn't any trace of emotion—almost as if she was reciting something she'd heard one too many times before.

"Then who are you with today?"

"Tino," she gave a tremulous smile, "but he has no time for me," she added dejectedly. "Can I see the drawing now?" she switched the topic immediately, placing her small hands on the bench and jumping in an attempt to haul herself up.

Seeing her efforts, Michele shook his head indulgently, a sad smile playing at his lips. He had the vague feeling she wasn't very cared for, and that broke his heart a little—especially since she was trying very hard not to dwell on it.

"Here," he placed his notepad aside for a moment as he swooped her up and placed her next to him on the bench. And before she could protest, he removed a pack of wet wipes from his bag, taking one out and dabbing it gently at her cheeks.

"Drawing?"

"After," he chuckled, feeling sorry for the state she was in. "Let's get you cleaned a little and then I'll show you the drawing."

She blinked, looking at him with such awe, he didn't know how to react. He'd always liked children, and he'd spent long periods of time with those younger than him in the hospital, so to an extent he was used to dealing with toddlers.

For some unknown reason, though, the state of this little girl, so dirty and neglected, tugged at his heart. In some ways, she reminded him a lot of himself.

A gentle smile on his face, he continued his ministrations, wiping the dirt smudges from her face and hands.

"Now you're good," he winked at her, grabbing his drawing and passing it to her.

"Wow," she inhaled sharply, staring at the drawing for a few seconds before turning to him. She scooted closer, a mischievous smile on her face.

"I love it," she exclaimed. "You're good. Very, very good," she praised with effusive enthusiasm.

He hadn't managed to draw much. There was the outline of the people and the casket, but he'd focused more on the forlorn surroundings—the tombstones and general atmosphere of the place. It wasn't his best work, but he couldn't deny her praise. More than anything, Michele found that he couldn't stop himself from smiling, her bubbly attitude intoxicating.

"Thanks," he chuckled.

"I'm Venezia," she offered slyly, grinning from ear to ear, the missing front tooth only making her more adorable. But Michele knew the little hoyden had something under her sleeve.

"Michele," he replied, taking her now clean hand and shaking it lightly.

"Can you draw me too?"

"Sure," he answered immediately, happy to indulge her. It wasn't often that he was asked to draw other people, so it was a good opportunity for him too.

"I want to be a princess," she continued. "I want a pink princess dress. And pink princess shoes," she scrunched up her face deep in thought, "*and* a pink bag," she squeaked.

"Slow down," he laughed. "Let me get some colors," he told her as he rummaged through his bag, finding some crayons.

"What type of princess do you want to be?" He asked when he had everything ready.

"Princess," she repeated, frowning.

"Like the ones on TV?" He needed some more information to work with, but she seemed even more confused when he mentioned the princesses on TV.

"Tell me where you saw this type of princess you want," he urged gently when he saw her befuddlement.

Her face fell even more and she fidgeted with her fingers.

"Hey, I need all the information so I can make you the prettiest princess ever, ok?"

She batted her lashes, slowly nodding.

"I saw this doll," she started, her words a little stilted, "she was wearing a pink dress. Everything was pink," her lips tugged up in a smile. "And she was so pretty," she gushed, the word pretty sounding more like pewtty. But Michele just nodded along, not bothering to correct her speech.

"Go on," he smiled.

"But the woman there told me to leave," she sighed. "She said it was for princesses, not for girls like me."

"Girls like you?"

"Unkept," she nodded sadly, probably meaning to say unkempt.

"She said what?" he couldn't believe someone would be so mean to a child so cute. But he supposed some people only saw the outside—and if she'd called her unkempt, it was likely a common occurrence for her to be this neglected. He thought back to the unkind words *he*'d heard from adults all his life, as well as those from other children, and he couldn't help but empathize with her situation.

"She was right," she continued, swinging her legs on the

bench. It was then that he noticed the scuffs on her knees, some red and angry. "No one keeps me," she said, still thinking the woman had called her *unkept*.

"She was just mean," Michele told her, "don't listen to her. Some people are just mean."

She stopped moving then, giving him an odd look.

"Can you make me a princess, then?" she quickly switched topics again, forcing a smile on her face.

"Sure thing," he agreed—he didn't think he had the heart to deny her at that moment.

"A pretty princess," she reiterated as she moved closer to him, raising herself slightly to peer over his shoulder as he worked.

His lips stretched into a smile, Michele started with a sketch. It wasn't hard to give her a princess-like look. He was sure that if she was more taken care of she would look every inch regal—especially with her adorable features.

"Am I doing good?" he asked and she readily nodded.

"Love it," she breathed out.

And so he continued with his sketch until he had everything done, her princess dress, her princess shoes and her princess bag. It was when he started adding the colors that she became a little too quiet by his side.

One glance and he found her watching him with a mix of awe, sadness and happiness all in one.

"Do you like it?"

She didn't answer, merely moving her chin up and down, swallowing hard and blinking even harder—almost as if she didn't think it was real.

"It's so pretty," she finally spoke, and he noticed she didn't consider *herself* pretty, merely the drawing.

"Like you," he smiled. "Pretty like you. After all, you were the model."

She blushed, her shyness coming to the surface.

"Here," he took hold of his pencil again and scribbled a few words in the corner.

From Michele to Venezia, the prettiest pink princess.

"It's yours now," he handed it to her.

"Really? I can have it?"

"Of course, I drew it for you."

She held it in both hands as if it was something precious, her eyes greedily drinking in the drawing. He'd tried his best to make her a pretty princess—one to rival any doll out there and any lady that told her she couldn't be one.

And by the look on her face, he thought he succeeded.

She continued to stare at it, but a glance at the crowd still gathered at the casket told Michele they'd dallied enough away from everyone.

Just as he was about to suggest he took her to her family, a low buzzing sound erupted through the silence.

Her hands went still on the paper, her chin tipped down in shame.

The noise continued, and Michele realized it was coming from her.

She was...hungry. And embarrassed.

"Are you hungry?" he asked in a serious tone. He'd only known her for a little while, but he could read her dire circumstances on her, and if she was *that* hungry, he doubted someone would give her food anytime soon. Especially since no one seemed that interested in her whereabouts.

A spark of anger ignited within him at the thought.

He knew what could have happened to him that night when he'd wandered off alone if not for Nicolo's help. She was a girl. A much younger and defenseless girl. Countless bad things could happen to her.

"Let's get you something to eat," he told her with a smile, all the while thinking to himself that he had to give her a talk about safety.

Clearly no one in her life had done it if she so easily approached a stranger. And he wanted to ensure he was the *last* stranger she approached.

Maybe he could even put in a word with Nicolo, since he *was* her uncle.

Venezia turned her huge eyes on him, biting her lower lip in apprehension.

"Come," he put the backpack over his shoulder as he stretched out a hand towards her. She eyed it for a moment before sliding her much smaller one into it, hopping off the bench and following him.

"I think I spotted a place to eat across the street," he gave her a smile.

She nodded, her eyes on him, unblinking. It was as if she was awestruck by him and the fact that he was considering her needs —as if that had never happened before.

He pushed down the rage he felt at that thought. He knew it on his own skin—knew exactly what the cost of such neglect was in the long run. And he was a boy—almost a man. She was just a small girl.

Her hand was warm in his, and he felt a surge of protectiveness over her. For a moment, he wished he could shield her from all the evils of the world—from everything bad that was out there, just waiting to strike at her. But just as the thought surfaced, he pushed it aside. It wasn't *his* job to do it.

He was just a stranger.

They reached in front of a small fast food restaurant, and he opened the door for her to come inside.

The staff took one look at her and their lips curled in disgust, undoubtedly at her messy appearance. Still, he didn't let that deter him as he led her at a table in the back.

"Wait here and I'll get some food, ok?"

She nodded at him, the drawing still in her hand as she clutched at it as if a precious possession.

That made Michele smile.

It was probably the first time he met someone who prized his art as much as he did.

"I'll be right back," he repeated, slowly leaving her side and heading to the counter.

He pushed one hand into the pockets of his pants searching for cash all the while perusing the prices on the board.

"Damn," he muttered as he felt around for money.

He didn't think he had enough for two portions. He had a meager allowance, and he used most of it on his art supplies. And so what was left was mere pocket change.

Still, he managed to pull together about ten dollars for a large menu, saving some coins to head to the pharmacy afterwards.

He wasn't that hungry anyway. Why, he'd already had breakfast. But her...he had no idea when was the last she ate if the people around her didn't even care enough to change her out of her dirty clothes.

After placing his order, he only had to wait a few minutes before it was done. Grabbing onto the tray, he walked back to their seats and placed everything on the table.

The large menu consisted of a massive portion of fries, a big burger, a side of salad and a drink. By some luck, it had been under ten dollars and he'd been able to also get a small chocolate muffin for Venezia.

Her mouth was hanging open as she looked at the food in front of her.

"Go on, eat," he urged her.

She seemed reluctant to dive in, and a few moments later he realized why. She was trying to wipe her hands on the dress.

"Give me your hands," he said as he took out the wet wipes and cleaned her hands until she was pleased enough with herself to start eating.

Immediately, she took a bite of a fry, smiling as she chewed it.

"Thank you!" she exclaimed. She was a bit of a messy eater, but he didn't mind it. She looked so cute in that moment Michele couldn't help but be glad he had the extra cash to spare.

"Why you no eating?" She asked when he saw him only watching her. "Here," she thrust a fry at him.

"No, I'm not hungry," he shook his head lightly.

"You don't eat," she pointed at him, almost poking his chest, "*I* don't eat," she pointed back to herself with a pout.

"Come on, Zia. You're the hungry one," he chuckled.

"Zia?" she stopped mid-chew as her eyes grew wide.

"A nickname," he offered. "Hasn't anyone called you that before?" He'd noticed she had a hard time pronouncing her name, most likely as a result of her missing front tooth. But he belatedly realized he should have bit his tongue. He was asking a child that, by the looks of it, barely had someone to care for her, if she'd ever been given a nickname.

She shook her head, pondering the word for a moment before nodding.

"I like Zia. It's easier to say than Venezia," she screwed up her face, making a funny expression before laughing at her own skewed pronunciation.

"There you have it, so now eat," he motioned her playfully.

She shook her head again.

"No. You eat, I eat," she continued, smiling in satisfaction as she leaned back to wait for his next move.

"You're quite the blackmailer, aren't you?" he couldn't stop himself from smiling at her antics. Still, he wanted her to eat.

"How about we do this? You have two bites, I'll have one. Then again."

She narrowed her eyes at him, probably thinking if he was trying to cheat her. Eventually, she nodded.

And so she would eat a little, then feed him a fry. It went on like this until the end of the meal. By the time the food was gone, both Venezia and Michele were full.

"Thank you," she sighed in pleasure, wiping her mouth with the back of her hand.

He tsked at her, cleaning her hand again before noticing her giggle.

"You're doing that on purpose, aren't you?"

She gave a shrug, smiling.

"You're a little troublemaker," he said, amused. But he quickly sobered as he remembered the topic he wanted to address with her. "Zia, from now on, you shouldn't talk to strangers again, especially men." he told her sternly. "And you should *never* follow them anywhere."

"Why?" she frowned.

"Because they can harm you."

"Harm me?"

He muttered a low curse under his breath, searching his mind for a way to explain it better. "There are a lot of people out there that want to take advantage of you. Hurt you. You don't want to be hurt, do you?"

She immediately shook her head.

"No. I fell yesterday and hurt my knee," she complained. "It hurt a lot. I don't like pain."

"Good. Then to avoid it, avoid strangers," he nodded at her, grimly reminding himself of those scuffs he'd seen on her knees.

"What about you, then?" she blinked, the question so innocent yet it felt like the ultimate test.

"I won't hurt you," he smiled. "And I'm not a stranger anymore," he winked at her.

Her lips spread into a blinding smile, even her tooth gap looking cute as hell as she looked at him adoringly.

"Now let's go. There's one more stop before I take you back to your family," he said as he stood up, getting his stuff and taking her hand.

He didn't miss the way her face fell when she heard about her family, and he felt bad for her situation.

If he had a sister her age, he'd protect her at all costs. Like Gianna and Rafaelo had protected him whenever they could. More so even. He would make sure that nothing and no one could harm her, and that she would never complain about being *unkept* again.

Swinging by a pharmacy nearby, he got some band-aids and some antiseptic cream with what little spare coins he had left.

"What's that for?" she asked in confusion as he brought her to sit on a bench by the road.

"For your knee, so it heals faster," he told her gently.

She didn't reply, merely watching him as he took some of the cream and spread it over her injured areas. She winced every now and then but didn't make a sound. When he was done, he put a band-aid over each knee and instructed her to do the same while handing her the rest of the supplies.

"If you hurt yourself again just do like I did," he told her, stretching out his hand to help her hop off, finally ready to return to the cemetery.

He hoped the ceremony had ended.

Zia was already yawning, her eyes droopy as she undoubtedly wished to go to sleep.

When they got back to the cemetery, they saw it was almost empty. The procession of people had already departed.

"What..." Michele blinked as he looked around. Everyone had left—including the girl's family.

Not wanting to let panic overtake him, he went back to where Nicolo had left his car, sighing in relief when he noticed it was still there. Upon noticing him, Nicolo opened the door, his sharp gaze skittering from Michele to Zia and their joint hands.

"She was hungry," Michele merely said, attempting a boyish smile.

Nicolo rolled his eyes and shook his head at them, motioning for the car.

"Valentino and his wife left already," he said when Michele helped Zia take a seat next to him.

"How could they leave and forget about her?" Michele asked, outraged.

Zia didn't seem too concerned about this turn, and she kept her eyes on the floor, quietly ignoring the noise around her.

"It wouldn't be the first time," Nicolo mumbled, his eyes landing on her. "My brother didn't really care for another child. Valentino doesn't have children of his own, and I don't think he *wants* any."

"Who's taking care of her then?"

Nicolo shrugged.

"Whoever can," he answered flippantly.

For some reason, his words made Zia uncomfortable as she snuggled deeper into Michele in search of safety, bringing her knees on the seat and placing them under her. She was so tired, she was struggling to keep her eyes open.

"Sleep," he smiled at her. "We'll take you home, but it's going to be awhile until we get there," he told her as he patted her head lightly.

She gave a small nod, wiggling closer and placing her head on his lap.

His eyes widened, but he didn't move her. She seemed right at home as she was.

Nicolo, though, gave him an odd look as he regarded them languidly.

"You have too big of a heart, son. And one day, that's going to be your downfall," he added cynically.

Michele frowned.

"Maybe," he eventually agreed. "But I'll have my conscience clean."

Nicolo's brows arched in surprise before he burst into laughter.

"You'll have your conscience clean?" he asked in amused outrage. "There is no such thing as a clean conscience in this world. But I guess you still have a lot to learn," he waved his hand. "Go on. Do you. At one point you'll have your wake-up call."

Michele grunted, not wanting to dwell on what his friend was saying. He'd survived for so long being exactly who he was—who he was comfortable being—that he knew he could continue on just like that.

The journey took some time, and in the meantime, Nicolo regaled him with some stories about his brother and the fact that he'd had four wives, and all had left him one way or another—the last being Zia's mother.

"She ran away," Nicolo told him. They didn't know how she managed, but they assumed she must have had an influential lover to facilitate her escape. She'd cared nothing for her daughter as she'd left her defenseless.

Michele looked down at the sleeping girl, and he couldn't help but compare how similar they were, a fact that served to make him feel even more protective of her.

They reached the Lastra mansion, and taking Zia in his arms, Michele exited the car. Nicolo signaled him to go ahead, and he merely nodded. He could gather his friend wasn't on the best of terms with his family.

She was light in his arms as he stopped at the front door, knocking lightly. A staff member opened the door, appearing quite disinterested as she saw Zia in his arms. She merely pointed the way to her room. And as Michele walked up the stairs and to the designated room, he couldn't help but feel the chill that went down his back when he saw her living conditions. They were...abysmal.

Everything was messy and dirty, as if no one had gone inside to clean in a very long time—as if no one had cared.

She was five, for God's sake.

Muttering a curse, he couldn't in good conscience leave her there. Turning, he found an empty bedroom where he laid her on a clean bed while he went in search of the house staff.

Clearly, her family hadn't returned home from the funeral so there wasn't anyone he could exchange words with—as if anyone would take a thirteen-year-old *crusader* that seriously.

Still, without even thinking, he found a few of the workers and asked them to clean her room. They protested for a while, but eventually Michele managed to convince them to do their job properly.

Half an hour later and the room was clean—or as clean as could be.

"It wasn't that hard in the first place," he shook his head in disgust as he went for Zia, swooping her up in his arms and taking her back to her newly cleaned room.

Just like him, she didn't have many possessions. Almost no toys, and certainly no dolls. He could see why she'd been so hung up on that one pink princess—she'd probably never had anything of the sort. She had very few clothes as well, with some she'd clearly outgrown and some that were too big for her small frame.

"Home?" she asked sleepily as he laid her down on her bed, startling Michele from his thoughts.

"Home," he attempted a smile that she could not return. Instead, she just sighed.

Did children sigh?

"Thank you for today," she told him in a small voice, watching him with big, innocent eyes. "Thank you for the drawing," she continued, and before he could reply, he felt her lips on his cheek. "I'll keep it safe," she declared with more pathos than anyone living in her conditions should have.

"I know you will, Zia," he added sadly, taking her in for one last time. "It's time for me to go."

The sadness was apparent on her face, but so was another thing—resignation. She'd known it was coming. This was a child used to people abandoning her, and that broke him a little.

"Maybe we'll meet again someday," he tried to placate her, though he knew it was unlikely.

She nodded, plastering a smile on her face, her hands clutching at her little drawing.

"Goodbye, Zia," he whispered as he laid a light kiss on her forehead. He heard a ghost of a goodbye behind him, but he was out of the room before he could come up with worse ideas—like confronting her family and demanding they took better care of her.

Yet, as he'd seen with Nicolo, her uncle, it might all be in vain.

twelve

AGE THIRTEEN

The way back was tense as Michele was quietly seething at the injustice of it all while Nicolo continued to sport a bored expression on his face. In his own words, it was not his business whatever happened to Venezia.

The car stopped a few streets away from Michele's home—all in an effort to *not* draw any attention to Nicolo's car.

"I'll see you soon," Michele nodded respectfully at him, taking his stuff and leaving.

Sneaking inside the house, though, was *not* such an easy feat. Not when Michele came head to head with Bass, his sister's bodyguard and secret boyfriend.

"Your sister wasn't aware you had to leave somewhere," he noted with a raised brow as he greeted him on the back porch.

Michele drew to a stop.

"Is she home?"

"She's taking a nap."

"Don't tell her, please," he burst out, not wanting his sister to worry needlessly.

"What are you doing, Michele? And dressed like that?" Bass nodded to his suit.

"It's nothing bad, I swear. I was just...with a friend," he blushed, lowering his head. It wasn't a lie. But Nicolo wasn't a friend people would easily approve of.

"A friend? He doesn't happen to bear the Lastra name, does he?"

Michele's eyes widened.

"Wha-what... How did you know?"

"It's not the first time I've seen that car around," he brought his big arms to his chest as he regarded Michele expectantly, waiting for an explanation.

"He's my friend," he said with a sigh.

"Michele," Bass looked a little concerned. "Why don't we go to my room. That way no one can hear us?"

He was hopeful at that, especially since he considered Bass a friend too. In a way, he supposed it was funny how none of his friends were his actual age. But as long as they accepted him, he did not mind it one bit.

He nodded, following Bass as he went up the stairs and towards his room.

Closing the door behind him, he invited Michele to take a seat at the table on the far end of the room. Reluctantly, he did.

"Now, want to tell me what that's all about?"

"I met him by chance at the hospital," Michele started, giving him a quick summary of his acquaintance with Nicolo as well as the fact that he'd saved him from a dire fate some time back.

"And you think he has your well-being at heart?" Bass raised a brow in question.

"He's been good to me," Michele nodded. "He challenges me, and I think I need that," he admitted.

"Michele," Bass took a deep breath. "You know I'm here for you too. Nicolo is a Lastra. You can never know what his true interests are. And you're still a child. Why would a grown man befriend a child? Have you asked yourself that? Unless..." his eyes widened. "He hasn't done anything inappropriate, has he?"

"No, no, no," Michele was quick to deny, putting his hands up. "Nothing of that sort, I promise."

But as Bass continued to talk, he realized how odd it may seem to someone on the outside that a teen would be friends with an adult. He supposed Bass was right to be worried.

"He's never even suggested anything of that nature."

"He could be grooming you. Be nice until..."

Michele shook his head. Yes, their friendship might be odd, but he was sure there was nothing to worry in that regard.

"Promise me you'll be safe? I can't do anything without risking a bigger conflict," he sighed in resignation, knowing that if he went to *anyone* about Michele's friendship with Nicolo there would be hell to pay.

"I promise. I'll come to you if there's anything," Michele said solemnly, before changing the topic. "But now I need *you* to promise me one thing."

Bass looked surprised at the sudden switch.

"My sister. I want you to promise you'll take her away from here. Away from her engagement, and...everything."

"Damn, boy," he shook his head. "That I can easily promise. Your sister won't marry that creep, of *that* I can assure you."

"Good," Michele nodded thoughtfully. "I want her to be happy. She's always been there for me, and I wish I could return the favor someday. So if you need *anything*, anything at all, please let me know. I'll help as I can," he told him sincerely.

Bass regarded him with interest and something more...something like pride.

"You've grown, Michele, haven't you?" he cracked a smile, but Michele simply blushed.

"Everyone grows up eventually," his lips tipped in a sad smile.

"Gigi's always done her best to shield me from everything. It's my turn to do it for her."

* * *

"She won't have to marry Clark, will she?" Rafaelo asked Michele as they sequestered themselves in a quiet corner of the house. They hadn't departed for the engagement ceremony yet.

"Bass won't let it happen," Michele replied confidently.

They had both been worried about their sister's impending wedding, feeling useless as the date approached.

"I hope so," Rafaelo sighed. "I truly hope so. He gives me the creeps."

"I know what you mean," Michele nodded. "I don't like him either. But I wouldn't like anyone for her who wasn't *her* choice."

"There's never a choice," his brother said dejectedly, taking a seat on a nearby chair and bringing his hands to his face. "We won't have a choice either."

Michele turned, surprised to hear the hopelessness in Raf's voice.

"Have you been thinking about this a lot?"

"Sometimes," he shrugged. "You know the tradition. I wouldn't put it past our parents to be already looking for women for us."

Michele regarded his brother thoughtfully.

He hadn't considered it before— marriage. Or, better said, *forced* marriage, because he doubted anyone would think of *his* well being. With Cosima's influence, Raf might make a better match—he might be allowed *some* input. But Michele? He already knew his father would use him for the first opportunity that arose.

Although he hadn't given it much thought before, he was

resigned to his future. It wasn't as if he could protest anything that came his way. He *was* the eldest, after all. It was his responsibility to help the family advance, socially and economically. At the same time, he didn't know how his future marriage would go, since he'd never had an interest in flirting or dating.

He was at the cusp of puberty, and he knew a lot of his classmates were already having their first relationships, some going further than others. Not him.

Not that he'd had much opportunity, seeing how he was mostly a pariah at school. But he'd never had the interest either. He knew there were a lot of conventionally pretty girls at his school, but he'd never seen them like *that*.

It didn't help that most were already crushing on his brother—at this point, he didn't think there was *anyone* who wasn't at least halfway in love with Raf.

He had an easy way about him that drew people in. Everyone flocked to him, both boys and girls. He was handsome, put together and well-mannered. He was also the smartest kid in their school. But instead of getting referred to as a nerd—the way Michele was sometimes called when he did a little better on his tests—he was referred to as a *god*.

Golden boy.

The boys envied him, but still approached him. The girls? They fanned over him and tried to get his attention any way they could.

He hadn't seen Raf respond to anyone in part, but he was never rude. Always with a smile on his face and a polite reply, even his rejections sounded awesome. Of course, the girls didn't see it as a rejection—just a chance to try again the next day.

Michele had no idea if his brother had gotten involved with anyone. He assumed he might have. Who in their right mind would refuse it when it was freely given? At least that's what the logical part of his mind told him. But he knew the truth. *He* would. Because girls didn't appeal to him that way.

Maybe something *was* wrong with him, but the first time he'd seen a couple locking lips in one of their breaks, he'd been repulsed—curious, but disgusted at the same time. The feeling had only augmented as he'd heard rumors of some upperclassmen having sex. *That* had repulsed him even more.

"Do you want that?" Michele asked, meeting his brother's gaze. "Do you want to marry whoever just to please father and Cosima?"

Raf took a deep breath before shaking his head.

"I want to marry someone I love," he replied, shocking Michele with his answer.

"Love?" He raised his brows in surprise. He'd never heard Raf talk about that before. "Are you in love?"

"No, no," he immediately shook his head, chuckling. "Not right now. But in the future? I want to be."

He said it like it was the easiest thing in the world. Falling in love.

Michele continued to study him, thinking if he looked long enough he could figure out some arcane mystery. He knew of love, and at times, he thought he *knew* love. But it wasn't the type Raf was hoping for—he didn't think he had it in him to entertain that type of feeling.

He loved his sister. He loved his brother. He also loved Nicolo and Bass. But it wasn't *love*, yet it was the only type of love he understood. It was a mix of affection, protectiveness and loyalty, all mixed in one.

"What about you?" Raf's question startled him.

"Me..." he stammered, fidgeting with his fingers. "I'm not sure," he answered—the only way he could.

Maybe he'd like a family someday. That didn't sound as bad. He liked children, and he'd make sure to be the best parent if that ever happened. It was the other bits that didn't sit too right with him. He couldn't imagine himself in the *making* of children part.

"It's too early to tell," he forced a laugh, hoping Raf wouldn't ask him more questions. He didn't think he was ready to reveal to anyone that he wasn't quite like the others—or at least, he wagered he wasn't. It would be another thing that made him different, another thing for which he would undoubtedly be made fun of.

He was already called gay, or sissy, or whatever derogatory terms his classmates had heard on the off chance and thought they fit Michele. Yet, the ironic thing was that he didn't think he was gay, either. He'd never had an interest in boys.

He was just...odd.

Sometimes he wondered if his cancer treatments hadn't somehow messed with his body. Maybe he just had a delayed hormonal response. Maybe...

He wasn't in any hurry to find out. And if he eventually found himself desiring those things, then he'd let things follow their natural course.

"We should get going. I'm sure Cosima will be looking for you," he changed the subject.

"True," Raf sighed. "I'll do my best to keep mother busy so she won't ruin things for Gianna. Although I doubt she would. She wants this marriage just as much as our father."

"It's better to be safe," Michele agreed. "I don't know how Cosima's mind works, but she *really* hates Gigi."

"That she does. You know, sometimes I feel so sorry for how she treated you both I can barely look you in the eye."

Michele blinked, not expecting to hear such a confession from Rafaelo. It had always been an unspoken understanding that his mother was the source of all their misery, with Raf doing his best to mitigate any conflict that arose.

"Especially after she ruined your birthday party, too..." he pursed his lips.

"It's not your fault," Michele was quick to correct him. "I've never blamed you for her actions, you must know that. Gigi would never, either. We know you always try to help us. It's just that she has her ideas," Michele grimaced, since those ideas meant making their lives a living hell. And though he disliked Cosima and hated what she'd done with their family, he couldn't truly hate her.

She was Raf's mother, and for that he would always give her his respect.

"I'm happy to hear that," Raf rose from his chair, coming by Michele's side and patting him on the back.

Michele's lips tugged up in a smile. He always enjoyed spending time with his brother, and would forever admire him for being so open when all his life he'd been taught to hate him and his sister. It was a hard line to tread—taking both his mother's side and theirs. But Raf had done it. Somehow, he'd done it. And he'd never behaved any less than a brother with them.

"It doesn't matter what my mother says," Raf continued, "you guys *are* my family."

And that...that was the only type of *love* Michele recognized.

Maybe family was a loose term since inherently it had done him more bad than good. But the good that did exist made him a little bit happier every day.

His sister and his brother were the reasons he was grateful his cancer hadn't killed him. It had taken him time to come to grips with life and death, the human condition and the lack of it. He'd never been particularly attached to the state of being alive since for him it had always meant pain. But them...having them gave his life a new meaning.

"Let's go," Raf nodded to his brother, "and let's pray Bass saves Gigi from that creep."

"He will. I know he will."

The engagement party was to be held at a fancy ballroom with over two hundred guests. Benedicto had gone overboard with spending to make sure everything was perfect and that everyone heard of his change of fortune—after all, having Clark as a groom would immediately lift him up from the genteel poverty he'd found himself in.

Between the two of them, Michele and Rafaelo decided to keep an eye on Benedicto, Cosima and Clark. They didn't know the particulars of Bass' plan, but he'd assured them that no engagement would take place. As such, they understood the evening to be of utmost importance.

Both mingled among the guests, and luckily, no one paid much attention to a pair of teenagers. And when they spotted Bass abscond with Gianna out of the ballroom for a moment, they nodded at each other, each taking their position.

Raf went to Cosima and Benedicto, who were deep in conversation with another couple by the refreshment table, while Michele decided to keep Clark, Gianna's fiancé, occupied.

He was already looking around the ballroom, trying to spot Gianna when Michele intercepted him.

"Mr. Clark," he called, a bright smile on his face.

Clark stopped in his trails, raising a brow as he regarded Michele with interest.

He had a certain allure on people, though he'd never realized it. While he thought people made fun of him for his effeminate features, most of the time it was due to the fact that his looks were bordering on unnatural. There was a beauty and purity that shined within him that made people mad—with jealousy, rage and envy. And so they hit, and hit some more when they were met with his unyielding attitude.

And on some people...that allure was dangerous.

Michele kept his attitude positive though he was unnerved

by Clark's presence. There was something about the man that gave him the chills.

His eyes were cold—dead. He looked as if he was dead inside.

He stifled a shiver as his feet dragged a step backwards, his body rebelling at the proximity.

"Gianna's little brother," Clark exclaimed, continuing to eye Michele in an odd manner. "We haven't spoken too much, have we?"

"No, sir," Michele replied, struggling to keep an even tone.

But he had a mission. And he wouldn't fail his sister.

"I wanted to congratulate you," he almost choked on the words, "and to ask you to treat my sister well."

Clark narrowed his eyes at him.

"What a nice little brother you are," he gave a low laugh. "I guess it's to be expected you'd want to be her knight in shining armor. But," he paused, coming closer. "What if I *don't* treat her well?"

There was something incredibly off-putting about his nearness—something that made Michele sick to his stomach. The feeling only augmented as he brought a hand, touching Michele's cheek and stroking it lightly.

"You're certainly her equal in looks," he commented. "Such a pretty boy," he mused, the words having an entirely different meaning than when some of the kids at school mocked him. This felt...creepy.

He strained a smile.

'Thank you," he mumbled, knowing he needed to stretch this conversation as much as he could.

"There's nothing to thank me for. I'm merely admiring beauty," he said, coming even closer. So close, Michele could almost feel his breath on his skin. "I think we're going to get along wonderfully, you and I."

"Really?" Michele's eyes widened in alarm. "I guess so... I'd love to visit my sister often."

"I'm sure that could be arranged," Clark murmured thickly. "Maybe you could even join us permanently..."

"I..."

Michele was spared a reply as a screen at the end of the ballroom flared to life. A video started playing, with an unknown person appearing and wishing the couple a happy engagement day in a distorted voice.

"But not too happy, is it? Not when the soon to be bride is fucking someone else—at her own engagement party, nonetheless. The drama," the person on the screen chuckled.

Immediately, the video changed, and Michele's eyes widened when he saw his sister and Bass together in a room. They were wearing today's clothes and they...

As if they had a life of their own, his feet took him towards the screen, getting closer and closer until he could convince himself that what he was seeing *was,* indeed, real.

Though there was nothing explicit on the screen, the camera was placed at such an angle one could make out exactly what was happening. Especially as his sister's and Bass' voices boomed in the speakers, the words the epitome of vulgar.

I own every hole in your body, don't I sunshine?

Every hole.

Every fucking hole, sunshine. You'll take all of me as I fucking breed you. Pump you so full of my cum you overflow with it. I want to see it spilling from every fucking orifice. Your mouth, your pussy, and your ass. Isn't that right, my dirty little slut?

Yes. You can do anything to me.

Michele was having a hard time reconciling the sister he knew with the one he was seeing.

Bass' hips were pumping in and out of her from behind, the sounds of their moans deafening. Even more deafening, though, were the murmurs that started to overtake the entire room, the shushed words that condemned his sister and branded her a *whore,* a Jezebel, and other outrageous insults.

He wanted to move. Turn and yell at everyone to shut up. That this was his sister they were talking about, not just anyone. He wanted to *harm* them for crucifying her, and for what? For being in love? For being forced to marry a creep?

No, Michele could never join their ranks in condemning her for something so natural. Even though he didn't understand it himself, even though he thought the entire act appalling—verging on disgusting—he would never think less of his sister for falling in love and giving in to that feeling.

Still staring at the screen, he was taken by surprise when soft hands covered his eyes.

"Don't," his sister whispered, her voice broken.

In that moment, Michele vowed that he would end whoever hurt her—whoever had to broadcast such a private moment for the word to see.

And he turned to tell her just that.

He might be just a teenager, but she was *his* sister. It was his turn to protect her.

As he opened his mouth to speak, though, someone yelled her name, the crowd parting to reveal Clark striding angrily towards them.

Instinctively, he sought to place himself in front of her. But it wasn't necessary. Not when the man dropped to the floor, foaming at the mouth.

One moment.

Two.

He seemed dead.

Gianna gasped, her hand seeking his and holding tight.

Everyone was with their phones out, recording everything and further criticizing the mess.

And there was Benedicto, who set his severe gaze on the two of them and suddenly, he knew that nothing good could await them.

A succession of confusing events later, and everyone was back to the house.

Gianna was locked in her room, on Benedicto's orders not to see everyone.

Michele was...shocked, distraught, worried?

He couldn't put his finger on what he was feeling. He was mad at the world, and to an extent, at himself.

When his father had shouted for the whole world to hear that Bass was a DeVille trying to ruin the family, Michele's gut had sunk to the ground.

He'd...he'd trusted the man. He'd trusted him with *his* sister —his most precious thing. And what had he done? He'd abused that trust and he'd hurt Gianna in unimaginable ways.

thirteen

AGE THIRTEEN

Waiting until nightfall, he snuck out of his room, knocking lightly on Raf's door. He needed someone to talk to. But more than anything, he needed a plan to help his sister.

Now that she'd been publicly dishonored, the entire world witnessing the family's shame, he knew his father was *not* going to be kind with her. It didn't matter if Clark was dead or alive, though the former was preferred. Michele knew that nothing but sorrow and pain awaited his sister if she remained here. As for Bass...Michele wasn't one to wish people ill, but for the first time, he wanted to do the man harm himself.

"Michele?" Raf's eyes widened when he spotted his brother still wearing his festive clothing.

"Can I come in?" he asked in a hushed voice.

Raf nodded, looking around before ushering Michele inside and closing the door behind them.

They hadn't been able to talk after the incident, but Michele knew Raf must have been just as affected by the video. He'd seen him by the sidelines, an expression of pure stupefaction and horror on his face.

"Are you ok?" He asked, his hand on his shoulder.

Though Michele was older than Raf by a few months, it had been his brother who'd always babied and protected him. This time, he felt it was *his* duty to ensure he was alright.

Raf nodded numbly, taking a seat on his bed.

"It's going to get bad, isn't it?" he winced as he voiced the question.

Michele nodded grimly.

"I don't know what father's going to do, but I'm sure it can't be anything good."

"I can't believe Bass would do something like that. That he'd lie to us like that," Raf shook his head in disappointment.

"I know. I really thought he loved her. I *trusted* him..."

"We all did, Michele. We all did," Raf sighed, gathering his knees to his chest.

"I don't know what to do," Michele confessed to his brother. "I feel so useless... Father is going to punish Gianna, of that I'm sure."

"What can we do?"

"She needs to leave. She needs to leave and never look back. This family, this world," Michele shook his head in disgust. "It's not for women. And it's definitely *not* for someone strong like Gigi."

"I agree. But how can she leave when father increased the security? Everyone is on guard while he's at the hospital making sure Clark, or rather his money, is still a viable option."

"She will try to leave," Michele said confidently.

"Then we can do our best to help her."

"She won't let us help," he shook his head at Raf. "You know she would never purposefully endanger us. But that doesn't mean we can't help her without knowing."

Raf blinked.

"What did you have in mind?"

Between the two of them, they started marking the schedule

of the guards as well as getting access to the video feed. When Gianna decided to make her move, they would simply act and make a diversion if needed.

It was a few days after that the plan was finally put in motion.

To Michele's chagrin, his sister came to him and asked him to leave with her. He knew that might be a possibility as they'd been inseparable their entire lives. But he also knew that she would *never* make it out with him as a burden.

And he *would* be a burden. He couldn't even protect her properly. He would only drag her down and ensure that his father's people would find them faster.

He'd thought about all that while still hoping she would choose to leave him behind. Otherwise...he knew he must do something drastic. Something that would change their relationship forever.

Michele didn't know if he preferred she broke his heart by trying to leave all by herself, or if *he* was the one who broke her heart. Maybe, to a certain extent, he would have wished for the former, because to break her heart was to break his *own* heart, but ten times worse.

The moment she showed at his door, late one night, he knew the fates were not on his side. Still, he knew what he had to do. He knew it as he dreaded it.

She looked so young but so weary despite her age.

Her mouth moved, her words rapid as her worry mounted at being caught.

He barely heard her.

He only heard the harsh beat of his heart against his chest as he opened his own mouth to say the most vile things he could think of.

The only things that would make her leave.

He blanked his expression. He blanked his mind. And for one moment, he killed his soul.

"No," he told her as she urged them to leave together.

"But Michele, you can't stay here..." the suffering in her voice was ravaging his heart. But he'd bled on the inside before. He'd known even greater suffering. And for his sister, he would know even more.

"No," he emphasized the word, holding himself cold and aloof. "I'm fine on my own. I've always been. But you..." he infused his words with disgust, saying the things that would break her heart but would set her free. "You've shamed us, Gianna."

She looked as if he'd slapped her, and on the inside, his wounds continued to weep blood. On the outside, though, he kept his resolve strong, his attitude unwavering and off-putting.

"Michele..." she whispered, blinking back tears.

"You know that they make fun of me at school. That I had a whore of a mother and a whore of a sister. I always defended you. But I shouldn't have, should I? Because it was true. Everything was true."

The only way for her to believe him was to imbue his words with half-truths. He spoke about his reality at school, but he lied about his feelings. And damn how those lies burned on his tongue.

"Michele, I know what you saw there..." her throat was clogged with emotion and he knew he was hurting her as he'd never done so before. He was hurting himself, too. God, how he was hurting himself with his own words.

"I know," he simply stated. "I'm not a child, Gianna. And like everyone else present that night, I had to see you—my sister—getting fucked from behind like a common whore."

She gasped, her eyes growing wide at his insult. It was a blow below the belt. It was a blow that cost him everything. But he willingly paid the price. And as he delivered his last line, he knew he lost her. He knew he lost the only thing that had given him strength over the years—the only person he could call her own.

And he did it with his own damned words...

"You've done enough damage to this family. You need to leave and never come back. I don't have a sister, much less a loose one like you."

He didn't linger. He didn't want to watch the disappointment on her face, or the way his words drilled a hole into her heart as he knew they would. He simply shut the door.

Seconds passed. He heard her hurry to her own room.

He held himself still.

One second. Two.

On the third, he couldn't hold it anymore.

The tears fell. Agonizing sobs racked his body as he crouched on the floor, gathering his knees to his chest and burying his head between them.

At that moment, he knew. Nothing would ever be the same.

Gianna successfully escaped that night. With their secret help, she managed to bypass all security and leave, surprisingly, with Bass in tow.

Michele watched.

That night, he watched as the car she'd stolen breezed through the gates, her presence becoming smaller and smaller until she was a dot on the horizon.

Until she was nothing at all.

He watched and he felt himself a part of himself die.

"It's for the best," Raf said as he patted him on the back, joining him at the window as they stared into the night.

"It's for the best," Michele agreed numbly.

Yet he still had no idea what that one event unleashed into his life—into their lives.

His heart cried out in pain. Soon, his soul would weep in agony.

* * *

His bedroom door was shoved open. Michele startled from his sleep, rubbing at his eyes as he tried to banish the confusion from his mind. He didn't have time to ready himself for the first blow.

It caught him under his jaw, harsh knuckles against bone, the pain erupting in a second and enveloping him whole. The force of it threw him backwards, and he couldn't even steady himself as he fell from the bed.

"Where the fuck is she?"

It was his father.

Michele blinked, his hand going to the spot his father had hit as he dared look up at him.

"I-I don't know," he mumbled, dragging himself back.

"The fuck you don't know," his father spat, his fist making contact with Michele's under-eye area.

Immediately, he sought cover, trying to crawl on the floor and under the bed.

"Fucking useless, that's what you are. Both you and your whore of a sister," his father's angry voice boomed in the room. He didn't bother to bend to get to Michele, simply using his feet to hit him, repeatedly.

Though Michele tried to avoid the incoming blows, he couldn't. Some caught him in his belly, some in his back. Others landed on his thigh and one caught him in the face, the tip of his father's shoe hitting close to his eye. Instinctively, he tried to move away, recognizing the danger if his foot actually made contact with his eye...

But he was too late.

"Ah," he yelped in pain.

Again and again.

Michele cried out.

Benedicto spat at him.

"Where is she?" His father asked the same question. On and on. And when Michele couldn't answer, he would earn another blow.

Blow after blow.

The pain was deafening—especially as his father scored a hit in his ear too.

More words. He stopped hearing.

Benedicto cursed him out, calling him and his sister the worst of names. All the while, he never once stopped hitting him.

"You fucking little shit. You cost me *everything!*"

More pain. He wished he could stop feeling.

Michele wasn't sure whether he could still feel alive. His mind was reeling, his body even more so. Pain on top of pain, moving from one site to another, so fast he couldn't get a respite to get his bearings together.

Even at the far end of the bed, plastering himself against the wall, his father's feet could still reach to hit him. Worse still, he had nowhere else to go.

"*Papa* leave him," he thought he heard Raf's voice, but he couldn't be sure.

More voices started speaking in hushed tones, the break enough to get him to finally wake up to the horror show that was his current situation.

He was breathing harsh, his lungs constricting with each inhale. He thought himself on the verge of fainting, or maybe a panic attack. He just knew his body was failing him like before.

He wheezed, bringing his hand to his nose and wiping away

the substance that poured out of him—the red substance that thrust him back in the past.

Blood. So much blood. It was everywhere.

Flowing from his mouth, nose, eyes... *Everywhere*.

Then there were the tubes. The needles that prodded his skin, the outside pain that only mirrored the inside one and the never ending question—am I going to die?

Now, too. The same question took over, echoing in his brain as his sight became foggy, the only object in front of him doubling, then tripling, then appearing as if it was a thousand figures at the same time.

He opened his mouth, trying to speak—trying to ask someone for help. But his throat was too clogged to work. He'd screamed so much at the pain of being hit moments on end, that his vocal chords had bruised, the only noise currently audible being a harsh, harsh breath. It was scratchy and groggy and so unlike himself he panicked even more.

"Michele..."

His name was being called out—or he thought it was.

Why was it so hard to react?

"Damn, Michele, stay with me," the same voice continued, gentle hands reaching out and grabbing his flesh. But even gentleness hurt—it was silent but ever so present.

"Agh," he yelped out, unable to open his eyes. "Agh," he repeated the sound, louder.

He wanted to speak. He did. But no matter how hard he tried, he could not spell out the words.

"Easy, I have you," his brother said, gently brushing his fingers over his forehead in an attempt to push Michele's hair aside.

His face was a mess.

Though he was teetering on the edge of the precipice, his eyes barely making out the light in front of them, he could make out the eerie quiet, the way Raf stilled as he got a better look at his features.

The entire lower half of his face was red—bleeding without stop. His cheeks were swollen, his eyelids so puffy it was a wonder he could make out anything at all.

But his face was the least affected. There, at least he'd had his arms to shield himself. The rest of his body, though? It had taken more hits than a grown man could have withstood.

"Michele, shhh," Raf whispered, gazing down at his brother and hurting for his pain.

But Michele couldn't see that. He felt himself trapped in his body, trembling from head to toe as the pain would not stop. As nothing worked to soothe the ache forming inside of him—right where the root of all his hopelessness resided.

He whimpered.

Minutes on end, the only sounds he could make were pained whimpers that gushed more blood from his nose and mouth.

Raf did his best to tend to him. He wet a towel with cold water and wiped his face down, doing his best to calm him down when he had no clue what to do.

He looked like death.

He sounded like death.

He might be soon…dead.

"Michele, you can't die on me, you hear?" his brother's voice penetrated the shrieking noise that echoed in his ear.

"N…N…N…" he wished he could tell him not to worry, but his lids grew heavy, blackness enveloping him.

In no time he went limp in Raf's arms, his consciousness slipping from him.

He couldn't hear his brother's cries, or his anguished screams. The way he called his name, so afraid tears started coursing down his cheeks.

He couldn't see how his heart broke for what his brother

suffered—what he was spared from by virtue of being the favorite.

He couldn't know that in that moment, Raf wished it could be him lying limp and bloodied on the ground. That it would be him who bore the brunt of the abuse and pain.

He couldn't know, would likely never know.

The next time he awoke, he couldn't be sure where he was, or how much time had passed. He could barely move. Everything ached. Even the simple act of breathing was too labor intensive.

His eyes swollen-shut, he could only make out particles of light and some movement.

"You're not taking him anywhere," Cosima's shrilly voice penetrated his foggy mind.

"He needs to go to a hospital, *mamma*. Look at the state of him. He's going to die on us."

"So?"

Rafaelo gasped.

"*Mamma!*" he exclaimed, scandalized.

There was a brief pause after which the conversation continued in shushed tones—too shushed for Michele to make it out.

But a while later, he felt hands roving over his body—cold, detached hands.

"His ribs are broken and he might have internal bleeding. We need to get him an x ray," a foreign voice said, and Michele supposed it was a doctor by the terminology he used.

"You mean at the hospital," Cosima, he did recognize. She was further away, but he didn't think he'd ever forget her condemning voice.

"Ma'am, he needs care."

"Do what you have to do. Here. You're not taking him anywhere."

And with that she was gone.

For what felt like hours, the doctor worked on him, cleaning his wounds and bandaging them where he could.

"Your face will be bruised for a few days, but it won't scar," the doctor noted when he saw Michele try to open his eyes. "You're lucky your brother insisted on getting you some care," he shook his head. "I've done all I could, but if you feel worse, or if you start coughing blood, get your brother to take you to the hospital immediately. You understand me?"

Michele blinked slowly, painfully, before nodding to the other man.

"Good. Now rest. I'll leave some pain medication here, but don't overdo it."

He nodded again—or at least what he thought was a nod.

With another few instructions, the doctor left, leaving the way clear for Raf to sneak in.

"Damn it, Michele. How could he do this to you?" Raf asked in an anguished tone, his hand coming to rest over his hair, gently stroking his head.

He was on his back on the bed, his limbs semi-paralyzed both from pain and from the stiffness of the bandages.

His ribcage was the worst, pain flaring at every small move.

"H-how," Michele paused, wetting his lips. It was hard to talk, but not as hard as the other day when he'd thought his throat had died on him. His voice was groggy, but at least it was audible. "How d-did you…get him t-to stop?"

Raf pursed his lips.

"I told him I would renounce him as my father if he did any permanent damage to you. He hasn't been home since then. I think he's trying to find Gianna and fix the problem with Clark."

"N-not dead?"

"No," Raf sighed. "He survived. If they find Gianna…" he trailed off and Michele knew exactly what would happen.

They would force her to marry Clark—the marriage still on the line. If not, she would be given to be used.

He had no doubt that both Clark and Benedicto would take their revenge for the humiliation at the engagement party in unimaginable ways.

That made Michele's resolve stronger. He could not allow his sister to end up in their hands. He could not allow her *anywhere* near them.

"Can't let them," he wheezed out.

He would rather die than let his father get his hands on Gianna.

"We won't," Raf agreed. "But you need to get well. You can't help her like this," he gave him a tight smile.

Michele tried to return it, his facial muscles were hurting too much so he only managed a droopy grin.

"I will," he promised.

"Good, I brought you a little something," Raf went back to the door, looking outside quickly before closing it and locking it. Shrugging a small bag from his back, he opened the zipper as he rummaged inside.

Michele was lying still, his swollen eyes on his brother as he removed some drawing essentials and showed them to him.

"You need to get better so you can get back to work," Raf told him, and tears stabbed at his eyes at his brother's thoughtfulness.

"Th-thank you," he said groggily, his throat filled with emotion rather than pain.

Raf gave him a comforting smile, hiding the supplies at Michele's instructions. Though his brother had wanted to make him happy with that gesture, he couldn't risk being found with anything drawing related. His father would *kill* him then.

"I'll let you rest now. You need to regain your strength," Raf told him, giving him one last look before leaving the room.

The first few days were the worst. His flesh swelled even more before it started healing. He had trouble going by himself to the restroom, at times depending wholly on Rafaelo to help him clean himself.

Any other time and he would have been thoroughly embarrassed. But this scenario helped the brothers become closer, and issues such as shame and privacy became a thing of the past.

Michele, for all his hopelessness around the people in his life, gained a new appreciation for his brother.

In the beginning, he'd thought that with Gianna's departure, he would be forever alone, closed off in a bubble *not* of his own making. Everyone hated him and everyone shunned him. He truly believed the beating would be the beginning, and at some point the end. How could he survive to be eighteen and independent when one beating threatened to be the last. And so, his body had not been the only one bruised, his mind losing hope, his heart bleeding more than his open wounds.

But there was Raf.

Sweet, dependable Raf.

For the first time, Michele gained a new appreciation for his brother.

Maybe in the past he'd been a little jealous of his perfect world—who wouldn't? He'd always justified it as being human nature, and he'd tried his best to squash those feelings. Now, as he lay on his back, staring at the white ceiling, he only felt shame at ever wishing he could have his brother's life. How could he not when he was the *only* one there for him? When he risked the wrath of both his mother and their father to be with Michele—to help him as he could?

Yes, his sister might be gone, but he still had his brother. And knowing Raf was there gave him strength.

He pushed himself despite the pain, and three days after the doctor had seen him, Michele was on his feet.

It wasn't pleasant, but he supposed nothing worth fighting for was. All he knew was that he didn't want to be the weak link. He didn't want to drag Raf down, too.

For once, *he* needed to be the strong one. Protect both his sister and his younger brother.

fourteen

AGE THIRTEEN

The days passed slowly, his bruises healing even slower. Still, Michele pushed against the pain.

A week after the incident, his father had still not returned to the house. Cosima was in a perpetual neurotic state as she screeched at Michele every time she saw him. Since Raf was mostly away at school or his activities, as decreed by Cosima, so Michele tried very hard to avoid bumping into her. He needed exercise to get used to moving again, but he tread carefully around the house to not get into trouble.

A few days later, on a cold, cold Saturday, when Michele's injuries had finally turned a more yellow color, his body halfway to recovery, Benedicto finally arrived home.

"I'll go check." Raf told him to stay put, wanting first to gauge their father's mental state.

Michele fiddled with his fingers as he stared at the mirror on his closet, his wretched state only making him more fearful should Benedicto decide he was in need of another beating. He'd barely recovered *some* of his motor functions, and as the doctor had said, he was extremely lucky to not have had any internal bleeding. He didn't want to push that luck.

"Michele," Raf's voice startled him from his musings. Slowly, he craned his neck to see the door pushed ajar as Raf half-entered the room.

"He wants everyone downstairs. Uncle Franco is with him."

"Is he... Is he still mad?"

"I don't know. But stick behind me?"

Michele gave a brisk nod, carefully lowering himself off the bed and heading to Raf's side. His brother was quick to grab his arm, steadying him and helping him carry his weight. Together, they headed downstairs.

Michele trailed slightly behind Raf as they all convened in the drawing room.

Cosima was sitting on the sofa at the far end of the room, her shrewd eyes taking in Michele and his condition as her lips tipped into a satisfied smile.

Next to her was another woman, dressed all in brown, the color only augmenting her plain looks.

"Aunt Aurora," Raf greeted, and Michele followed his brother's cue.

She nodded at them absentmindedly.

Their uncle Franco was sitting by the fireplace, one elbow on the marble finishing as he looked at the two boys languidly. Benedicto was by his side, his gaze one that could put fear even in the bravest of souls.

The two brothers looked nothing alike. Whereas Benedicto's looks were light and pleasant, Franco's were darker and harsh. Yet in spite of that, Benedicto's personality was the frightening one while Franco's was more pleasant.

Michele had always thought his uncle a nice enough man, certainly better than his father. Growing up, he'd wished, once or twice, that Franco was his father instead of Benedicto. As far as he knew, he was a very indulgent father to his cousin Antonio.

Speaking of cousin Antonio...

A moderately tall figure swept through the doors, entering the room with much enthusiasm as he looked around, taking everyone in. Cousin Antonio was a younger replica of Franco, his features nondescript and bordering on harsh. He did his best to mask that, though, and for as long as Michele had known him, he'd always had a smile on his face—forced or not, it made him look more approachable.

He was in his twenties. While they didn't regularly see Franco and his son, news traveled, especially since as the couple's eldest son, Antonio's achievements were always talked about and praised. He had just finished a famous theological seminary in Naples, having studied under famous teachers of the scriptures and canon law. He was a lawyer by profession, but he'd decided to dedicate himself to the church. He'd recently obtained a post in Rome and was aiming high—for the Vatican.

The family was ecstatic about it, having such an eminent figure in their midst.

Though to any outsider a career within the church might seem plain, or unimportant, it wasn't that way in the Guerra hold—or anywhere within their circles in Italy.

Faithful to the Catholic faith, the Guerras had always prided themselves on being close to the Church, donating and helping whenever possible. They could be downright broke, but if the Church needed help, they were there to provide it. It didn't matter that the money was obtained through suspicious means. It didn't matter that they were known outlaws and enemies of the Italian state, with the local *polizia* on their trails and watching their every move—the main reason they'd entirely relocated to the United States. The Guerras *always* backed the Church.

They still had their ancestral lands in Italy, owning a big portion of Northern Sicily which had been passed down from generation to generation. The lands and edifices, however, were in poor condition and had even poorer prospects of making a profit. They still bore the Guerra emblem, but they were rich in name only. The area was forever left to the mercy of its surroundings, but the perpetual conflict between Guerra and DeVille made it a wholly hostile environment. That coupled with their sordid reputation and they could never capitalize on much in that region.

But. There was always a but. With Antonio's new position and swift rise through the ranks in Rome, the family hoped to regain its reputation in Italy, the Church providing the ultimate shield for the Guerra to start all over with its businesses in the Peninsula.

"Uncle Benedicto," he exclaimed, going to him for a hug. They kissed each other's cheeks, exchanging small pleasantries. He turned to Cosima, affording her the same respect before settling his eyes on Rafaelo and Michele.

His smile was strained, and Michele took one step back before steeling himself lest he look weak. With his bruises out in the open, he already knew he was being judged. And so he strived to make himself look strong by meeting Antonio's gaze head on.

"Rafaelo and..." he narrowed his eyes. "What happened to little Michele?" he asked in a concerned tone.

"You know, at school," Benedicto waved his hand. "He is our resident troublemaker," he lied, and everyone laughed at that one statement.

Everyone but the two brothers.

"Thank you so much for having us here, Ben," Franco suddenly said.

"It's been so long since I've been in New York. Thank you for the invitation, uncle," Antonio added.

Benedicto cracked a polite smile.

"Franco, Aurora and Antonio will be staying with us for a few months. They'll have the east wing of the house," Benedicto grunted, his gaze scanning the room. He wasn't speaking to anyone in particular, he was just making his decision known.

"We're still on the lookout for Gianna, so this is the perfect time to have some more help."

"Of course, brother. I'm here, at your service. You know you can count on us for everything."

At that moment, a few more people trickled inside the room.

Michele looked around bewildered. He recognized some as his father's men, but others not so much.

"We have a change of plans. Clark is still in the hospital and after that humiliation he refuses to have anything to do with our family and the Guerra name," he gritted his teeth at the statement, his eyes glinting dangerously as he met Michele's.

"Change of plans, sir?" A man in the back asked.

"Do you know them?" Michele asked Raf in a whisper.

"They are father's soldiers," he replied. "They're probably the ones in charge of finding Gianna."

"Then what..."

"Yes, change of plans. You are not to capture Gianna anymore. You are to kill her and bring me her body."

Both Michele and Raf stilled, their eyes growing wide at the pronouncement.

"Kill her?" Michele whimpered.

"Kill her? *Papa!*"

"Shut up, Rafaelo," he snapped, a rare occasion of him raising his voice at his favorite son.

"We need to show everyone that we're not going to stand for this shame. And that is exactly what Gianna has done. She has *shamed* the family in the most undignified way possible. I want her dead and she will serve as a lesson for the entire *famiglia,* and anyone who thinks to go against us."

The words were unspoken. If Benedicto was capable of killing his own daughter, then he was capable of doing anything to his enemies. It was both a show to their family *and* to DeVille.

Michele's body started trembling. No matter how much he tried to hide his tumultuous feelings, he couldn't. Every single thought was written all over his face.

"See, boy," Benedicto switched his attention to Michele. "If you'd told us where she was, it wouldn't have gotten to this. This is on *you*," he sneered.

"Don't," Raf whispered, tightening his hold on Michele's hand.

The words were haunting.

He'd tried to protect her and in the end he'd still caused her hardship. God, but how had things turned up this way?

He blinked repeatedly, his mind quick at work. There was absolutely nothing he could do now except pray they would never find her—that they would never...

"Tell everyone about the change of orders," Benedicto instructed his soldiers.

"And you," he then addressed his family, "tomorrow we're going to church. *All* of us. We're going to show a united front, understood?"

Everyone nodded. Antonio smirked.

Michele didn't know how he got back to his room, or how he managed to get in his bed. The physical pain was irrelevant as his mind honed in on one thing. Gianna.

Had he failed her? Had he sentenced her to death, even if inadvertently?

He did not know. He could not make sense of anything happening around him.

That night, he barely slept.

And when the morning came, dark circles accentuated the

bruised flesh of his cheeks. Raf was by his side as he tried to help him into a clean suit for church.

"Do you think he'll..."

"He won't find her," Raf said with great conviction. Where he got that confidence, Michele didn't know.

"Won't he?" he asked softly, guilt already churning in his stomach.

"He won't. Trust Gianna. She's smart enough to evade all detection. I know it."

"You're right," Michele said after a moment. He couldn't give in to the desperation he was feeling. He needed to be strong —for her.

"Let's go," Raf tugged him along as they headed downstairs, the entire procession waiting to go to church.

Oddly enough, Cosima's remarks were few and far in between. She never even criticized Raf for helping Michele, as per usual repertoire. Everyone was simply quiet.

They arrived together at the church, right before mass. Benedicto was the first to enter the building, with his brother behind him, then Antonio followed by Michele and Rafaelo. The women were last, and they were all seated in the order they entered.

Michele was squeezed between Rafaelo and Antonio, and he bit his tongue in pain when his cousin's knee bumped into his injured leg.

"Are you alright, little Michele?" Antonio asked, looking down at him with tenderness.

Michele raised his gaze, nodding stiffly. He didn't like the way Antonio always addressed him, *little* Michele making him seem much younger and not at all the eldest son that he was.

He assumed it was because, physically, he was smaller than Rafaelo. But his growth spurt had just kicked in so he was sure in no time he would catch up to his brother. Still, it was a sensitive spot since he'd always been made fun of for his frail appearance and smaller frame.

"Yes," he answered.

"Good, tell me if you're uncomfortable, ok?" he brought his hand to Michele's cheek. Instinctively, he flinched at the echo of pain, but Antonio didn't rebuke him. His lips tugged up in a saccharine smile, but it didn't quite reach his eyes. He didn't back down either. He moved his hand again, one finger touching Michele's cheek as he trailed it down to his jaw. "Such a pity for your face. It won't scar, will it?" he murmured softly.

Michele strained a smile as he shook his head.

"The doctor said it won't scar."

"Good. That would be a sin against creation. Against *very* beautiful creation," he continued, his eyes focused on Michele's face.

Antonio looked like a man on the brink of starvation, and Michele could not understand why he was gazing upon him in such a way.

Soon, though, he dispelled those thoughts as mass began. He tried to be present, follow the words being spoken and root himself in the moment, all the while saying a mental prayer for his sister. It was very hard, however, to keep still when Antonio's body kept brushing against his own. One movement here, one there, and their skins were always in contact.

His cousin apologized, repeatedly. But his expression didn't seem apologetic in the least.

He just continued to watch Michele with a relaxed but assured look.

"You should stay away from Antonio," Raf mentioned when they got home, closing themselves in his room.

Michele blinked, his brother's words taking him by surprise.

"Why? He's not as bad as the others," he answered, squaring his shoulders. Their other relatives all regarded Michele with contempt, mostly ignoring him and on the off-chance they deigned to talk to him they belittled him. Antonio had done neither.

"I don't know. There's something about him... I don't like how he looks at you."

"It's fine," Michele gave him a smile. "I don't think he means bad, no? He's training to become a priest."

"So?" Raf shrugged. "That doesn't mean he can't be bad."

"But it has to mean there's some good in him, no?" Michele retorted in a hopeful tone.

Truthfully, he did think Antonio was a little odd, but nothing too worrisome. He was just older, more worldly and had heaps of experience on both Michele and Raf.

"You're too trusting," Raf shook his head. "Just...take care, ok?"

"Don't worry about me," Michele winked. "I think I've had enough pain to last me a lifetime," he feigned a sigh.

"Hey," Raf poked him gently, mindful of his physical state. "Don't joke with things like that, ok? I don't want you to get hurt."

"I know you don't."

The conversation turned more playful as they started talking about comic books and Michele showed Raf the latest drawing he'd done—one with Lasso and his new love interest.

"I thought you didn't believe in love?" Raf raised a brow.

"Maybe I don't," he shrugged, "but I know *you* do."

"It's for me?"

Michele nodded.

"For me too. If Lasso with his hidden identity can find someone who complements him in all ways, then I can too. I don't have any worries for you, seeing how all the girls swarm around you.

"Don't remind me," Raf complained, scrubbing a hand over

his face. "If only they liked me for *me* and not for my credentials."

"Have you let someone in for that to happen?"

Raf stilled, turning to look at Michele thoughtfully.

"You're right. I haven't. Maybe I'm romanticizing this too much, but I've always wanted..." he trailed off, a hint of a blush erupting on his cheeks. "I wanted to know it straight away. I wanted *something*," he grumbled, not knowing how to put into words what he wished for.

Michele, given his lack of interest in the subject, could not understand what he was implying.

"But how can you just *know*?" He asked, seriously pondering the topic. "When I think about love, I think about trust, comfort, and... I don't know," he frowned, "companionship. Something that's built on, not something that just exists. You get what I'm saying?" he asked, afraid he'd given away too much.

"Yeah," Raf leaned on his elbows, his head in the air as he closed his eyes on a pleasant sigh. "I know. But what if there is... more? What if you see someone and you just *know*?"

Michele didn't answer. It wasn't an area he had experience *or* interest in. All the same, he didn't think he could look at someone and *know*.

"Maybe Lasso can help us," Michele chuckled, grabbing his pencil and adding a few details.

Since his beating he'd been more careful than usual with his precious supplies, knowing that if his father saw them he would go nuclear. Instead, Raf had proposed to keep them in his room, and Michele could come get them whenever he wanted.

It turned out to be a wonderful experience, with most times Michele coming to Raf's room where they would both hang out and think up stories with Lasso that Michele would ultimately put on paper.

"Here," he shoved the paper in front of Raf, showing him the rough sketch of the comic strips and the meeting between Lasso and his love interest.

"Maybe if you add something here," Raf noted, explaining how he saw the scene unfolding from his point of view.

Michele listened quietly, his pencil poised as he made the necessary adjustments.

"I should go," he sighed a while later after they'd put aside everything. "I don't want Cosima to catch me here."

"She hasn't been that bad lately," Raf admitted hopefully.

"I don't want to take any chances. I'll see you tomorrow," Michele hugged his brother before leaving the room.

He tiptoed towards his own room, quite a distance from Raf's. At such a late hour it was imperative no one caught him, least of all his father, otherwise he would get another beating. To get to his room, he had to pass through the east wing where his uncle and his family were staying. He tried his best to keep quiet, but it was in vain as he came face to face with Antonio.

He was sitting in the hallway by an open window. He had a cigarette in his mouth, his eyes spotting Michele as his lips curved around it.

"What do you have here? Shouldn't you be in bed, little Michele?" he asked in an odd voice.

"That's where I'm going," Michele strained a smile, ready to bypass Antonio.

"Wait," he called out.

Michele turned, raising his eyebrows in question.

"Stay with me to finish this?" He offered, his tone friendly.

Michele shook his head, knowing he couldn't afford to be caught.

"Come on, what's five minutes? If anyone comes I'll tell them you're with me," Antonio winked, all but backing him into a corner to agree to stay.

Michele put on a pleasant smile as he kept a small distance, his hands in the pockets of his hoodie as he waited for Antonio to finish.

"You're thirteen now, aren't you?" He suddenly asked, taking a drag off his cigarette and blowing the smoke out the window.

Michele nodded.

"Already a young man, aren't you?" Antonio gave a laugh. "And how is it with the ladies? I bet someone with your face must be very popular with the girls, no?"

Michele didn't like the topic, but he did his best to mask his discomfort with a lazy shrug.

"I don't really have time for that," he answered vaguely.

"What? No girlfriend?"

He shook his head.

"Come on, you must have at least someone," Antonio pushed. "Lots of boys at your age are already doing it."

"Doing it?" he frowned.

"You know, having sex. You can tell me if you are, I'm not going to report back to your parents," Antonio smirked at him.

There was a duality in his cousin that Michele could hardly grasp. His words tried to be assuring, soft-spoken even. But his facial expressions belied that intention.

"I'm not having sex," he murmured, his cheeks already heating up.

"But don't you want to?"

His lashes fluttered in confusion.

"Not particularly, no," he admitted honestly.

He didn't know why Antonio would be so interested in what he did and whom he did it with. He found it odd. But maybe he was just curious...

"Damn, when I was your age..." he trailed off on a whistle and Michele's eyes widened.

"But to be a priest don't you have to be chaste?" The question flew from Michele's mouth before he could help himself.

"After you take the celibacy vow, yes. Before..." Antonio just smiled.

Michele regarded him perplexed. He didn't see how that made a difference. If you decided to embark on such a journey, why would it matter *when* you take the vows? Shouldn't you exhibit the principles you preach from the beginning?

"Oh, I see," he replied stiffly, his eyes on the cigarette as he willed it to burn faster.

"But I can tell you I had my fair share of..." he smiled again, his white teeth gleaming in the darkness of the hallway. There was something incredibly off-putting about the way he would accompany every sentence with a smile.

Michele didn't reply, merely tapping his foot lightly as he waited for the green light to leave. He supposed he could have left before, but he didn't want to be rude.

He *never* wanted to be rude. Maybe that was an issue, he quietly mused. He'd always tried to cause as little inconvenience as possible since he'd never been desired in the first place, that it had become a habit to comport himself beyond reproach—even to his own detriment.

"I can teach you, if you want," Antonio suddenly said, taking another drag of his cigarette.

"What," Michele squeaked before he caught himself. "No, thank you," he declined politely, though on the inside he was uncomfortable at Antonio's words.

"Are you sure?" Antonio flung the butt of the cigarette out the window, taking a step towards him.

He was so close Michele could feel his breath, a mix of cigarettes and alcohol that was entirely unappealing as he tried to turn his head to the side.

"I could show you a lot of things, little Michele," he said, his hand on Michele's cheek, his finger brushing against his flesh, slowly, deliberately.

Michele stifled a grimace at his proximity, keeping himself still.

"Yes. I'm not in any hurry."

"Hmm," Antonio mused.

His mouth was too close to Michele's skin, and closing his eyes, he held his breath, counting to ten until Antonio stepped away.

"Good night, little Michele," he heard his voice followed by footsteps drifting away.

Immediately, Michele dashed to his room, disconcerted by the events in the hallway and resolving to heed Raf's advice to avoid Antonio from then on. Maybe he wasn't with ill intent, but he was making Michele uncomfortable, nonetheless.

For the next few days, he tried his best to avoid being alone with Antonio, though his eyes always followed Michele around, his gaze predatory. He didn't approach him, though. He didn't try to interact with Michele.

Not until one evening when the entire family was seated for dinner, the topic of conversation landed again on Gianna.

"They will find her soon," Cosima said smugly. "And it will be a lesson for everyone that we're not to be trifled with."

Michele met Raf's eyes as his brother willed him to stay silent—not provoke Cosima's wrath.

"She was very close with Michele, wasn't she?" Antonio asked, leaning back in his seat and throwing a bored glance in Michele's direction.

"She was," Cosima answered dismissively.

"You could help everyone and tell them where she is, little Michele. Wouldn't that be better?" He addressed Michele in a smooth voice.

"And get her killed?" Michele burst out, belatedly realizing he'd walked right into a trap. "I don't know where she is," he amended. "I've already told father as much."

"Is that so... Why is it that I don't believe you?" Antonio chuckled.

"Michele understands it's not in his best interest to keep things from the family," Benedicto interjected calmly, but his countenance spoke of hidden dangers. "Isn't that right, boy?"

"Yes, sir." He replied quietly, hoping they would find another topic of conversation. He might not know where his sister was, but he couldn't bear to listen to everyone maligning her character and making her out to be something she was *not*.

He kept quiet for the rest of the dinner, retiring upstairs when everyone did. He didn't get to close the door and Antonio lodged his foot inside.

"Antonio?" Michele blinked in surprise, a sliver of fear going down his back.

"You love your sister, don't you?" He suddenly asked.

Michele could only stare at him, slowly nodding.

"What if I could find her for you? Warn her about Benedicto's plans?"

"Wh-why would you do that?"

"For you, little Michele," he smiled, pushing the door open even more.

Michele reacted quickly, placing his own palm against the wooden door, holding it in place and not allowing Antonio to come inside.

"Why?"

"Because I like you. I don't want to see you suffer for your sister."

Michele wasn't convinced. He kept his grip on the door regarding Antonio with suspicion.

"You barely know me."

"We're family," Antonio replied, his hand on the edge of the door as he dragged it lower until he could touch Michele's fingers. "And we could be more..." his lips tipped up in a dangerous smile.

Alarm bells rang in Michele's mind, and before he could think of a thorough reply, he simply kicked at his foot, closing the door in his face and nabbing his hand in the process. Antonio yelped in pain, and only then did Michele call out.

"It's late. I'll talk to you another time," he said quickly, making sure to lock the door before taking a few steps back.

His heart was racing in his chest, his forehead covered in sweat.

Until that moment he hadn't let himself think that Antonio might be...deranged. He was definitely not normal to imply something like that. Though Michele was completely innocent, he knew *exactly* what Antonio wanted with *more*.

"Raf was right," he whispered to himself, suddenly terrified about his situation.

He'd avoided Antonio so far, but he was getting bolder. Could he really avoid him forever? Or at least until they moved *out* of their house?

He didn't know how he would do it, but he must.

Otherwise....

fifteen

AGE THIRTEEN

The more Michele tried to avoid Antonio, the more his cousin made it a game to catch him alone and make him more and more uncomfortable. He'd ask him intimate questions, and one time he even put his hand down Michele's pants, cupping him and asking him his size. Michele had been so flustered he'd been unable to move for a good minute before he'd ran away. That hadn't deterred Antonio. It had only made him amused, and Michele could see the hidden smirk or the way he looked at him when no one was watching.

He'd meant to tell Raf about it a time or two, but then he'd decided against it. He didn't want to come across as weak—again.

He needed to take care of himself for once. How else could he grow and become the independent person he wanted to be? His face was a curse he'd have to live with, and seeing how Antonio was not the first to comment on his appearance, he knew he won't be the last. Some reviled him for the way he looked while others...others wanted to do things to him, things that Michele could not even think about without getting the urge to puke.

As time passed though, it seemed as though Antonio was making a game from putting Michele on the spot. He derived pleasure from seeing him squirm, especially as he sneaked small touches in his private areas or whispered some sexual joke.

Michele didn't share the amusement, and the more he experienced it, the more he became restless and afraid in the house. If before it had been hell on earth, now it was... He wasn't sure if running away from home wasn't the best option, regardless of the fact that he'd promised Nicolo he wouldn't.

Because everyone was still so alert with Gianna's disappearance, Michele, too, was under constant surveillance lest he get in contact with her. As such, he hadn't been able to meet with his friend, or with anyone at all.

His room was his only sanctuary. The only place he was still at peace and safe.

Until it...wasn't.

He'd just left some food in the backyard for the kittens his sister used to feed and was returning to his room. He'd chosen that particular moment because everyone was off to a social event, leaving Michele home alone.

Or so he thought.

Opening the door to his room, it was to come face to face with Antonio.

He was sitting on his bed, one of Michele's drawings in his hand as he perused it with interest.

The moment Michele entered inside, Antonio's eyes took on a different glint—a dangerous one that made Michele want to run. Retrospectively, he supposed he should have.

"What are you doing here?" He asked, steeling himself. He needed to show he was strong—enforce boundaries and make Antonio understand he couldn't talk to him as he wished.

"I was looking for you, little Michele," Antonio smiled

smugly, discarding the drawing carelessly before jumping off the bed.

Michele took a step back, ready to bolt. But Antonio had expected that, and faster than Michele, he pushed against the door, locking them inside the room.

"W-what are you doing?" Michele whispered, his voice trembling.

Fear coursed to him as well as dread—so much dread. He'd already developed a thorough dislike of Antonio, but there was something about his nearness that made Michele want to gag. Especially as he came closer, crowding him and pushing his body against his own.

"I've been waiting for this for a long time," he said, smacking his lips together and looking Michele up and down with sick appreciation.

"What do you mean..."

"You think I don't know you've been avoiding me?" Antonio's voice boomed, startling Michele.

Suddenly, his arm shot out, grabbing Michele's still bruised one and dragging him from the door.

He tried to push the heels of his feet into the floor, pushing his weight behind so Antonio couldn't move him. It was in vain.

He was just a boy of thirteen—a small boy of thirteen—against a grown adult. Antonio wasn't only more than one head taller than him, but he was also much, much heavier.

Michele gasped as his face made contact with his mattress, a hand on his nape holding him captive.

"Let me go," he mumbled, panic taking hold of him.

He didn't want Antonio's hands on him. He didn't want his cousin *anywhere* near him. Maybe he couldn't grasp it wholly, but deep down he knew exactly what the man meant to do—what he'd been wanting to do from the beginning.

It was slow, but once realization reached the surface, his eyes widening in terror, he started thrashing, yelling at the top of his lungs.

Surely...surely someone could hear him.

Smack.

The blow caught him in his neck. It was a blunt type of pain that made his eyes roll in the back of his head.

"I didn't want it to get to this, little Michele, but I've been patient enough. I wanted to be kind to you. I wanted you to want this. But you couldn't go along with my plan, could you? You just had to avoid me."

"Please let me go," Michele whimpered.

Antonio was behind him. He could feel the warmth of his body right behind him, his hands holding tightly onto Michele and immobilizing him to the spot.

"Please let me go," he cried again. "I won't tell anyone, just please..."

"You won't tell anyone, what? That you're a little slut and you've been trying to seduce me for weeks?"

Michele's eyes widened at his words. What in God's name was he talking about?

He renewed his struggles.

Smack.

This time the blow was to his ass, hitting him so hard he couldn't help but howl in pain.

"That you've been looking at me with those cute eyes of yours, blushing at my words and inviting me to sin? Is that what you'll tell them?"

"You're crazy..." Michele whispered, unable to believe Antonio could sprout such nonsense.

"What did you say?"

"Please... Just leave me alone..."

"We can do this two ways, little Michele. You can fight me all you want, but that's going to hurt *only* yourself. Or you can *not* struggle, and I'll even do you a favor."

Michele shook his head, trying to push himself off the mattress and shrug Antonio off. Easier said than done when Antonio's weight rested on his back, keeping him pinned down. No matter how much he tried, he knew it would be in vain. Frustration gnawed at him, tears pricking at his eyes as he realized the futility of the situation.

"You didn't even hear what I was offering," Antonio chuckled. "Before you hurt yourself, why don't you listen to my bargain?"

"Please..." Michele pleaded again, turning his head before Antonio pushed him down further, his cheek stuck to the mattress. Tears coursed down his cheeks, his entire body seized by monumental fear.

"If you're a good boy and don't struggle, I won't tell your father where your sister is," Antonio said in a smug tone.

Michele startled.

"W-what..."

"I won't tell him where she is or how low she's fallen. Working as a waitress..."

More panic swelled in Michele's chest.

No, it couldn't be...

How could Antonio find his sister when his father and entire army of soldiers had been unable. No, it had to be a fake.

"I don't believe you," he wheezed, pushing against him again in an attempt to weaken the hold.

"You..." Antonio trailed off on a laugh. "What about this?" He asked, one hand momentarily off Michele.

He took the opportunity to wildly move around, all in an attempt to make Antonio lose his footing. He needed one second. One second where his strength wasn't focused wholly on him and he could escape. He would dash out the door and... He could hide somewhere until everyone else got home. Until he could go to his brother and tell him and he would help him. Yes...Raf would help him, he knew he would.

The idea was sound, but the execution of the plan was lacking. Not only was Michele much, much smaller than Antonio, he was still suffering from the injuries inflicted by his father a few weeks past. His body still ached, his strength still diminished.

And so the opening passed, and instead of gaining ground, Michele only got another slap on his ass, the hand on his nape back in position. This time, however, Antonio brought his other hand in front of him, holding out a phone and showing him a picture.

A picture of...

He couldn't believe his eyes.

That was...Gianna. That was his sister, Gianna.

"But how... Why?" He couldn't even speak because of the shock that reverberated in his body.

"So you see, little Michele. One word from me and she's dead. Is that what you want for your beloved sister?"

"No...no," he shook his head, still staring at the picture.

She had dark hair now, but her features were unmistakable. It *was* Gianna. Michele could recognize his sister anywhere. But if Antonio had the picture, that meant...

"Why?" he croaked in pain. "Why are you doing this?"

Why would he be so cruel, and why with Michele who'd never harmed another soul? Why would he be so bent on causing him pain?

"There's no *why*, little Michele. I want you. But I don't want you fighting me. I want you to take me, fully take me," he cooed, the words foreign to Michele but familiar at the same time.

He knew what was going to happen, just as he knew he was going to say yes. Because the alternative...

A dry whimper escaped him as he couldn't even cry his heart's pain in peace, the weight on his body the same size as the weight on his soul.

"You promise you won't tell?"

It cost him everything to ask that question. He knew that. Maybe he wasn't familiar with the implications, but he knew this would change everything.

"I promise," Antonio murmured from behind, bringing his face closer to Michele's and inhaling deep. "As long as you do what I tell you to, your sister is safe. How does that sound, little Michele? Will you do what I say? Will you be my little toy?"

His breath fanned over Michele's cheek, his lips moving over his flesh. Michele wept on the inside, every little touch on his body killing him a little further.

But he'd been dead a long time ago, hadn't he? His body had already gone through everything a human could withstand. It had been beaten and defiled. What did it matter if it happened again? At least his sister would be safe. His father wouldn't find her and... It was only for a little while, no? He could withstand it for just a while, until his uncle and Antonio left the house.

He did his best to rationalize his actions, telling himself that it couldn't be that bad. All the same, in his innocent mind, he had no idea what he was agreeing to. He had no idea he was about to sell not his body, but also his soul.

"Swear... Swear you won't tell," he pleaded again, needing the assurance—needing to know he was doing this for the right reasons.

"I swear. Do you swear, too?" Antonio asked, his tongue swirling around his earlobe.

Defeated, Michele could only nod and whisper a soft.

"Yes."

That moment, the fight left his body. It went into hiding, locking itself in a deep place within him. He let his body sink limply against the mattress, closing his eyes and hoping whatever Antonio planned to do to him would end fast.

The faster the better...

There was rustling behind him, Antonio getting off him and stepping back.

He was waiting to see if Michele would hold up his part of the bargain. This was his chance to leave—dash before anything happened. He was giving him an out, but that route meant his sister would be the one getting in trouble. She would...

Michele didn't move. He just waited.

Half his body was on the bed, his feet firmly planted on the ground, his cheek still plastered to the clean sheet covering his mattress.

Antonio was slow, almost as if he wanted to prolong Michele's suffering.

He could hear the sound of a zipper, just as he could feel the man's hands on his pants, undoing them and pushing them down his legs together with his underwear.

Michele grabbed fistfuls of the sheet as he tried to ground himself, anything to shift his attention from what was happening and from what he, himself, had agreed to.

He felt Antonio's hands on his ass cheeks, touching him in areas no one had touched him before. Every contact of his skin against Michele's brought a fresh wave of nausea and disgust and he didn't know how he stopped himself from emptying the contents of his stomach right then and there. And it only got worse.

Antonio spread his cheeks, his one hand dipping to his hole as he pushed a finger inside, playing with his opening.

It hurt. But he didn't make one sound. Michele just squeezed his eyes shut, mentally praying it would be over soon.

But how could he be so lucky? He'd never in his entire life been lucky, why would he start now?

And so he withstood, minutes on end, as Antonio pumped his fingers in and out of his body, prolonging his shame and his suffering.

He was saying things too. Calling him his dirty slut and how he couldn't wait to fuck his ass. All lewd talk that Michele tried to ignore—push it out of his mind.

He didn't know how much time passed like that, and for a while, he even thought that was everything there was to it.

There was some pain when he put his fingers inside of him, but it wasn't as bad as he'd initially thought. For that brief second, he thought he'd gotten away as easy as he could.

But that all changed when he felt something much bigger and thicker trying to breach him—successfully doing so as Antonio forcefully pushed himself into his body.

Michele gasped, his eyes growing wide with unshed tears and pain, so much pain he thought his soul left his body.

His fingers tightened in the sheet and he barely stopped himself from crying out, from yelling at what he could only see as the most painful and debasing violation of his life.

Suddenly, he understood.

As Antonio slammed himself inside of him, again and again, Michele understood.

He'd never stood a chance.

From the beginning he'd been primed for the worst, had endured the worst *everyone* had to offer. This was just the missing piece—the last drop that finally rattled him awake to a new reality.

To the *true* reality.

For so long he'd tried to see the good in people and the positive side of his situation. He had people in his life who loved and cared for him while others didn't even have that. So he'd overlooked the bad in favor of the good.

Now, as he felt Antonio gleefully rip him apart, his hand back on his nape as he held him down while he grunted on top of him, Michele finally realized.

The world wasn't a good place—and it might never be.

sixteen

AGE FOURTEEN

His limbs trembled as he stared down his bloody hands. Blood was everywhere. On his clothes, on his face, and on the floor. It was staining the entire room, the walls dripping with red. He felt it on his tongue, the taste bitter and tangy, his vision swimming with red until it was coating his tongue and the back of his throat.

Raising his gaze, he saw the lifeless bodies on the ground leaking more blood.

He inhaled sharply, his surroundings morphing before him. The room shook with him, circular motions that threatened to make him lose it. He didn't know if he was gazing at reality, or some type of nightmare his sick mind had conjured up.

"Breathe," he whispered to himself. "Breathe."

A whizzing sound penetrated his foggy mind—his own harsh, barely restrained breathing.

He was still staring at his hands, sticky with someone's life force—at the life he'd taken wittingly or unwittingly.

He took a step back, losing balance as he tripped over something. He didn't have time to stabilize himself, and as he fell to the ground, it was to come face to face with unblinking eyes.

He startled.

"Fuck this shit!" someone cursed behind him. "There are still a few hiding in the back. Get them!"

"Yes, sir," a choir of voices assented.

Hands reached out for him, dragging him backwards. Shaking himself from his reverie, he looked up to see some of his father's soldiers, equally covered in blood and other injuries as they tried to drag him to safety.

In front of him, bullets flew from all directions, the sound deafening, the sight sickening.

"Stay here, Raf," one of them mentioned as he ran back into the open field, pistol in hand as he started firing at the people on the other side.

Raf was still in a semi-shocked state, but as clarity slowly returned, he wiped his hands over his formerly white shirt, staining it with even more red. But as he dragged his palms down his front, he winced at a stab of pain—one that hadn't been there before.

His fingers started trembling, and with measured movements, he lifted the material to reveal blood stained skin. Yet not all was from foreign sources. A threatening gash to his side leaked blood like a raging volcano, the red substance flowing down his torso.

He blinked, unnerved.

Had he been shot?

He couldn't remember.

He could barely remember what happened.

Since their return to penury, his father had resorted to more dangerous ventures to make up some of his lost money. One of said ventures had been getting involved with some gangs from the city. But as outsiders in that sphere, they hadn't been welcomed with opened arms.

Benedicto had the marvelous idea to get involved in a drug

ring. To avoid stepping on other big player's toes, he hadn't gone to point zero. No, he'd gone for the intermediaries. Yet he hadn't counted on them being just as territorial and as zealous about their business as the other big fish.

And now?

Maybe they'd recouped some of their losses in the year that had passed since Gianna's broken engagement and disappearance, but they'd also gotten themselves involved in inane conflicts that often ended up with bloodshed.

Benedicto had taken Rafaelo along to all their important meetings, citing it as push for him to grow and become the leader Guerra needed.

But he hadn't learned anything about the business side. He'd only learned how to shoot a gun out of fear, how to use a knife when death knocked at the door and how to clean himself of blood when it was all said and done.

He'd never wanted to be part of this life—had always dreaded it. Now? It was his perpetual reality.

He could have withstood it if it had been like before, when they had rarely gotten their hands dirty. But after their finances took a big hit, a lot of their workers abandoned them. Only the soldiers and made men, the ones who'd sworn their fealty to Guerra, remained, fighting tooth and nail for the restoration of the family to its former glory.

Rafaelo, as Benedicto's designated heir, had to stay by his father's side and face all the dangers everyone else did. But more than that, he had to exercise the same violence he abhorred onto others.

Was he a good shot? No. Was he good with a knife? No. Did he know how to fight? A resounding no.

What he did know was how to behave out of fear—how to use the resources at his disposal to avoid becoming a body in a bag, while at the same time damning someone else to that fate.

He was *not* fit for the life, but the life was all he had.

So he persevered.

He kept his worries and fears to himself and he strove to become better.

There were three things that made the situation more bearable and the fact that he was risking his life on the daily at barely fourteen.

First, he was helping set an example for his father's soldiers and paving the way for his eventual succession as was his father's wish. One would not follow someone who did not have the courage to risk his life alongside his subordinates. This fake bravery he put on earned him their respect and their future support.

Second, he was doing this for his parents, who had placed their hopes in him and had been broken ever since their situation had fallen to such extremes. His mother, in particular, had fallen into a quiet depression as a result of their bankruptcy and having to sell a big part of her jewelry collection and things she considered dear to her heart.

The third and probably the most important reason was that he was doing this for his brother. Since Gianna had left, Michele had not been the same. He retreated deep within himself, rarely smiling and preferring to keep to his room at all times. Rafaelo knew Michele could *never* deal with this side of the family, and he was happy he could keep him away from it.

As long as Rafaelo did his duty, Michele would never have to. He would never suffer and he would *never* have blood on his hands. *That* was the driving force behind his resolve.

But it didn't mean that his resolve was strong at all times.

He tried for it to be. He did his best to put on a strong façade, at home, at school, at work. He changed himself so thoroughly sometimes he wondered who he was—if he even knew anymore. Always tough, always resilient, there was absolutely no space for other emotions—or emotions, period. Rafaelo built himself up according to the expectations around him, burying the sensitive side of him so deep, he feared he might never find it again.

"They're running," someone yelled, heavy footsteps resounding in the distance.

Rafaelo's eyes were on his open gash as he continued to search his memory. Was it a knife wound, or a bullet one? If the former, then he needed stitches, but if it was the latter...he needed someone to remove the bullet from his body since he could not detect an exit wound.

In his befuddlement, he barely realized when the rest of his father's people reached his side, helping him up and telling him they needed to leave before the police came.

He was loaded in a car, no questions asked. Though he tried to look around for his father or uncle, he could not spot either, and he could only hope nothing happened to them.

It was only when they all got back to their compound that he spotted the familiar figures running up and down to help the injured men. A doctor was on call, looking around bewildered as he tried to decide who to treat first.

This time, there were too many injured. Not that usually that didn't happen, but casualties were a given when they went head on with local gangs.

Rafaelo had tried to speak to his father about it—that he was prioritizing money over the human capital. Already, he'd lost count of the people that had died in the span of a year.

Benedicto had refused, decidedly telling Rafaelo they needed to find their way back to their formal glory. He'd cited his mother's feeble state and the mounting debts as a way to rope Rafaelo into doing more for the family—what more, he didn't know.

Until he did...

Of course Benedicto didn't care who he lost in this

maddening search for gold. He wasn't the one notifying the bereaved families of their loss. It was Rafaelo.

"You need to get used to being in charge," his father had told him the first time. Though Raf had vehemently refused, he'd eventually found himself with another soldier in tow in front of an older woman's door, emotionlessly telling her she was now a widow.

In the beginning it had been hard. But as the corpses abounded, he managed to lock that part of himself away too. In the process, he'd also discovered something else.

His parents were *not* who he'd thought they were. He could no longer find any strength in them and his admiration was starting to turn into resentment.

Especially as he realized the quest for riches took priority in *all* their life avenues, both his mother and his father slaves to material goods.

It had been a wake up call to realize the people he'd looked up to his entire life would be so easily swayed by money, or lack of money.

One year.

Exactly one year since they'd fallen into poverty and *everything* had changed.

Rafaelo felt old. Too old for his age, and certainly too old to be the one taking care of his parents, more often than not minding their sensibilities instead of the other way around.

They should have shielded him from this side of life. Instead, they threw him at it head first, wanting a fourteen year old boy to resolve all their issues.

Around the compound, he spotted his father deep in conversation with his uncle while they directed the doctor right and left as the need arose.

Moans and groans of pain permeated the air, and all around, he only saw blood. Blood and more blood. Based on his experience, at least one person wouldn't make it through the night.

His walk was stilted from pain, but he didn't give it away as he walked to his designated room at the compound, a small, closet-like space that had one bed and a few drawers and a mirror.

Rafaelo opened one of those drawers, withdrawing a small kit.

It wasn't the first time he'd gotten injured, and it wouldn't be the last.

He'd been stabbed and nicked by blades before, the injuries having different degrees of severity. Yet he'd learned pretty early on that complaining about them and asking for help would get him exactly *nothing*.

"You're my heir, Raf. You need to show them you're made of sterner stuff. If you can bear the pain, so will they."

Those had been his father's words when he'd gotten stabbed in the back during a brawl.

The next time, he hadn't told him of his injuries, preferring to tend to them himself than face another disillusionment regarding his father—and the carelessness he now displayed.

He knew his parents loved him. He really did. But sometimes he had to wonder if they didn't love money *more* than him.

Rafaelo tugged his shirt off, wincing as he pushed it over his head. He laid it on the back of the chair, slowly trudging to the mirror to take in the damage done.

His chest was covered in purple bruises, all of which hurt like a bitch as he tried to make any sudden movements. And then there was the main culprit. The gash in his side.

He assessed it quietly or a minute, checking the angles and the extent of the damage. Maybe it wasn't a bullet wound. It certainly didn't feel like one and he'd been shot once before, at one of their first gatherings. It had been a clean shot, luckily, and it had gone straight through the muscle of his shoulder. He'd been patched nicely by their resident doctor and now he barely had a small scar on left shoulder.

Though his father had told him to be strong and take it like a man when it had happened, he'd still made Rafaelo swear he wouldn't tell his mother. Raf guessed that for all his bravado, his father had *one* thing he was truly scared of—Cosima's opinion.

It had been hard to convince her in the first place to allow Rafaelo to participate in their new venture, and though he exposed his son to daily dangers, Benedicto did not want his wife to know the full extent of it.

Rafaelo sighed at that thought. He didn't like lying to his mother, but he didn't like partaking in these events either. Somehow, though, he knew that if his father put his mind to it, he could easily convince Cosima to let Raf get involved in such dangers—all for the ultimate goal of turning Rafaelo into Benedicto's official heir.

His mother loved her son dearly. But she also wanted power for him—it was what she'd wanted from the beginning and why she'd been such a bitch to his other siblings.

Taking a clean cloth, he placed it in his mouth before grabbing a bottle of disinfectant and pouring generously on the wound. The clear liquid mixed with blood, flowing down his body and wetting the side of his pants too. Considering the amount of pain he was in, he didn't think he could care about such details now.

When the blood was mostly gone, he was able to assess the damage better. It was a cut, likely from a blade. It wasn't too deep, but it still needed stitches.

Shaking his head lightly, he placed the disinfectant bottle on the side of his bed while he grabbed some items from the medical kit. He had everything he needed to patch up the wound for himself. Though, it was likely going to hurt.

Just as he was getting used to the thought of threading the stitches through his skin by himself, the door to the room snapped open.

"Raf," Marco frowned. He had an open gash on his forehead and a few bruises all over his face. It seems his turn to see the doctor had not come—likely because there were others in worse conditions to be seen first.

"Good lad," he chuckled when he saw what Rafaelo was about to do. "You're missing one important item," he drawled, his words slightly slurred. Before Raf could ask what he meant, he was gone, only to return a few moments later with a half full bottle of cheap whiskey and slamming it on the bed's frame.

"That's gonna hurt like a bitch," he winked before he wobbled out, closing the door behind himself.

Rafaelo stared at the door for a moment before redirecting his gaze to the bottle of whiskey.

Though he'd been part of the life as an official member for over a year now, he'd never developed a taste for alcohol—just like he hadn't developed a taste for smoking, whoring and killing.

Debating between the sharp pain his intact awareness would yield and dulled senses, he decided Marco might be on to something. He grabbed the neck of the bottle, wincing in preparation for the bitter taste to hit his tongue and he chugged. He chugged and chugged until he almost wheezed as he took a deep breath, the alcohol inflaming his throat.

When he thought he'd had enough, he quickly got to work. He needed to have *some* of his faculties about him if he were to patch himself up.

Pinching his skin between two fingers above and below the gash, he threaded the needle through his flesh. His teeth clamped down on the cloth he'd put back in his mouth, sweat accumulating on his forehead as he willed his body not to give up in the face of such pain.

The liquor helped—or he supposed it did. He didn't think anything could take away the biting touch of the needle on his skin, or the feel of the threat as he dragged through his flesh.

Still, he persevered.

He wanted to howl, but he persevered.

Luckily, the gash wasn't too big so he was able to sew it together quickly. When he was done he bandaged the area and leaned back on the bed, his eyes on the ceiling as his mind started swimming.

The alcohol finally got to his head.

The room started spinning with him and he thought he saw double—or triple—until he finally fell asleep.

It was later in the evening that he awoke, a monumental headache descending upon him the minute he opened his eyes.

He quickly dressed in the spare clothes he kept in the room before going out and assessing the damage to their men.

Most were blackout drunk, having applied the same treatment as him to bear the pain.

There was, however, a body in a bag at the end of the great hall, and he grimaced as he realized his prognosis had come true. Someone hadn't made it through the day.

He found his father easily, and he was surprised to see he didn't look much worse for the wear.

"There you are, son. Looking good," Benedicto commented, his mouth full of food.

He was seated at a table with Marco and Franco, both looking like they'd actually participated in the fight, not stayed on the sidelines and cheering people on like he presumed his father had done.

His lips flattened into a thin line. He'd always known Benedicto wasn't a very physical man when it came to fighting or any type of combat. Though he was the de facto leader, Rafaelo had never seen him get his hands dirty. Now, he had to, to a certain degree. But he still kept himself aloof from the more demanding part of the job. After all, that befell to his son, who, in Benedicto's words, had more to prove than he did.

Rafaelo muttered a low curse, his annoyance with his father growing the more he regarded him.

"Come, sit," Benedicto invited Raf, motioning to the end of the table.

"We lost one?" he asked as he took some bread and ham from the food laid on the table, making himself a sandwich.

"Two," his father answered nonchalantly. "We lost Levi on the way. They already disposed of the body," he continued to munch as if he didn't just state one of his most loyal soldiers had died.

Raf's hand stilled on his food, his insides rebelling at everything.

He was in pain on the outside, but he was in pain on the inside too. Yet it wasn't expected of him. No, of course not. He had to be immune to everything. He couldn't even mourn a good man because it would be perceived as weakness.

He slowly brought the sandwich to his lips, biting into it and chewing drily. All in an effort to look as nonchalant as his father wanted him to be—as everyone else expected him to be.

"Your son has a bright future ahead of him. Caught him stitching himself up in his room," Marco observed, looking at him with admiration.

He managed a smile.

"He's made of tough stuff, my Rafaelo. He'll be a good leader once I'm ready to retire," his father chuckled, though Raf didn't share the amusement.

For a moment he wished his father would retire *now*. If Raf was good to take wound after wound at only fourteen, surely he was good enough to lead too. He definitely did more than his father. And if he admitted it to himself, he *knew* he could do more than his father. At least he wouldn't make the same idiotic choices Benedicto had done, thereby placing the family in a path of financial ruin.

Their bankruptcy wasn't a thing of fate, or bad luck. No. It was the direct consequence of Benedicto's poor financial choices over the years, all amounting to the stinking debt they had now—one they couldn't hope to be out of any time soon.

"Why don't you let me do a trial period? See if I'm a good fit," Raf found himself suggesting.

He was shocked at his own words, or the fact that he was practically begging for more responsibility than he already had even though he dreaded all of it.

But he supposed that he was already suffering for the position he found himself in. If he undertook more tasks—more suitable to his intellect—then maybe he could be of *actual* use to the family.

Everyone knew he would never be a great fighter or a famed marksman. That was a given since many had tried to teach him over the years, all failing vehemently. He wasn't suited for *that* part of the life. But maybe he could be for another.

Benedicto frowned. Franco did too. Only Marco grinned at him with a hint of pride in his eyes.

"What are you talking about?" Benedicto's quick words conveyed he felt an attack was incoming and he was already gearing up for defense.

"Why don't you let me weigh in on the *important* decisions? I'm never going to make a difference in these brawls you send us into. But maybe I can help with other stuff," he shrugged. Then, for good measure, he added the one bit of information that might sway his father. "That way I can prove to our men I have what it takes to lead the *famiglia*. That I'm not just a pretty face," he joked, cracking a smile and waiting for everyone else to laugh.

His father didn't.

Franco didn't.

But Marco took the lead, making Franco jump in before his father faked a laugh too.

"You want to make the decisions?"

"I want to help the family," he stated.

A moment of silence as Benedicto's stare bore into Rafaelo.

One second. Two. He could hear the ticking of the clock on the wall behind him, holding his breath as he awaited the verdict.

"Fine. Why not," his father finally relaxed, leaning back in his chair. "I'll give you three months. If I see a difference, you'll have more," he said so dismissively, he didn't think Rafaelo could do anything good.

Raf smiled.

Three months. He aimed to change his opinion.

His first order of business was to put a stop to the gang involvement. Next, he had to find a new source of money.

Fast.

Seventeen

AGE FOURTEEN

Rafaelo returned home with his father and uncle Franco sometime at night. He was tired, his head still pounding from the alcohol while his body was stiff with pain.

Absent-mindedly, he walked upstairs to his room, all the while hoping his mother would not witness the state in which he found himself in. She had an inkling of what went on, but Raf supposed she didn't need the visuals. Especially with her beloved son covered in bruises and gashes, stinking of blood and alcohol. As he put one foot in front of the other, all he could think of was a hot shower to wash the stink of the dead off his body.

His gaze was to the floor when a sudden noise startled him. He blinked, turning just as he was about to reach his room. The noise was coming from the other side of the hallway, and for a moment he wondered if Michele was still up, mayhap worried about him.

Michele had already voiced out concerns about Raf's schedule of late, and he wanted to put his mind at ease, maybe have a small chat before bed.

He was dead tired, but he reckoned a minute with Michele

could invigorate him and remind him of his purpose—why he was doing all this in the first place.

He pivoted, taking a few steps in the direction of Michele's room when he suddenly stopped, his eyes wide in confusion.

The door to Michele's room was ajar, and not a moment later Antonio came out of it, a greasy smile on his face as he preened forward, adjusting his belt before closing the door with a resounding snap.

He didn't see Rafaelo at the end of the hallway. So lost was he in his thoughts that he merely rounded the corner, going to the wing he and his father shared.

At once, alarm bells sounded inside Raf's mind, and he didn't spare a moment as he dashed to Michele's room, pushing it open in an attempt to catch his brother unaware—all to get an honest reaction out of him and banish the thoughts that took root in his mind.

He was almost trembling, with rage, worry, and something so sickening he wanted to howl.

Pushing the door open, it was to find his brother on the floor, his knees to his chest.

He was wearing a pair of flimsy cotton pajamas, his black locks on his face as he stared at empty space. He only reacted when he heard the door open, his eyes growing wide with horror —a genuine reaction—before he masked his feelings, apathy descending on his features.

"Michele?" Raf uttered his name with trepidation, the sight of his brother like that worrying him.

Michele blinked, almost as if he was willing away whatever thoughts had been occupying his mind a moment before. With great effort, he stretched his lips into a fake smile.

"Raf, you're home," he said softly, raising his head to get a better look at him.

"What's wrong? Why was Antonio in your room?"

Michele blanched at the question. His features paled before he forced another smile.

"He wanted to borrow something," he lied.

Raf didn't know how, or why, but he *knew* his brother was lying about Antonio.

Closing the door behind him, he took a step closer.

"Has he been bothering you?" Raf asked as he stiffly bent his knees to lay on the floor by his brother's side.

His wound hurt at the movement but he ground his teeth, trying to push it out of his mind.

"No, not really," Michele shrugged.

"Hey, you can tell me," Raf reached out to touch Michele's hand, surprised to see his brother flinch away so suddenly. "Michele..."

"Nothing is wrong, I swear," he said vehemently, though he wouldn't meet Raf's eyes.

He stared at the carpet, his features tight.

"Things will get better, you'll see," Raf felt the need to assure him. "I'm working with our father for a new strategy and we should be back as before in no time."

"That's awesome," Michele replied, but the words held no meaning—they were just empty platitudes.

The more Raf stared at his brother, the more he sensed something was wrong.

"You'd tell me if anything happened, no?"

"What do you mean?" Michele blinked.

"If Antonio did anything improper..."

"No, nothing of the sort," Michele shook his head, the vehement denial startling Raf.

"If you say so..." he trailed off, unconvinced.

He'd been busy with his father lately so he hadn't been as present at home. He'd go from school to the compound, sometimes not even getting home for some sleep. He realized that maybe he'd ignored some red flags along the way because he'd been too caught up in his own issues. Now, as he regarded his brother a bit more attentively, he realized he needed to pay more attention.

"I'll leave you for the night," he said as he got up, glancing one more time at Michele before leaving for his own room.

"Goodnight, Raf," his brother's soft voice reached his ears as he grabbed the door knob.

"Goodnight, Michele."

He went about his nightly ablutions, taking a hot shower and once more tending to his injuries before going to bed. Still, his mind would not calm down.

His mind replayed the image of Antonio exiting Michele's room and he couldn't help the shudder that went down his body at remembering the man's smug expression.

From the beginning, Rafaelo had tried to steer clear of him, Antonio's presence always giving him the creeps. That decision had only solidified after a few encounters with the man.

The first times they had interacted, he'd been harmless enough, though his words could easily be misconstrued as double entendre. Rafaelo, who was already well on his way to becoming a cynic due to his early exposure to how trash the world could be, had immediately realized Antonio wasn't trying to *bond* with his cousin, merely laying the foundation for him to potentially act despicably later.

It was the reason why he'd warned Michele so many times to be careful with him. Something about the man didn't sit right with him.

Michele was much more innocent about the world than him, both in experience and ideology. His brother preferred to see the good in everyone, oftentimes at the expense of his own wellbeing. It was an odd thing to consider, seeing how Michele had been treated his entire life by those around him, including the circumstances of his illness and ghost of a childhood. Still, he'd retained a childlike quality about him, an openness that invited others to take advantage of him.

Rafaelo had seen that at school, everyone taking a shot at bullying Michele with him *never* minding it, even excusing the behavior of his bullies.

Raf, on the other hand, was the exact opposite.

He'd witnessed enough in his short life to be wary of everyone's reasons. He supposed he had his parents to thank for that, since for all their avowals of love, they were quick to push him head first into danger for their own advantage.

Maybe that had soured his perception a little.

What he'd then witnessed within the mob, including the men they were dealing with on a daily basis, had simply woken him up to reality. The world wasn't a nice place. No, it was a horrible pit of suffering and only the strongest could survive.

So he knew Antonio's type. He knew there were people out there who thrived on others' suffering—who thrived on being in a position of power over someone weaker. But more than anything, Raf knew there were those who had odd predictions—unnatural urges.

He'd met one such person before—a man in his forties who'd been found to have abused his young daughter. The *famiglia* didn't have mercy for those like him, and he'd met a gruesome death at the hands of the collective.

Antonio gave him the same vibes. Unlike that man, however, Antonio was related with the leadership, and Rafaelo had to wonder if anyone would go against that. For all the famiglia's distaste for certain practices, they were still a group of hypocrites who only applied their principles when it suited them.

Franco was Benedicto's right hand—the one who did *all* the

dirty work. He didn't know how his father would react if Antonio did, in fact, prove himself guilty of anything.

Shortly after the few failed interactions with Rafaelo, Antonio had escalated his behavior, cornering him one day when no one was about. He'd been more handsy, his words more crass, and alarm bells had rang in Raf's mind. He'd known to get out of the situation as fast as possible, putting distance between him and his cousin and deciding never to find himself alone with him again.

He'd even tried to hint to his father that something was seriously wrong with Antonio, but he hadn't wanted to hear any of it.

And *that* brought him to the current dilemma. If Antonio was guilty of anything, and by God, he hoped he wasn't, he didn't know *what* to do. He was terrified for his brother but did not have a clue how to help.

His worry intensified the following day at school.

Due to their difference in academic performance, Rafaelo and Michele had not been placed in the same class. Though in the same school, it wasn't often that they crossed paths now.

With his mind still on the issue from yesterday, Rafaelo headed to Michele's classroom. He needed to talk to him in a more neutral environment and make sure that Antonio was not behaving inappropriately.

He trudged his way across the school, pain flaring up in his side every now and then. He'd taken some painkillers, but for the beating he'd taken he imagined no amount of medication could help. Another thing that brought to mind Michele, and his frequent beatings at the hands of their father. The last one, when Gianna had left, had been so bad Raf had feared Michele wouldn't make it.

Now, having experienced such debilitating pain on his own skin, he didn't know *how* he'd withstood it. It made him gain a new appreciation for his brother. He might be too naïve, but he was also resilient—a quality one certainly needed in their walk of life.

Reaching the classroom, he was disconcerted to find Michele gone. Immediately, his mind went to his bullies, but some of them were present inside, snickering at Raf the moment they saw him.

His panic only rose as he strode to the courtyard, finding Michele alone, in an empty alcove. He should have been relieved nothing was wrong with him. But as he took in his brother, *everything* was wrong with him.

Michele was wearing a dark hoodie, the material pulled over his head and obstructing his face. There were visible shadows under his eyes, as if he had not slept in days—perhaps weeks. But what shocked Rafaelo the most was to see him bring a lit cigarette to his lips, taking a deep drag before releasing the smoke—doing it as if he'd done it countless times before in the past.

Since when was his brother smoking?

"Michele," Raf called out, taking a step closer.

Michele's eyes widened and he quickly put out his cigarette, squashing it with the tip of his boot.

"What are you doing here?" His brother blinked, taken aback by Raf's presence.

"I was looking for you. Damn, what's wrong with you? You're smoking now?" Raf frowned, coming closer and pulling the hoodie down to reveal his brother's face.

He was so pale, his skin almost translucent. There was an ethereal quality to Michele's features, and Raf supposed he could understand why some decided to use his looks against him out of jealousy. He *was* prettier than a girl.

"When did this start?"

Michele shrugged, but he had the decency to look guilty.

"It's just something I picked up," he answered coyly.

How was it that Michele had picked up smoking when Raf had not, and *he*'d been the one surrounded by smoking mafiosi for the last few years.

"It's not good for you," Raf pursed his lips.

He didn't know how to deal with this version of his brother. He seemed so withdrawn, but more than anything so forlorn, his chest constricted with hurt.

"I know," Michele took a deep breath, and Raf noticed he kept a modest distance between them. No matter how much he got closer to him, Michele would step back to ensure they weren't too close.

The way he'd flinched the night before came to his mind and he frowned.

"Michele, I worry about you."

Raf didn't know how to approach the issue without putting Michele on the spot and making him go on the defensive. He'd seen how he'd reacted when he'd asked about Antonio point blank, so he decided to circumvent the issue for now.

"Don't. Really," he raised his head to give him a tight smile. "I'm just trying out new things."

"And if they aren't good for you?"

His brother *was* too trusting. Raf didn't want to imagine someone plying *him* with alcohol or drugs. It was already alarming enough that he was smoking, and he knew it was easy to go from one to another.

"Then I'll quit, eventually. I won't know until I try it."

Raf frowned, studying his brother.

"What brought this on? Is it because of Gianna?"

Their sister's departure had taken a toll on Michele, and Raf had to begrudgingly admit that was when he'd started to change.

Damn it... If only he hadn't been so busy with his father. He could have paid more attention to his brother and how he was faring. Because at the moment, he truly feared for Michele's mental health.

He shrugged.

"I miss her," was all he said. "But I know she's better off away from here. For that alone I wouldn't want her to come back, regardless of how I feel."

"You can talk to me, you know." Slowly, he lifted his arm, placing his hand on Michele's shoulder. He was tense, but he didn't flinch away. He simply raised his gaze to meet Raf's. "I'm here for you."

"I know," Michele gave him a tight smile. "Don't worry for me. I'm fine, truly. You have enough on your plate as it is..."

"That doesn't mean I don't have time for you," he interrupted.

Michele gave a tremulous smile, and Raf decided to drop it for now. They made small talk until the break between classes was over, at which point they went their separate ways.

Rafaelo, however, was still unsettled about the whole matter.

In an unprecedented gesture, he skipped his last few classes as he hurried home, intent on having a discussion with Antonio without anyone around.

While he was staying with them, Antonio didn't have much to do except attend some weekly theology seminaries. As such, he was mostly at home.

Raf's lips flattened into a thin line as he thought about Antonio's religious *inclinations* and how his persona had nothing remotely in common with it. The hypocrisy was so astounding, his resolve only grew stronger on the way home.

According to plan, his parents were not present. That would make the confrontation much easier—for now. But he knew he had to tread lightly. If Antonio was as dangerous as he suspected, Raf couldn't confront him in an open field—certainly not anywhere Antonio would have the upper hand.

Thinking fast, he decided the best location would be the drawing room.

Setting up the speaker set and playing some music, he took a seat on the couch, thinking *that* should lure Antonio out of his cave—the potential presence of a victim too hard to resist.

He was right.

It didn't take much time for Antonio to come down.

He was dressed in a pair of washed up jeans and a black shirt. His hair was cut short, his features harsh—or made harsher by Raf's perception of him.

"Rafaelo," he smiled in that slithery way of his, and Raf pushed down the wave of nausea that hit him at thinking this man could have done something to his brother. Something...

"Antonio. What are you doing?"

"I should be asking you the same question. Shouldn't you be in school?"

"They let us out early," he replied, his shrewd eyes taking everything in.

His left arm was resting on the top of the couch, in full sight, while his right hand clutched tightly onto the knife hidden behind him.

Antonio strolled towards him, sporting a carefree attitude as he attempted to make Raf at ease.

Does he do that with all his victims?

In Raf's mind, his suspicions were so strong, he'd already branded Antonio as guilty. The only thing left to do was to ensure he kept his distance from his brother, or else...

He settled on the couch next to Raf, placing his leg on top of his knee as he leaned back, turning his head to appraise Raf.

"Don't tell me you're skipping school, Raf. I didn't peg you for a bad boy," Antonio chuckled, his eyes roving appreciatively over Rafaelo's uniform.

"What if I am one?" Raf maintained his smile, internally cringing at Antonio's form of address. His nickname was reserved only for friends, and he'd never given Antonio leave to use it.

"Is that so?" He asked with a knowing smirk, and before Raf knew it, he was coming closer, shuffling until his spread arms were almost touching Raf's arm.

Strike one.

"And how bad are you?" Antonio continued on a silken voice, his eyes hooded.

"Very, *very* bad," Raf replied through gritted teeth.

Antonio was in position and ready to move. That was when Raf struck. One moment they were side by side, the next he was on top of Antonio, his blade at his neck, the sharp edge digging into his skin and drawing first blood.

"I hear you're much *worse* than me, Antonio," Raf said smugly when he saw the man's eyes go wide in surprise.

He likely couldn't do much, but he would try all the same. Though Rafaelo was much bigger than Michele, he was still slightly smaller than Antonio and he was sure that difference in size would prove decisive if he were to engage in any type of combat. As it were, his plan was to say his piece then leave.

"What do you think you're doing, Rafaelo?"

Antonio's voice took a dangerous edge.

"Giving you a warning, dear cousin. Leave my brother alone," he stated, doing his best to imbue his words with as much confidence he could muster. "If not, then don't blame me if your head becomes separated from your body."

"Bold words, Rafaelo," Antonio laughed. "Bold words."

He pushed the knife deeper into Antonio's neck.

"Stay away from Michele, or I *will* fucking kill you," he threatened.

"What if your brother can't stay away from me?" Antonio

chuckled, as if he didn't take Raf seriously. "What if *he* is the one you should have a chat with."

"What are you talking about?"

"Hmm... What am I talking about? Do you want to find out?"

Raf kept his grip on the knife, staring into Antonio's unfeeling eyes and blinking. A shudder went down his back.

There was something seriously wrong with the man. So wrong, in fact, that he felt he was staring into the face of evil personified.

"This will be the first and last warning I give you. Next time, this," he cut alongside his throat, "will be slashing from ear to ear. When you least expect it."

Raf was aware those were big words for a fourteen-year-old dealing with an adult man. Yet he needed to show him he was in earnest—that he *would* kill him regardless of their family association.

"I'm sure you will," Antonio murmured, and to Raf's surprise, he leaned closer, his face a breath away from Raf's. He inhaled deeply. "Continue being bad, Raf. I happen to have a taste for bad, *bad* boys," he purred.

Before he knew it, Raf found himself on the floor, his ass hitting the ground with such a force that all his injuries rebelled at once.

He expected Antonio to pounce on him, but to his surprise, he didn't. He simply winked at him before leaving the house.

Raf stared at the empty room, confusion swarming his mind.

Just what kind of monster was he?

The question was answered for him a few days later. Though he'd continued to be absent from home due to his involvement with his father, he was extremely vigilant when he was at home, making it a point to spend all his time with Michele.

The differences in his brother's behavior became more

pronounced the more Raf studied him. He was less talkative, often in his own world. He flinched whenever Raf reached out and caught him by surprise, only allowing him to touch him when he could prepare himself mentally for it.

The worst, though, was that Michele had stopped drawing. That was all the confirmation Rafaelo needed to know something *bad* had happened to him.

Michele had kept his passion alive through countless beatings from their father, never giving up his dream to become an artist. For him to suddenly stop doing it altogether meant something was seriously wrong.

Raf had asked him why, but he'd only received a noncommittal answer that he was on a break.

He knew his brother. His art was *never* on a break.

Under Raf's vigilant gaze, Antonio had seemed to behave too, rarely spending time at home. But it was all a ruse.

It was past midnight when Raf was showered and ready for bed. He'd had another exhausting afternoon sifting through alternatives for their family—both in an attempt to save what was still salvageable, but also to prove to his father he could do it.

He jotted down a few thoughts in his notebook, some ideas already coming to mind to explore the following day. As he went to turn off the light before getting into bed, he noted a folded sheet of paper on the floor that had been slipped under his door.

Picking it up, he frowned as he unfolded it, his eyes immediately going wide as he scanned its contents.

A drawing.

Michele had drawn something for him. A scene from the comic they had been talking about some time back.

He felt his pulse pick up, happiness blooming inside him.

Maybe not everything was lost.

Placing it safely on his desk, he put on a loose hoodie before exiting his room. If Michele was still up, he needed to thank him for it.

His hands clammy, he realized he hadn't felt that excited in a long time—in more than a year. But this was it. A sign that the old Michele was still somewhere inside. He missed his brother and the comfortable camaraderie they used to share.

Tiptoeing around the hallway, he raised his hand, ready to knock on his door. His brother was not one to sleep too early, so he was confident he wouldn't' wake him up.

Just as he was about to know, though, something stopped him.

The sound of someone speaking.

He stilled, frowning.

Leaning forward, he placed his ear to the door, trying to make out the words.

The moment he heard the word *slut*, though, knowing who the voice belonged to, he couldn't stop. He pushed the door open. Slowly.

Dread accumulated in the pit of his stomach, his brain knowing what to expect but hoping he'd be proven wrong all the same.

He was careful not to make a noise because if his suspicion was right, then he wanted to catch Antonio in the act. In...

The door was halfway open and he got his first eyeful of what was going on. And by God, he wished he hadn't.

eighteen

AGE FOURTEEN

His stomach rebelled. His heart lurched in his throat. Dizziness overtook him.

Antonio was with his back to the door. Raf could make out his figure perfectly well. He was dressed in a pair of sweats that were now to his ankles and the same black shirt he always seemed to go for.

In front of him was Michele. On his knees. His mouth on...

Raf felt himself get sick, the urge to run away overwhelming him. But he couldn't. He couldn't do that to his brother. If he was experiencing this, then Rafaelo should at least have the balls to witness his brother's agony.

Antonio's hand was in Michele's hair, his fingers tightened around his scalp as he forced him to suck on his dick, pushing him into his crotch so hard, Michele's eyes were tearing up.

Yet he didn't make one sound of protest.

He just stood there, hands on his knees, mouth open as he let Antonio use him.

Antonio's groans, harsh breaths and pejorative terms were the only thing Raf could hear.

It was like his brother was a doll without *any* agency.

He was frozen to the spot, could not avert his eyes from what was going on—from the fact that he'd been right all along. Antonio *had* been taking advantage of Michele...

But how? Why would Michele not say anything? Why would he allow him to do something like that, likely more?

Spit dribbled down his chin as Antonio thrust into his mouth. He was pushing his dick so far into Michele's throat, Rafaelo didn't know how his brother held himself so still...

He took a step forward, ready to act. Ready to kill the bastard. Ready to...

Michele's eyes met his, and he stopped.

He saw everything in his brother's expression—the fear, the shame, the disgust. Yet there was more, as Michele moved for the first time of his own volition. Only to shake his head.

Raf opened his mouth and closed it, disbelief painting his features.

Michele was telling him to not intervene. Why, he couldn't tell. Raf only knew that he could never ignore what he was seeing.

He took another step.

Michele's gaze turned tortured, so much anguish hidden in those depths that Raf felt it hit him right in the chest.

He shook his head again.

Antonio was oblivious to the small exchange as he drew back.

Raf saw a flash of his dick as he removed it from Michele's mouth, his fist working his shaft up and down before his cum shot all over Michele's face. His eyes wide, mouth agape, he was still looking at his brother—in shock and pain. So much fucking pain.

He shook his head again, this time ushering him away with a small sign of his fingers.

Raf was split into two, the shock of such a scene making it

much harder for him to reach the right decision. Michele was asking him to leave. Everything inside him told him to go inside while the evidence was still fresh—catch Antonio in the act and...

And what? What could he do? The answer was a resounding nothing. At least not then. After he'd thought things through? Maybe.

He stepped back.

A look of relief crossed Michele's face, the tips of his lips tugging up in such a sad smile, Raf felt himself tear up.

Michele signaled Raf again with his hand, sending him away.

And at last, he finally respected his wishes.

Closing the door as slowly as he'd opened it, Raf left. He dashed to his room, making it straight to the toilet before he cast his accounts, tears streaking down his cheeks. For as long as he lived, he didn't think he could *ever* erase the image of his brother abused like that from his mind.

"Raf?" He heard Michele's voice through the door, followed by a quick knock. He put himself together before he opened the door.

Michele walked in, his shoulders squared, his entire body stiff. He stopped at the bed, sinking on the mattress and resting his elbows on his knees, he buried his face in his hands.

Raf could only stare at his brother, unable to utter a word—not knowing what he *could* say.

Michele had washed his face, he noticed. He'd changed his clothes too.

Sitting on the bed as he was, Raf couldn't help but feel his heart contract in his chest. His brother looked so young—much, much younger than his age. That someone would do that to him...

A sob broke the air. Michele bent down, his arms going to his belly as he started crying.

"Michele..." Raf whispered, and taking a tentative step forward, he crouched in front of him. Now knowing the cause of his flinching, he slowed his movements, giving Michele time to shrug his touch aside. When he didn't, he simply wrapped his arms around him, holding him tight as he cried out in pain.

Raf's soul hurt too. How could he not when he'd witnessed the most depraved scene, something he hadn't seen even in his dealings with the underground world?

"Let it go," he whispered, wanting to provide a small haven for his brother.

God, but how long had this been going on?

How long had Raf been too busy with his issues to notice that Michele was being abused in such a way? That he was being raped by their own cousin?

Somehow, that knowledge hurt even more. He could have helped. He could have done more. From the beginning, he'd known there was something amiss with Antonio and he hadn't pursued that haunch. And now...

"I'm sorry," Michele mumbled. "I'm sorry," he continued, his hands wrapped in Raf's shirt.

"What?" Raf was taken aback by Michele's words. "What are you sorry? What..."

"That you saw. That..."

Raf drew back, regarding his brother with bewilderment.

"You have *nothing* to be sorry about. Damn it, I should have done something before," Raf tightened his fists in his lap. "I should have done something the moment I suspected him."

"You couldn't have known," Michele shook his head.

"Why didn't you say anything, Michele? Why..."

The questions abounded in Raf's head. Why had his brother not come to him? Why had he allowed this to go on for so long? Why hadn't he trusted Raf to help him?

"He knows where Gianna is," his brother whispered in a soft yet resigned voice.

Raf's eyes widened and it finally dawned on him. There was only one reason Michele would have suffered in silence all along —why he would have sacrificed himself.

Gianna.

He thought he was doing it for Gianna.

Rafaelo froze, his mouth agape as he couldn't find the words to reply. In his brain, the information flowed and was duly processed, the conclusion unmistakable.

Antonio could *not* have known where Gianna was. It was impossible. His father and Franco had not been able to find out and they had scouts everywhere, but Antonio could? Antonio, the lazy son of a bitch that only dawdled around the house and pretended to go to his theological seminaries so he wouldn't be called out on his indolence. That Antonio? There was absolutely no way in hell he could have obtained that information.

But how could he have fooled Michele to such a degree?

Raf knew his brother was smart—too smart to have fallen for such a trick. At the same time, he had to remind himself that Gianna was his weak spot. From the beginning he'd done everything he could *for* her, to help her. It stood to reason that his loyalty and love towards her would blind him to Antonio's words.

"What do you mean?" With great difficulty he managed to slow his words and not startle Michele with his rage.

Michele then recounted everything that had happened. How Antonio had shown him a picture of who he thought was Gianna and he'd threatened Michele that if he fought back he would give it to Benedicto, ensuring their sister would be killed by the *famiglia*.

Then the worse came, the details of the abuse. Rafaelo had already gotten an eyeful at how Antonio abused Michele, but to hear it was worse than that? That his brother had been raped for the better part of a year and no one had known about it? No one had seen the signs?

His heart broke for Michele. But more than anything, he was angry at himself for ignoring what was going on—for not questioning his brother's changed behavior sooner.

"I'm so sorry, Michele," he said, the words heartfelt, though he reckoned he could never succeed in conveying just how sorry he was. "I'm so fucking sorry I wasn't there for you. That I didn't realize..."

"I tried my best to keep quiet," Michele lowered his head, fidgeting with his fingers. "I didn't want to take any chances that he might act on it."

"Michele," Raf took a deep breath, unsure how to break it to his brother. "I don't think Antonio knows where Gianna is. Think about it," he urged gently. "If father and his men couldn't find her, how could Antonio? He's been manipulating you."

"But it was her," Michele protested. "He showed me a picture. It *was* her."

"Pictures don't always reflect reality," Raf countered. "There must be a way we can confirm if it's her or not. This can't go on..."

"But what if it *is* her?" Michele's lips trembled as he raised his eyes to meet Raf's. He was terrified of the consequences, Raf could see it in his gaze. "As soon as the family's business is back on track, Antonio and Franco will be gone. I can bear it until then. I can..."

"What? Of course not," Raf's voice came out harsher than intended, and Michele flinched. "You're not going to allow that sick bastard to put his hands on you again. We need to figure out a different solution," he sighed heavily, bringing his hands to scrub his face. "I can help with the business side, and I can try to sway father to send them away. But there must be another way to prove he's lying about Gianna."

Michele was quiet for a moment, merely staring at the ground.

"I'll try to see if I can find something," he eventually agreed, but Raf could tell the prospect of angering Antonio into revealing what information he had on Gianna worried him a great deal.

"I have some money," Raf came up with an idea. He had a small stash of money set aside for emergency purposes, and he didn't think there would ever be a greater emergency than this one. "We could hire someone to check into his claims. Then we'll know for sure," he gave Michele a hopeful look. "In the meantime, try to avoid Antonio…"

"I don't know if I can. He comes to my room unannounced. I never know when he's going to be there…"

"Use my room instead," Raf offered. "You know I'm gone most of the time. So come here and lock the door."

Michele nodded his agreement, but his features were still pale.

"Thank you," he whispered, the ghost of a smile playing at his lips.

"You don't have to thank me for anything. We'll get through this, trust me," Raf gave him a tight nod.

That night, Michele didn't return to his room. They both went to bed together, and though Michele tried his best to put on a strong front, Raf could see the glaring differences. From his countenance, to the way he talked and interacted with Raf, everything was different. He was no longer the jovial and unrestrained brother Raf had always admired for his optimism and empathy. In its place, there was only the shadow of a boy that barely held on. And *that* broke Raf.

Antonio hadn't only stolen Michele's innocence. He'd broken down his spirit.

The following day, they left for school together, with Raf sticking to his side during breaks. Though there was no danger of Antonio showing up there, Raf was worried about his brother's mental state and the fact that there was no trace of anger, of frustration, or anything of that nature. Michele was simply resigned to his fate, waiting faithfully for the guillotine to fall down on his neck.

It was a startling thing to realize that there was something wrong with his brother besides the abuse. Or, more aptly put, as a direct result of the abuse.

Rafaelo was no expert in human psychology, but any time he would think of Antonio and what had he been doing for so long, he couldn't help the rage that erupted within him—rage that he expected to find in Michele as well. After all, *he* was the one suffering.

Instead, Michele appeared serene, going through the motions as if he no longer cared whether the rapes stopped or not. The only thing he seemed remotely interested in was Gianna, and whether Antonio had the power to harm her. His own person, though, came last—or not at all.

Raf tried to talk with him about his feelings, wanted to let him know he was there should he want to open up. Yet Michele's sole reaction was a careless shrug, his expression shrouded in mystery and apathy.

That is how Rafaelo knew that something was seriously wrong with his brother. Something he doubted would be magically fixed even if Antonio died a thousand gruesome deaths. Worst of all? He didn't know how to fix it. That feeling of uselessness got to his head as much as the hurt at Michele's plight inundated his heart.

He was a fixer by nature, doing his best to help those around him be their happiest. Rarely did he think of his own self as much as he considered his loved ones. And his greatest goal in life was to make people happy—it was what he'd been doing from childhood. He was only happy if those around him were happy. To know there was one person he'd failed was akin to personal torture and his very definition of hell.

At school, he went through the motions, still putting together the plan he'd come up with for the business but unable to fully concentrate because of Michele. And when classes ended, he instructed his brother to go to his room and wait there until Raf came home, lock himself inside if need be.

He would have forgone the meeting with the famiglia, but it, too, was one step closer to getting rid of Franco and Antonio. Their father had invited Franco and his family to join them at the house so they could work closer together towards his goal of refilling the family's coffers.

Franco's ideas had proved as futile as his father's marvelous plan to intervene in gang activity. Now, it was Raf's turn to see if he could turn the situation for the better—for everyone involved.

A car waited for him after school, taking him to the compound where all the main figures in the famiglia were present, everyone watching him expectantly. Raf didn't think any of them had high hopes for him, but they would indulge Benedicto this time—they would probably indulge him anything as long as he put a stop to the gang involvement. They'd suffered so many casualties in the last year, that the future of the family looked bleak.

"There you are, Rafaelo," Benedicto addressed him in an official manner, motioning him to take a seat before turning to the other people present.

"As you know, my son is my designated heir," Benedicto started, but already someone cut him.

"But he isn't the oldest, is he? What about the other one?"

"Yes, what about your other son?"

More questions about Michele and tensions swiftly rose, Benedicto looking on the brink of an apoplexy. He abhorred mention of Michele in the context of the famiglia, and though he was indeed the eldest and the official heir according to tradition, Benedicto would have none of it.

"Michele's always been a little sick, as you well know," he explained, quickly outlining all the reasons why Michele wasn't fit for the life before switching to the reasons why *Raf* should. "Rafaelo has been getting his hands dirty with us from the beginning. The know knows no fear," he grunted in satisfaction.

Silence descended, all eyes on Rafaelo as everyone at the table quietly assessed him.

"He's worked alongside our soldiers and has helped with every task assigned to him, no matter how daunting. It's why I've decided to give him the ultimate test."

People regarded them curiously, but Benedicto paid no mind.

"For three months, he's going to take over the leadership and show you that *he* is the future of this organization. That *he* is the one who can carry the Guerra name to great heights. And he has a plan, don't you, son?" he turned to Rafaelo, giving him the stage.

"Thank you," he nodded respectfully, putting on the best act of his life. He *needed* to convince everyone he was the best choice. The alternative was to subjugate his brother to even worse tortures, and he would give anything to spare him that.

"Benedicto is correct that I have a plan moving forward," he started, addressing his father by his given name in an attempt to put a distance between them and their relationship. He needed people to take him seriously as his own person.

"We're listening," Franco said from across the table.

Raf stood up, and taking his backpack, he removed a folder

full of sheets of paper that he distributed to everyone at the table.

"I've made an analysis of our performance for the last year, taking into consideration our overall profit as well as our losses, both financial and casualties that occurred due to our *excursions*," he added dryly, and his father gave him a sharp look. It wouldn't do to antagonize his father's past plans, so he quickly moved to the main topic.

"As you can see, our profit has increased, but the costs far outweigh the benefits in this case. So if you look on the other side, you'll see we are actually in the red with all the expenses accumulated."

Some curses, eyes bulging and heads shaking.

Raf stifled a backhanded comment as he guessed neither his father nor Franco had tried looking at facts, assembling the data before making any decision. Looking at everyone's expressions right now, including his own father's, Raf realized just how bad things were.

He shook his head, keeping his calm as he continued with his speech.

"Not only are we in the red, but we've also taken needless risks that could have put the entire organization at risk," he went through some instances where a few of their men had gotten arrested, and though they had not snitched, the possibility is always there.

"We can never predict if someone is going to betray the organization..."

"Now wait a moment," someone called out. "Are you saying we are a bunch of traitors? Everyone took an oath and you..."

"I'm not saying that," Raf leveled him with his stare. "I'm not accusing *anyone* of anything. In a perfect society, everyone would be, well, perfect," his lips tipped into a smile. "But we don't live in a perfect society. We live in a perfectly *flawed* society. Which means that unless we account for the worst that could happen, then we're just setting ourselves up for failure."

People blinked in confusion.

"Let me put it another way," Raf cleared his throat.

How was it that a fourteen year old was lecturing grown ass men about the way the world worked and he was still met with bewilderment? Slowly, Rafaelo realized *why* their organization was in such abysmal shape. It wasn't that Benedicto was a bad leader, though he wasn't a great one either. It was simply that everyone on the board was a moron.

"I'm not accusing anyone of anything. I'm merely stating that in our line of business we have to be vigilant. You cannot fully control a person, therefore you could never know when someone decided to snitch. As such, we need to have some safety mechanisms in place."

He went over a list of items he'd marked as important, such as making sure people knew only as much as they were required and not a bit more.

"The people in this room are the only ones who will have access to the full picture. Everyone else will only know as much as their task requires."

That this hadn't been implemented before baffled Rafaelo. Everything was so chaotic within the organization that most people did what they wanted, and they ran their mouths whenever they wanted too.

He'd noticed that while he'd been mingling with the soldiers. No one shied away from saying too much, including things they weren't supposed to. And *that* was just another issue that had to be dealt with.

"Fine. You've made your point," Benedicto eventually grumbled after Raf listed all the things they were doing wrong and should hereafter change. "And the plan? If we don't do this, we don't do that, how the hell are we going to make *any* money, let alone clear the debts with the Russians?"

"But that's just the thing. We need to do the *one* thing no one else has monopoly over."

Everyone was staring at Rafaelo as if he'd grown a second head. For God's sake, moron was an understatement.

"We're going to launder money," Raf continued, expecting some excitement from the table.

"Launder money?" Franco blinked.

"How?" someone else asked.

Raf barely controlled his rage as he realized he needed to spell everything out for these people.

"Look on the next page," he sighed, pointing to the documents he'd given them. "I've built a diagram of the organization in the shape of a triangle, from soldiers to leadership. We're going to use *only* the people at the bottom, and we're going to recruit more that are completely unrelated with our organization."

He explained his reasoning that the further they separated themselves from the people committing the *actual* crime, the better chances they would have to escape detection.

"Ok, I get this," someone interrupted. "But I don't get *how* we're going to launder the money..."

"Simple," Raf smiled. "We're going to hire *only* married hands to help, and we're going to use their wives instead."

As if he were explaining the scheme to a toddler, he went step by step how the wives were going to shop for expensive items, pay with fake cash, and then return the items and receive the real money as a refund.

By the end of the explanation, everyone finally understood and was in agreement. Even Benedicto looked thoughtful but pleased, decreeing that *this* is exactly what they would be doing.

"And you're going to oversee it, son. Good job," Benedicto patted him on the back, pride shining in his eyes.

But as he found no happiness at being so readily appreciated by Benedicto and his men. He might have presented a strong and collected front, but inside he was seething. That he hadn't snapped at Franco at any point during the meeting had been a miracle. All throughout he could see himself jump out and demand what his son had been doing, if he had any knowledge, or worse, if he condoned that.

He kept a pleasant smile on until he finally got home later that evening. Yet it wasn't to find Michele in his room. He wasn't in his own room either.

Panic rose in his chest.

Immediately, he went to Antonio's room, ready to confront him.

He wasn't there either.

That was enough to make Raf go crazy as he looked everywhere within the house where Antonio could have hidden Michele. To his mind it was a forgone conclusion that Antonio had taken his brother somewhere, doing who knows what to him.

It was all in vain.

Aside from Franco and his wife's room, as well as his parents' wing, he looked everywhere. No sign of either Antonio or Michele.

"They must be somewhere around," he clenched his fists in frustration.

Antonio was daring, but surely he wouldn't be as daring as to take Michele anywhere off property. That would trigger alarm bells for anyone. And so Raf had to think strategically.

Where else could they be...

His foot tapping impatiently on the floor, he realized there was one more location he hadn't checked out yet.

The gardener's shed.

Behind the main house, it was a tiny cabin meant for the gardener to store his tools and some of the greenhouses. The gardener came a couple of times per week, and aside from him no one else in the family frequented the place.

Mind made up, he put on his shoes and exited into the night.

It was cold out, shivers enveloping him as he walked out dressed only in his shirt.

As he neared the shed, he heard voices. More than one voice, and none belonging to his brother. Belatedly, he realized he should have taken a weapon—anything should he find Michele in danger.

Sneaking around it, he went to the tiny window in the back, raising himself up slowly so he could gaze inside.

First, he saw Antonio. He was smoking furiously as he argued with someone. He didn't recognize that person, but Raf supposed he was a man around Antonio's age.

The man's hands were in his pockets as he searched for something, pulling up a bunch of wrinkled banknotes and slapping them into Antonio's hand.

What were they doing?

Raf's thoughts went to a drug business. Maybe this was Antonio's way of making a quick buck since they'd all been struggling during this time.

But then they moved, and he saw Michele.

He was sitting in a corner, his arms around himself as he didn't dare gaze up at the two men. He was sitting there at the mercy of fate.

Raf couldn't believe it. He'd told him *not* to go with Antonio anymore—to refuse him and barricade himself in Raf's room. And now...

Slowly, though, Raf understood *what* had been traded for that money.

Antonio made some quick commands, gesturing with his hands and Michele moved, going towards the big table in the middle. He was with his back to the window, his hands on the band of his pants as he pushed them down his hips before laying on the table with his ass in the air.

The other man stepped forward, his hands on his zipper.

Antonio stayed back, watching with a smug expression how the stranger pulled down his pants and underwear, gripping his dick with one hand as he positioned himself behind Michele.

Raf watched, flabbergasted, as the man pushed himself into Michele, his brother's body going limp from pain yet never crying out. The man thrust in and out of him, raping his brother under Raf's very eyes. He couldn't stand by and let this happen. He couldn't...

His gaze suddenly met Antonio's who was casually stroking his dick while smiling at Rafaelo. Startled, he fell back. But he didn't have time to put himself together as the door to the shed opened, Antonio strolling forward and grabbing Raf by the arm and jerking him inside.

"Look what I found," he jibed. The other man half-turned to look behind, his eyebrows going up with interest at spotting Raf struggling within Antonio's grasp.

He moved back, only the tip of his dick remaining in Michele's ass.

"No," Antonio put a hand up. "This one isn't for you," he said with a knowing smile.

Raf blinked. Even more so as he spotted Michele's terrified expression, their eyes meeting and holding, the events of the moment holding them tighter together than any experience in the past.

And for the first time, Raf finally panicked.

Gone was the brave boy from before who'd thought he could go against the whole world to save his brother. Gone was the confidence he *could* do it. Now? It was all replaced with paralyzing fear as he could barely will his limbs to move.

The man kept fucking Michele, leisurely looking back at Raf.

Far from the house, no one would think to look for them *there* at that time of the night. And now, Raf would meet the same fate as his brother. He knew it deep in his gut, just as he recognized his lack of reaction as a sign of fear—so much fear his mind blanked on him.

God, but how could he have judged Michele before for not putting up a fight? For not saying or doing anything?

He recognized in that moment that not all things were black and white—brave or cowardly. There was only survival. And Michele had chosen it not only for himself but for his sister too.

Their eyes held, and he read in his brother's gaze everything he'd felt the first time he'd seen Antonio rape Michele. There was an understanding there that was unshakable. Just as was the heartbreak at what was happening.

It felt like an eternity passed. In fact, only moments did.

"This one's mine, aren't you, Raf? Because you're a bad, bad boy, aren't you?" Antonio crouched next to him, his tone mocking as he stared at him.

His pants were still undone, his dick hard, the danger looming right in front of Raf. He shoved himself back, suddenly kicking back at Antonio.

He just laughed.

"How about I make you a deal?" Antonio's hand shot out, his fingers wrapping around Raf's neck.

"Wh-what deal?" He felt ashamed of his stutter, but the adrenaline ran so high his head swam with confusion.

"Do you want to save your brother?"

Raf nodded slowly, his limbs trembling.

"Then why don't you take his place? If you do, I'll let him go."

Raf blinked, his eyes widening in disbelief.

"No," Michele finally spoke. "Raf, don't do it!" He cried out, finally struggling against the man. A loud smack permeated the air as he slapped Michele, his hand on his nape as he held him down, railing him even more violently than before.

Raf couldn't speak. He was frozen to the spot as he stared between Antonio and the stranger hurting his brother. Michele's arms were flailing up and down as he tried to shrug the man off but couldn't, his screams getting louder and louder.

"Gag him," Antonio snapped at the stranger. Some shuffling, and the man punched Michele so hard, his screams stopped completely before shoving a dirty cloth in his mouth.

"Change your mind? I can let him go. You just have to take his place and earn me my money," Antonio continued, his palm on Raf's cheek as he stroked him. Before he realized it, his other hand was between his legs, grabbing his penis.

Raf tried to struggle, pushing at Antonio's chest. His mind was a whirlwind of what-ifs, countless scenarios going through his head as he tried to clear his mind enough to choose one path.

To take his brother's spot though... Could he do that? Did he have that in him? He didn't know. He truly didn't know...

A second later, Antonio was off him, sparing him from making such a monumental decision so quickly. But the break wasn't necessarily a good thing as he walked towards the table, nodding at the stranger.

"Ever done a double?"

The man frowned, shaking his head.

Antonio turned to Raf, his eyes glinting dangerously.

"Congratulations, Raf. You've made your decision, just as I knew you would."

He did? When had he? Had he said something in between his lapses in awareness? What did Antonio mean? He was shaking so badly from fear he couldn't even move. He barely controlled himself from not wetting his pants, the urge overwhelming him the more he stared at the disaster in front of him.

He couldn't run, yet he couldn't offer himself up in exchange. What kind of brother was he?

Tears stabbed at the corners of his eyes, his teeth rattling with the power of his terror.

Antonio saw all that—he counted on that and was getting increasingly more aroused by it. He wanted their fear, he wanted them to see him as fear itself.

The man moved, withdrawing from Michele's body. His brother wasn't moving anymore, and in the back of his mind, Raf remembered the punch he'd gotten. He was limp as they maneuvered him around, his body pliable—too pliable.

The man smirked as he exchanged some hushed words with Antonio, agreeing with whatever he had in mind. Pulling some rope, they tied Michele's hands behind his back in a tight hold, using some of the rope to add over the dirty cloth and tying it at the back of his head.

Eyes wide in horror, Raf could not understand what was happening. Especially as the man laid himself on the table, Antonio placing Michele's limp body on top of him.

The man grabbed his dick, positioning it at Michele's entrance and impaling him in one swift thrust. At that moment, his brother reacted, flinching back and moving wildly against his bounds.

Antonio gave Raf a sick smile before he stepped between the man's legs and he...

Raf blinked. He wasn't sure he was seeing right. Because Antonio was...

He pushed his own penis inside Michele's body, and even gagged, Michele's cries of pain could still be hurt.

Both men were pumping in and out of Michele, the entire scene obscene.

"What do you say, Raf. Will you save your brother now?" Antonio had the gall to turn, smirking at him as he beckoned him with two fingers.

Raf's stomach rebelled. Fear took hold of him to such a frightening intensity that he couldn't control himself anymore. Wetness appeared to the front of his pants, his entire body shaking so badly, he could barely move. Yet move he did.

He managed to wobble to his feet, backing away until his hand was on the doorknob.

Right at that moment, Michele's tortured eyes connected with his, and to his great shame, he averted his gaze. He looked away, opening the door and dashing into the cold night air.

And when he reached his room, he took just long enough to calm his errant heart before he did what he should have done from the beginning.

He went to someone for help.

nineteen

AGE FOURTEEN

Michele went utterly still when he heard Antonio's words.

"Then why don't you take his place? If you do, I'll let him go."

He could never let his brother do that for him—not when this was a mess of his own making. He'd been gullible enough to buy Antonio's threats, and that was his fault. Hadn't Raf advised him to lock himself in his room? To wait for him, for then they would be safer together? He should have stayed put. But one word from Antonio and he'd felt guilt overwhelm him—the what-ifs killing him on the inside. They didn't know yet if he was lying or not about Gianna, and Michele would never play with his sister's fate. So he'd gone along with Antonio.

He hadn't known what he was signing up for. As usual, he'd thought Antonio would use him and then let him go. He'd certainly learned to tune that out and pretend he wasn't present when it was happening to him.

Michele had experienced so much pain over his short life that he'd become inured to it—mayhap even desensitized. From the cancer treatments, to his father's beatings and his classmate's bullying, he'd learned to ignore it. And though Antonio's actions were in a class of debauchery of their own, the pain often accompanied by shame and revulsion, he'd learned to ignore that too. His body had always known pain—what was a different kind? Or so he told himself as he willed himself to be strong.

Because even if he took the pain well when it happened, the repercussions flared up *after*. When he was alone in his room, staring at the ceiling and feeling a thousand hands on his body, ant-like movements under his skin that threatened to make him go insane. He'd scratch and scratch, giving way to more pain, yet the sensation never left. Not until he'd first taken a blade to his leg, stabbing at the imaginary creatures that haunted his flesh.

It didn't stop.

It never stopped.

There was only pain. More and more pain, never to be assuaged.

"No," he cried out. He'd do anything for his brother to avoid the same fate. "Raf, don't do it!" He yelled, and for the first time, his body reacted. No longer limply taking everything happening to him and accepting all the ignominies done to him, Michele moved. He struggled against the man currently holding him from behind—anything to get to his brother and avoid he end up in the same position.

A slap landed on his flesh, quieting him. The man's hand reached for his nape, holding him down as he impaled him on his dick even more violently than before. And now that his awareness was at the surface, he couldn't help but gasp in pain, the violence on his body registering as never before.

"Gag him," Antonio barked the order and Michele started panicking. If before it had been painful, now that he was actively fighting against the other man, it was ten times more so. Just when he thought he was gaining some ground, a punch caught him in his jaw, his eyes rolling in the back of his head, his breathing growing labored. His limbs, too, felt heavy and he could not move no matter how much he tried to. It was enough for the stranger to easily maneuver and manhandle him.

Antonio spoke again, addressing Raf, but Michele couldn't focus on the words. He was stuck in a battle for awareness, his own mind shutting down on him, that one punch he'd taken to his face enough to knock him out. Yet by sheer perseverance alone, he resisted. He tried to ground himself, anything to ensure his brother wouldn't meet the same fate.

"Congratulations, Raf. You've made your decision, just as I knew you would," Antonio suddenly said. Michele blinked, almost as if in a dream. What decision? God, he truly hoped his brother hadn't traded himself for him...

Suddenly, the man raping him stopped. He pulled out of Michele's body, and that action alone made him slump on the table, all strength leaving him. There was a trail of pain left behind by the rough handling of the man, his entire backside hurting.

He had no notion of what was happening around him. He only felt the hands on his body, accompanied by something rougher—rope. His hands were pulled to his back, the rope digging in his wrists as they tightened them over his flesh—so tight they cut his circulation. But that wasn't all.

The gag they'd stuffed in his mouth was suddenly accompanied by rope, all in an attempt to make sure the cloth was unmovable and Michele couldn't scream. That alone made his panic grow. Yet he still felt himself trapped inside his body, unable to move or do anything. He was fully paralyzed as the two men did things to his body, painful, degrading things.

More movement later and Michele found himself on top of the stranger, his eyes making contact with the man's perverse ones. This time, it wasn't only the pain of being penetrated that registered in his mind. It was also the sweaty skin touching *his* skin. He felt the man everywhere, and that made him sicker. It was a worse invasion of privacy than *just* being raped. This was a violation of his entire body and everything that made out his physicality on this earth—everything that he was at an atomic level. He felt invaded by repulsive man, infected with his stench.

Bile rose up his throat, and he would have vomited if not for his gag.

But in a moment of pure self-preservation, he knew he had to calm himself. He could easily choke on his own vomit and then... Michele didn't want to die. Not yet. He might abhor the present and the situation he found himself in, but he *couldn't* die. Not while he still had to protect his siblings.

Yet his conviction came too prematurely. In his mind, that invasion was the epitome of bad. He didn't think things could get worse, and as such, it was just a matter of taking it all and withstanding until the man was done—until he'd had his fill of Michele.

Michele's consciousness kicked in when he felt another body behind him, yet another erection prodding at his opening, pushing forcefully inside.

In spite of the gag, in spite of everything, Michele tried to scream. His throat hurt, his vocal cords raw as he attempted the futile. He couldn't take it... He couldn't...

"What do you say, Raf. Will you save your brother now?" Antonio asked, and only then was Michele reminded of his brother. How was he? Had something happened to him? It took him herculean strength to will himself to move, craning his neck to look behind.

Raf was shaking as he fitted himself to the door, his hand on the handle and ready to open it. He hesitated one moment as their gazes collided. To Michele's shock, his brother looked away. He purposefully looked away before darting out of the shed.

For one moment, relief filled Michele at seeing his brother safe. But that was short lived as he was once more aware what was happening to his body—that *two* men were violating him in such a debasing manner.

He squeezed his eyes shut, willing himself out of the moment as he let everything happen, his body limp, his soul tired.

Time passed. He didn't know how much. He only recovered much, much later to find his hands unbound, his naked body on the table. Antonio and his friend had already left.

With great difficulty, he moved. His limbs ached, his bottom even more so. He felt so beaten down, he didn't know how he found the strength to bring his hands to his mouth and untie the rope holding his gag together. He certainly didn't know how he jumped off the table, searching for his clothes and donning them on.

It was only when a little movement grabbed his attention that he stilled. Until then, his mind had still been blank. On autopilot and blank. Slowly, his movements stopped being mechanical, his focus more clear.

"Michele," his brother's voice finally penetrated his mental fog.

He blinked.

Looking down at his naked chest, he saw the marks of use, the burn of the rope and the prints of foreign hands. He was slender, maybe *too* slender. Maybe that's why he couldn't fight them off... Maybe he could have done something else

"Michele," Raf's voice snapped him out of a vortex of vicious thoughts. "How are you?"

Michele took a step back, unable to connect the voice with safety. Why, he didn't know.

Raf was staring at him, a worried expression on his face as he held a blanket in his hands, inviting him to snuggle inside.

He wanted to. God knew, he longed for warmth so much. But he didn't think he could bear having a body that close to him—regardless of the fact that this was his brother. He didn't want to think about body heat, sweat or touch. His entire being rebelled at that thought.

"Hey, are you ok?" Raf repeated, and Michele nodded, his arms extended as he took the blanket from Raf with utmost care not to brush his fingers against his brother's.

Wrapping it around his shoulders, he followed Raf into the house.

"Here, sit," Raf pointed to the bed, and Michele carefully took a seat though his bottom hurt at the contact. He winced, but he forced himself to bear it.

"I'm sorry," his brother suddenly said, dropping to his knees in front of him, slowly advancing until his hands were on Michele's. Everything in him screamed for him to let go, yet one look at Raf's expression and he couldn't bring himself to reject him.

"I'm so sorry, Michele. I shouldn't have run. I shouldn't have..."

"And what were you supposed to do? Take my place? I would have never asked that of you," Michele told him squarely.

If anything, what had hurt the most had been seeing his brother avert his eyes, as if seeing what Michele was going through had shamed him. *That* had drilled a hole into his heart.

Objectively, he knew there was nothing to be upset about. He would have never wanted Raf to experience what he had. Yet he couldn't say that the way the events of the night had unraveled hadn't hurt him inside to some degree. At that moment, while he knew something was wrong—that something had irrevocably changed—he couldn't understand what.

He only knew a bleakness in his heart as everything replayed in his mind with slow exactitude. And for some reason, the moment Raf had dashed out in the night was the one moment he remembered clearer than anything else.

"Still," Raf pursed his lips, regret infusing his features. "I'm sorry."

Michele tried to force a smile, his first instinct to placate his brother. He found he couldn't.

He hurt. And it wasn't just physical. It was so much more than that. He wanted to cry but his tears had dried up. He wanted to yell, but his throat was clogged. He wanted... Sometimes he just wanted to cease existing, though he knew that wasn't fair to the people around him.

Yet the more time passed, the less people he seemed to have around—less people to ground himself in. And if he wasn't living for someone else, then how could he live for himself? What did he have left then?

His sister had left. Bass had betrayed them.

Nicolo seemed to have disappeared from the face of the earth, rarely giving any sign of life—almost as if he forgot Michele existed.

He still had his brother. But as he regarded Raf, truly regarded him, he felt a pinch in his heart that hadn't been there before.

But he pushed it all down.

"It's ok," Michele eventually said—a half-truth.

It wasn't ok.

Nothing in his life was ok.

"We need to do something about this, Michele. It can't go on. It truly can't go on."

Raf's eyes were filled with unshed tears—an emotion Michele was starting to become familiar with on a constant basis. He wanted to cry—he always wanted to cry. But the tears failed to come. Day after day, his eyes pricked with tears, yet they never flowed.

They were...stuck. Just like him. Just like his will, which had been stolen from him over a year ago. And he didn't know what to do to get it back.

Was it even possible? If things stopped, if Antonio got what he deserved and finally left Michele alone, could he return to the past? To his old self that still had feelings, dreams and ideals? Could he...

He wasn't sure.

At that moment, he wasn't even sure he was a person anymore. He was just a body that continued to live on while his mind slowly retreated deeper and deeper into a dark corner, never to see the light of the day again.

"What can we do?" he asked softly.

He no longer had strength to argue, or to do anything. He wanted to stay steadfast—to protect his sister. But he felt weary. So damn weary that he was one sway away from collapsing, both mentally and physically.

Forgive me, Gigi, his mind screamed at him. *Forgive me for not being strong enough.*

"We need to tell father. He can do something about this, send Antonio away, *anything,*" Raf said, and Michele's eyes widened.

"Father?" he whispered, the word paining him even more. He wasn't sure their father would ever understand, might end up blaming Michele for everything instead.

"We need to do this. I'll back you up. I'll say he touched me too," Raf continued, and suddenly the idea didn't seem so bad. Surely if Raf confessed to improper behavior from Antonio, then Benedicto was bound to do something—take the claims more seriously.

"Ok," he agreed. "But I need to make sure Gigi is safe first."

"Of course," Raf nodded. "The moment we know Antonio

has nothing on Gianna we tell them. Until then, *please*, don't put yourself in danger again. Don't..."

"I don't know how," Michele croaked, some emotion spilling to the surface. "He's always there, always cornering me. I don't know where to hide anymore because he *always* finds me."

By some stroke of luck, as Michele was returning from school the following day, Nicolo intercepted him, apologizing for keeping his distance for so long and citing some issues that had arisen with his own family after the death of his brother.

Michele, though disappointed his friend had not deigned to send him a message in that time, saw this as a golden opportunity.

"Could you please look for my sister? I know you have resources and..."

"Gianna? Of course," Nicolo readily agreed, promising to do whatever he could to get some information on her.

They spent some time catching up, and though Michele felt the burden of his secret overwhelm him, he didn't dare say anything out loud. He didn't want his friend to think him weak or cowardly, though he *was* all that. Instead, he only hoped Nicolo would find some information on Gianna that could finally set Michele free.

A week passed before he heard again from Nicolo. A week in which he did his best to avoid Antonio, though he couldn't do it continuously. For all his efforts, he still found himself used by his cousin a few times. At least he hadn't invited someone else to join him, Michele thought to himself as he tried to look at the positives. Yet in a situation such as his, how could there be *any* positives?

Raf continued to be a staunch supporter, and every time he was at home, he spent time with Michele, trying his best to comfort him.

Michele could tell his brother felt guilty for what happened that night and for how he'd run away from the shed. Although in his mind he knew he could not blame him, he couldn't help but feel a tiny fissure in his heart.

It was a tiny thing, yet it was a crack that had the potential to grow—at any point.

Nicolo's information, however, was a game changer. Michele's spirits soared as he read through the report Nicolo had compiled.

Gianna was fine. She was safe and she had recently gotten married to Bass. That meant...whatever issues they'd had in the past had been solved, and she was well protected.

For the first time in too long, a tear made its way down his cheek. It wasn't a tear of sadness. On the contrary, it represented all the happiness he felt at knowing his sister was living the life she deserved. But more than that, he *knew* neither Antonio nor Benedicto could touch her. Not when she'd married a DeVille.

They might have tried to ruin them before, but he reckoned her marriage to Bass changed things.

She was safe.

He finally breathed out in relief.

Raf, too, was immensely relieved to hear the news about Gianna. And so finally, they started planning how they were going to tell Benedicto and Cosima. The best time would be on Sunday, during lunch time—the only time the family sought to behave peacefully and *like* a family.

The more Raf assured him of his support, the more Michele was confident that they could do something about it. That Benedicto would not stay still if both his kids had been abused by that monster. And more than anything, he was *sure* that Cosima would ensure Antonio got his due for daring to touch her son.

Michele might be on Cosima's bad side, and he might *not*

like her as a human being. But even he had to respect her for the mother she was—for the mother he wished he could have had. Against all odds, she was always there for Raf, making sure he was loved and protected. That alone gave him the courage to push forward with the claims.

He might be the unwanted child, but surely, rape wasn't anything to be scoffed at.

That's what he tried to convince himself as the days passed and Sunday loomed closer.

He was apprehensive about it, was embarrassed and ashamed to have to recount everything that had been done to him. But he needed it to stop!

Since he'd gotten the information that his sister was safe, he'd finally started fighting back against Antonio. The few times his cousin had caught him alone since, Michele had bitterly fought until he'd escaped, kicking and punching and doing whatever he could to ensure he never again fell prey to that monster of a human. And *that* was even more proof.

The last time they'd crossed paths, Michele had scratched Antonio's arm so badly, he'd drawn blood, a scar forming all along the length of the man's forearm.

As such, Michele couldn't help but be sure that Benedicto would believe him and that he would take action. Maybe he hadn't been the best father until then, but Michele was sure he wouldn't value a rapist more than his own son.

Sunday morning, Michele's nerves were killing him. He'd had a nightmare the night before, everyone shunning him for daring to speak out. He knew it wasn't likely to happen, had seen the family's attitude towards child molesters was *not* flexible, everyone condemning such behavior. He knew that, or he *wanted* to know. His limbs wouldn't stop trembling, his palms clammy, his vision swimming.

He wasn't sure what to expect from the discussion. Did he

want Antonio kicked out of the house? Definitely. But did he want him to suffer?

He brought a finger to his lips, nibbling at one nail anxiously.

Michele had never been one prone to violence, but in this case, he could see Antonio get his due.

He might even enjoy it.

He didn't know what that said about him as a human being, since he'd always made an effort not to wish ill on anyone. But God, how he wanted to see Antonio suffer for everything he'd put him through. For all the moments he'd stolen from him—moments that would haunt him for the rest of his life.

One year.

One year he'd been at Antonio's mercy and in that timespan he'd changed irrevocably. Something had died within him. Something he'd always held on so tightly.

His humanity. Or, rather, his appreciation for humanity.

Before, he'd always tried to look on the bright side of things, find positives where there were none. He'd never liked to categorically brand people as monsters because he knew how he'd been labeled his entire life without there being a seed of truth to it. And so, he'd done his best to *not* judge people too harshly. Not as he'd been judged himself.

But now...

Monsters existed. And there was *nothing* on this earth that could excuse their behavior. There was absolutely nothing positive about some people, and the realization hurt.

Not only had his entire life changed in the span of that one year, but his bubble had been burst. The way he saw the world was forever altered, the stench of evil staining it to such a degree Michele wasn't sure he could ever trust someone again—at least not fully.

He felt at the mercy of fate. A cruel, and fickle fate that chose him as her plaything. And for that, he resented *her*. For someone who'd never known true hate—who'd never even known true resentment—that negative emotion stained his soul, laying its small seeds that now had a proper environment to grow and prosper.

His body wasn't the only thing that had been defiled. His soul had, too.

twenty

AGE FOURTEEN

That morning, the entire family went to church. Michele trailed behind his brother, doing his best to avoid Antonio and his roving hands. Yet for all the anxiety that was clouding his judgment, he felt that something wasn't quite right.

"Raf, are you okay?" he asked his brother as he followed him to his room the moment they got back home. "You look a little pale."

"I'm fine," Raf strained a smile.

Michele frowned. Something was wrong with his brother. He didn't know what, but he could feel a certain distance in the way he'd interacted with him all morning.

Maybe he was also afraid for the confrontation. After all, it would be the two of them against everyone else in the house. Raf was probably scared of how their parents would react. Maybe he was ashamed as well. God knew, Michele was filled with so much shame and self-loathing at the things that had been done to him that he didn't want to ever think about himself as a physical being again. The mere thought of his corporeality, or his body's interaction with the outside world disgusted and revolted him to such a degree, he wished he could close himself in a new bubble

—one where he didn't have to partake in the fakeness of society. He wanted to shut himself in his own little world where he knew he was safe—where *no* one would hurt him again.

As he noticed his brother's discomfort, he knew he had to be strong. He'd promised he would do this, and for the first time he would do his duty as the older brother. This time, *he* needed to be the one to protect Raf. As much as he wanted to believe Antonio would eventually stop if he fought hard enough, he was afraid he might change targets. He'd already touched and taunted Raf. It would be entirely too easy to escalate that. And for his brother to experience what Michele had...

Already, the events with the man who'd paid for him weighed heavily on Michele's mind. Since then, his aversion to people had only become worse, now extending to his own family and people he regularly trusted.

Yet he needed to be strong—stronger for Raf, too.

"If you say so," Michele returned the smile, reaching out with his hand to squeeze his hand. It took everything in him to steel himself for the contact.

Raf just nodded, seemingly not understanding how hard it was for his brother to withstand touch, much less to initiate it himself.

"I'll get ready for lunch," Raf told him, "you should, too."

For a minute, Michele could only stare at his brother, his previous smile frozen on his lips. He hadn't expected to be dismissed, but he duly nodded, taking a step back and slowly removing from his brother's room.

Quickly checking the hallway, he ran to his own room, locking himself inside. And as he changed out of his church clothes, he went over his lines, anxiety eating at him as he imagined his father's reaction.

He was afraid. At the same time, he knew this needed to be

done. Raf was right that Antonio could not continue like this unpunished, and Michele wagered that if it wasn't him, it would be another boy. Antonio was much too confident in his actions to not have done this before and much too careless to not do it again.

Retrospectively, Michele understood more about their initial interactions. From the beginning, Antonio had wanted Michele to submit to him, not fight him. He'd sought to convince him to allow Antonio to touch him of his own free will. He didn't know why something like that pleased Antonio so much, but every time Michele had fought back, he'd been met with a cruel side of Antonio that had nothing to do with what the abuse wrecked on his body.

Pulling a shirt over his head, he went to the mirror, taking in his expression.

He'd lost weight.

Consistently over the last year, he'd lost weight. First, it had been because he'd been too ill to eat—every time he tasted food he felt like he would throw it back out. Then, Antonio had prohibited him from getting too big.

With a clearer mind, Michele could see Antonio simply wanted him helpless and unable to put up much of a struggle when he overpowered him.

A loud sigh and he convinced himself to exit the room. The quicker this would be over, the faster he could find some sense of quiet in his house.

For so long, he'd been under continuous stress that he didn't know any other state. His body was forever primed for fear, pain, and anxiety. There was nothing else for him. He could barely remember the last time he'd smiled or had a good time— to his mind that felt like a lifetime away.

Armed with as much conviction as he could muster, Michele

exited his room. Raf, too, was closing the door to his room, and their eyes connected across the hallway.

Raf averted his gaze.

Michele frowned, puzzled at his brother's reaction.

"We'll do as planned, no?" He felt the need to ask, catching up with Raf as they both went down the stairs.

"Of course," Raf nodded, his eyes never meeting Michele's. His tone was flat, too, but Michele assumed Raf was as nervous as he was.

They walked into the day room, the table already spread. Benedicto and Cosima were sitting side by side, with their father at the end of the table as befitting the head of the family. Franco, his wife and Antonio had not come down yet.

Michele and Raf took a seat on the side opposite to Cosima, Michele sitting next to Benedicto as they had planned, though that seat was usually reserved for Raf.

Benedicto noticed the change but he just narrowed his eyes, his forehead creasing as he studied Michele.

The urge to squirm was unnerving. Michele mentally said a mantra, trying to convince his own self that this was for the best—that it was the *only* option. Next to him, Raf was stiff, his gaze forward as he looked at Cosima with an inscrutable expression.

The cold atmosphere did nothing to calm his nerves. Especially as Franco, his wife and Antonio came down to lunch.

They had all changed out of their church clothes, opting for more comfortable outfits.

Antonio sported a smug smile as he winked at Michele. All at once, he felt a lump in his throat, a disgust at himself and the situation. But with that revulsion came the unwavering conviction that he *needed* to do this.

"Maybe we shouldn't," Raf turned to him to whisper.

"We will," Michele stated confidently. He wasn't going to

cower in front of him anymore. He wanted to be free. "We'll do it."

Conversation flowed at the table as everyone started eating, and Michele simply bid his time, trying to find the right moment to interject.

That moment arrived as Benedicto declared that their business had been doing better, lightly praising Rafaelo for his ideas. Seeing his father in a good mood, Michele knew that was the perfect time to say his piece.

"Father," he cleared his throat.

Suddenly, everyone's eyes were on him. Particularly Benedicto's who was regarding him as if he'd sprouted a second head.

In a way, he supposed he had since he'd never once interacted at the table, always keeping quiet out of fear of saying something wrong. This was the first time he'd talked, but more than anything, the first time he addressed Benedicto so directly.

"Yes?" The sound was harsh. Michele's body trembled as the echo enveloped him. Everything he'd rehearsed fled his mind as he found his gaze clashing with his father's unyielding one. He was scared. Infinitely so. But he couldn't give up. He didn't know when he might have such a chance, or when he'd muster up such courage again.

He swallowed hard, wiping his sweaty hands on his trousers as he pushed his chin up.

"I have something to tell you."

There was a pause as Benedicto narrowed his eyes at him.

"Is that so?' He leaned back in his seat.

Michele opened his mouth to talk, but Raf's hand was suddenly on his, squeezing tightly. Turning to his brother, it was to see him shake his head, a bead of sweat on his forehead as he whispered the word *no*.

Michele faltered for one second. Just one. Because he realized Raf was as afraid as he was, but that only meant that one of them had to be stronger—braver. He'd been the weaker brother for too long. It was his turn to protect Raf. And so he nodded at him, his expression peaceful as he tried to relay that he had it—that he was going to handle everything.

Suddenly, it wasn't just some other boy Antonio could abuse. His brother could very well be the next one once he tired of Michele. Antonio had already started laying the groundwork for that, and to Michele's mind, that was where the danger was.

Before he lost himself to the trembling of his limbs, or the incessant need to go to the bathroom and empty his stomach, Michele told his father.

"Antonio raped me."

Silence descended at the table. Cutlery fell, the sound of metal clinking against plates. A gasp at the end of the table—Antonio's mother. Cosima, too, was blinking rapidly, staring at Michele before her gaze swung to Raf, her eyes sending a quiet message.

Franco sputtered, while Antonio could simply stare at Michele with malevolence.

"What did you say?" Benedicto asked, an incredulous expression on his face.

Michele didn't dare lose momentum, so he simply started speaking. He recounted from the beginning what had happened, how Antonio had blackmailed him with Gianna's location and how he'd sold him to another man...

"You mean to tell me you knew where your sister was all along?" Benedicto's thundering voice made Michele flinch.

"What... No... Antonio..." He stammered, suddenly looking around the table and at the accusing eyes settled on *him*.

"Antonio what? What in the fucking hell is this Michele? What you're accusing your cousin of is a *very, very* grave. You shouldn't lie about this."

"I'm not lying!" Michele cried out. "I swear I'm not lying. He'd been forcing me to do stuff to him and..."

"Antonio, what do you have to say?" Benedicto interrupted, nodding at Antonio as if he expected the man to be the only one telling the truth.

"What do you expect me to say, Benedicto? I'm appalled that Michele would make up something like this. I've only been kind to him, and to hear him say that about me?" He shook his head, feigning a sad expression as he looked at Michele with disappointment. "Is this how you repay me for everything I've done for you? For being your friend?"

"What... No," Michele shook his head, unable to believe his father would buy Antonio's words rather than his. More than anything, he could not believe how Antonio could look so calm while spouting such lies. What kind of monster was he to do all that with a straight face? Nary a trace of guilt?

"He *raped* me," he choked on the words, tears already threatening to make their appearance—he could only hold the strong façade for so long. "He held me down and he...he..." Michele stammered, unable to put into words what had happened, or the fact that Antonio had defiled him in such a manner.

"He did what, Michele?" Benedicto asked in a bored tone, barely resisting rolling his eyes.

"Father, you know what I mean..."

"No, I don't think I do. Why don't you tell us? What did Antonio do to you?"

Put on the spot, Michele blinked, his mind going blank.

"H-he..."

"He?" Benedicto raised his brows. Everyone was quiet at the table as if they were waiting for Michele to make a spectacle of himself. Michele couldn't believe he had to say the words out loud—words that pained him as much as the act itself had.

"He put his penis in me... He forced me to suck on it..."

Silence.

"Is that what you did, Antonio?" Benedicto asked his cousin, who of course, denied it with an awkward laugh.

"Is this your way of telling me something, Michele?" Benedicto then turned his icy glare at *him*, regarding him as if he were nothing but the dirt on his shoes. "That you might have some," his face scrunched up in disgust, "deviant tastes?"

Michele shook his head, opening his mouth and closing it as he could not utter more words. The incredulity of the situation overwhelmed him, pushing him into a corner. He looked around the table.

Cosima's eyes were on her plate, but her smile was unmistakable. She was having a laugh at his expense. Antonio was pretending to be scandalized, but deep down he was also amused at Michele's meager struggle. Then there were Franco and his wife, who both let out nervous laughs as they pretended the situation was wholly of Michele's making—a ridiculous statement, maybe one borne out of a sense of inadequacy or a need for attention.

The entire house knew that Michele had both in spades.

His body was shaking, and he just saw everyone laugh at him.

"Raf," he turned to his brother. "Raf can tell you. He saw us," he said out loud, remembering his brother's promised support. "He saw everything," he continued, and turning to his brother, it was to come face to face with someone foreign. Someone who looked at him with no reaction.

"Right?" a tremulous smile appeared on his face. "Tell them what you saw, Raf. That he touched you, too. That he..."

Silence.

More silence.

Then Benedicto laughed.

"Goddamn," he chuckled dryly. "Do tell us, Raf. Did you happen to see this interlude Michele speaks about."

Raf blinked. He was pale, his gaze skittering around the table in an attempt to divert attention from him.

"Raf?" Benedicto repeated. Raf's gaze collided with Cosima's before it met his father's.

"Yes, father?" He asked innocently.

He was nervous, too, Michele could tell. But together they could put an end to this ruse. They could ensure Antonio got his due for the lying scoundrel he was.

"Is it true what your brother says? You've seen Antonio take advantage of him in such a way?" Benedicto's voice was tense—serious. That's how Michele knew his brother's words were the missing piece. Once he said everything he'd seen, his father would believe them.

"I..." Raf faltered.

For a moment, their eyes met, and he saw something in his brother's gaze that he could not decipher. Raf looked nervously around the room, his teeth raking over his lip.

"I..."

"You don't have to cover for your brother, Rafaelo. Just tell the truth. Did you or did you not see Antonio rape Michele?"

Raf didn't answer, his lips trembling.

"Tell them, Raf. Tell them what happened. That he tried with you too..."

Cosima was frozen at the table, her eyes on her son as she waited breathlessly for his answer. And for the first time, she spoke.

"Is that true, Raf?" Her voice held an edge to it, and Raf swallowed uncomfortably.

"Rafaelo!" Benedicto snapped. "Speak!"

"No."

Michele stilled, that one word leaving him open-mouthed and in a state of pure shock.

"No, it's not true," Raf continued, his voice trembling.

Michele could only stare at his brother.

"Raf..."

"It's not true," he repeated, guilt lacing his tone. "It's not true," he shook his head.

"Raf..." Michele called his brother's name numbly, the blow to his heart making him stagger in pain.

He... He... He couldn't even think of the words, much less say them out loud. His brother had lied. He'd betrayed him... He'd...

A sob broke through the air.

Belatedly, Michele realized it was coming from him as his father's palm connected with his cheek, the blow so strong he was flung from his chair. His body fell to the ground with a loud thud.

He was still in a state of shock and he could barely register what was happening around him. Even the pain in his body as his father landed blow after blow on his flesh became inconsequential.

He heard the words though.

Liar. Degenerate. Abnormal.

"What the fuck did I do to deserve someone like you," Benedicto spat out. "This is all payback, isn't it? I should have fucking beat it out of you a long time ago..."

He couldn't understand what his father was talking about. Not until he heard the other words.

Gay. Homosexual. Deviant.

His father, and the entire family believed he was doing this because he was in love with his cousin and had an affinity for men. And through more blows, he heard Antonio confirm it too by saying he'd noticed a pattern with Michele and how he would seek him out all the time.

Everyone was lying. About Michele. About what happened. About everything.

They were all lying but branding *him* the liar.

"Father stop! You're killing him," Raf's voice penetrated the fog in his mind.

His lungs constricted with so much pain he couldn't help but howl out loud.

His brother. His only ally. His only...

He'd lied.

"Please stop," he continued.

Raf *lied*.

That was the last thought Michele had before he passed out.

twenty-one

AGE FOURTEEN

Michele came around hours later, finding himself back in his room, a cold compress against his cheek. He was dazed as he struggled to keep his eyes open, his body radiating with pain.

He blinked fast, all in an attempt to dispel the mental fog that had laid siege on his mind. At the same time, he wished he hadn't. Because then, the events of the day came rushing in.

"It's not true."

His brother had lied. Raf had promised he'd have his back and then...he hadn't.

With great difficulty, he managed to get up, his entire body stiff.

His father had spared none of his strength when he'd kicked at him. Luckily, used to such treatment, he'd brought his arms and knees to his stomach to protect the area since that was the most dangerous one. He'd experienced it before when he'd had broken ribs, when he'd been kicked so hard he'd spit blood for days on end. Now, only his extremities hurt, bruises already forming on his skin.

He took a deep breath, and heading to the bathroom, he splashed some water on his face.

His lip was split. A dark bruise appeared under his eye. One on his right cheek.

He looked thoroughly beaten.

Black damp locks fell over his forehead, his lush hair a curtain to obscure the severity of the damage. All at once, he was thrust back to the time when he'd had no hair—when his life had been so bleak his last worry had been whether people made fun of his baldness of not. Yet even in those moments he remembered wishing he were normal—wishing he looked and behaved like all those other kids.

Yet what had all that gotten him? Pain and disappointment.

He continued to peruse his form in the mirror. Without even realizing, he took a pair of scissors, holding tightly on to his hair as he snapped the strands from their roots.

He didn't stop. He cut until only a mess of wild wisps of hair remained. All easily remedied with a blade.

Michele wasn't himself anymore. He only saw the reflection in the mirror—all he hated and abhorred. He saw himself staring back and thought only about one thing.

Enemy.

For so long he'd been his own enemy and he'd been unable to recognize that. He'd convinced himself that he could forge his own path in the world, that as long as he was kind to others kindness would be done onto him in return. He'd been so sure of his philosophy in life that no matter how many obstacles he'd faced so far, he'd continued on.

He'd thought that as long as his conscience was at peace, he would be too.

Yet it was the reverse.

The more apathetic he was towards the evil things done to him, the more his mind became ridden with echoes of anguish and pain.

Nicolo's advice rang in his mind.

The world was *truly* kill or be killed. And Michele was the perpetual victim. Because of his weakness, or his idealistic perception of the world, he didn't know.

All he knew was that it needed to stop.

He needed to change in order to bring change onto himself.

Taking a deep breath, he winced at the physical pain. At the same time, though his soul wept torturously with misery and so much anguish he could barely ground himself in the present, his conviction shined strong—stronger than ever. He *must* change.

But first, he needed to know why. He needed to understand what could have led his own brother to behave in such a way—to throw Michele to the wolves and sit by watching while he was eaten alive.

Taking care not to exacerbate his injuries, he applied some soothing gel to the tender areas before shrugging on some clothes.

He sneaked out of his room with care. The last thing he needed was for Antonio to catch him alone. In the state he was in, he could *not* put up a fight.

Limping down the hallway, he stopped in front of his brother's door. Three breaths later, he knocked.

He didn't know what to expect—what would happen once the door opened. There were so many things he wanted to ask his brother, to demand an explanation on. Yet as he watched the door rattle, opening to reveal Raf, his face devoid of emotion, he could only muster one word.

One question.

"Why?"

His voice was harsh, the pain as he swallowed unbearable.

Raf didn't answer.

He stared at Michele as if he'd seen a ghost—but even those people showed more reaction than his brother did.

Michele didn't want to believe this was it. That *this* was the moment he lost the last person he could call his own.

"Why?" He croaked, louder, more painfully.

Raf shrugged.

"I tried to tell you *not* to go on with it."

"What... When?" Michele stared at him in bewilderment.

"We can't afford for our family to be divided right now. Especially since Franco is in charge of our new operation. We can't let something like..."

Raf continued to talk. Michele stopped listening.

He only looked at his brother in shock, the events of the day finally catching up with him—the horrors he'd lived through and the horrors he would *still* live through registering on his battered mind.

Raf hadn't just betrayed his trust. He'd destroyed *everything*.

That one lie he'd uttered not only sullied Michele's experiences even more, or the fact that he'd shared them with him when he'd been at his lowest. No, that lie would end his entire life. Michele knew it. His father wouldn't take it lightly—had already come to his own conclusion that Michele was a deviant and that he'd been lusting after the only holy person residing in their home. Everyone had formed an opinion based on that lie. And Michele *knew*. That would eventually destroy him—or what was left of him.

After Raf's desertion... He didn't think there were worse things in life.

"Who are you?" Michele uttered the words on a broken whisper, shaking his head as he took a step back.

"We need to prioritize our family, Michele," Raf told him.

"I am your family, too. I..."

"We need to get our priorities straight, Michele. And right now, we can't afford to lose Uncle Franco's support," Raf stated resolutely, his eyes boring into Michele.

"Raf... What's going on?" Michele stammered, looking at Raf's face for any sign of deceit—for any sign that he'd been forced into this.

"If that's all..." Raf nodded at him before turning back and slamming the door in his face.

Michele reeled back, his eyes wide and full of hurt.

He was so shocked, so steeped in disbelief, he couldn't move from the spot. It was like his feet had sprouted roots, digging into the ground seeking to keep him to that spot for an eternity. Maybe not his body, but certainly his heart.

Beat after beat, it echoed in the deafening silence of the empty corridor. And beat after beat he felt it hit his ribcage with such a force, he felt his entire being fail him.

How...

How had he gotten here?

How had everyone he'd ever trusted turned their backs on him? How had everyone he'd ever loved taken his love and thrown it in his face?

He struggled breathing.

He struggled *existing*.

And when he finally managed to get back to his room, locking the door behind him, it was to sink to the ground, his hands on his throat as he tried to get it to work again.

He'd always thought that despite the fact that the bad moments far outweighed the good ones in his life, at some point the balance would work in his favor. If he withstood the bad, he'd be deserving of the good—and much, much more appreciative of it.

But Michele was at a point where he didn't think there would ever be good.

Blow after blow, life showed him how merciless it was, fate choosing him as unworthy of her rewards. And time after time, though he tried to measure up to something—to some ideal—it was to be hit back, kicked to the ground and reminded that his ideals weighed *nothing* in the real world.

Still. He'd hoped.

Now, as he breathed in and out, wheezing sounds coming out of his mouth as he tried to calm himself, he saw that hope slowly slip from him.

Before his eyes, he saw *it* materialized, its physical form as solid as the furniture that graced his room. He saw it tall and mighty, raising up against the odds. It only took one wind—one man's malicious breath to send it crumbling. And just as it rose, it started shaking, the entire foundation turning to dust before his eyes.

Michele reckoned that if his own spirit had a physical form, it would also crumble down like that, mercilessly ground down and eroded until only dust remained. Dust that could be blown away by yet another breath.

Terrified, he watched.

His dreams, hopes, ideals. They all crumbled to the ground, disintegrating as if they had never before existed.

In their place, there was only bleakness. The absence of essence, and the void that should have been there in the first place. The void that Michele had attempted to nurture all along. Yet as understanding dawned, he stopped. He cut the thread that connected him with that source.

Eyes wide, he continued to watch the play of shadows on the wall, all the while feeling the shift within him—feeling the slow death of his being, only to be reborn as he *should* have been, as the entire world had forced him to be.

Empty.

Slowly, yet precisely, he felt himself slip.

And as his teary eyes closed with the power of his emotions —the last outburst and ultimate catharsis—he was free.

Empty, and free.

To Michele's everlasting relief, Antonio didn't try to come to his room that night, nor any subsequent one. No one did. After the beating he'd taken from his father he'd thought at least Raf would come by to check on him, as he'd done in the past. But as soon as that thought crossed Michele's mind, he was reminded of his brother's stance towards the whole fiasco—that he'd decided the family business was more important than Michele.

The hole in his heart caused by that *hurt*. Every time he thought of Raf he hurt. So he decided to thrust him out of his mind. To dwell on that matter would only mean going down the mental road of no return, and Michele knew his state was already precarious as it was. If he went deeper...he would likely become trapped in his own mind, together with his misery and anger at the world. And it would all turn into an echo that would only hurt *him*.

The best recourse was to *not* think about it. Or at least try not to. Though he'd already decided to harden himself against the world, it was easier said than done, and he already yearned for some human contact. For at least someone to *see* him and not dismiss his issues as inconveniences.

A few days later and after his injuries had healed to an acceptable extent—at least to one where he could move freely around—Michele returned to school.

Everyone was regarding him strangely, and crude whispers reached his ears. The words his father had spewed at him echoed through the hallways, the upperclassmen laughing at him and pointing at him with their fingers in derision.

He'd thought he'd escaped his hell at home only to be swallowed whole by another at school. Everywhere he went, the rumors followed. He simply had no respite from all the hate thrown at him.

And for what? For daring to stand up to his abuser? For trying to go to an adult with his concerns and the fact that he'd been abused months on end by a sick individual in his own home. Instead, he'd been branded the guilty one.

Somehow, the school had found out too. Yet here the information had been distorted. He didn't know how anyone would have heard, but he supposed any of the staff could have spoken out—especially given Guerra's perceived status in society. He was sure everyone in the house had heard the confrontation at lunch and how Michele had taken the beating of his life for being *abnormal*.

That was exactly what the rumors were saying. That he was into boys. That he'd tried to seduce his own cousin and made sexual advances towards him. The fact that Antonio was supposedly a man of the cloth amplified the nature of the rumors and made for juicier content, as some people had taken to point out in his face.

To Michele's relief, though, he'd only gotten a few punches here and there at school. It hurt, as his previous injuries were far from healed. But it was better than he'd expected considering everyone knew his shame and had distorted it, making it a source of entertainment.

His lip split and bleeding, he trudged his way back home. He hadn't interacted with Raf at school, had barely seen him all week as he was always away and working with their father.

Michele felt angry at himself for hoping it was all just a big cosmic prank and that Raf would somehow return to him and apologize. He even supposed he would accept the apology, after he'd heard his brother's reasons, of course.

He was just so desperate for a little bit of attention—for *some* affection—that he would even forget his brother had sold him out when he needed him the most.

The loud honking of a car startled him, frowning as he took in the car that pulled to a stop in front of him. The passenger door opened to reveal Nicolo who looked him up and down, his mouth drawn in a snarl as he realized the state Michele found himself in.

"Hop on," he ordered.

Though Michele was bewildered at his friend's sudden appearance, he didn't contest the command. Not when he wanted someone to talk to so badly, he felt like bursting into tears the moment he settled on the bench across Nicolo. The mere nearness of a person who didn't mean him harm was like a balm to his battered soul. His body rebelled at the proximity, as it had done for so long now, but his heart rejoiced in his chest.

He needed a friend. And Nicolo *was* that friend.

"What happened to you?" The brusque question took him by surprise.

"Of, this," Michele's hand went to the purple bruises on his face, his mouth drawn in a tremulous smile. "Just a squabble," he tried to shrug it off.

Why was he trying to be strong when all he wanted—all he'd desired for so long—was to unload himself and the burden that held him down.

Nicolo stared him down, the explanation clearly not cutting it. He knew something was wrong. Something that Michele wasn't yet saying.

"What happened, son?" he asked in a softer voice—so soft that though Michele opened his mouth to lie again, he found he couldn't.

He blinked. Once. Twice.

Tears gathered at the corner of his eyes—tears he'd been unable to freely shed before. Instead of placating words and flimsy excuses coming out of his mouth, a sob escaped him.

A loud, heartbreaking sob.

He finally cried. He cried so hard, his breaths turned into hiccups, his entire body shaking with the force of his sorrow.

Nicolo was shocked at his display. He wasn't one prone to

displays of affection, or sentimentalisms—not like Michele, or at least the *old* Michele was. Still, he couldn't sit by while the boy was crying his heart out.

In a gesture of unprecedented kindness, one that shocked both Nicolo and Michele, the older man moved on the back seat, taking Michele in his arms and holding him tight as he continued to cry.

He cried for so long that even though the car drew to a stop, Nicolo didn't interrupt him. He let his emotions run their course, sensing it was exactly what the boy needed.

Only when Michele had calmed down a little did Nicolo take him to his office inside the gym.

There, Cami was present as usual, having a laugh with some of Nicolo's men. When she spotted the two of them, though, her features tightened with alarm.

Nicolo nodded at her, walking by the other men who showed their respects with a small bow and heading straight for the isolated room at the end of the gym. He settled Michele on a chair, taking his backpack from him and urging him to make himself comfortable.

Cami was quick to dash through the door, already holding a cold compress in her hand and a pack of tea in the other.

"Dear Lord, how many times will I have to see you with your face busted up like this?" She shook her head at Michele, her words chiding but her gestures gentle as she pressed the compress to his cheek.

"Who did it this time?"

Michele strained a smile, shaking his head.

"I swear," she cursed softly, grabbing a bottle of water and filling the kettle on Nicolo's desk. She was quick and efficient as she made him tea before taking a seat in front of him. She was worried about him, and that worry only grew as she saw with what difficulty Michele moved.

"Good Lord," her hand went to her mouth in horror, her eyes searching Nicolo's. "Please don't tell me..." she trailed off at Nicolo's grim expression.

"There's more, isn't it?" She pointed to the discoloration that started on his neck and spread down, under his shirt.

Michele stiffened, his gaze on the floor as he gave a brisk nod.

"What happened, son? Can you tell us?" Nicolo spoke, all the while having a silent conversation with Cami with his gaze. They realized the precariousness of the situation and the fact that they had to tread carefully.

"I can leave if you'd prefer to speak with Nico alone," Cami offered, wanting to put Michele at ease.

He was clutching at the tea cup in his hands, the steam traveling up and enveloping his features.

"Stay," he said in a low, resigned voice. "I..." Taking a deep breath, Michele found the strength to talk.

He related the events as they had happened, doing his best not to forgo any detail for fear he might be called a liar again. Though it was difficult for him to describe what Antonio had done to him, he *needed* to do it. This was a safe environment, and both Nicolo and Cami had never been anything but nice to him. He could trust them.

You thought you could trust your brother too...

He ignored that small voice inside his head that told him only disappointment awaited him. Instead, he took a chance—one last chance—that at least someone would believe him.

Michele's gaze was still on his mug as his lips moved, the words in some parts mechanical while in others too full of emotion he thought he might choke on them. He didn't look at the people around him. If he had, he would have seen the open-mouthed horror with which Cami was regarding him, or the quiet seething that took over Nicolo.

He would have seen that there *were* people who believed him and empathized with his situation.

But he didn't dare.

Not even as he finished talking did he raise his gaze, waiting for them to talk first—for them to relay their verdict.

"Goodness, Michele," Cami spoke first.

Before he knew it, she was on her knees before him, her kind eyes watching him closely, her hands in the air as she waited for permission to touch him.

She knew.

Somehow, she understood.

He blinked back the tears that assailed him. After all he'd cried, he thought he'd emptied his reserve of tears for an eternity, yet it turned out to be such a renewable resource, he found it hard *not* to cry anymore.

He gave her a small nod, and her hands finally touched him, gently stroking his forehead and the area where his hair had been before.

Nicolo was still quiet. But once their gazes connected, it was to hear a resounding curse escaping the older man.

"Fuck! Fuck! Fuck," he yelled, twirling around in anger before exiting the office.

He took a few long moments outside to calm down before he came back, his breathing still harsh, his eyes still signaling murder.

"You... You believe me?" Michele felt the need to ask.

"Believe you? Dear boy, how could we not?" Cami exclaimed horrified. "I'm so sorry, darlin'. You should have *never* had to go through something like that. And for your own family to say you're a liar..." she trailed off, her eyes swimming with tears.

She was...crying. For him.

Once he saw he could trust them with his narrative, he continued, detailing how his own brother had let him down and how the entire school had somehow found out details of what went on and thought he was trying to perv on his cousin.

"He said that? Nicolo asked in a harsh tone. "He said business is more important than what happened to you?"

"Yes."

"Fuck... I get it now," Nicolo added bitterly. "I just can't fucking believe it..."

"What do you get?" Michele inquired innocently.

"Don't you see? Your brother did this all for one reason, and one reason only. To cut you out from the succession order."

Michele frowned.

"But I've never had an interest in that. He'd always been the one to entertain our father with his schemes. I never cared about that side of the business."

"You might not have cared, but his men sure did."

"I don't understand," Michele frowned.

"It's simple, son. You're the eldest. By default, everything *should* go to you. Unless they found you lacking in some ways."

Nicolo went on to explain how important the tradition of the first born was and that if Benedicto tried to force Raf's leadership down everyone's throats he would only meet hostility.

"He wouldn't," Michele whispered. He *knew* his brother. It was impossible that he would have backstabbed him just to get a position Michele hadn't wanted in the first place.

"He wouldn't?" Nicolo raised an eyebrow, the situation in front of him undeniable.

"But..." Michele stammered, unable to believe Raf would have sold him out for *that*.

"I'm sorry, Michele. But from where I'm sitting, that's the most likely explanation. You just told us he saw you. He witnessed everything and still lied. Why else would he do that unless he had something to gain?"

"Why convince me to come forward then..." he mumbled, his disillusion growing by the second.

"Why else if not to discredit you?"

Michele felt numb.

For days after the incident he'd tried to find excuses for Raf, yet here it was. The truth staring him in the face. Was that it? Had his brother used him to advance his own position?

He didn't want to believe that was the case, but at the same time he couldn't ignore Nicolo's words either. Logically, there was no other explanation.

twenty-two
AGE FOURTEEN

Cami was by his side, gently cleaning his wounds while Nicolo paced up and down the room. Since hearing the entirety of what had transpired and what Michele had suffered, he'd been restless, muttering a string of curses not fit for the current company.

"Cami, be a dear and make an appointment for him with doc. I have to do something," Nicolo finally addressed Cami, giving Michele one last look before exiting, his phone to his ear as he gave a barrage of orders.

"Doc?" Michele blinked, the words sinking in. "What do you mean?" He asked with wide eyes.

"We need to get you tested," Cami said, pursing her lips. "I'm not sure our doctor will be able to come down here until the end of the week, but I'm clearing his schedule so he can get you tested."

"I don't understand," Michele blinked innocently.

Cami froze, her expression one of pity as she regarded him. It was even worse as she explained the dangers of unprotected sex and the fact that a lot of diseases were transmissible through sexual contact.

"If he did this to you, there's no telling how many others he's done it to," Cami continued.

Michele only stared at her dumbfounded. Once more, his cheeks heated with shame, not only at what had happened to him but also at his own ignorance. He'd never once thought about *those* repercussions, and suddenly, he felt sick to his stomach.

By God, but he hoped he wasn't so unlucky as to have contracted something. Wasn't it enough that he would most likely never live a normal life again? That he was unlikely to ever look upon another being with sexual interest since he the mere thought of giving someone access to his body sickened him? Wasn't that enough? Now he could...

He stifled a sob at the realization that his life might very well be over.

"Shh, don't cry," Cami cooed. "It's just a precaution, okay? We can't know..."

"Okay," Michele nodded, his heart heavy.

At that moment, he hated himself. He hated that he'd been so naïve—so complacent with everything that had happened. Retrospectively, he supposed he could have done things differently. He could have reached out to Nicolo sooner to check on Gianna. Instead, he'd been so paralyzed by fear he'd only thought of one thing—protecting his sister.

He was happy Antonio had lied, but he wasn't happy with himself for buying those lies.

Cami tried her best to comfort him, not letting any of the other men come into the office and spending the time distracting him with some silly stories. She dressed his wounds and made sure all his injuries were looking good and on their way to recovery. It was the only thing she could do, but even that proved difficult as Michele couldn't help but flinch every time she touched his body. He wasn't as bothered if she touched his face, since he could track the movements of her hands. The moment she went lower, where his eyes could not see, he started shivering, revulsion choking him. It was the hardest thing to keep still even knowing she meant him no harm.

In his mind, all touch equaled pain.

It was later in the afternoon that Nicolo returned.

And he wasn't alone.

A loud shrilling scream resounded in the air, startling both Michele and Cami.

"Stay behind me," she told him, her expression serious as she opened the door to the office. Michele followed after her.

Nicolo was in the middle of the gym, a beat up man at his feet groaning in pain. He was covered in dust and dirt and one could see the foot prints all over his body—he'd been trampled on.

Michele took a step forward, ignoring Cami's warning.

Despite the messy appearance, he would know that person everywhere.

It was *him*.

Antonio whimpered on the ground, barely moving. Raising his head, he spotted Michele, blinking repeatedly as he took him in. Then, looking around, understanding dawned on him.

"Michele, please," he begged.

"Oh my goodness," Cami gasped behind him.

"He's all yours, son. What do you want to do with him?"

Michele just stared at the man writhing in pain on the floor.

"I can do whatever I want to him?" He asked, almost mechanically.

He was barely aware of what was happening, or what this meant for him. He understood that Nicolo wanted him to take whatever revenge he wanted from Antonio. Though he found himself in a position of power over his abuser, he found he could not move—nor could he think besides the paralyzing fear that overtook him at seeing him.

It always happened.

His limbs froze whenever his eyes connected with Antonio's, dread coursing through him.

"Of course. You can kill him in the most gruesome way. I can offer some ideas," Nicolo grinned.

Michele was barely aware of what went on around him, his eyes on Antonio's pitiful form.

Nicolo's men joined the conversation, having a laugh at Antonio's expense and coming up with different scenarios fit for his deeds.

"No," Michele suddenly said, raising his eyes. "I won't kill him. Death isn't the answer," he said confidently, though he didn't know where that certainty came from.

Nicolo's brows went up in surprise.

"No?"

Michele shook his head.

"Death is too easy. Death is a way out," he said. Though, if he were perfectly honest with himself, he didn't know whether he had what it took to murder a man in cold blood—including the man responsible for his nightly terrors.

"Then what do you propose, son?"

"Castrate him," he simply stated. "So that he can *never* hurt another again. So that he can suffer the consequences of his actions for the rest of his life."

Antonio howled, his eyes wide, his body spasming in an attempt to get himself free.

"No, Michele, please," he cried out.

Michele paid him no mind.

His attention was wholly on Nicolo.

"I want him to feel the pain," he continued, "but not to death," the hint of a smile peeked through.

"I'll be damned," Nicolo whistled, seemingly pleased with that turn of events. "Boys," he held a hand up, signaling his men. "Undress him and tie him to the chair."

The men immediately obeyed the command, gagging Antonio and proceeding to get him ready for the procedure.

"I'll do it myself," Michele took a step forward.

"Of course you will. I'll bring over the utensils. To make sure he doesn't die we'll need to cauterize the wound after..."

"I'm aware of how that works. He will pass out from the pain, won't he?"

Nicolo nodded.

"Good."

A serenity descended over Michele at the prospect of seeing his abuser suffer, as well as an additional idea to give the last blow.

He wanted Antonio to bear the consequences of his actions physically, but also mentally. And there was only one way to ensure that.

Antonio was stripped of his clothing, his arms tied behind his back, his legs spread apart and tied to the chair's legs. A cloth was in his mouth, his face red, his eyes puffy.

All over his body, Michele could see the injuries he'd sustained at Nicolo's hands. Oddly enough, he couldn't muster any satisfaction at his pain.

He just wanted this to be over—to stop living in fear of what his cousin would do next. And more than anything, he never wanted another person to suffer what *he*'d suffered, though as Cami had suggested, he may have done it to others in the past.

Michele abhorred violence. But it seemed this was one more step towards leaving the old him behind—to freeing himself from the shackles of his own ideals.

"He's all yours," Nicolo was suddenly by his side, pushing a mobile cart towards him. All the necessary items were laid there.

Michele pushed down any disgust he might have felt and he picked up a sharp knife. Antonio was thrashing against his bounds, making low sounds in his throat—probably begging for mercy. But there was no mercy to be had when he hadn't afforded the same treatment to Michele too.

Michele crouched in front of Antonio. He faltered for just one moment before he let his conviction seep into every pore of his body.

This wasn't him torturing someone for the sake of it. No, this was justice. And he would take his justice out of Antonio.

Yet this would not be normal castration. Not when that meant there was still a chance for Antonio to have an erection in the future. No, Michele would ensure that *everything* was cut off—as befitting the offense.

Pushing all other thoughts from his mind, he honed in on his objective. With mechanical movements, he tightened his grip on the knife, grabbing on to Antonio's flaccid dick with the other. Starting at the base, he brought the blade against the flappy skin, pulling towards him as he cut.

He cut and cut. Antonio bucked against the chair, but Michele did not spare him one glance.

He was solely focused on his task. After what seemed like an eternity, the organ gave way, the body of penis completely detached from its base. Blood immediately gushed out.

Nicolo was by Michele, helping him and handing him the items he needed to cauterize the wound.

His balls were next until a mess remained of his pubic area. Placing a flat iron over a flame, he waited until the metal was hot enough before placing it on Antonio's skin.

The pain was so intense that his cousin passed out at the first contact with the hot metal.

Sprayed with blood from head to toe, Michele took a step back.

His eyes were bleak, his soul even more so.

"Cami, come take the boy," he heard Nicolo bark the order. He was unable to move, his attention arrested by the blood—blood *he* had drawn.

How had he gotten here?

He hated it. He hated his circumstances. Most of all, he hated himself.

"Darlin', come, let's get you cleaned, shall we?" Not even Cami's soothing voice was enough to get him out of his stupor.

Moments later, he found himself on a chair, Cami carefully wiping some of the blood from him.

"What's going to happen to him?"

"Nico's going to drop him off at some hospital. He's going to get care in time to survive, but they won't be able to do much else."

Michele nodded.

He truly didn't want him to die. For all his hate of the man, he didn't want his blood staining *his* hands—not more than it already was at any point.

Michele simply wanted...justice. Odd to think of it as justice, though, when it barely aligned with his previous ideals. Yet it was the only thing helping him to move on—the fact that he could at least dole out justice with his own hands if the entire world failed him.

He might hate to do so, might hate himself even more for being deserving of abuse but undeserving of justice, but that only meant he had to forge his own path.

No one had understood him to that point, not his qualities nor his dreams—no one had sought to. For that reason, no one could understand his woes either.

If they couldn't love him at his best, he doubted they could at his worst. And he reckoned the road towards that destination had gotten a bit more slippery.

It was moments like this, when his entire life flashed before his eyes that he questioned his existence and his purpose on earth.

Why? Why was he so unlovable? Soon, though, the question morphed. Why was he so hard to love but so easy to hate?

He'd always done his best to be good, thinking his actions would cancel the stigma around him. If he tried hard enough, people would surely see there was something more to him than the identity of his mother, his frail and unhealthy body, or his feminine features. He'd tried to overcome his condition, prove that he was not the *monster* Cosima had branded him since childhood.

And what had he gotten in return?

They'd called him a monster and a monster he was becoming.

He set his unblinking eyes on his hands. There was still blood under his fingernails, with some streaked over the inside of his palm.

Michele was smart enough to understand he was heading down the path of no return. There was still the essence of *him* inside—the *him* that he'd sought to nurture all along. The natural, good *him* that he knew to be his real self. Yet it was slipping from him.

Dark thoughts, like a violent storm, gathered in his mind, spreading to every corner and inundating every little nook he tried to keep safe.

It was akin to an infection. And he was infected.

"All done. Let's wait for Nico and he'll take you home, ok?" Cami's voice startled him, and he found himself nodding.

A few hours later, and he found himself back home. Just as Cami had said, Nicolo had dropped the barely conscious

Antonio in front of a hospital and he'd been rushed into urgent care. According to the last information, they had him stabilized.

Michele didn't doubt his uncle would find out, and by default, his father too. Would they blame him for it? He didn't know, but if another beating was forthcoming for it, then he would simply accept it.

He didn't regret it.

He didn't regret making sure his cousin would never harm another human being.

And for that, he would take any beating, and any pain. In the end it would have been worth it.

By some stroke of luck, nothing happened. The house was quiet the entire evening, and even as Michele left for school the next day he didn't detect anything out of the ordinary.

Appreciative of any reprieve he might get, he decided it was high time to put some effort into school, too.

The moment his brother had ceased to be his friend and confidante, Michele had realized he needed to work on his plans. As he'd decided in the beginning, the moment he was eighteen, he'd leave the house and everyone behind. He didn't want to continue where he was not welcomed. But for that to happen, and for him to have a future, he first needed to lay a strong foundation. That meant taking his classes seriously.

He'd always been in his own world before, preferring to daydream to listening in to his lessons—especially since he had the advantage of his memory and the fact that he could memorize the lessons with no problem. But he'd done that before, and he'd just been accused of cheating. Therefore he knew he needed to change his entire attitude towards his studies to be taken seriously. And though he'd always hated his father for forcing him on a path of numbers and exact science, he was smart enough to realize that would help him more in the future than art.

Of course, he wasn't about to give up his art. But first he needed to make sure he could support himself before dedicating himself to it.

A satisfied smile pulled at his lips. He had a solid plan and as long as he didn't stray from it, he was sure he could succeed. He would then leave, go far, far away where no one would recognize him and reinvent himself.

Then, he wouldn't be a monster anymore. And maybe, he could stop himself from becoming one.

He breezed through his classes, managing to avoid some of his bullies. Getting older and switching from middle school to high school had not meant that the bullying had stopped. If anything, it had gotten worse and bolder. Older boys had no qualms doing atrocious things for the sake of *fun*. It was something Michele couldn't wrap his mind around, and did not want to try. His goal was to get through high school unnoticed, ace his classes and build his future.

As the bell rang, signaling the end of the school day, Michele gathered his things, ready to go home and change before meeting with Nicolo a while later at the gym—anything to not stick around at home where he might bump into his brother. Though Michele didn't hate him, he couldn't help the pain that surfaced in his heart every time they met, Raf's indifference and new attitude cutting him deep.

Shrugging his backpack on, he hurried down the corridor, exiting the school and losing himself among the masses of other students—all just as eager as him at leaving the premises.

What he didn't expect, though, was the blow to his head that made him reel, stumbling forward and falling as his eyes rolled in the back of his head.

He'd thought himself lucky too early. That was the last thing he thought of as he slumped to the ground.

When he regained consciousness, he didn't know how much

time had passed. He was barely aware of his own surroundings. Squinting, he saw the shadows on the old brick wall, the dead end in the back of the school where all the dilapidated buildings were. It was also the playground for the delinquents—the bad seeds of his high school.

It had only been a couple of days since his last beating, when some guys had mocked him for his clothes and had made fun of his alleged sexual orientation. He supposed he couldn't exactly breeze through high school when he was *the* pariah. This time, he didn't even know which of the guys had taken him.

Was it Jonas? Or Galen? Those two in particular hated Michele for a reason he did not know. But from the first day of high school they had sworn to make his life a living hell. And that was before the rumors of him and his cousin had started swirling around school.

Michele let out a tired sigh. He'd get a few punches, maybe a few kicks and then they would leave him alone. That was the usual.

So used he was with such treatment that he decided it wasn't worth it to put up a fight. He'd take the hits and then move on. Maybe Cami would dress his wounds again. She was very good with that and Michele found her touch soothing.

As his focus slowly returned, he could make out the giggles behind him and the hushed words.

His eyes went wide as he heard the words fag, weirdo, and it's what he deserves in the same sentence. It was then that he attempted to move and he realized he couldn't.

He was laying on an old table thrown in that corner—a dirty old table that smelled of rust and rot and made him sick to his stomach. One of the boys must have used his tie to secure his hands behind his back.

The position was awfully familiar, and a pit of despair formed in Michele's stomach.

He started thrashing.

"Let me go," he cried out, only to be met with a slap, one of the upperclassmen coming into view.

It *was* Galen.

But he wasn't alone.

There were at least three more boys behind him going by the sounds they were making. Maybe more.

"Look at him how innocent he looks," Galen laughed in his face, his palm cupping his cheeks as he forced Michele to meet his eyes. "Your brother told us you'd put up a fight. But that's how you like it, isn't it?"

Michele blinked, unsure where this all was going. What had Raf told them?

"I don't understand..."

"He told us you were taking clients," he chortled. "But that's to be expected, isn't it? Everyone knows your family's good as bankrupt. I guess I can admire your thinking. Any business is good business, isn't it?"

"Ask him how much he charges," another chimed in from behind. Michele recognized the voice. It was Allan, one of the upperclassmen who'd made fun of him in the past but had never been violent towards him.

"No, that's not..." Michele shook his head.

He couldn't believe Raf would say that about him, that one encounter when Antonio had sold him shaming him more than anything. It was a stain on his soul he didn't think would ever be erased.

Galen didn't let him continue, however, as he whipped out his wallet, counting a few hundred dollar bills and throwing them at Michele.

"That should cover it," he smirked. "I'd even say we're paying above market price."

What?

What was happening?

Michele's eyes widened in shock, but the more he tried to move against his bounds, the angrier Galen became, punching him in the face until his entire head spun. Still, it wasn't enough to completely dull his senses.

He was still aware of someone yanking his pants down.

No! No! No!

The words echoed in his brain, but he could utter neither out loud. The most he could do was whimper in pain when one of the guys spread his butt cheeks apart before thrusting into him without a care for his pain.

His mouth opened on a scream, but his voice was dead. Just as sounds vibrated in his throat, a hand was slapped over his face.

He felt everything.

For a moment he wished the blows he'd taken before would have knocked him out. Instead, they made him even more aware of the pain that threatened to splinter his being—just as he was being split into two as the first guy finished, only to be followed by the next one.

He thought it a small mercy that the semen from the first guy's release was making it less painful for the second person, but that didn't mean inside he wasn't hurting—maybe even more so.

Once more he found himself at the mercy of fate—that hateful thing that seemed to have it out for him. What had he done to anger her, he didn't know.

He lay on that old table, his eyes blank as he tried to retreat within himself. But his body still felt every invasion—and as a consequence his mind did too.

One finished, another one took his place. It went on forever, or what felt like forever as all the guys took their turn at using him, only to laugh when they would finish, calling him names and telling him he was primed for his future job.

He didn't realize when it was over, only that cold air caressed his backside, the tie on his wrists gone. Still, he didn't move.

He didn't think he could. Frozen to the spot, his eyes lingered on the brick wall, his mind counting each one in an attempt to erase what had happened to him.

When he finally moved, it was to fish a napkin from his bag to clean himself. Semen was running down his legs mixed with blood from the forceful invasion. He was sore and aching. The pain was already something he was used to, but that didn't make it any easier.

A sob racked his body, but no tears would come. Only the trembling that usually accompanied the feeling of being drained to the point of collapse.

More bloody semen flowed out of his ass. He kept wiping.

It was dark by the time he finally made his way back. He didn't drop by his house, going straight to Nicolo's gym.

"There you are darlin'," Cami was the first one to receive him. "Nico is busy for a bit, but you can play in his office. I have some matters to tend to," she prattled on for a little and he was thankful she didn't notice his new bruises. He didn't think he was ready to answer more questions.

He wasn't ready to talk.

Quietly, he made his way to Nicolo's office, closing the door behind him and going to the far end of the room where a makeshift bed was. From experience, he knew he wouldn't be able to sit for a while. Considering the degree of abuse, which went far beyond Antonio's M.O., he wagered it would take more than a *while*.

Through all that pain, though, Michele was numb.

His body was numb, his mind number.

How could Raf do something like that to him? How could he

tell them... And there was only *him* who knew of the exchange, because he hadn't told that part to anyone else, except Nicolo and Cami. How could he betray him even more?

He couldn't cry.

God, but he wanted to, yet he couldn't bring himself to. His tears had dried up, his entire being so numb he could barely muster *any* sort of feeling.

The disappointment he felt at his brother was foremost in his mind, but even that was slowly fading.

Just like before, Michele knew it was time. He needed to let himself go—the old himself. It was imperative to do so...

His eyes snapped open, his gaze honing in on Nicolo's study. He'd seen his friend hide many things there, including...

He rose. Ignoring the way his body ached, he pushed on. Opening one drawer and then the next, he found what he was looking for.

A gun.

The gun.

The one that would end everything.

He didn't know how he'd come to that conclusion. From hurting from his brother's betrayal to feeling himself descend into a pit of madness, he only knew that this was the only way he could cease *feeling*.

Otherwise, how could he keep going forward? How could he bear to see another day when the same thoughts would invade his mind, the same heart wrenching pain at knowing his loved ones had turned their backs on him—that they considered him little more than dirt on their shoes? How could he go on the same as before when his heart refused to listen to his mind?

He wanted to change. He really did. But he knew it just wasn't him... And the only way to change—to stop his pitiful self from existing—was to wipe that self from existence.

He sneaked the pistol in the band of his pants, and leaving

his backpack behind, he slid out of the gym and to the inner courtyard.

There was one place he enjoyed spending time in, and he supposed it was the perfect place for him to go.

His steps were measured. Too measured. Because for all his conviction, there was also fear.

"I need to do this," he muttered to himself, the only way he could convince his cowardly self to go through with it. After all, he knew no one would mourn him. At home, they would probably laugh at him, calling him a deviant and other names, mocking him and his entire pitiful life before they decided it was good riddance—one less mouth to feed and one less blow to the family reputation.

Isn't that all they cared about?

From the beginning he'd been crucified for the sins of his mother, branded a monster before he even knew the meaning of the word. After that, things got progressively worse.

Every painful moment of his life flashed before his eyes and it became easier to convince himself the gun was the way out.

He was tired of the pain. He was tired of *living*. And now? He had no one else to live for.

He could finally go in peace. He could finally...

Grabbing on to the gun, he pulled the safety off—that much he knew about how to use a gun. He'd seen movies, and he also knew what the next step was.

Opening his mouth wide, his fingers trembled slightly as he aligned the barrel of the gun to the back of his throat.

Now for the last bit...

A tear slipped down his cheek. The first one he could release and the final one. Mentally, he started a countdown.

I'm sorry, Gigi...

His sister was the only one he knew would miss him. But she would move on. Everyone did eventually. As for the others...

"Michele!" A voice thundered, Nicolo's form appearing in sight.

His eyes widened as he took in Michele and the precarious position he found himself in.

"What... Michele, don't..." He put a hand up, slowly coming closer to him.

Michele shook his head. It was in vain. No one could convince him otherwise.

He just wanted to shut it all off—all his emotions, the good and the bad. Because the good borne out the bad. And he was tired. So fucking tired of the bad.

He'd only had good intentions in his life, and he'd only received the bad in return.

That alone made him wish he were someone he wasn't—that he wasn't good, empathetic, or *anything* positive. He wished he could be bad, but as he'd seen with what happened with Antonio, he was lousy at that. He just couldn't shut himself off.

But this... This was the only way his mind would *stop* thinking. Every bad memory would go—along with his dreams and hopes. Maybe it was a steep price to pay, but it was one he would gladly pay.

For nothingness.

Nicolo talked. He kept on talking, telling Michele he was young, that he had his whole life ahead of him and that he should not squander it for nothing.

He was wrong.

He wasn't squandering anything since he'd never had anything in the first place. The only thing he owned, in that moment, was a sea of emotions that threatened to drown him. He was doing this to escape the madness...

"Michele, don't, please," Nicolo kept pleading.

"I'm sorry," Michele said, the sound muffled.

Nicolo advanced, gaining speed as he saw Michele's finger tighten on the trigger.

"No!" he yelled.

Michele pressed the trigger.

Closing his eyes, he said his final fuck you to the world as he pulled the trigger.

Nothing happened.

Another tear fell, then another.

Nicolo rushed towards him, taking him in his arms.

The last tear fell. The last he'd ever shed.

That day, Michele died.

Too bad he was still alive.

twenty-three

AGE FIFTEEN

The rain hit the window, small drops lingering as they descended upon the wooden windowsill. The storm kept raging outside, making ravages of the trees and violently snapping their branches. The wind howled, and Rafaelo felt the foul taste of nature's cry—it was a cry for help he knew all too well because his own soul was soundlessly vibrating with it.

He watched the abysmal weather and he felt the parallel with it inside himself.

It was in times like this that he cursed his messed up senses, the way he experienced the world on the outside, but also on the inside. Though he was safely ensconced in his home, away from the direct effects of the storm, he felt dumped in its middle—in the eye of the storm.

He closed his eyes, inhaling.

For one moment, he wished he could stop his senses from going into overdrive. Wasn't enough that he was suffering on the inside—that his self-loathing had reached such heights he barely stood to look at himself in the mirror? Wasn't it enough that he was living in a small prison, trapped within himself with his shame, regret—God, but it was so much regret he could barely function. Now, he had to experience that anguish on the outside too.

His soul was dying.

His mind was clamoring.

There was no quiet to be had—no respite from the raw grief that straddled his shoulders, a weight that had been glued to his back never to be lifted again. That was one thing he was sure of —his guilt would *never* disappear.

A sudden bang on the piano startled him.

"What's the matter, darling boy?" His mother turned towards him, raising her eyebrows in question. "You've been staring out the window for a while now. Is it something at school? I've already talked to your teacher and you've been doing great. If you keep this up, he is sure the valedictorian position is yours."

"It's not that," Raf shrugged, though he didn't take his eyes off the storm outside.

'Then what is it?" She moved then, getting up and coming to sit next to him on the sofa. "You should be happy dear, not morose as you are now," she shook her head in disapproval. "Our situation has changed, too. We're not beholden to others for money. That is a cause for celebration, not sulking."

One year of the newly implemented money laundering scheme and their coffers were starting to fill up. Franco and his wife had left, finally able to return to their home without worry that some debt-collector would come calling. Luckily, though, Antonio had left soon after the incident with Michele. He'd been called to Rome urgently, and had finally taken his priestly vows. Raf scoffed mentally at that, hating the thought of Antonio as a man of cloth. But that was yet another repercussions of his actions. When he'd lied, he hadn't only doomed his brother, he'd also given Antonio a free pass to continue doing as he pleased.

"Have you..." he swallowed the lump forming in his throat. "Have you noticed a change in Michele?"

"And why would I?" Cosima exclaimed, affronted. "I don't care about that hooligan and neither should you, darling boy," she said in a stern tone, her hand on his shoulder as she squeezed his flesh in a gesture of comfort.

"He's not the same, is he..." Raf continued, his eyes glued to a tree branch that was at the mercy of the wind, waving precariously in the air.

His brother had ceased to be the same since Raf had ruthlessly backstabbed him. He grimly acknowledged he'd committed the gravest sin. Especially as the result was staring him in the face.

Michele had changed. And it wasn't only in the physical sense, though his growth spurt was hard not to notice, especially since he'd shot in height almost overnight. The true change, however, was at a deeper level. He was no longer the sweet, positive boy he'd once been. He was no longer...anything. There was a coldness emanating from him that made Raf's skin crawl on the off-chance they found themselves in the same room. Because that had changed too... Michele was barely at home, and when he was, he stayed out of everyone's way.

Gone was the well-mannered brother Raf knew, too. If Benedicto or Cosima picked on him, he fired back. Before, he'd never dared to raise his voice in front of their father—had never *tried* to defend himself even in the worst conditions. Now, it seemed that even Raf's parents were afraid to offend him since he was *that* unpredictable.

That wasn't the only difference.

He'd simply stopped talking. He rarely interacted with anyone in the house except if provoked, and he most certainly never interacted with Raf anymore.

The last time they'd spoken... Raf couldn't remember—or, he

didn't want to. Remembering would mean reliving the words he'd spewed at his brother—the careless words he'd been forced to utter.

Michele hadn't sought him out anymore after that.

Out of shame, Raf hadn't either.

That didn't mean he wasn't aware of his brother. On the contrary, Raf was ever more attuned to Michele's situation, for the guilt inside of him would not let him behave otherwise.

"Don't worry your head about that, Raf. It's done," she pressed her lips to his cheek.

"But it's my fault..."

"It's no one's fault, dear. You might have said a small, white lie. But it was for me. And you have no idea how much I appreciate that you protected me," she whispered lovingly.

Raf didn't move, nor did he acknowledge her words.

In spite of what his mother thought, he hadn't done it for her. Far from it.

He'd done it for his brother.

Yet at the moment he had to wonder whether he'd chosen well.

His mother was right in one regard. It was done. He couldn't change the past, and going by the present, it was unlikely he could alter the future, too. Not with how Michele had embarked on his very own path towards self-destruction that no one could save him from.

Raf might pretend he was above gossip, unmoved by the social life at his school and his peers' opinion of himself. He liked to think himself immutable in that regard, *and* for others to note it in him as well. That in itself lent him an untouchable air—the epitome of his golden boy persona. People respected him. They wanted to be *near* him. They valued his opinions and they thought him the coolest person in the school.

He wondered what they would think if they knew the true

him—the one he'd hid all along, as well as the other one he'd slowly morphed into?

If they only knew...

He was composed only as far as appearances allowed. Inside, he was a mess of anxiety, shame and guilt. So much fucking guilt sometimes it was hard to breathe.

Raf was suffocating. But on the outside, he always had a pleasant smile on.

There was also the small detail of his obsession with his brother—or rather, with what he'd done to him. But Raf did not have to seek out gossip for it found him anyway.

So he heard. That despite being considered a freak and a loner, Michele had gotten involved with some dangerous gangs. That he'd gotten in fights, beating a few students to a pulp and putting them in the hospital. Oddly enough, none had filed charges.

There was also another issue—the one that worried Raf the most.

Drugs.

According to rumors, Michele was doing hard drugs.

Raf already knew his brother had taken up smoking to cope with what happened to him. But drugs...?

He was worried—deadly worried. And he could not do a damn thing about it.

"You need to stop thinking about him. He's only going to bring you down," Cosima droned on, though he was only listening with half an ear.

"I never understood, mom," he looked her in the eyes, his gaze haunted. "Why is it that you've *always* hated him? You know he would have never harmed anyone. He was the kindest person I've ever known. And the things that happened to him... They should have never happened to *anyone*, least of all someone as innocent as Michele," he stated in a deadpan voice.

Cosima drew back, her eyes narrowed. She didn't answer for a moment, merely regarding her son.

"You know why. You know *very* well why, Raf."

He frowned.

"I don't care how kind, or nice, or what an awesome person Michele is. I don't. I never have," her chin went up a notch, her eyes glinting with fierce conviction. "For me he's always been one thing, and one thing only."

"What..."

"He was an obstacle in *your* path. It could have been anyone for all I care. But his only sin is having been born months before you. That is why I'll never be sympathetic towards him—why I'll never look at him with compassion. I can't. Not when I know he's what's standing between you and the Guerra legacy."

"Mom..."

"You may think me a monster for it. If that's so, then so be it. But I have only one goal in life, and that is making sure you get your position—your inheritance. Nothing else matters."

"And no one else, is that right?"

"Correct. Judge me all you want. As long as I achieve my purpose, I'll have no regrets."

"What if it was me, too?"

"What do you mean?"

"What if Antonio did that to me too?"

"He wouldn't have dared," Cosima replied confidently.

"And why is that?" Raf blinked, his heart beating painfully in his chest. "Why would he have not *dared* when he did so with Michele? What makes me so different?"

Retrospectively, he could see all the opportunities Antonio had had. He'd never acted on them though. He may have taunted Raf and tried to instill fear in him, since, it was clear fear was what he got off on, but he'd never gone beyond that even when he'd had the chance.

Realizing she made a blunder, Cosima blinked.

"What makes me so different, mom?" Raf asked again, this time more pronounced.

"You're my child. That's what makes you different," she replied with a dignified huff.

Raf froze.

"Mom," he whispered, his features pale.

He'd never once thought she would have had a hand in what happened—had never believed her capable of such cruelty. Was she mercenary? Absolutely. But she was *not* a horrible human being. At least he hoped so...

Now, he didn't quite know.

"Tell me you didn't know," he uttered the words, feeling the harsh consonants against his tongue, the sounds breaking like glass and stabbing his tongue with unbearable pain. "Tell me you didn't know," he repeated, almost as if in a trance.

Cosima opened her mouth to reply, but then she closed it.

She had no reply.

"I had to protect you," she eventually said, her voice holding none of the previous strength.

"You had to protect me?" Raf shot up from his seat, rising to his full height and watching terror envelop Cosima's features.

Michele wasn't the only one who'd experienced a growth spurt. And though he still had to fill in his big frame, he still cut a terrifying figure as he looked down at his mother with so much disdain, her eyes started watering.

"You knew what he was doing... You knew he was... Fuck..." he swore.

Raf *never* swore.

"Raf, you have to understand..."

"Understand what, mom? What?" He yelled. "That you covered for a fucking pedophile? That you thought it was ok if he was raping someone else as long as it wasn't your son?"

"Raf..." Cosima flinched.

"How?" He shook his head in disgust. "How could you do something like this? I get that you want me to take on the Guerra legacy. I get that you've been playing your hand in the most unorthodox ways. But *this*?"

Cosima blinked back tears. It was the first time she'd seen her son reacting so vehemently to her. He'd never yelled at her.

"Raf, please," she whimpered.

"*This*, mom? This isn't some business strategy. It's someone's life. That *you* ruined. You knew and you..." He choked on his own words.

He looked and looked at her and he could not recognize her anymore.

"You tried to convince me not to tell. Fuck," he swiveled, his fingers massaging his temples. "Did Antonio *really* have anything on you? Or were you just scared that father would find out you were an active participant in it?"

"It's not like that, I swear to you. I just wanted to make sure he..."

"That he *only* raped Michele," he cut her off, his words grave, his features even more so.

"I can't believe this. I never expected you'd be so...so," he stumbled over his words, his eyes misted with tears, his throat clogged with emotion and so much pain.

Damn, but the pain was proving too much. Even for someone with Raf's unusual composure, he found he couldn't keep it all in anymore.

How could he have been so blind to it all? To the fact that he was living in a fucking den of vipers and that he'd damned the only innocent person in their midst?

How could he live with himself now when he realized he'd been played? And he'd been played to such a degree he was disgusted by himself and by everyone around him.

And his mother...

"You're despicable, mother," he eventually said, the foul taste of her lies inundating his being.

"Raf, my dear, please," she made to grab on to him but he shrugged her off. He didn't think he had it in him to let her touch him after what he'd found out.

"I know I can't do anything now. That it's too late," he took a deep, ragged breath. "But I can do something from now on. And don't..." he closed his eyes in agony, "don't you dare ask anything of me again. You're my mother, and I love you. But even loving you is not enough now." He took a deep breath. "I doubt it will ever be."

With that, he turned his back on her.

She cried his name, begging him to forgive her, begging him to reconsider.

He closed his ears.

He ignored everything around him as he ran out of the house, into the storm—into the fucking raging storm. But it was all in vain.

Not even that rain could cleanse him of his guilt, of his sins, and of the agony that now seeded his soul.

One mistake and he'd lost his brother.

Too late he realized he hadn't *just* lost his brother. He'd lost everything.

Like an island slowly drifting in the ocean, he felt himself split apart, carried by currents until he was wholly isolated from civilization.

It was later, much later, that he found himself in the gardener's shed—the place that marked the beginning of the end. Huddled into a corner, he was a wet mess as he stared at the table in the middle of the room. All he could do was wonder how the hell had everything devolved into this hell...

That night, when he'd gone to his mother, she'd promised

she would help. She'd given him her word that she would help them come forward to Benedicto and his father would take action.

How wrong Raf had been to put his faith in her, especially since it concerned Michele directly.

All throughout, he'd been so sure that was the best recourse, yet when the moment had come, he'd been unable to go through with it...

His mother thought it was because of her.

Raf's mouth twisted in a sick smile as he gave a dry laugh. Of course she'd think it was because of her. After all, Raf was ever the obedient son and he would never do anything to harm his mother.

A few days before that infamous Sunday dinner, Raf had gone to his mother to ask for guidance. He was afraid Antonio would do something to retaliate against Michele and he hadn't wanted to put his brother in harm's way. Especially after Raf had been the one to convince him to come forward.

When he'd first seen his mother, he'd known something was wrong. Like the dutiful son he was—perhaps for the last time—he'd asked her if he could help her with anything.

It was then that she'd confessed that she'd tried to argue with Antonio on Michele's behalf and ask him to leave him alone. Raf had been surprised at her initiative and had thought the world of her that she would put aside her differences and do something good for his brother for a change.

Except... It had all been a ruse.

She'd put on a show, her acting skills worthy of an Oscar. She'd bemoaned how Antonio had threatened her and how he'd come into possession of a few tapes of Cosima before her marriage.

"But why does that matter?" Raf had asked. To his mind, if it was before her marriage then certainly no one would mind them.

"You don't understand dear," she'd said, a tear going down her cheek in feigned pain. She'd then gone on an extensive tangent about her life before she met Benedicto and how her family had needed the money and she'd taken any acting gig she could find. Including semi-naked ones. But according to Cosima that wasn't the issue. The main problem was that she'd continued to do that even while dating Benedicto.

"You know how stubborn Italians are," she'd waved her hand. "Your father would have never married me if he knew. It didn't matter that I came to him untouched. The fact that other men had seen my naked body would have been an insult he would have never recovered from. More than anything, no one in his family would have approved of me. And you already know how hard that was when they thought I was just an opportunistic gold digger," she'd sighed, going on about her woes and how that could ruin her.

All so she could get to the main point.

"You can't go against Antonio. The moment you do..."

Raf had been taken aback by her attitude. Surely, someone's safety was more important than her reputation. She'd been in such hysterics, though, that Raf had been unable to give her anything but a positive response.

As soon as he'd left her, however, he'd decided he needed to take matters in his own hands.

If he couldn't count on his mother's support, then at least he could count upon himself. That night, he took one of the guns his father kept locked up and making sure it was fully loaded, he went to Antonio's room.

Raf was a fixer, and fix the situation he would. If he couldn't stop Antonio, then by God he would kill him. Maybe all his training had been leading to *that* moment—so that he could be capable of looking his cousin in the eye when he killed him. If so, then he was glad he'd set aside his principles and his feelings to become what he'd never wanted to. Because in the end, it would help protect those he cared about.

He would end Antonio.

That had been the plan until Antonio had laughed in his face. Even with the gun pointed at him, the man hadn't cowered. He'd simply come close to Rafaelo, pushing his forehead into the barrel of the gun and daring him to shoot.

"You can't, can you, you bad, bad boy?" Antonio had mocked.

"I can," Raf had retorted, taking the safety off and returning Antonio's stare with an unflinching one of his own. "And I will."

"You might think twice about that," Antonio had laughed. "If you want your brother to survive..." he'd trailed off.

"What do you mean?"

"It's simple. The moment I'm dead, everyone will know *all* my secrets."

"I don't..."

"You don't understand. Of course," he'd nodded thoughtfully, taking a step back and waving a small tape in front of Raf. "You see, I'm nothing if not resourceful. If anything happens to me, copies of this will reach *everyone*. And it's not only Cosima who will pay the price for her erotic poses. Your brother will pay the steepest price. As will everyone whose secrets I own."

He'd smiled then. A smile so sickening, Raf's gun shook in his hand.

"What are you talking about?"

"Of course you don't know. But don't tell me you haven't suspected?"

"Suspect what?" Raf had demanded, confused at Antonio's mad man talk.

"My, my," Antonio had whistled. He was enjoying the show

and having Raf at his mercy. "You haven't *once* suspected that your brother might," he made an oops sound ,"not be your brother?"

"You're lying."

"Am I? Why does Benedicto treat him like shit, then? Why does *everyone* treat him like shit?"

"But that would mean that father knows and..."

"He knows alright. But he would never let it *be* known. Not when he still has his reputation to protect. Imagine that, a proud Italian man raising his wife's bastard. Everyone would have laughed at him. Everyone *would* laugh at him."

Raf hadn't been able to move from the spot. The news had taken him by surprise, shocking him.

"Then why would you make it known?"

"Simple. If I made it known, not only would your father and the entire family become a laughing stock, but do you think little Michele would survive? He would be the first killed to keep face—whether by Benedicto or by someone high up in the famiglia. No one would want an outsider claiming any rights to the Guerra name, would they?"

Antonio had kept on talking, explaining everything that would happen should Raf go through with his threat—or worse, tell anyone about what Antonio had been up to.

And so Raf had found himself with the biggest conundrum of his life.

For him, it didn't matter that his brother was not his *blood* brother—he'd never been anything but his beloved sibling and would continue to be so. But as he ruminated over the details Antonio had imparted, he realized he *was* right.

If anyone found out that Michele wasn't Benedicto's son, then...

The days passed and his dilemma only increased.

The choice was brutal. Either he helped his brother punish

that scum that dared call himself a human being, or he denied any knowledge of Antonio's misdeeds and protected his brother from a future fallout.

How could he make such a decision? How could he, when both meant hurting his brother. The former would endanger his life, while the latter would ensure Michele would hate him for his entire life.

But at least he'd be safe. And so would his secret...

That Sunday morning, as he left Michele behind to retire to his own room, he reached a decision.

He would bear the brunt of it all.

Now, a year after the incident that had forever seared itself on his retina, the words exchanged setting fire to his ears just as they coated his tongue in the bitterest taste, Raf didn't know what to do... He didn't know what *else* to do.

He'd made the decision and for a while he'd stuck by it, thinking that anything would be better than have people out for Michele's life. But as he saw him descend further and further into misery—into a hell of Raf's making—he couldn't help but hate himself.

He'd done that.

Raf had been the one who'd condemned Michele to the existence he now led, and he found he couldn't live with the consequences.

It hurt.

It *fucking* hurt.

"How can I make this right?" He whispered, leaning against the cold wood of the door as he continued to stare at *that* table.

But the answer was not in his favor. He could *never* make it right. Michele would likely never forgive him. And if he were honest with himself, he realized he wouldn't forgive himself either. Regardless of Raf's motivation, regardless of the fact that he only meant well.

How could one choose between *bad* and *worse*? How could anyone choose well and live with a clean conscience? He might have spared Michele from a worse fate, but he'd condemned him to a crueler existence.

That choice would forever haunt him.

twenty-four

AGE FIFTEEN

Raf's relationship with his mother became more and more strained. Cosima tried to interact with him, putting forward her best self in an attempt to prove to him she was still his mother—the same one who'd loved him from infancy.

But that was the issue.

She was his mother, and her way of *loving* him had meant hurting others. Rafaelo wasn't sure that was the kind of love he wanted anything to do with.

How could he when he *knew* his mother had been the cause of the rift between him and Michele?

Maybe in the past he'd overlooked her behavior because he told himself she hadn't meant it *that* way—that in her attempt to be protective of Raf she'd ended up hurting his siblings. He'd always told himself it hadn't been intentional, for surely his mother wasn't that kind of a monster.

Raf had always thought himself self-aware, and *generally* aware. He'd known his mother's nature and he'd accepted it. But he'd been fooling himself from the beginning, hadn't he?

He'd told himself she was just ambitious—that she wasn't downright evil.

Now, faced with the evidence of her actual crime—of the one crime that would make anyone despicable—he had to take a step back and assess the situation again.

Benedicto, too, noticed the rift between mother and son, and in his attempt to placate Cosima, he tried to offer Raf advice.

It all started and ended with *you know how much she loves you.*

Raf took it all quietly, merely nodding. Yet inside, he was seething.

How was that love? Or if it was, what kind of fucked up love was it that she'd ruin someone else *just* for his sake?

And it wasn't even for his sake, was it? He'd never been a fan of the crime life he'd been born into, but he'd accepted his lot. He'd known his legacy from the beginning and had taken to honoring it in his own way. But his mother had never been satisfied with *just* that. No, she'd wanted the Guerra name and Rafaelo to become synonymous. She didn't just want the leadership for him, she wanted *everything*. And by extension, she wanted everything for herself.

Raf cursed himself daily for being such a blind fool all this time. He'd always taken his mother's side when his siblings had been right all along.

She was out for blood.

And she didn't care whose it was as long as blood was spilled, and riches were gained.

As time passed, everyone sought to give him advice. More than ever, though he was surrounded by so many people, he felt all the more alone.

He did well at school. He did his job at the organization. His efforts alone had brought the family back from ruin, yet even that wasn't properly acknowledged.

Raf supposed his father might want him to succeed him, and

for him to be seen as a competent future leader, but that didn't mean he'd let Raf steal his own glory.

Bit by bit, he was seeing flaws where before had been none.

And *that* was his father's. Hubris. The type that didn't allow him to accede that his much younger son could have done much better than he ever could.

Though the initial deal had been to let Raf lead for four months, more if he did well, his father had quickly resumed his position once he'd realized Raf's plans had materialized and were bringing real cash in. In a way, he'd claimed Raf's achievements for himself. Not that Raf had minded that, secretly hoping it would mean less engagement with the organization and more time to be...well, to be.

He didn't know what it was like to be a teenager.

Before, he'd had his parents to please. Now, he lost everything.

Before, he'd had his responsibilities. Now, he only had his unsurmountable guilt. And it was unlikely it will let him live normally.

He could never allow himself that—not while knowing what it had cost him.

And so he slowly felt himself become a shell of his former self. If before he'd put on an act, behaving as it was expected of him and keeping up the appearances that he could do no wrong, now he couldn't bother anymore.

Everyone at school noticed, too, and they gave him a wide berth for it.

Soon, Rafaelo simply closed himself in. At home he ignored his parents. At school he ignored his peers. And at work...as laughable as that might sound for a barely fifteen year old, he put on an emotionless mask and he did what he did best—work.

"You're worrying me, Raf," his father took him aside a week later. "I thought it was a phase, but it's not is it? What the hell is wrong with you?" he asked, shaking his head in frustration. "And your mother, what did she ever do wrong? How can you treat her like she doesn't exist? You know how much she loves you..."

"Then why don't you ask *her* what she did?" Raf snapped. "Why don't you ask her why I can't even look at her anymore?"

"She won't tell me," his father grit out. "It has to do with Michele, doesn't it? That little shit causing trouble again..." Benedicto cursed under his breath.

"Causing trouble again?" Raf blinked, taking a step back to contain his mounting rage. "He's *never* done anything wrong, *father*. He's only done that which you *decide* he's done."

"Did he turn you against your mother? Is that it? Fucking hell, I thought I taught him to keep his fucking mouth shut..."

"Why?" Rafaelo suddenly couldn't contain himself anymore. "Why should he keep his mouth shut? You know he was telling the truth about Antonio."

His father's eyes widened.

"Oh, come on, spare me the theatrics. That's what both you and mother excel at. You know what Antonio did to him, and he's still the guilty one?"

"For fuck's sake. You didn't see how Antonio left the country. That little shit mutilated..."

"If he did, then all the better. Antonio deserved that and more."

"Rafaelo," his father drew back, scandalized.

"You think I don't know why you're doing this? Why are you trying to alienate Michele from this family? What did you think? That you could make him hate us so much he'd finally disappear from our lives? That he'd run away?"

"What..."

"I know he's not your son."

Benedicto blinked, then faltered. His mouth opened and closed and still, no words came out of his mouth.

"Right," Raf smiled derisively, "and that is the issue, isn't it? You couldn't possibly broadcast it to the world that he's not your blood, that would have been too shameful. Instead, what did you do? You let an *innocent* boy be abused by everyone around him."

"Why should I care about someone else's bastard?" Benedicto finally burst out, his true colors showing.

"Indeed, why would you," Raf shook his head. "He might have been someone else's bastard, but he was still just a child. One that grew up in this house, together with all of us. If blood's your only criteria for family, then..." He took a step back, his entire body shaking with anger. "I want no part of your definition of family."

"Raf, wait," his father called after him, but he didn't stop.

Everyone looked askance at him as he ran out of the compound, his raw emotions evident on his face.

Raf didn't know where he was going. He only knew that he couldn't stand to face his parents—didn't think he could ever forget what they'd done.

This wasn't just some question of honor, as Benedicto had tried to made it seem. It was a matter of being humane, and both his parents lacked that in spades.

His father, the fool who prided himself on being the impervious head of the Guerra family, but who'd lost their family's fortune time after time with idiotic business ventures. His mother, the Anne Boleyn who'd enchanted Benedicto for his name and influence. As opposed to Anne, though, she'd delivered on the much wanted son and had successfully secured her claim. Then there was his uncle, who was solely moved by his interests. Why, their entire extended family was that way. It was why Antonio had been allowed to walk free for as long as he had, because Raf had no doubt Michele was *not* his first victim. Everywhere he looked, they were all the same. Awful, awful people. And it wasn't in the nature of their business, though that mostly skirted the lines of legality. They were simply terrible people.

Why was it that only now his eyes were opening to the true reality of his family?

His heart was breaking as everything he'd lived until then shattered before his eyes. All his memories become tainted by the knowledge that there had always been a hidden motive for his parents' behavior.

He'd loved them dearly. And now, faced with all these realizations, he wondered what he was to do with that love...

For hours, he didn't go home. He wandered the streets alone, even as the night chill descended upon the city, the wind cutting at his skin. Yet that pain was but a fraction of the pain he felt on the inside.

All this time, he'd tried his best to be the person his parents wanted—burying his true self deeper and deeper until he didn't know how to dig it back up.

For Raf, this was more than *just* the disappointment of the people whom he'd looked up to all his life. It was the loss of his own damn self.

Who was he? Who the hell was he anymore?

From the beginning, he'd been groomed to be the next Guerra head. His mother had ensured that he received a stellar education, that his manners were polished and that his reputation spoke for itself. To the outside world, he was just that—the golden boy. The polite, respectful and sociable golden boy. The absolute perfect son, perfect student, perfect boy.

He was so fucking far from perfect he felt his chest constrict with the weight he felt on his shoulders. His entire body bent forward as he gasped, his features taut, his face red with tension.

He wasn't perfect, far from it. He was an illusion—*just* an illusion.

Yet the worst part was that he was an illusion even though he'd started believing.

Who the hell was he?

The answer came easily, though he didn't want to heed it. He was an impostor.

He'd practiced being *good* his whole life, he'd assumed it would come naturally to him. But the one time he *should* have been good, he'd failed. He'd been bad...so fucking bad he wanted to rip his hair out, pull at his skin and shed the weight of his own persona—the fake, manufactured one he'd been forced to assume his entire life.

But...he couldn't.

He could only live with the knowledge that he wasn't good. Maybe he'd never been good. And now? He felt like the worst.

It was past midnight when he got home. No one was there to greet him, but he heard the sound of footsteps retreating on the second floor. His mother, no doubt, had stayed up to make sure he *came* home.

A sardonic smile pulled at his lips, disgust filling him to the brim as he squared his shoulders and slowly walked up to his room. Before he could wrap his fingers around the knob, though, something caught his attention.

A room at the end of the hallway teetered open, the barest hint of light peeking through.

Raf stilled.

For a moment, he was afraid Antonio had returned.

His feet took him in that direction, his fists clenched as aggression rolled off him. If he dared to come back...

He opened the door.

The room was swathed in darkness. The only beam of light was coming from a lit cigarette.

The window was wide open, Michele lounging on a chair in front of it, his feet propped up on the window sill. His head thrown back, he was half-angled towards the door, his gaze catching Raf's the moment he stepped into the room.

A smirk played at his lips as he twirled with the chair, the cigarette still in his mouth as he leaned forward, his feet back on the ground, his elbows resting on his knees.

He watched Raf with a strange expression. One he couldn't interpret, and at that moment, Raf didn't know whether he really wanted to.

He was tired—so fucking tired that the last thing he needed was a confrontation with his brother, though it was what he deserved.

"Close the door behind you, will you?" Michele drawled, his voice heavy.

He'd changed. Not only in his attitude, but appearance-wise too, puberty slowly revealing its effects on him. He no longer wore his hair long either. For a year now he'd been sporting a buzz cut. He'd pierced his ears, and he'd even added a piercing to his nose—all in an attempt to change the way people looked upon him.

And it had worked. At least to the extent that he'd stopped getting bullied after he struck back. Now, he was the resident loner of the school. People called him names behind his back, especially given his recent goth-like style. But they didn't dare insult him to his face. Not when the last kid who'd called him a fag had been taken to the hospital with broken ribs and a disfigured face. It had been a miracle that Michele hadn't been charged with assault. How he'd managed to escape any type of repercussions was beside Raf. All he knew was that *this* Michele was *not* the same one he'd grown alongside with.

He wasn't his beloved brother anymore. A sad smile pulled at his lips. He guessed he wasn't Michele's beloved brother anymore, either. And *that* was solely his fault.

"I didn't know you were here," Raf finally found his voice.

They were staring at one another. Like two predators trying to gauge the other's strength before an attack, neither was willing to back down.

It had been close to a year since they'd last spoken properly. A year in which they'd avoided each other and the matter of their division.

Raf was embarrassed to admit to himself that he'd barely tried to interact with him, regret eating at him as well as the guilt that made him ashamed of himself.

"Michele," he called his name, the first step in what he knew would be the next phase in the annihilation of his self. "I..."

Michele put a hand up, stopping him from talking.

There was something oddly disturbing to his manner, the way he was so calm and collected yet one look into his eyes and Raf could see a deadly storm waiting to be unleashed.

"You have two options, Raf. Either close the door on your way out, or come join me," he said, his mouth tipping up. He was daring him to come closer, playing on Raf's guilt and the fact that Michele knew he wasn't indifferent to how the events of the past year had played out.

One second. That's how long it took Raf to make his mind, his foot kicking the door closed as he stepped closer to Michele.

He pulled another chair closer to him, and he took a seat.

Neither spoke.

Michele held his relaxed pose, puffing his cigarette and blowing clouds of smoke.

"Here," he took out his pack, offering Raf one.

His first instinct was to refuse. He rarely smoked, and that was only when he was at the meetings with his father. But he saw this as an opportunity to engage Michele, so he quietly accepted, taking a cigarette and lighting it.

They were quiet for the longest time.

"What are we doing, Michele?" Raf asked softly, a sigh

escaping him as he gazed into the night. He was giving his brother the power of decision—the least he could do given his crimes.

"What does it seem like we're doing? We're having a smoke at night, like two naughty teenagers," Michele chuckled.

Raf blinked, Michele's words unexpected.

"Or at least that's what we're supposed to be, isn't that right?" he followed, his tone doing a one eighty as he turned, his eyes boring into Rafaelo.

"What do you want from me?"

"What are you willing to offer?"

Raf stared at his brother for a moment.

"I can't take back what happened, I..."

"Let's not speak of the past," Michele stopped him. "Why don't we talk of the future. That seems much more appealing."

"I don't understand what you mean."

"I think you know exactly what I mean, Raf," he took a deep drag of his cigarette. "I want it all. Are you willing to give it to me?"

There was no trace of emotion as he asked the question.

"All? You mean..."

"Yes, I mean everything. The top position, the business. Everything. Will you give it to me?"

"Why would you want that?"

Michele had never had an interest in the family business. He'd barely been exposed to that side of things, and Raf was sure he did not have a genuine interest in it.

Michele shrugged.

"I want to see if it was worth it," he added cryptically.

"Worth it?"

"Throwing me over for it," he smiled then. A smile so sick, Raf instantly knew.

Michele was not the brother he knew anymore. And the

worst? Raf had done that with his own hands. He'd been the one to kill him and make him into what he was now.

"You think..." Raf's mouth opened in shock. "You think that's what happened?"

"What else?" Michele countered, yet his tone wasn't accusatory. If anything, it held the same bleakness as before.

"I..." Raf wanted to tell him what happened—why he'd done something so unforgivable. But to tell him he wasn't Benedicto's son might be stripping away the last bit of identity Michele possessed. And though Raf wanted to take some of the blame off his shoulders—to feel lighter again—he couldn't bring himself to do that to him. He couldn't give him another blow like that. So he simply kept quiet.

He was guilty. That much was true. Would Michele knowing the truth change the fact that Raf had betrayed him? He doubted it...

"You can't answer that, can you?" Michele smiled. "It's ok. If you won't give it to me, then I'll just take it for myself."

Throwing the cigarette out the window, Michele rose. He gave Raf an odd look before he made to move. Yet he didn't.

Raf only heard the sound of wood breaking before he found himself on the ground, looking up in shock to find Michele looming over him, his features contorted in such torment, he felt it in his own soul.

"You owe me, Raf," he said as he brought his hand to Raf's throat, leaning in until his mouth was close to his ear. "And soon I'll come to collect. But when I do..."

Raf exhaled a tortured breath.

"When you come to collect I'll be there," he replied, resigned.

Michele didn't move off him yet. Leaning back, he regarded Raf for a moment, his pale eyes glinting in the dark room. There was confusion and something else in his features—something that gave Raf hope for a moment, before Michele opened his mouth and dashed it.

"I could have forgiven you anything," he started, loosening his hold around his throat. "I could have forgiven you anything, Raf. Anything but what you did," he said with a sad smile—one that was reminiscent of the old *him*. "This is the last time I'll behave civilly. For old time's sake," he mentioned ruefully. "But from now on, I have no brother. Or at least, I have no brother by your name."

The words weren't said in anger. They held such disappointment to them that Raf simply held his breath as he watched Michele get up and walk away.

And when he did breathe, it was to feel the weight on his shoulders increase in size, the cage around his heart growing smaller and smaller until it suffocated that organ that tried to keep him alive.

Until that moment, Raf had managed to hold on.

Yet Michele's disavowal tore at him worse than anything he'd experienced before.

For the first time, in the darkness of that room, he couldn't stop the tears from flowing down his cheeks, explosive sobs racking his body and making him curl in a fetal position on the ground.

Alone. He was so alone.

Not unlike Michele. But in Raf's case, it was of his own making. He had no one to blame but himself. Before, he'd been blind to his parents' machinations, excusing them every time they treated Gianna or Michele badly—or at least trying to. In his young mind, he'd thought them the ultimate moral authority, with everything they were doing being for the best. After all, they knew better. Now, though? He saw the truth for what it was. He'd been blinded by his love for them and he'd been blinded by everything else around him. All of it leading to that Sunday lunch, the time when everything had fallen apart—the moment Raf's eyes had started opening. He blamed himself for everything, for it had been his inherent weakness to stand up to those he loved that had led to this. And ultimately, that same weakness had hurt someone else he loved—yet this time it was someone who was truly blameless.

The following days were worse. At school, the only place he saw Michele these days, Raf couldn't help the way his eyes would always search for him.

Though he was the younger brother by a few months, he'd always been Michele's protector. Now, watching the humanity seep out of him one step at a time, Rafaelo didn't know if he could deal.

Deep down, he knew he should step away and leave Michele alone. It was the least he could do after ruining his life. But he couldn't.

The *fixer* in him would not allow that. Because to let Michele truly go off the rails would mean he'd truly failed. And for someone who'd never failed at anything in his life, the prospect of that terrified him. Almost as much as the reality he found himself in.

Slowly, though, he started calibrating himself. It was that, or simply lose himself to the grief bottled inside of him that threatened to be let out. And if there was something Rafaelo knew, it was how to push his problems and worries away—how to bury his own wants and desires as well as his sadness and his sorrow. He'd done that for as long as he could remember.

So he tried it now, too.

Instead of focusing on everything that was wrong in his life —that his mother was constantly trying to pretend nothing happened or that his father was becoming more and more demanding of Rafaelo in an attempt to bury his own fault in the whole debacle—he decided he could focus on making sure Michele was ok.

He didn't know how he intended to do that, but he decided it was his duty. He'd pushed him that far, it was up to him to lend him a hand and bring him back to a modicum of normalcy.

As those thoughts arose in Raf's mind, he didn't realize how entitled that sounded, or the fact that he wasn't putting Michele's well-being first. Rather, he was only looking for ways to lessen the guilt *he* felt. And that was the only way he knew how.

He didn't realize that his brother kept his distance for a reason—that every time Michele gazed upon Raf, it was to remember everything that had happened to him; that he was reliving every bit of that torment all at once. He couldn't know, because like the former Michele, Raf was also in a bubble. The only difference was that Michele's had burst sooner. Raf's bubble had been deflating steadily over the years, but it was far from destroyed.

The *main* difference was that Rafaelo still had hope where Michele had none. But he was too young and inexperienced to read that on his brother. All he saw was someone in need of saving. And wasn't that what Raf did best? Save, please, fix?

Over the years, he'd become what everyone wanted of him, never what *he* wanted of himself. In this instance, the pattern was merely repeating. Instead of accepting that his deeds likely could never be forgiven, at least not without the proper explanation that he was reluctant to give, he decided to mold himself after what Michele needed.

And the first order of business was saving his brother from his own self.

One afternoon, before classes even finished, Rafaelo decided to follow Michele. For a while now it had been a mystery where his brother was going when he was skipping school. As he had no friends that Raf knew of, he was afraid he might be involved with bad people.

He was careful to keep a distance as he saw Michele head to the nearest bus station and getting into the first bus that came. Raf, not wanting to be overly conspicuous, took a cab and paid the driver to follow the bus.

To his everlasting relief, Michele didn't seem to know he was being followed. As he got off the bus in the Bronx, he walked until he reached a gym, going inside.

Raf frowned. He didn't know his brother to be interested in working out, and his physique didn't show any signs of exercise.

He stepped closer.

twenty-five

AGE FIFTEEN

The doors opened, and Michele came out again, this time accompanied by a gentleman. Both were smoking and talking, Michele seemingly hanging on every word the older gentleman was saying.

As Raf got a better look at him, he was shocked that he recognized him. He was... But that couldn't be right, could it? How would Michele know Nicolo Lastra?

As part of his training with his father, Raf had been given information on all the players in the city, and he knew all the other Italian families and what their stakes were. In principle, it had been a way of getting to know the enemy but also to know *not* to step on any toes when doing business. The Italians were extremely territorial of their interests, and they preferred to have business monopoly over whatever industry they were interested in. There were exceptions, of course, when two families would decide to unite their capital and work together. But that was usually done through marriage, and as far as he knew, Nicolo had no children. Valentino, the current head of the Lastra family, had no children either.

The more he racked his brain for an explanation for why

Michele would be meeting with Nicolo, he could not come up with anything. So intent he was on figuring that out that he heard the buzzing sound of an incoming bike too later. He jumped out, startled. The biker cursed him before going off again.

The commotion got everyone's attention. And as Raf looked across the street at his brother, it was to lock eyes with Michele. He scowled at Raf. Putting out his cigarette, he exchanged a few words with Nicolo before crossing the street, his stride determined as he walked towards Raf.

Raf straightened his back. He'd gotten this far he wasn't about to back down. Especially since he was afraid Michele might have gotten himself in trouble. If Benedicto found out he was hanging out with Nicolo, his son or not, he would *not* be kind.

"What the fuck are you doing here?" Michele gritted his teeth as he reached his side, his finger jabbing in Raf's chest.

They were similar in height, puberty doing wonders for both of them.

Raf blinked.

"What are *you* doing with Lastra? What the hell, Michele?"

"Is that it? You're spying on me?" His lips drew up in a sardonic smile. "Are you going to tell daddy that I'm hanging out with the enemy? Maybe make a traitor out of me, too. After all, that's the only thing I haven't been accused of," he laughed, but his eyes were unsmiling.

"I wouldn't do that," Raf was quick to defend himself since he would *never* hurt Michele that way. But his words lodged in his throat as he realized he already had.

"Right. You wouldn't," Michele mocked. "Go home, Rafaelo. There's nothing for you here. Go and do your worst," he spit at Raf's feet before he backed away.

So shocked Raf was by the turn of events that he could only

react when Michele was already across the street, entering the gym.

He might have gone after him if it hadn't been enemy territory. He might have done a lot of other things, but God, he felt his guilt eating him on the inside so badly he could barely react to a confrontation with his brother. And while it wasn't in his nature to be so subservient, his shoulders felt too heavy with the weight of his sins to be able to stand up straight—to have any more dignity left.

One last look at the entrance of the gym, and he made his way home. He couldn't tackle the issue anywhere but at home. Regardless of what it took, he wasn't about to lose his brother—though deep down he knew Michele was already lost to him. But as he looked around and he saw the desolation and the emptiness, he couldn't help but hope. His logical mind faltered at that, but his soul was unwavering. He *needed* to be absolved of his sins. An undeserved mercy, but one that his soul needed to continue to function Otherwise... he didn't know how he could live with himself.

When he got home, he quickly scribbled a note, sliding it under Michele's door.

It was a long tradition of theirs to sit and talk on the roof, and Raf hoped Michele would remember those good times—remember that despite their different positions in life, they had *been* brothers.

And though Raf now knew Benedicto wasn't Michele's biological father, he didn't think of him any less of a brother. They'd grown up together for God's sake. They'd been through so much...

With a deep sigh, he returned to his room, finishing his homework and making sure everything was done by the time night came around.

His heart in his throat, he made his way to the roof. He just hoped Michele would show up. That he would listen to Raf...

He opened the attic trapdoor, climbing up before hauling himself on to the roof.

A lone figure stood in the distance, cigarette smoke wafting from him and into the night. He was wearing a tank top and a pair of jeans that rode low on his hips. Michele had always been on the skinnier side, but with his increase in sight, he looked even leaner.

"I got your note," Michele said as Raf came closer. He didn't turn. He didn't move. He continued to puff his cigarette, his head tilted back as he looked at the gathering of clouds marring the sky.

It was going to rain.

Raf quietly made his way to Michele, taking a seat by his side and looking into the horizon.

"I'm sorry." He uttered the words, his voice full of shame. When Michele didn't reply, he continued, steeling his voice. "What you want, I'll give it to you. But in exchange..." he drew in a harsh breath, his voice trembling.

"In exchange?" Michele turned, lifting a brow and narrowing his eyes at Raf.

"Stop hanging out with Lastra. Stop this rebellious act you put on. I'll give you what you want, but please, go back to the old you..."

Michele laughed.

Raf drew back, blinking furiously as Michele kept on laughing.

"Old me?" He took a step forward. "Old me, Raf? What does that mean? The pushover from before? The one who took every type of abuse in silence? That old me?"

"No," he shook his head. "The old...nice you," he attempted a smile.

"Nice me?" Michele mocked. "Hear that," he chuckled. "I'm sorry to tell you but that me is forever gone. That me died the moment you decided to betray me yet again. Again and again. Because once wasn't enough, was it? You had to do it again and again, wipe out every bit of humanity out of me."

Raf's eyes widened, and he couldn't believe his ears.

"What..."

"That's what you did, Raf. You betrayed me until I had nothing left. Nothing but pick up a fucking gun and end my goddamn life," he accused bitterly.

Raf stared into his face, the truth there for him to see. God, and it was a truth that shamed him until he was barely coherent.

"I-I d-don't know w-what you're t-talking about," he stammered. His skin erupted in goosebumps though the weather was pleasantly warm.

"Of course you don't," Michele sneered. "Was it worth it?"

"W-what?"

"Becoming heir? Taking everything. Was it worth it?"

"I..." he faltered. "I didn't do it for that," he whispered, but there was no one to hear him. Not when one look at Michele's face told him there was no way his brother would ever believe a word that came out of his mouth.

Thunder boomed in the distance.

Michele's fingers were wrapped in Raf's shirt, holding him close yet so far away.

"What did you do it for, then?"

There was a pause as rain started falling, big drops landing on their skin. The sounds of thunder intensified, light flashing into the sky.

They stared at each other, both breathing hard with the intensity of *their* emotions.

"What did you for it, then, eh?" Michele repeated, his voice raised to make up for the background noise.

"I did it for you!" Raf yelled. "Goddamn it, I did it for you!"

Michele's eyes widened for a second before he burst into laughter.

"Is that why you spread the rumors, too? For me?" The laughter turned manic.

"Rumors? What? What rumors?" Raf frowned, but he didn't get to ask more as a punch landed on his face.

He didn't avert his face, taking that blow and the one that followed. He kept himself still. If Michele wanted to work his demons on him, Raf would let him. God knew, he deserved every bit of that and more.

The more Michele hit, the less Raf moved, not even making a sound of pain.

"Oh no, you don't get to play the martyr," Michele sneered. "You don't get to sit there all saintly. You don't get to fucking make *me* the bad guy!"

Raf didn't answer. He couldn't. He only knew he was getting what he deserved, nothing less.

"Fucking fight me, damn you!" Michele shouted, throwing him back. "Fight me!" He yelled, aggression rolling off him, but something else too.

Raf saw it. Just like he saw this was all his fault. It was in the pain that marred Michele's features, the agony that oozed every time he shouted at Raf.

He recognized the pain because he shared part of it. But he could never share it all, not after what Michele had been through. He closed his eyes and he took it.

Another blow.

"Fight me!" Michele demanded.

Raf shook his head.

"Beat me if that's going to help you. Fucking kill me!" he cried out. "But I *am* sorry, Michele. And I'm willing to give you everything. Everything," he breathed out, blood pouring out of his nose and split lip.

He hurt physically, but it was only a shadow of the pain he felt inside.

"Just do it!" he squeezed his eyes shut as he saw Michele's raised fist, his body getting ready for the upcoming pain.

It never came.

His hands in his shirt, Michele hauled him up again, bringing Raf's bloodied face close to his.

"Goddamn you, Raf. Why?" He asked the question, his voice broken. "Why?"

"Hate me if that's going to help you," Raf finally uttered, the words taking *him* by surprise.

From the beginning, he'd set out to get his brother's forgiveness—to make him see that the path he was embarking on was the wrong one; the dangerous one. But as he looked at Michele —as he *truly* looked, he realized that nothing could right that wrong.

Ever.

Their relationship was doomed—had been doomed from the beginning.

The more he clung on to Michele, the more he tried to bring him back, the more he pushed him over the edge.

He *finally* realized. His help wasn't helpful for his brother. It was only for his conscience's sake—a very selfish reason that was just registering. And it was all because he was witnessing the raw pain on his brother's face and the fact that it seemed to be the default expression whenever he looked at Raf.

"Hate me," he repeated, almost numbly. "Hate me but don't destroy yourself for my sake," he told him.

Michele shook his head, his lips flattened in pain.

"Too late, Raf. Too late."

He let go. Taking a step back, he let go of Raf.

"Please, just leave me alone. I told you, and I'll tell you again. You're null to me." His emotionless mask was back on. Then he turned to walk away.

"Then why did you come here? Why did you come if I'm nothing to you?" Raf asked. In Michele he saw what he himself felt. They both had a hard time letting go, even though holding on was causing too much pain.

Michele didn't answer. He took another step.

"Liar," Raf called out. "You're a fucking liar, Michele, and you're not going to fool me."

His brother was still there, and damn if he wasn't going to keep holding. Because he saw traces of the old Michele. And while *he* was there, then Raf would still be there too.

When Michele didn't answer, Raf grabbed on to his shirt in an attempt to pull him back.

"Did you hear, you're a fucking liar."

"Fuck off, Raf," Michele burst out, turning just to jab his elbow in Raf's side. The push wasn't too powerful, but the rain had already stained the ground, making the entire surface slippery.

One moment Raf's feet were planted on the ground, the next he was thrown back. Everything happened so fast, he barely had time to grab on to the ledge as his legs dangled in empty air, a gasp escaping his lips as he looked down, at the distance between where he was and the ground.

Michele's eyes widened, and before he could think about it, he thrust himself forward on his belly, grabbing at Raf's hands, holding tight.

"Fuck, Raf," he cursed, his voice tinged with worry. "Don't you dare," he muttered. Raf didn't hear. His heart was drumming in his ear, the storm raging in the background. He could only hear his throbbing pulse and the fact that he was one step away from death.

He looked up, his gaze terrified as it met Michele's equally so.

"Don't let go," his brother gritted out, doing his best to pull Raf back.

But Michele barely had any strength. More than anything, Raf's weight was pulling *him* down. And as he slid on his belly until the edge of the roof, Raf realized it wasn't going to work.

"Let go," he said, trying to get his hands free.

The more Michele held on, the more Raf panicked. He was going to fall—he knew that. At this point, regardless how many seconds it took, it was a certainty. But he wasn't going to take his brother with him. He'd be damned if he was going to hurt Michele again.

"Let go!" he yelled, pushing at Michele.

"I'm not letting you die, you little shit," Michele retorted, his face taut from effort. He tried once more to pull back, but the friction only caused him to slide down further.

Further and further until...

"No!" Raf's eyes widened in horror.

The rain continued its assault, and they were both drenched from head to toe.

"Let go, please," Raf pleaded.

If Michele tried to pull him again... If he didn't let go...

"I won't, Raf. You're not dying today," Michele bit out, flexing his arms and getting a better grip on Raf. Taking a deep breath, he tried to pull again.

Raf closed his eyes, tears and blood mingling with the rain. He only opened them when he heard the snapping sound.

He was falling.

His brother with him.

He'd held on until the very last moment. In that split second, Raf realized that if by a miracle, they survived, he would let go. Like he should have done from the beginning.

He would finally let go.

* * *

When Rafaelo opened his eyes, he had no idea what had happened. His mind was a whirlpool of confusion. Only the smell of bleach and sanitizer registered, his eyes slowly honing in on the bare walls of the hospital room.

Someone was arguing next to him, the words bitter on his tongue.

At least one thing hadn't changed.

"How could this happen, Beni? *How?* Our Raf hasn't woken up in days. *Days!* And that devil spawn got away with only a few scratches. By God, I'm going to kill him with my own two hands..."

"Control yourself, Cosima," Benedicto grabbed his wife's hand, his tone shushed. "You can't say shit like that in public."

"What? That I'm going to kill that son of a bitch? Because I will, Beni. Mark my words, I will. I'm sure he was behind Raf's accident. Otherwise why would he be on the roof in the first place? In the middle of a storm, too? That monster must have lured him somehow..."

"Stop. Just...stop." His father said in a resigned voice. "There's nothing we can do now, is there?"

"Of course there isn't. You let him get away. How could you?"

"He was discharged from the hospital, Cosima. There was nothing I could have done about that."

"I still can't believe that he got away with nary a scratch while my baby's languishing in this goddamn bed. What if he never wakes? What if..."

Raf moved, a low moan escaping his lips.

His mother turned, her eyes widening as she saw him awake.

"Raf, thank God!" She spared no time in dashing to the door and yelling for a doctor.

Awareness slowly trickled in, as well as the fact that his arms and his left leg were in a cast. He wasn't even sure he had any feeling in them until he tried to move them, pain radiating everywhere.

In spite of everything, his mind was quick at work. He realized he'd banged himself pretty badly in the accident. Still, by all intents, he had been incredibly *lucky* to survive such a high fall. The fact that he knew Michele had been even luckier filled him with so much joy he wasn't bothered anymore about his lack of mobility, or the close to intolerable levels of pain he was in. If anything, that pain told him he wasn't paralyzed, which was yet another good thing.

And as the doctor came in to check on him, he was told exactly what injuries he'd sustained—broken limbs and a pretty severe concussion. All mild for the height he'd fallen from.

"You were very lucky, young man," the doctor declared, telling him he'd make a full recovery.

Raf hadn't spoken yet, and though his mother badgered him for it, the doctor said it was normal for him to be in a state of shock. The fact that he reacted to words and he understood when spoken to meant there was nothing wrong with him. Just shock.

It wasn't shock as much as quick thinking on Raf's part. He understood the moment he found himself in as one given by fate —both in the fact that he'd survived, *and* that he could now pay his dues. He could finally repent for everything he'd done, and in the process, maybe, his soul would become *slightly* lighter, too.

For the rest of the day he didn't speak.

No matter how much his mother prompted him to, how much she cried by his side and cursed Michele, he didn't say one word.

Ironically, now that he was locked within his body and forced to sit alone with his thoughts, his mind was clearer than it had ever been. Maybe the fog had been removed by *that* rain, or maybe, the pain chased it away. In any case, for the first time, he saw his situation with startling clarity.

He was guilty. No matter the circumstances, he was guilty. And all this time, he'd only attempted to assuage his *own* guilt by trying to convince him to forgive him and go back to who he used to be. Laughter bubbled in his throat as he realized how entitled he'd been.

Instead of letting Michele heal at his own pace, leaving him to his own devices, Raf had held on. He'd pushed and pushed, wishing things could go back to normal when there was no such thing as normal—not anymore. He'd been so focused on his pain that he'd disregarded his brother's.

But now... With a heavy heart, he knew it was time to let go.

Of everything.

The following day, when the doctor came to check on Raf, he unwrapped some of his head bandages to check on his wound and asked him some questions.

"You know what happened?"

Raf opened his mouth, closing it and opening it again a few times before finally forcing the syllables out.

"I-I f-fell."

The doctor frowned.

"How did you fall?"

"S-S-slipped," he eventually said, pretending he was having difficulties speaking. He stumbled over his words, losing track of his thoughts and mistaking meanings. All in an attempt to make people around him believe something wasn't quite right with him.

"How old are you, Rafaelo?" The doctor asked, all the while jotting down his observation.

"F-Fifty o-one," he answered, his face straight, his eyes wide and innocent.

Everyone faltered around.

His mother drew in a stilted breath. His father paced around before exiting the room while the doctor kept his professional cool.

"I see," he simply nodded, continuing to ask various questions that had to do with his life, as well as with media, current events and commonly known historical facts. Raf got them all wrong somehow, but not in a blatant way. He was simply off, suggesting he had an idea what he was talking about but his brain couldn't access the necessary knowledge and put it into coherent words.

He managed to keep his act up for the entire time, making it seem like he had difficulties not only speaking but also concentrating.

Cosima became hysterical by his side when the doctor announced his concussion had likely caused more damage than previously thought, and ordered a new series of tests.

"Raf, my baby," his mother cried after the doctor left. "What did that devil did to you, my darling boy," she kept bemoaning, holding on to him and whispering how much she loved him, and how she would never do anything wrong again as long as he got better.

He didn't get better.

Tests came and went. Diagnosis changed, but no one could figure out what happened to Raf.

"The brain is a complicated organ, Ma'am," one doctor said, implying the injury was beyond doctors' abilities.

After weeks in the hospital, when his casts were cleared, his limbs slowly working again, Rafaelo was discharged.

Yet when he got home, nothing was ever the same. Starting with his own life.

At school, the change was most significant.

Overnight, his status as the *golden boy* was gone, replaced with slurs like retard, stupid, weirdo, among others. Where once he'd criticized his brother for not standing up to his bullies, he learned it wasn't as easily done as said.

People who used to like him left him. People who used to admire him now spat insults at him. Everyone saw him as weak, a *freak* and everyone laughed in his face.

He took it in stride—it was what he'd signed up for.

His brother, though, avoided him. He saw Raf get picked on, he saw the change in his life, and he never once asked him if he was fine. Which, in Raf's opinion, was better. It was easier for him, too, to make a cleaner break—to finally let go of their bond.

At home, Benedicto was visibly distressed by the turn of events, though he did not want to admit. He pretended everything was fine and that Raf would eventually get better and resume his previous lifestyle. More than anything, he didn't want to let Raf know that the *famiglia* was already talking about him, saying that no one like that should ever hold a position of power.

Yet *that* was exactly what Raf had wanted in the first place.

By retreating into his own self and by changing the way people were regarding him, he was finally free from everyone's expectations of him.

He could finally be...him. Or, at least, given the current limitations, he could try.

His mother was the only one who didn't change. After the initial shock wore off, she accepted his condition as permanent and she devoted herself to taking care of him, fussing over him and showering him with all her love.

Raf felt bad about deceiving her, but he also knew what she'd done. *That* was his dilemma. How could he reconcile the loving mother who accepted even her handicapped son to the vile person who'd wanted to hurt his brother in the worst way imaginable?

He couldn't.

And so he settled into a status quo. He neither accepted nor rejected her help, treating her with a neutrality that was killing her on the inside—almost as much as his changed mental ability did.

"N-no," he shook his head, slumping his shoulders as he found himself in one of the secluded corners of the school courtyard. Travis, one of the boys who'd once been his friend was now mocking him openly.

They had dragged him off in one of their breaks, and he'd had no way to avoid them. If at the start they would only insult him and give him a shove here, one there, this was the first time they'd physically assaulted him.

Only a few months after his accident had passed, and his limbs were not completely healed, though he could now move enough to go to school and resume some of his old habits.

His teachers had made allowances, giving him extra time for his assignments and enrolling him in special classes for students with learning disabilities.

If in the beginning it had been harder to keep up his act, the more he did it, the more he became accustomed to be this *new* Rafaelo. And there was the added benefit of seeing everyone's true face. No one stuck around him. Everyone laughed, one way or another. Or like Travis, mocked and pushed him around. He saw it, the envy that had been masked before by obsequiousness. And God, was he happy to be rid of those people, even though the current circumstance didn't appeal that much to him.

"You thought you were the best, didn't you," he laughed. "Let's see if you still think that now."

On his knees, Raf simply cowered back, hunching his back

and stammering his words in question. He didn't even look at his new bullies, simply waiting for them to say their piece and leave. Except, this time they didn't.

They didn't mock him. They just...

His eyes on the ground, he felt the first jet of piss hit him in the head, drenching his hair. Travis was the first to do it, the other boys following soon after.

Raf stood, unmoving, his eyes wide in shock.

What...

The laughter continued as they mocked Rafaelo, bringing up all his past achievements and how those wouldn't help him now.

He didn't know how much time passed before they left, but he only dared look up when the snide remarks echoed in the distance. His body trembled, his injured leg aching while his mind was simply numb. Yet as he turned his head around, he noted a dark figure at the end of the alleyway, leaning against the brick wall and watching him with narrowed eyes.

Michele.

His brother.

He brought his cigarette to his lips, taking a deep drag while he maintained the eye contact, only to throw the butt to the ground, stomping on it as he backed away.

As if he'd never been there in the first place, he was gone.

Loneliness crept into Raf's heart. He'd chosen his way. He'd knowingly gone down this path. Now he needed to bear the consequences of his decision.

Even if that might kill him along the way.

twenty-six

AGE SIXTEEN

"Are you sure there isn't anything else? Something you haven't found yet?" Cosima demanded of the doctor.

"As I told you, Mrs. Guerra, the brain is unpredictable. Your son is physically healthy. The problem is entirely mental."

"But you must *fix* him," she added in a tremolos voice, her feet turning to jelly as she grabbed on to the table for support. "You must fix him," she repeated, sneaking a glance behind her to find her son lost in his own world.

"I'm sorry. There's nothing I can do," the doctor sighed.

"Doctor," she hissed, pulling on his white coat as she motioned towards Rafaelo who was currently at the far end of the room. "Look at my son. Look at him! He's black and blue. His classmates bully him. He might not tell me, but I can tell that's where the bruises are from."

"I can sympathize with your situation, Mrs. Guerra. But I can't do anything on my end. You should probably look into transferring him to another school."

"He's my child, doctor. *My* child," her voice broke as she watched her son and the state he found himself in.

A year had passed and instead of getting better, her darling

Raf had gotten worse. Not his condition—that was forever the same. But his morale had fallen to the ground, and Cosima could see the signs of abuse at his school.

He never told her anything, of course. He'd rather invent the silliest excuses, like he'd tripped and fallen, or that he'd accidentally hit himself with the door. But she knew the truth.

Rafaelo, her darling Raf, was being bullied.

And she could do nothing about it.

"Can you also check if his arm is dislocated? He's been having difficulties lifting it," she added to the doctor.

Shaking his head at her fussiness, he proceeded to give Raf a full body consultation, noting the various bruises and the wounds he claimed he'd gotten from *accidents*.

"This is serious damage, young man. You could report it..."

The doctor didn't get to finish his sentence for Raf suddenly drew back, a look of pure shock on his face.

"N-o," he shook his head. "I-I'm j-just c-clumsy," he confessed, lowering his chin in embarrassment.

Everything hurt.

Everything had been hurting for so long, Rafaelo didn't know what it was like to *not* hurt anymore.

Funny how everything had changed in the span of a year. Michele, who had previously been the pariah of the school, was now the untouchable. Not because people respected him, but because he struck back. Most were worried they'd get their asses handed to them so they stopped picking on him.

He was just...there. When he was present, which wasn't very often.

Rafaelo, on the other hand, had taken his place at the bottom of the school's hierarchy. As such, everything that had been previously done to Michele had simply changed targets, and was now done to him.

The worst was that he couldn't even defend himself—though

sometimes he desperately wanted to. No, to do so would be letting his act slip and he could not afford to do that. It only took one person to realize he was faking everything for the rumors to start, which would ultimately reach his parents.

From the moment he'd taken his quiet vow, wrapping himself in the guilt he felt deep in his heart, he'd known what he was embarking on. Over the years, he'd witnessed how vicious people could be to those who were *less*.

Odd how Rafaelo had always tried to be inclusive with everyone, regardless of their disabilities. Now? Even those people he'd been nice to in the past were awful to him. He understood why, to a degree, since being nice to Rafaelo would make them pariahs as well. They were protecting their own social status.

And that was the most important lesson he'd learned.

Everyone was looking out for themselves.

When he'd decided to atone in the most extreme of ways, he'd known all that was to come—mayhap he'd also wished for it.

After all, it was nothing more than he deserved.

Pain, pain and more pain.

So much pain until he could finally breathe out with relief—sometime at the end of the tunnel.

It wasn't the physical pain that crippled him, though that was nothing to scoff at. It was the mental one—the fact that he felt trapped within his own body with all his mistakes on replay. More than anything, there were those images that had become seared on his retina. Of his brother being abused. Of everyone laughing and discounting Michele's story—including himself.

Then there were the threats.

He wagered he'd never had the time to come to grips with everything that had happened and Antonio's overtly lewd suggestions hanging over his head. He was ashamed of that, since he knew what his brother had been through. Yet he couldn't help but feel sick every time he remembered Antonio grabbing his dick or touching him inappropriately.

There were also those times, deep in his mind, when he wondered what would have happened if he had accepted to switch places with Michele.

Could he have saved his brother? Could he have lessened his burden at least a little?

But just as soon as those thoughts arose so did the realization that he was a coward—the *worst* type of coward.

He'd balked at being fondled a little, how could he have withstood what Michele had?

For that, he was deeply ashamed.

Once Cosima finished with her harangue of the doctor, Raf was given some pain medicine and some soothing cream for his injuries.

Not a few days later and he was back at school—his new personal hell.

He knew he could easily tell his mother about the bullying and she'd take measures—after all who dared to disregard Cosima Guerra. But he saw that as taking the easy way out.

Michele had kept quiet all along and he'd never had anyone to champion him as Rafaelo did. For that alone, he didn't want to make a mockery of his brother's experiences by asking for help.

The conflict with Michele had affected Rafaelo in such a way that he couldn't differentiate between right and wrong, fair and unfair.

In his mind, it all came down to evening out the scales.

He knew he'd likely never be able to suffer everything his brother had. But he could try.

Worst of all, it wasn't for any acknowledgement from Michele, or hope for a future reconciliation once his brother saw the extent of Rafaelo's penance.

No, it was strictly for him.

Because Rafaelo couldn't live with himself knowing what he'd done.

The only way he could be at peace with himself at some point in the future was if he paid for his transgressions with his blood and tears—the same blood and tears his brother had repeatedly shed.

Rafaelo might have a highly developed sense of justice, but he kept himself to an even higher standard than other people. He didn't realize that he was killing himself with his own hand— that step by step, his so-called evening of the scales was taking such a toll on his psyche that he was becoming a shadow of his former self.

He only saw the end goal and the harrowing journey that would take him there.

All his life, Rafaelo had wanted to be good to others and make them happy. Yet time after time, he'd done the exact opposite.

Whoever said the road to hell was paved with good intentions must have had him in mind. Every time he acted in good faith, someone got hurt. Every time he tried to help, he made things worse. Maybe it was better that he kept to himself— creating an outer persona that the world shunned and abhorred. That way, he could protect himself and those around him.

He wouldn't mess up again, and he wouldn't be tortured for it in return.

Despite all the suffering, he supposed there was light at the end of the tunnel. He just had to work hard to reach it.

The first week that he was back, though, things were better than they'd been in a long time. So good, in fact, that Raf started suspecting something might be afoot. But all that suspicion went away when problems arose in his own family. As such, he could only be grateful from the respite at school while he mentally and emotionally dealt with what was happening at home.

It all started when he overheard a conversation between his father and his mother—one he knew very well he should have *never* heard.

He was going downstairs to grab a glass of water when he heard some noise coming from his father's study. Usually, he would have avoided it, but this time he heard his own name.

Curious, he tiptoed until he reached the half-opened door, sticking his ear right next to the wooden frame.

His mother's voice was the first to reach his ears.

"You need to calm down, darling. The doctor said he's optimistic. Maybe we can..."

"For fuck's sake, Cosima. Look at me!" Benedicto shouted. "Do you think I have the time to wait around for my handicapped son to become even more handicapped? People are waiting for me to make a decision. You know that. They've been on my back for too fucking long."

"Well," she took a deep breath, "just tell them Rafaelo's health is coming along and..."

"They don't want him. No one wants him. No one but you," Benedicto said in a weary voice. "No one but you," he repeated as he released a sigh.

"That's not true," his mother said on a hopeful tone. "You want him, too, right? This is just temporary. You know that our Raf is a bright young man with an even brighter future. You know how kind and smart and special he is."

"Maybe he was. But he's nothing right now, Cosima. *Nothing*. He's just..." Benedicto gritted his teeth. "I should have killed him that night. I should have killed him and spared us from this shame. You don't go out anymore so you don't have to hear the rumors, the whispers. But I do. And it's not pretty. Everyone is pitying us. They say we don't have what it takes to lead."

"Don't say that, darling. Please..."

"You shouldn't have stopped me, love. You shouldn't have..."

Rafaelo drew in a stilted breath, barely able to comprehend what he was hearing.

Kill him?

His father had wanted to...kill him?

No, surely he was hearing it wrong. His father loved him. He was sure of that. Benedicto may have become more aloof since Raf's diagnosis. But his father loved him.

Didn't he?

"I could have done it. One second and he would have died. He would have spared *us* the disgrace, and he would have spared himself the humiliations he's going through right now."

"How can you say that?" Cosima asked on a broken sob. "He's our child, Beni..."

"He's nothing more than a waste of space. More than that. He's bringing us down just by existing," Benedicto said through gritted teeth. "You think I don't know about the bullying? About what people are saying?"

"Then why... We need to help him—change schools. Anything to make this go away."

"And have people brand us as cowards because our son couldn't even withstand a few high school boys?" Benedicto sneered. "Categorically no. He brought it onto himself when he jumped from that roof and when he tried to help that monster. He did this with his own hand," he paused for a moment before delivering the last blow. "You didn't let me kill him then. Maybe those boys will finish the job for us. Then we'll be seen as grieving parents. Not the parents of a retard."

Rafaelo couldn't listen anymore. His heart thumping in his chest, he hurried to his room, making sure he was quiet enough to not attract any attention.

The last thing he needed after hearing his father speak like that was for a confrontation. And what could he even say?

That maybe his father was right.

Rafaelo shouldn't have survived that night.

Deep down, he knew that, maybe even wished for it. But he also recognized that death was the easy way out—the coward's way out.

Maybe he'd been cowardly before when he'd been unable to make a decision regarding his brother. But he wasn't about to live his life like one anymore. He was going to face life and his mistakes with his head raised high.

That didn't mean that his father's words didn't...hurt him.

They did.

They cut him on the inside like little else had done until then—not even the bullying or the horrifying insults he was forced to listen to on a daily basis.

His own father wanted him dead. He'd just been unable to get the job done.

Until that moment Rafaelo hadn't realized how his condition had affected the family. And as he closed himself in his room, sliding to the floor and watching the play of shadows on the wall, he couldn't help but wonder why life was so hard.

Why were people so superficial and self-absorbed?

He supposed now he could add another person who'd turned his back on him at his lowest.

It was moments like this that made him wish he could cease to exist—simply erase himself from everyone's thoughts. He wagered they would be much happier without his existence marring their lives.

His brother, Michele. His former friends who were never really his friends. His father.

And even his mother. Despite the fact that she continued to stick by him, Rafaelo didn't fool himself that it would be forever.

Eventually she would realize he was truly a lost cause and he could do nothing to prevent that—not while still holding to his oath.

As he went to bed that night, his father's words haunted his mind, paining him more and more.

Though initially he tried to explain Benedicto's sentiments in a rational manner—that anyone would scoff at having a burden of a child—eventually he lost all sense to simmering anger.

Rafaelo was Benedicto's child. His *child*. How could he think about killing his own blood? The person he'd raised from infancy?

He couldn't fathom how anyone could do something as atrocious, by deed or by thought.

If Rafaelo ever had a child, he knew he would never be capable of something like that. Hell, he couldn't even do it against his bullies and the people who wanted to hurt him. But to act against his own child?

He couldn't conceive something more preposterous.

That anger lingered, and the following day at school it threatened to spill.

Though he'd been given a small reprieve from his bullies, it seemed they were ready to pick up right from where they left.

Class ended sooner than expected, and Rafaelo slowly made his way to the exit, ready to head home. It was at that time that he was intercepted by one of the kids who often picked on him, and the insults didn't take long to come.

Retard. Idiot. Stupid. Brainless.

Soon they'd have to search for more insults since the current ones had become too basic. Certainly, Rafaelo was already too used to them to pay attention. He just kept his head down and sought to keep his calm until they got tired of picking on him and they allowed him to leave.

"Why are you still alive, freak?" Another boy joined, sneering at him. The words, this time, were accompanied by physical blows, and Rafaelo lost his equilibrium, falling to the ground.

His injuries from last time had barely healed, some bruises still tender. The pain radiated in his body, making him visibly wince in pain.

Mocking laughter and violence.

The two constants in his life.

"You should have let me kill him."

His father's words rang in his brain, and in an unprecedented show of strength, he defended himself, placing his hands over his face before swinging his fists forward. He didn't aim for anyone in particular. He just aimed at his fate and the pitiful sight his life had become.

"Fuck," one of the boys spat at him. "He's fighting back isn't he?"

"You dare fight back?"

Just as he thought he hit one of the guys, he felt his entire skull reel with the force of a punch, his eyes rolling to the back of his head before his entire body became limp. Falling to the ground, he continued to hear the laughter and feel the spit landing on his face.

Yet he found it hard to move. Or, the sudden rage he'd felt at the world had slowly subsided to a pathetic resignation.

He clung to the hope that they'd get bored of him soon and let him leave. But that didn't seem to be the case when two boys grabbed him, one holding his arms, the other his feet.

Dragging him back to the school building, Rafaelo's sense of self preservation slowly started to kick in.

It may have taken him a few seconds to shake off the shock, but when he did, he started flailing his limbs in an attempt to get out of their grip.

But it was a few seconds *too* late.

Before he could get his bearings together, the guys swayed with him, gaining momentum before throwing him inside a dark room, the clicking sound of a lock alerting him he was all alone.

More laughter and promise of retribution before the voices became more and more distant.

But Rafaelo couldn't think about that—couldn't even recall his bullies' words. Not when the most putrid smell assaulted him. Even worse was the realization he was sitting on something soft. Something...

His stomach rebelled, and before he could help himself, he turned his head to vomit on the side.

The entire room was dark. The entire room was filled with feces and bodily fluids and now his own vomit. It was even worse as all those smells accumulated not only in his nose, but also in his mouth, his tongue coated with the most putrid taste. It was in times like these that he regretted his awful condition and the additional pain it brought him.

He was stuck inside. The door locked. Discomfort seeping into his skin.

First, panic took over, as did the sickness at being around all those noxious smells and feel the substances coat his entire body. No amount of mouth-wash, or soap could chase away that feeling.

He supposed it was a small mercy he couldn't see himself covered from head to toe in shit—one more sense to add to the cacophony of the others and the way his misery increased by the moment.

But that thought went out the window as he banged his hands against the door, yelling for anyone to let him out. He did that until his voice became hoarse, until the tears dried on his face.

Everything became more tragic when he realized his phone

was nowhere to be found. The boys must have taken it before they'd dumped him in the room.

His pulse sped up, and the stench coming from everywhere around him threatened to make him ill again.

Still, he wasn't going to give up.

Everyone might want him dead, but he wasn't about to give them that satisfaction.

He might have his own sins to pay for, but he was still alive—and would continue to be so.

A new resolve took shape within him. The more he thought about the satisfaction people would get at his expense, the more he decided he wasn't going to give it to them.

He would survive, and he would prevail. And once he'd paid his dues, he would just disappear somewhere into the world where no one knew him. He would start a new life and would finally live on his own terms.

Maybe the guys had thought they would wear him down with their disgusting tactics. But they hadn't counted on the opposite effect as his current circumstances only showed Rafaelo what to expect from the world—nothing.

Absolutely nothing.

He could only depend on himself—*would* depend on himself.

He was only indebted to his conscience and no one else. And once that was washed clean, he would live for himself and no one else.

Finally, he would show his family, too, that he wasn't just a tool to gain power. That he wasn't a puppet to be used and abused for his parents' goals.

His determination soared as he realized this journey was more than just repenting for his past mistakes. It was also about avoiding the worst fate of all—submitting to his father's wishes.

Why would he, when Benedicto would rather wish him dead than useless to his plan?

Though Rafaelo had been shocked by his father's words, he supposed it was what he needed to drop his last bit of guilt towards his family and harden his heart against them.

They would never get him.

No one would.

He would just bide his time until he could finally be free. Of every obligation and responsibility—everything that wasn't of his own free will.

Until then, he would close himself to the world to maintain what little sanity he had left.

Expectation bred disappointment.

And he was done with being disappointed by everyone around him.

If only he could force his heart to stop feeling...

twenty-seven

AGE SEVENTEEN

The raucous noise coming from outside woke him up. Groggily, he brought a hand to his face, scrubbing his eyes in an effort to chase sleep away. His head pounded with the pain of too much vodka and a few pills here and there that he couldn't remember the name of.

It took him a few moments to finally open his eyes and take in his surroundings. He was in a utility closet, the fluffy end of a mop cushioning his head, some aluminum sheets covering his body. He groaned at the realization, but he supposed it could have been worse. The space was small, enough to accommodate his supine form, but it did not allow for additional movement.

He winced as he lifted himself in a seating position, his muscles aching, his stomach rebelling at every slight motion.

"Fuck," he muttered.

Nicolo had organized one of his raves at his club, and Michele had dutifully attended. He wasn't a fan of the parties his friend threw, but Michele knew how to placate him with his momentary presence before he made himself sparse.

Over the years their friendship had developed into mentorship and lately he'd allowed Michele a glimpse into his business, promising to initiate him in it.

As the newly appointed official Guerra heir, he would one day take the reins of his father's business, and he wanted to be ready when that time came. He wanted to prove to everyone that he could succeed, regardless of the hurdles in his path. And so he'd become serious about his studies, investing time and effort into an area that otherwise held no interest to him. But with Nicolo's guidance, he was on the right track.

It was also the reason why he was so careful not to disappoint his friend. After everything Michele had been through, Nicolo had been the only one who'd always stuck by his side, supporting him and pushing him forward to reach his potential. For that alone Michele wanted to do whatever he could for his friend.

Times had changed since the accident on the roof. Benedicto wasn't thrilled to replace Raf with Michele, but the organization demanded it for stability. As such, he'd reluctantly announced that Michele was going to be his successor. Michele knew his father was only biding his time, though, waiting and hoping for Raf to get better so he could resume his position. And Raf... Michele didn't see him recover any time soon.

His brother hadn't only sustained quite severe physical injuries in that accident, but his mind and speech had also been affected. Since then, he'd developed learning disabilities and a bad stammer. Overnight, their places had swiftly changed, with Rafaelo becoming the bullied one at school and the unwanted one at home.

Michele, however, had distanced himself from everything.

He felt bad for his brother, and he knew the longer he stayed at the house, seeing him and his difficulties would only strain his conscience. As such, he'd all but moved out, only spending the

Sundays at the Guerra mansion as Benedicto dictated that was the family time.

Nicolo had given him lodgings at his gym, which had some habitable rooms. Though their condition was passable, Michele enjoyed spending his time there, having already made friends with most of Nicolo's men. There was also Cami, who in such a short time, had become like a mother figure for Michele.

He knew she didn't necessarily agree with a lot of his choices, particularly the more recent ones, but she was kind and gentle in making her point of view known and in caring for him in her own way. For that alone, Michele tried not to upset her too much.

Well...she would definitely be upset if she saw *now*.

Since his failed suicide attempt, and with Nicolo's guidance, Michele had tried to find different mediums to cope with the intrusive thoughts in his mind—the way his brain never seemed to quiet down. He'd taken up boxing, shooting, karting—anything adrenaline rushing that would help redirect his thoughts. And it worked—momentarily. It worked only as much as he gave himself to the situation, pushing his limits and living *out* of his body. The rest of the time...he was forced to live *in* his body.

That was his tragedy.

The worst were his nightmares. They had started during the time Antonio had abused him, and with time, they'd only gotten worse and worse. All his memories—all the nasty, disgusting memories—rolled in his head like a damn movie on a loop. He could barely close his eyes at night for fear he'd relive his rapes again and again. It also didn't help that he'd developed an aversion to people—or, more specifically, people's physicality.

He abhorred being in close quarters with another person. But more than anything, he hated when someone's naked skin touched his own. Just one touch was enough to bring all those memories back to the surface—make him relive everything that had happened to him. More than anything, it was *that* night he always relived, when he'd been caught between two bodies, the sweat dripping down his flesh, the suffocating heat permeating his skin.

His condition and the numerous triggers that, well, *triggered* it, made it hard for Michele to live like a normal human being. To that effect, he was mostly a loner. He kept to himself in his small room at the gym, interacting when it was necessary but otherwise occupying his time with his studies, and sometimes, his art.

Unfortunately, even that had taken a blow. The more unstable his mental state became, the more stifled his creativity was. He would stare for days at the same piece of paper, trying to draw something but he could not.

He was still living in hell, but for the people who had hope in him—the people who'd extended kindness when no one else ever had—he was willing to stay alive. Michele didn't have any goal for himself. Everything centered around making his *new* family happy.

In the Guerra household, everyone thought Michele had tried to kill Rafaelo for the position of *don*. It couldn't be further than the truth.

Though he'd thrown it repeatedly in Raf's face, Michele had no interest in that damned position other than spiting everyone who'd wanted to take it away from him. If anything, it had been Nicolo who'd advised him to be careful and not throw away the opportunity to claim his legacy. He'd been the one to nudge Michele in that direction, telling him he would love to see him where he belonged. And with Michele's still set ways about violence, he'd implied that it would be the best revenge on the family that never wanted him.

He'd agreed.

After all, Nicolo's opinion mattered so much to Michele that he sought to push himself to his limits to make sure he wasn't disappointing his friend.

If Nicolo invited Michele to a party, he went. If he asked Michele for a favor, he did it. It was that simple.

And *that* was the reason Michele presently found himself in a closet, sleeping on a goddamn mop and with a throbbing headache. He'd wanted to please his friend. And in the process he'd probably disappointed Cami.

If she found out...

Which Michele hoped she wouldn't. She already disapproved of his smoking, though he'd repeatedly told her it was like a nervous tic. When the urge to do *something* arose, a drag of the cigarette calmed it down. It wasn't a cure, but it was a temporary fix. And by God, he did need something to keep him from constantly wanting to blow his brains.

He hadn't intended to go too far.

When Nicolo had told him he had a rave planned for the weekend, Michele hadn't asked too many questions. He'd been to some of the other parties his friend had organized and he'd always found himself a secluded corner in the VIP section from where he watched people—his favorite activity.

This time, however, things had been a little different, starting with the venue. Nicolo had rented a much bigger one. The downside? It was on one level, all open space—no secluded nooks or corners. The VIP section was by the stage where everyone could bump into Michele and rub themselves on him.

In the beginning, he'd told himself that he could withstand it for a little bit before excusing himself and leaving. But when he'd approached Nicolo that he was ready to go, the older man had told him no, that he expected Michele to have a good time and stay until the event ended.

Michele, being Michele, had been unable to tell him no.

So his nightmare had truly begun. The only way he'd managed to withstand it had been by overindulging in alcohol, and anything else he'd been offered in an attempt to numb himself and his overactive mind.

He was seventeen now, almost a grown man, and although on a daily basis he avoided men and women alike, in *that* setting, he couldn't. People had bumped into him, they'd touched and they'd groped—everything he detested. But Michele didn't realize that even though he tried to make himself as unappealing as possible, with his buzz cut and his piercings, or with his nails painted black, he still oozed a certain kind of magnetism that made people want to get closer. His face alone, though currently holding an edge with all the changes he'd done to himself, still appealed to both men and women.

It probably took him all of five minutes to know he couldn't stay until the end of the night—at least not sober.

At first, he'd been plied with vodka by Nicolo's men, all of whom wanted to make a good impression with the boss. Michele had lost track of how much he'd drunk, but it hadn't been enough. So when he'd been offered some interesting-looking pills with the promise of numbness, he'd readily accepted.

Only he hadn't counted on *one* consequence—the loss of control, which he dreaded as much as touch.

That realization had hit him approximately half an hour after he'd ingested his last pill. His sight had dimmed, his coordination had taken a hit, and his overall focus was close to non-existent. People he'd never talked to before had suddenly come up to him, being a little *too* friendly. And so he'd *known* he couldn't continue there. Nicolo might be disappointed, but better that than find himself *again* in a position where his choices were taken from him.

He had a vague recollection of how he'd gotten out of the

crowd, his memories jumbling in his brain. But he'd still had enough control to know he needed to isolate himself until he was well enough to take care of himself. And so he'd gone from door to door until he'd found what he was looking for—a secluded room that could be locked.

That is how he'd ended up in the utility closet, where he'd promptly passed out.

"Fuck, Cami will have my head," he squeezed his eyes shut, resting his head in his hands.

She would no doubt hear of his behavior and would give him one of her sad smiles. She wouldn't tell him off, but he would see the disappointment in her eyes anyway. And that was enough to send him into a panic.

The disturbance outside grew louder and louder. There were voices arguing accompanied by all sorts of other noises, and Michele finally found it within himself to move.

Turning the lock on the door, he stepped out, the light hitting his eyes and making him grimace in pain. His headache was mounting just as the yelling grew louder.

"I need coffee," he mumbled, teetering on his feet.

Maybe the excess indulgence from last night was *not* completely out of his system. Still, he knew he needed to get himself together. He would likely have to explain his whereabouts to Nicolo and help him deal with the aftermath of the rave.

As he stepped inside the venue, the first thing he noticed was the trash. There were bottles, glasses, confetti and even used condoms thrown on the ground. His nose twitched in disgust as he made his way towards the stage where Nicolo with a few of his men were arguing, a few other guys already on the floor, their faces covered in bruises as they moaned in pain.

"Michele," Nicolo turned sharply, looking him up and down for a moment before he nodded, as if to himself.

"What happened, Nico?" He asked as he reached him. They've become so close that he was now allowed to use Nicolo's nickname, a fact that made him very proud as it put him among the few that had that honor.

"You snuck off somewhere last night, didn't you?" Nicolo's expression was amused, not at all annoyed as Michele would have thought. "There didn't happen to be a woman, too?" he wiggled his eyebrows suggestively.

Michele scowled.

"No. I passed out somewhere in the back," he said matter of factly, not wanting to make a big deal out of it.

"Well, son, while you were passing out somewhere, we had a bit of an issue with some unwanted visitors," he stated, his nose wrinkled in disgust.

The unwelcome visitors, it seemed, were some of the gangs from the area, who'd heard of Nicolo's raves and had rightly assumed there would be a lot of demand for drugs. Whether they'd thought it would be a chance to expand their own business, or that someone was encroaching on their territory didn't matter, as Nicolo explained. They had entered the rave and had caused trouble, assaulting some of the women and getting into fights with other men.

"You know I have a very strict attendance policy," Nicolo nodded towards the men groaning in pain. "It's very easy to lose control of an event like this, which is why I don't allow outsiders."

"Where were they?" Michele motioned to their men, who were supposed to monitor the influx of people coming into the club.

"They swear they didn't leave their positions. That they simply overpowered them," Nicolo shook his head.

There were eight men, all on their knees in front of Nicolo as they swore up and down that they didn't leave their positions and that they tried to keep them from entering but were unable to—as evidenced by the injuries on their faces.

One of them, a guy about Michele's age, found the courage to speak up.

"I swear, sir., I didn't leave my position all night," he raised his chin, looking Nicolo dead in the eye. "When they came... I just couldn't hold them off," he sighed.

He looked the worst from the bunch. Both his eyes were swollen, and bruises were forming down his neck.

"Did they do that to you," Michele pointed to the bruises.

He swallowed, his eyes wide as he debated how to answer.

"Yes. I told them they couldn't come in..."

Michele nodded.

"Were you alone?"

His eyes widened, and he looked at his fellow colleagues, almost as if for help. They gave him an odd look, one that Michele didn't miss even in his hungover state.

"No, sir. We were all where you assigned us. It was just too much..."

"Damn it," Nicolo cursed, bringing his fingers to his temples. "I can't let this slide, you realize that," he told them sternly.

Michele narrowed his eyes at the line of men.

All sported bruises and had seemingly been injured in this incident. Theoretically, the fact that they'd tried to stand up to the outsiders put him in the clear, at least from the worst punishment he knew Nicolo would not hesitate to implement—death. But they would still be punished. Still, Michele had the vague impression something was off.

"How many outsiders were there?"

"I don't know. About five that I spotted on the CCTV."

"What about the CCTV at the entrance?" Michele asked, though he knew Nicolo would not be holding this meeting if he'd seen the evidence of what had occurred.

"They destroyed the camera when they arrived. We could only check the inside of the venue."

"Five against eight," Michele remarked, his eyes glinting with suspicion. He moved closer.

The men made to move too.

"Tsk, tsk," his tongue clicked against the roof of his tongue, his gaze enough to make them to stop.

The youngest was the one who'd spoken. The rest, he reckoned to be in their twenties.

He crouched in front of them, his shrewd eyes quick at work as he perused their faces and made note of their injuries.

"Don't bother," Nicolo called out with a resigned sigh. "I'm just going to give them a month at the docks as punishment and that's that," he added dismissively.

A month at the docks wasn't that bad, but it wasn't good either. It was the type of work that could put a man in the hospital if he was unused to that type of labor. And it would definitely not bode well for the smallest of the bunch.

"Let me check something," Michele added, giving Nicolo a look.

"Suit yourself," he shrugged, the shadows under his eyes visible. He was tired—had likely not slept at all yet. For that reason, Michele decided he needed to be fast—confirm or rebut his suspicion so Nicolo could go rest.

"What's your name?" He asked the youngest one, all the while fishing into his back pocket for the pair of gloves he usually had on hand. Cami had been the one to give him that idea when he'd confided how hard he found it to even shake hands with people. She'd gifted him a beautiful set of thin leather gloves that he used in his daily interactions.

The boy blinked.

"Andreas."

Michele shrugged the gloves on, coming closer to them.

The men flinched, looking a little out of their element. Michele narrowed his eyes.

"Tell me, Andreas, did you fight them off?" He asked as he leaned in, taking Andreas' hand and examining it. Scratches were present around his knuckles, the skin peeling away. There were other bruises too, and Andreas winced as he pressed on the tender skin.

"Yes, I tried, sir," he answered dutifully.

He nodded.

"What about you?" He asked one of the other men, randomly stopping in front of him.

"Of course! I tried my best," he said, a little loudly, before swallowing uncomfortably.

Michele repeated the same action, taking his hand and looking at the knuckles.

There were bruises, but the color was off—a few days off.

He did the same with man after man, realizing that most of them had clean hands, and those who did not had days, or weeks old worth of bruises. Nothing as recent as Andreas did.

His head still pounding, he found the strength to smile as he sharply turned towards one of the men. Before he could move, Michele wiped his gloved hand across his face, right in the spot where his *bruise* was.

The man startled, jumping back and falling on his ass.

"My, but that's one contagious bruise," Michele chuckled, turning his glove and noting the specks of dust, some quite shimmery, that were left on the black of his leather.

"Anyone else share this affliction?" He asked, amused.

"What are you talking about?" Nicolo suddenly voiced out his question, coming closer.

"It seems we have our answer to the five to eight dilemma. It was a rather five to one fight, wasn't it?"

"What?" Nicolo frowned.

Michele explained his theory, that the other men had left the youngest alone and then forced him to lie that they had all been overwhelmed in a fight. To make it more believable, the others had drawn bruises on their skin.

"I'll be damned, son," Nicolo whistled in admiration. "I guess we have to switch punishments a little, don't we?" He chuckles. "You're good to go, Andreas, but don't think I'm letting you off the hook. You did lie to me..."

"Why don't we do it a bit differently? Why don't you let Andreas help me? You were already talking about finding someone to work for me, and he could be a good fit," Michele put forward the idea, appreciating how the man had not betrayed his colleagues and had stood steadfast in front of danger. Loyalty, in any shape or form, wasn't something to scoff at.

"Is that so?" Nicolo murmured pensively. "Fine, he's yours. Now let's see what we're going to do with these..."

As Nicolo found a fitting punishment for the other men, Michele gave his new subordinate his first orders.

"Can you drive?"

"Y-yes, sir," he nodded fervently, his eyes wide and looking at Michele as if he were a god descending among mere mortals.

Andreas was a fine looking man with black hair and brown eyes. But he was also a *young*-looking man.

"By that I mean, are you of age to drive, Andreas?"

"Yes, sir, I am nineteen and I have a driver's license." Andreas promptly answered.

"Good, then let's go."

Nicolo had a few cars in the parking garage, and spotting his valet, Michele asked which one he could use. He was given the keys and he threw them at Andreas, giving him a nod as he climbed in the backseat of the chosen car.

Immediately, he sprawled himself on the couch, his eyes closing. Damn but he needed some pain medication. Otherwise he didn't know how he was going to survive the day.

"Stop by a pharmacy," he gave a languid order, dictating to Andreas a list of items to buy.

The last he heard was a *yes, sir,* before he fell asleep.

The next time he opened his eyes, he was still in the car. The sky had already darkened and he noticed they were in the parking lot of the gym.

Andreas noted he was awake and was quick to tell him he hadn't wanted to wake him up and incur his wrath, and that he'd bought everything he ordered from the pharmacy.

"Good," Michele grunted, getting out of the car and rummaging through the pharmacy bag. He took out the box of ibuprofen he was looking for and thrust the rest to Andreas.

"For your bruises," he mumbled before he made his way to his room at the gym.

He turned so quickly he missed Andreas' expression and the awe with which he was regarding Michele. He also missed the look of pure adoration Andreas gave him for no one had ever done something so nice to him. Indeed, the young sir had cleared his charges, had taken him under his wing and now had given him medicine? Andreas didn't know how to react to someone so kind. Immediately, he vowed he would do his best to be a model employee so that his young sir would never complain about him.

Growing up, he'd never found his place in the world, but he reckoned he was about to.

When he'd been just five, his mother, Paulina and his uncle, Juan Fernando, had decided to cross the border from Mexico to the States. His mother had been shot during an altercation at the border, and he'd been left with his uncle, who wasn't fit to care for a child. He'd more or less raised himself while his uncle worked an odd job here, one there, and when he'd gotten involved with the mob, he'd taken Andreas with him.

Juan Fernando had met his end by going against some debt collectors when Andreas was only fourteen. Luckily, by then Andreas had already met some of the people from the Lastra family and had resolved to work hard to earn his place. For years now he'd been doing small work where he was needed, and so far, it had been enough to put a roof over his head and food in his belly.

But with his new boss... Andreas had a feeling that things were going to change—and he was very excited about that.

twenty-eight
AGE SEVENTEEN

It took Michele a little more than twelve hours to sleep off the effects of the alcohol and pills he'd ingested—making him vow to never mix them again.

Upon waking up, he did his morning routine, changing into fresh clothes and getting ready for the day. It was already summer vacation, which meant he wasn't going to school. And as he'd promised Nico, he was going to help him with the management of the gym.

Nicolo had various businesses, and while the gym was his place of comfort, sometimes he didn't have enough time to go over its management. Michele had been the one to volunteer. After all, he was living on the premises, might as well earn his living by proving himself useful.

Sneaking a glance at the clock, he noted it was seven in the morning. The gym wouldn't open for another couple hours, even to its employees. When he realized he wasn't in a hurry, he pulled some of his sketches, grabbed a pencil and tried to complete his latest drawing.

There was one thing he hadn't given up on, though he would never admit it to anyone. Though he found it hard to draw most days, he didn't want to give up. Lasso was the only thing he *could* focus on, and though the story was etched in his mind, it was becoming harder and harder to materialize it on paper.

A few strokes on the paper and he put the paper back in his drawer, muttering a curse as he scrubbed his face with both hands. Knees drawn up; he took a shaky breath as he stared at the white wall.

Some days were harder than others. Some days he didn't know how he got out of bed. And some days...some days he wished he were anyone but himself.

The clock ticked as seconds, then minutes ticked by.

His breathing grew more labored before it calmed. Only when his attack subsided did he pull himself up, donning his gloves. He was ready to face the day when he wrenched the door open and stopped in his tracks.

"What?" His eyes widened as he spotted Andreas not far from his door. He was on the floor, using his jacket as a pillow.

At Michele's raised tone, he opened his eyes, recognition slowly seeping in.

"Sir," he jumped to his feet.

"What are you doing here Andreas? Why are you sleeping on the floor?"

"I live pretty far and I didn't want you to wait for me in case you needed something..." he made the excuse, a hesitant grin on his face as he scratched the back of his head.

Michele merely cocked his head to the side, studying him. The clothes he was wearing weren't bad, but they were tattered and worn out. He'd probably been using them for too long.

His shrewd eyes took in Andreas' jeans and the too short hem. He wondered how long he'd owned that particular pair.

"Nicolo said you're to work under me from now on, which means I own you, you understand that, don't you?" Michele drawled, leaning back against the wall and watching the young man squirm under his scrutiny.

He wasn't a fighter, that much was for sure. But he seemed to have a good sense of loyalty.

"Yes, sir. I work for you now," he nodded emphatically.

"Good. Now that we got that out of the way, let's go shopping. You're going to represent me and that means you need to look your part."

Andreas tried to argue, but Michele put one hand up and all chatter ceased.

He simply got in the backseat of the car and told Andreas to drive to the nearest mall. In the meanwhile, Michele asked him a few questions, wanting to get a sense of his situation.

Andreas lived somewhere in Long Island, sharing quarters with other six men, and had lived like that for the past two years. He'd had no formal schooling, but he knew how to read and write in Spanish and English as courtesy of his roommates, who'd taken pity of him and taught him the basics. He knew his way around numbers and could do basic arithmetic, but so far he'd only been hired for menial jobs—like guarding venues or cleaning.

Andreas enthusiastically told him all about his past, and Michele noted another thing about him. He had a bright, positive disposition. He could definitely use that.

More than anything, for brief moments, he could see his old self in him. Yet he pushed that thought aside. He was going to give Andreas a chance to prove himself.

At the mall, they strolled around, browsing the choices. Michele noted Andreas looking longingly at some of the items, and made an excuse to get him whatever he needed, one way or another. Nicolo wasn't stingy with money, and he'd given Michele a card with an unlimited spending limit. Since he wasn't using much on himself, he was sure Nicolo wouldn't mind this little spending spree.

After Andreas was fitted with a new suit, shoes and updated cell phone, they were ready to return to the gym.

"Thank you so much, sir. I promise you won't regret it," he added fervently as they got into the car.

"Good. I'll hold you on to that," Michele answered noncommittally.

As soon as they reached back, though, Michele pointed Andreas to a door down the hall from his own.

"You take that from now on, since you said you live too far away. This way you're always there when I need it."

"Sir..." Andreas blinked. "Thank you," he swallowed painfully.

Michele waved his hand.

"Good, get yourself comfortable. I have something to do."

"Yes, sir," Andreas replied before heading to his assigned room.

Leaving Andreas to his own devices, Michele headed to the office wing of the gym. Cami had already arrived, punctual as always.

"There you are, darlin'," her face brightened when she spotted him. "Come, let's get coffee, shall we?"

She didn't wait for Michele to reply, busying herself around the table that housed the kettle and instant coffee.

The gym wasn't luxurious, and that included its rooms and equipment. It was used more for the training of Nicolo's men, and it was rarely accessible to the public unless they were directly recommended by someone within the organization.

"Morning, Cami," he finally said, giving her a hesitant smile as he took a seat at the small table crowded in the corner.

"I heard from Nico that you had quite the night," she chuckled, raising a brow at him.

He felt his cheeks heat in shame, and he just nodded.

"We had to deal with some of the men," he mumbled.

"You know that's not what I'm talking about."

She handed him his coffee in a paper cup, taking a seat opposite him.

Popping a cigarette in his mouth, he lit it up, waiting for her comments. He wasn't looking forward to them, necessarily, but he was glad someone cared for him enough to give them to him.

"Nothing happened. I just had a little too much to drink."

"Nico says it wasn't just alcohol," she added quietly, but her eyes were down-turned with worry.

He swore softly under his breath. It seems Nicolo had been quite attentive to what Michele was doing.

"A few guys offered me some pills," he shrugged. He didn't want to make a big deal out of it, but he didn't want to upset Cami either. "It wasn't the best experience."

"I'm glad. I wouldn't want you to... You know," she smiled.

"I didn't realize our section would be in the pit. And you know my issues with too many people."

"I know," she nodded. "But I'd rather you avoided those events than force yourself to take God knows what to cope."

He didn't answer. Pursing his lips, he focused on the steam wafting from his coffee.

"I never told you how I met Nico, did I?" Cami suddenly said, and he whipped his gaze up to meet hers, slowly shaking his head.

She was such a pretty woman, but not in the conventional way. Her beauty came from her kind and soft manner and how she nurtured everyone around her. When Michele had first met her, she'd been in her early thirties and had already been with Nico for over a decade.

"I was eighteen when I moved to L.A. with some of my girlfriends, all of us having our dreams of independence," she smiled fondly. "We partied, we had fun. It was quite the time of my life, or so I thought. I met this guy, Leo. He was so charming and sweet in the beginning, inviting us to parties and paying me a lot of attention. Back then I was so starved for attention that I would have done anything to impress him.

"He was the first one who introduced me to drugs. Back then ecstasy was the party drug of choice. And honestly, in the beginning, it was the best thing ever. We were young, having fun, and the pills only enhanced that state."

She paused, taking a cigarette from her pack of slims and lighting it.

"What happened?" He asked, a little afraid of the outcome.

From the way her fingers trembled as she took a deep drag, he knew the story unsettled her.

"It all started with molly. But when we had no money for it—it was quite expensive, you see—we took whatever we could. It took me a couple of months, I think, to get hooked on meth." She smiled sadly. "And if there's something that goes hand in hand with meth, it's prostitution."

"Leo was your pimp, wasn't he?"

"In the beginning," she nodded. "He got killed on Skid Row in a gang altercation. After that, I moved from one pimp to another. Honestly, I was high out of my mind most of the time, I hardly remember a lot from that period. But at some point I ended up sold to one of the higher end brothels from outside the city.

"That's where I met Nico." A lightness appeared on her face. "He told me he recognized I didn't belong there, and he bought my freedom. He brought me with him to New York, and we've been friends since. He helped me detox, and I haven't touched any drugs since."

Michele nodded thoughtfully.

"It's so easy to get addicted to that shit, darlin', and it's so fucking hard to quit it. You have no idea how long it took me before I could even say the word *drug* without craving some."

"I know," he sighed. "I know the dangers. I don't want to make a habit of it either."

He didn't add that he craved the state of numbness the drugs gave him. He wouldn't go down that path because it meant so much more than just forgetting his existence. It would be forfeiting his fate, and that wasn't something up for negotiation —not ever again.

"Addiction isn't the only danger, unfortunately. And trust I'm saying this with the utmost love, darlin'," she reached out, her hand grazing his gloved one. "I don't even know how many hands I've been passed through. Everything blurred together at some point. But there were men. Many, many men that I would have never said yes to if I'd been aware."

Her voice was filled with pain as she blinked not to shed a tear.

"You're an attractive guy, darlin'. There will be those who will try to take advantage of you. I just want you to take care of yourself, ok?"

He nodded, his throat clogged. He couldn't speak because he knew very well what she was talking about. It was only now that he realized their pasts were more similar than he'd thought.

"Nico was my saving grace," her expression changed, turning sweeter, a dreamy look descending on her face. "He showed me I was worth more, that I *should* demand more."

"So... Are you lovers?" Michele hesitated to ask the question, but he'd always wondered about their relationship. He knew Cami was a regular in Nicolo's life, but he'd never been able to find out in what capacity.

"Sometimes," she shrugged. "Nico is a difficult man. He doesn't do steady."

"Doesn't that bother you? That he may have other lovers?

You love him, don't you?" Michele had observed as much. Cami looked at his friend as if the sun rose and set with him.

Cami chuckled.

"I've always loved Nico. And he loves me, too, in his own way. But it's not *that* type of love. He's not capable of it anymore."

"Because of that girl, no? The one he wanted to marry?"

"You're pretty astute," she smiled. "Yes. She's always been his obsession. In life and in death... But that's his story to tell. If you're curious, you'll have to ask him," she winked.

"Did you meet her?" Michele probed. He'd always been curious about Nicolo's private life. He was not married, had no children, and seemed to be the consummate bachelor. Yet he knew of that one woman who could have owned him, a long, long time ago.

"Once. It was right before she died. She wasn't...well. But I believe she loved Nico, too. She just had the misfortune to catch his brother's eye first. And that man," Cami shuddered. "He was a sadistic fuck who took pleasure in hurting women. Poor Liliana, I don't want to imagine the life she led."

That was the last Cami imparted about Nicolo and his great love, quickly switching the conversation to less morbid subjects. They took their time with their coffee and Michele told her all about Andreas, his new subordinate.

"He's a good one, I can tell," he declared confidently.

And that prediction would, indeed, come true. Andreas wasn't just a good one. He was the only one who would stick by Michele's side—through thick and thin.

* * *

A week later, Michele was intently studying Nicolo's books

when he realized he'd smoked his way through an entire pack of cigarettes.

He sighed.

He hadn't even realized he'd been cooped up in the office for so long.

Though he was good with numbers, mainly because of his excellent memory and an ability to do complicated calculations in his mind, he didn't necessarily enjoy it. But he knew that in this field of work, such skills were valuable, and Nicolo trusted him with a lot of confidential information from his businesses, so he resolved to do the best he could.

It was also something, he reckoned, that would help him in the future, when he would—willingly or unwillingly—take the reins of the Guerra businesses.

He picked up his phone to call Andreas, ready to send him on an errand to get him more cigarettes. He didn't answer.

Frowning, Michele got up from his desk and went out. Andreas wasn't likely to be far away. He'd only been working for Michele for a week, but he didn't have any complaints about the man. It was visible that he was doing his best to please Michele, and he valued his position. That made Michele a little uneasy about his absence.

He crossed the hallway into the main gym, stopping just as he reached the double doors that led towards the boxing ring. Raised voices told him to be on alert, especially as he heard some racial slurs and a bunch of other sexual innuendoes.

He pushed the door open.

Two men well in their thirties were standing in front of Andreas, their stances overconfident as were the smirks on their faces.

Careful to not draw any attention to himself, Michele stayed in the back, simply listening.

One of the men was pushing Andreas around, asking him if he got his position by offering sexual services.

"Come on, you can tell us," he laughed.

"N-no," Andreas denied, staring at the ground and shaking his head repeatedly.

Michele narrowed his eyes. There were fresh bruises on his skin, around his neck. He couldn't see too well from his position, but he wagered that they were hand prints...

"You're not fooling us. No one would hire someone as dumb as you for that position," they mocked.

Michele supposed that working directly under him was considered a lofty position by mere foot soldiers. Yet that didn't excuse the way they were handling Andreas.

And if he *was* Michele's subordinate, then it was his duty to make sure he was safe.

He casually strolled inside, reaching for his boot and pulling out a pocket knife. Juggling it around his fingers, he sported a bored expression on his face as he stopped right by the trio.

"I heard you have questions for me? If that's so, you can ask directly," he addressed the older men.

They blinked. Then, they laughed.

Michele wasn't sharing the amusement.

"I'm sorry, sir," Andreas immediately added, coming to his side.

"If you're sorry then I need you to tell me exactly what happened, and what they did to you."

Andreas' eyes widened. Slowly, he nodded, and leaning in, he whispered what had occurred.

He'd been cornered by the two men as he was coming to the office to ask him if he wanted coffee. Andreas had tried to get them to leave him alone, but he'd heard these people didn't take well to outsiders, so he'd gone along with them for fear they would do worse, or put a bad word for him.

Michele listened, his face expressionless.

It was true that there was some sort of inner circle even among Nicolo's men. Depending on their position and proximity to him, some were more important than others. Given that Andreas was Michele's *only* man, that put him in a somewhat higher position than those men. Clearly, they hadn't taken it too well, especially considering Andreas' age, ethnicity and physical form.

Probably the most important thing to note was that he was *not* Italian, as were the two men and ninety-nine percent of the people within the inner circle. It was almost unheard of to allow anyone else that close to the core of the organization, which Nicolo had done by allowing Andreas to work under Michele.

The more Andreas spoke, the more Michele realized the issue was all Cosa Nostra politics, and the fact that they did *not* take well to any non-Italians. Luckily for him, though, he cared nothing about tradition or conventions.

"Say that again," he nodded to the men, both still regarding him with arrogant smirks.

"What? That we're wondering how he got the job? It's no biggie..."

He didn't get to finish his words as a scream permeated in the air.

Michele's knife lay firmly lodged in his eye. While he was still lean since boxing was only a pastime rather than something he was good at, he had one thing going for him—his aim.

"What was that? Why don't you start from the beginning?" Michele narrowed his eyes at his companion. "Say it to my face. Why do you think I hired him?"

He'd overheard enough to know what they were suggesting. After all, hadn't he heard the same thing his entire life? He wondered if he had a neon sign over his head that simply spelled out *gay*, regardless of whether he swung that way or not. People saw his pretty face, his lean body and how his tastes for clothing and jewelry ran and immediately assumed that he was gay.

In the past, it would have upset him. Now? He'd had plenty of time to exorcize those demons. He was who he was, and he had no issue with it. He didn't care that he came across as *this* or *that*.

"I..." He stumbled over his words when he noted Michele's serious demeanor. Though his friend was howling in pain, he kept himself still, quiet.

"Not so brave now?" Michele raised a brow.

They could take a swing at him—they were almost double his size. But even they recognized the chain of command. They could pick on Andreas. On Michele, however, they could *not*.

"What's going on here?" Another voice boomed from the back.

Michele didn't have to turn to know Nicolo had entered the gym, no doubt taking in the blood pouring from the man's eye and the shrilling screams of pain.

"Son, you have something to tell me?" Nicolo narrowed his eyes at what was obviously Michele's knife sticking out of the man's eye socket.

Michele shrugged, merely leaning forward and plucking the knife, unfortunately taking the eye with it. The man collapsed to his knees, his screams already getting too much.

For someone who'd always eschewed violence, Michele was showing a great nonchalance for it. And that didn't escape Nicolo, who found himself intrigued by the scene in front of him.

Michele gave him a quick round up of what he'd walked into, and Nicolo nodded pensively.

"Lorenzo, you know Michele has full authority over this place in my absence," he said in a smooth voice. "That you'd question his decision is akin to questioning mine."

"No, *signor,*" Lorenzo was quick to apologize, gritting his teeth through the pain of losing his eye.

"Hold," Michele suddenly said, instructing him to put out his hand. When Lorenzo did, Michele slid the eye to him. "Go to doc, maybe you can still salvage that."

Michele doubted it was possible, but he wanted to show Nicolo that he was not a slave to baser impulses. He might be engaging in violence, but it was *calculated* violence. After all, he was obsessive about his control, growing even more so as the days passed.

Nicolo gave them a short speech about respect, after which he told Michele to follow him in his office. Andreas stayed behind, but he looked at Michele as if he were his savior.

Nicolo was the first to enter the office. Michele walked behind him, taking a napkin and cleaning his knife as he closed the door with one foot.

He was about to make a joke when Nicolo suddenly turned, his palm connecting with Michele's cheek in the most unexpected slap.

The knife fell from his hands.

His eyes widened as he blinked and blinked, unable to believe his friend would...

"Do not, *ever*, apply punishment to *my* men yourself. You come to me first, you understand?"

Nicolo said in a stern voice.

Immediately, Michele understood where he'd gone wrong, and duly nodded, accepting his fault.

He'd been so incensed on Andreas' behalf that he had forgotten that small detail.

"I apologize," he simply stated.

Nicolo nodded, rounding his desk and taking a seat, inviting Michele to do the same.

"Now that's out of the way, I had something to discuss with you."

Michele raised a brow.

"I know you already had the conversation with Cami, but I wanted you to hear it from me too."

"If it's about the drugs, then I know," he nodded. "I promised Cami I won't make a habit of it."

"You're a good kid, Michele, but you're not living," Nico added with a sigh. "I see you and the lengths you go to avoid people, that you barely socialize. I'm not criticizing your work, since you know that's flawless. But you're not *living*, son, and that worries me."

Michele nodded.

"What exactly do you mean by living?"

"What do you do in your free time?"

He shrugged.

"I study and sometimes I draw."

"In your room."

"In my room," he agreed.

"I'm glad you chose Andreas since he seems like a nice lad. But, son, you don't have any friends."

"I have you and Cami," Michele protested. "I don't need anyone else."

"You're a teenager, Michele. You *do* need friends. And you need to live like a normal teenager. God knows, when I was your age I was doing all kinds of things," he chuckled. "Mistakes. It's called youth for a reason. It's the only time in your life when you can get away with *anything*."

"But I don't *want* anything. And you know people my age are different," he answered quietly. "They have different interests and besides... It's not like there's a line of people wanting to be my friend."

Michele refrained from adding that though the bullying had

stopped, his reputation as pariah continued. They still made fun of him, just not to his face anymore.

"What about girls? You're at the age to date, experiment, have fun," Nicolo continued, and he seemed almost incensed on Michele's behalf because he wasn't out there living it up like everyone else.

It was on the tip of his tongue to point out that he *wasn't* like everyone else. That he'd been different before what had happened with him, too. He'd never had an interest in girls like *that*. But he didn't want to disappoint Nicolo further, especially since he seemed concerned about Michele's wellbeing. And after his impertinence earlier...

All Michele wanted was to please his friend—show him he had no reason to regret taking him on when he didn't have to. But more than anything, he was grateful for everything Nicolo and Cami had done to him—more grateful than he could ever put into words.

"You know my problem," he said softly.

Nicolo knew Michele had an issue with touch, that skin to skin contact revolted him more often than not—as evidenced by the fact that he never left his room without his gloves.

"I know son," Nicolo sighed. "But you need to get over it one day. You can't shut yourself out like this. Have you ever kissed a girl?"

Michele shook his head, slowly.

twenty-nine
AGE SEVENTEEN

"Damn it," Nico cursed under his breath. "If you haven't even kissed a girl, I doubt you've done much else."

Again, Michele wanted nothing more than to tell Nicolo that he didn't *want* to. That there was something wrong with him because he had absolutely no interest in girls, or kisses, or more. He'd never had. But he kept quiet.

"Listen, son," Nicolo started, a little exasperated. "If you want to put the past behind you, then you need to take a step forward. You will never be able to move on if you don't take a leap."

"What... What do you mean?" Michele blinked.

God, but how he wished he could be normal... But he knew it wasn't something on the table for him—not with how his past had shaped everything in him, but also how he seemed to be naturally built.

If before he'd had no interest in dating, after what had happened to him, he found it nothing less than disgusting. To think of someone else's skin on top of his, of their sweat mingling with his...

He could barely keep a straight face as that image arose in his mind.

"Why don't you try it?"

"Try... What?"

"Come on, don't make me say it," Nicolo shook his head, a light smile on his lips. "Take the leap, fuck a girl, or two..." he trailed off when he noted Michele's reddened cheeks.

"When I was younger than you, my father took me to a brothel to make a man out of me," he chuckled. "I was scared out of my mind; I'll give you that. But the woman who took care of me was kind and patient. Once you get that first time out of the way you'll gain more confidence," he explained.

Michele listened, holding himself stiff as he intuited what Nicolo was going to say next.

"I'll take you to a high-end place in Jersey."

"But..."

"Come on, son, it's high time you became a man, don't you think so?"

Nicolo's tone was friendly, almost concerned. But Michele didn't miss the slight edge to his words.

He knew *why*, too. Just like Lorenzo and the other man were talking about him and his sexual orientation, so were a lot of other people in the organization. That question had hung over his head his entire life, at home making him his father's disappointment while at school making him the butt of jokes after jokes.

Since Nicolo had taken him under his wing, trying to make something of Michele under his mentorship, he knew the rumors would never be truly squashed unless Michele did something to put an end to them. And the more they persisted, the more they undermined his ability in front of Nicolo's man, and by extent, it reflected badly on Nicolo, too.

Though Michele didn't find anything wrong with it, homosexuality was highly frowned upon by made men. Not only did it go against everything *manly* they stood for, but they always found reasons to condemn it by using their religion as a weapon.

For a man in their world to come out openly as gay would likely be suicide. To have rumors of that nature swirling around him? Just as bad.

As Michele noted, Nicolo was getting increasingly impatient with him and his currently reclusive lifestyle. And the more he pondered it, he realized that Nicolo's insistence that Michele attend his parties and raves had all been in hopes that he would let himself go—behave as everyone else did.

But he hadn't.

"You know my problem with touch..." he mumbled, embarrassed. Nicolo was well aware of Michele's issue, and so he put forward another idea. One that told Michele his friend had been giving this serious thought, and all the more made him feel guilty about his shortcomings and inability to be like everyone else.

"I can provide the perfect environment for you. No one will touch you. No one will try to," Nico assured him.

"Nico, I appreciate it, but..." Michele strained a smile, a little at a loss as to how to decline his friend's offer.

"Try it first, and we can talk later," Nicolo interrupted dismissively, his tone sharp.

Michele regarded him carefully before he slowly nodded.

"Fine. I will try," he accepted the offer reluctantly, guilted into it by Nicolo's unusual manner. He didn't want Nicolo to be disappointed in him, or to be inconvenienced by the rumors going around about *his* protégé. Michele owed him far too much for what Nicolo had done for him, and he supposed he could *try*...

If Michele thought Nicolo would forget his idea he was sorely mistaken.

Not a few days later, he sent Michele the instructions, including how to get to the *location* and what to do once he was there.

The appointment wasn't until the end of the week. Still, Michele dreaded it all the same.

Andreas noted the change in his moods and made the courage to ask what was happening the day before he was supposed to present himself to the high end place Nicolo had scheduled him at.

Michele, though usually private about his business, especially since it concerned a part of himself that he wasn't quite comfortable with, recounted what Nicolo had asked of him.

"So he wants you to go to a prostitute and lose your virginity," Andreas blinked, though his expression was devoid of judgement.

Michele nodded.

"If it's a good place, then you don't have to worry about disease or other things," Andreas said thoughtfully.

"That is the last of my worry," Michele muttered under his breath. He was sure Nicolo would never put his health at risk, especially after the scare they'd had with his assaults. Luckily, his tests had come back negative back then. A small mercy.

"I don't see the problem, then. It's not that hard," Andreas shrugged in that simple manner of his. He proceeded to tell Michele of how his first time with a prostitute had gone.

Michele's curiosity got the best of him and he proceeded to ask all sorts of questions, none of the answers helping him with his anxiety.

"It was a mess," Andreas laughed. "I made such a fool of myself the first time. But the lady was kind enough to not laugh in my face," he recounted.

All Michele heard was fluids, fluids and more fluids. Bodies tangled together. Sweat meeting sweat.

His face paled.

"You'll be fine," Andreas assured him.

"Right," Michele forced a smile.

He wasn't so sure anymore...

The following day, Andreas was driving. Michele was in the back of the car, toying with his gloves and wondering what Nicolo had prepared for him.

Just that morning, he'd called Michele to guarantee that everything was prepared to accommodate him, and that he should just trust Nicolo.

Michele had taken the call as a backhanded warning. It displayed both Nicolo's thoughtfulness, and the fact that the decision had been made for Michele. And knowing his friend, he didn't discount the fact that whoever he'd hired was also paid to report back to Nicolo how everything had gone.

He was on pins and needles. Literally. They pricked at his skin, sweat glistening on his forehead as his mind went into overdrive.

He didn't want to do it. Hell, he wanted to continue as he was—away from people regardless of what rumors swirled around him. Michele had never really cared about his reputation. Odd, since it was the thing that had *always* hurt him. But he knew himself—or, at least, the person who he was deep down. He had no control of how others perceived him.

"You ok, sir?" Andreas asked, one hand up as he righted his mirror to regard his boss. He noted the paleness of Michele's features and his chapped lips. He looked like someone going to the guillotine instead of a pleasure house.

"Yes, of course," he muttered, but he didn't meet Andreas' gaze. He seemed to be in his own world, and Andreas was sharp enough to realize there was something wrong with his boss. He didn't react as a normal horny teenager would, and Andreas knew plenty about that, still being one himself.

He'd also heard the rumors about Michele, that he might *not* be interested in women. Seeing how he was behaving, he wondered if there was some truth to that.

They reached the location a while later. As Nicolo had told him, it was a luxurious place. As soon as Michele and Andreas entered, they were greeted with champagne and a hostess came to see to their needs.

"I'm here for an appointment," Michele swallowed his awkwardness as he told her Nicolo had set it up for him.

The woman, recognizing Nicolo's name, nodded.

"Yes, the appointment with special accommodations."

She described in detail what Nicolo had ordered and Michele was, indeed, surprised to hear that his friend had given this a lot of thought.

The girl Michele would be seeing was forbidden to touch him. She would also be bound for the duration of the appointment.

Michele listened to the woman mechanically list all the things he was allowed to do to her, barely able to hide his discomfort.

"We draw the line at violence, sir," she told him sternly. "You cannot mistreat the women under any circumstance. If a problem arises, you call the front desk and someone will come to help you. Each room is equipped with everything you might need. Condoms, lube, toys..." she droned one.

"I understand," he said.

When she was done talking, she required his signature on a document before she led him to the elevator. Andreas followed closely behind, and the woman kept giving him odd looks.

"He's my bodyguard. He's going to stay outside the door," he mentioned. She didn't seem particularly thrilled about the notion but eventually nodded.

"I must confess, sir, I've never seen something like this. It's *really* high end." Andreas whispered.

"It is," Michele grunted, his eyes taking in every little detail of the place.

And Michele couldn't wait to be out of there.

Damn Nicolo and his ideas. And damn Michele for feeling like he *needed* to do it because he didn't want to disappoint his friend.

Reaching the door, the woman opened it with a special key before inviting him inside.

"You have two hours," she said in a business-like tone and left.

Andreas winked at him.

"You got this, sir," he said as Michele stepped inside the room.

Suddenly, the door closed behind him, the sound startling him.

"Fuck," he muttered in a low voice, feeling trapped.

His eyes went about the room in an effort to ignore the figure resting on the bed, her hands and feet tied in such a way that her ass was sticking out—only her ass.

The room was a luxurious bedroom with an ensuite bathroom. It resembled a five star hotel room, except the entire area was decorated with obscene drawings and paintings. There was a big TV in the middle of the room, a silent porno playing on it. Like the lady had mentioned, there were toys, whips, cuffs and other things Michele could not name as well as a bowl filled with condoms and lube.

He took a deep breath.

He couldn't pretend anymore. He was fucking petrified.

More than anything, he was scared because looking around, seeing all the sexual stuff strewn about the room, he didn't feel *anything*.

Even as his gaze finally landed on the woman in the skimpy, see-through lingerie tied to in the middle of the bed, he felt absolutely nothing.

Putting one foot in front of another, he went to the TV, took the remote control and hit the volume up button. Moans and grunts permeated the room.

Yet they didn't have the intended effect. Instead of arousing him, they disgusted him further. He quickly shut the TV.

"Damn it all to hell," he closed his eyes, taking deep breaths as he brought his fingers to his belt.

"I am ready when you are, sir," the girl spoke. She had a soft voice. Still, that did nothing but increase Michele's anxiety.

He was close to shaking, his hands already trembling as he imagined going closer...

His eyes squeezed shut.

I can do this. I can do this.

He kept chanting it in his mind, slowly building up the courage. After all, he was absolutely sure Nicolo would get a full account of what went on.

Slowly, he managed to pry open his belt, tossing it aside and unbuttoning his pants.

But how was he to do anything when he wasn't even hard?

He took a step closer to the girl, forcing himself to look.

Come on...

Nothing.

Absolutely nothing happened. It didn't matter how much he looked, or how he convinced himself he could do it. The girl did absolutely *nothing* to him.

And *that* terrified him.

He must have spent twenty minutes just building up the courage to do something. Yet at some point he had to admit to himself that he was fighting a losing battle.

One more scan of the room, and in a moment of insanity, he made up his mind.

He couldn't disappoint Nicolo.

Picking up the remote control, he turned on the video again, bringing the volume to the maximum. Then, browsing the assortment of toys and accessories laying around, he grabbed a blindfold.

Michele barely held himself together as he neared the girl just enough to place the blindfold over her eyes.

"Shh, it's ok," he whispered, hoping she wouldn't freak out on him. When she nodded, he stepped aside, opening the door to the apartment and dragging Andreas inside.

"Wh..."

Michele lifted a finger to his lips, motioning for Andreas to be quiet. Then, to be sure they wouldn't be heard, he took him to the bathroom.

"Sir... What..." Andreas was bewildered as Michele closed the door to the bathroom.

"Just one question, Andreas," Michele swallowed, going straight to the point. "Do you want to fuck that girl in my stead?"

"W-what? But..."

"She's paid to fuck someone. She didn't see me, she doesn't *know* me. She just needs to fuck someone because she will later be asked if she fucked someone," he was hyperventilating, his speech almost incoherent. "I can't do it. And I mean, I can't *physically* do it," he pointed towards his crotch and the lack of *any* reaction. "I'm not going to make you do it if you don't want to. But do you?" The last question was on a hopeful yet hopeless tone, a grimace painted on his face. Michele was so out of his mind in his panic that he didn't realize how he sounded—how frantic, scared and absolutely terrified he came across to Andreas.

Andreas blinked, the words slowly sinking in.

"Ok," he nodded. "I'll do it."

Michele sighed in relief, feeling a weight being lifted from his chest.

Getting out of the bathroom, Michele went to the window. He took a seat on the windowsill and tried to calm his errant heartbeats.

Andreas simply gave him a nod before he set about removing his clothes. Then, going to the girl, he started touching her, stroking her.

Michele's eyes widened for a moment before he looked away, his cheeks red, his heart pounding in his chest.

The noise from the TV was so loud, he didn't hear anything else. He only saw a few flashes from the corner of his eye, how Andreas was mounting the girl, thrusting in and out of her.

The entire thing lasted maybe another quarter of an hour.

When he was done, Andreas disposed of the condom before donning his clothes back on. They exchanged a couple of words before he was gone, leaving Michele to remove the blindfold from the girl and pretend it was *him* who'd been with her minutes before.

She thanked him for being gentle as she fished out a robe and put it on herself. Michele kept his distance as he nodded, muttering a low thanks.

The girl chuckled, but luckily, she departed soon after, allowing Michele and Andreas to leave the establishment too.

For a long time, they didn't talk. They didn't address the elephant in the room, or the fact that Michele was still reeling from his inability to do something so simple—to act like a fucking man.

It was only when they were back to the gym that Michele spoke. He invited Andreas to his room, taking out a bottle of whiskey and pouring generous amounts in two glasses.

"You're probably curious what happened inside," Michele finally said, though he was dreading the conversation. Still, he knew he had to address the situation, if only to ask for Andreas' help if such a situation would further arise. And knowing Nicolo, it might.

"I wouldn't dare," Andreas shook his head.

"I don't do well with...skin to skin contact," he raised his hands, pointing to his gloves.

"I see," Andreas simply nodded, taking a big gulp of his drink.

"That's not all. I..." Michele grimaced. He hated having to explain that part of himself—the one even *he* didn't completely understand. But he figured if he were to ask Andreas for his help in the future, it would do to have all the facts.

"You don't have to tell me," his subordinate was quick to mention when he saw Michele had a hard time putting his thoughts into words. "It's okay if you...like men," Andreas blushed, dropping his gaze to the floor.

"I don't like men," Michele was quick to say before frowning. "Or, I don't think I do," he sighed.

Why was his existence so complicated? Why couldn't he just...know? He didn't find girls attractive like that, but he'd never found guys attractive either.

"You don't think?" Andreas inquired softly.

Michele shrugged.

"I had a few things happen to me that screwed with my perception, I suppose." He gave him a brief account of what had happened to him, but without getting into details. Just that he'd had some non-consensual encounters in the past that had left their mark on him.

He didn't know why he was telling Andreas all that. He barely knew the man. But God, did it feel good to talk with someone his own age about this—someone who didn't laugh or point fingers at him.

Sure, Nico knew about his past, as did Cami. But they both approached it from different perspectives. Nico wanted him to grow stronger, while Cami wanted him to heal.

He just wanted to...be. He hated that his trauma defined him so much, that it hindered him daily. Yet he found it hard too hard to connect with people, to *try* to move on. Because they all saw the same thing—always the same thing. And they *all* judged him for it.

Maybe that's why he felt more comfortable with Andreas. In their short acquaintance, he hadn't judged him once. And he'd had plenty of opportunity, Michele's idiosyncrasies being far too many.

"Why don't we test it out?" Andreas suddenly said.

Michele frowned.

"I know this club downtown," he continued, telling Michele about a famous club for queer people. "We could try it out. I'll have your back," Andreas smiled.

Michele's lips trembled as he strained to return the smile. He was quiet for a second, mulling over the offer. But before he could overthink it, he said screw it and accepted.

That night, after imbibing some liquid courage, Michele allowed Andreas to take him to the club. But he still took his own measures of safety. On a summer night, Michele wore a long-sleeved shirt and his faithful leather gloves, all in an effort to avoid any skin to skin contact.

When they arrived, they showed their fake IDs before being allowed in. The inside of the club surprised him. Flashing lights everywhere, the loud music took a little to get used to. It was the makeshift stage, though, that got his attention, and he watched riveted as a few ladies came down the podium, dancing around the club-goers and lip-syncing to the song.

Andreas leaned in to whisper that they were drag queens, giving him a quick explanation when he didn't understand the concept. Michele nodded his appreciation and he sought to make himself comfortable at the bar—or as much as he could.

He was fine with observing. At least for a while.

Andreas was on the dance floor, clearly enjoying himself. And as he noted a while later when he spotted him getting a little handsy with another guy on the dance floor, his knowledge of the bar didn't come by accident.

Michele nursed his drink as he tapped his foot to the music. Suddenly, though, someone occupied the chair next to him. He half-turned, taking in a guy he assumed to be in his twenties, with brown hair and blue eyes. He wasn't bad to look at. In fact, most of the people in the club were reasonably attractive—just not attractive *to* him.

The other guy ordered himself a drink but kept sneaking glances at Michele. At some point, he just went straight for it, leaning in to address him.

"You have lovely eyes," he said in a semi-yelling voice, enough to get his words across over the loud music.

Michele's lips tipped into a hesitant smile.

"Thank you," he said, unaware of the etiquette in such cases.

The guy continued to look at him with a languid smile, asking him questions such as his name, age and occupation.

It soon became clear to Michele that he was interested in him. And just to give this a chance, he studied the man better, hoping for something—a flicker of something.

He was a fine-looking man—objectively. But Michele could stare all he wanted and he wouldn't find what he was looking for. He wouldn't find it anywhere in that club.

He did his best to socialize, only withdrawing when the man went to touch his gloved hand.

"Sorry," he muttered an excuse about going somewhere as he

went in search of Andreas. Their little experiment wasn't very conducive, unfortunately.

He had to make his way through the crowd of people, always alert about not making *too* much contact. Yet he still kept his eyes wide open, hoping he could find at least someone attractive that way. If he did, then maybe there was nothing wrong with him. He was just...*picky*.

He saw individuals that were, by all standards, stunning. Yet he felt not one stirring of desire. It was then he realized he'd never so much as wished to kiss someone, let alone go further, and the thought of it simply sent him into a mental spiral.

"Andreas," he yelled when he spotted his friend—weird how from his subordinate, the man had turned into his friend.

Andreas was grinding against a larger man, a huge smile on his face as he nuzzled his face in the man's neck.

As he got closer, Michele stopped in his tracks.

The world around him continued to have a good time, dance, laugh, make love on the floor.

He just stared at his friend in awe, at the free way in which he was embracing the other man and accepting caresses in return–at the way he seemed to *revel* in those interactions.

He stared, and he didn't understand.

Andreas finally spotted him, and waved him over.

"Can we go?" Michele asked, his eyes skittering from Andreas to the other man. "You can bring him if you'd like," he said on a whisper.

Andreas just shook his head, a happy smile still on his face.

"Let's just go."

They both managed to find their way out of the crowd and exit the club, going around the building to reach the spot where they'd left the car.

"Damn that was fun," Andreas sighed happily.

"I'm glad at least you had fun," Michele replied, resigned at his situation.

"Nothing?"

He shook his head, getting a cigarette from his pack and lighting it. He offered one to Andreas too, and he accepted.

"I didn't realize you…"

"That I like men?" Andreas filled in the words. "It's not something I advertise, for obvious reasons. You know what the men in our cultures think about that."

"You took a risk with me, didn't you?"

"You didn't strike me as a homophobe. Which is odd, considering the rumors about you," Andreas narrowed his eyes playfully at Michele.

Michele took a deep drag of his cigarette.

"I've heard the same thing all my life. And it's all for the way I look, because, as it seems, I don't think I'm into men, either."

Andreas nodded quietly.

"How did *you* know?" Michele propped himself on the ground, looking up at Andreas.

"I think I just did?" He laughed. "I don't know how to explain it, other than that one day I saw a boy and I got hard for him," he said with a slight blush. "It's not something I've talked about with anyone, and it took me the longest time to come to terms to it because of the way I was raised."

The more they got into personal stuff, the more Andreas became more comfortable speaking with Michele, as if now both had secrets tying them together.

"Have you…" Michele cleared his throat. "Have you fucked a guy?"

Andreas nodded.

"Is it different than being with a girl?"

"It's just…different. Both were pleasant because I was into both of them."

"I've never been into anyone," Michele admitted.

"No one? Ever?" Andreas blinked.

Michele pursed his lips, slowly shaking his head.

"Do you jerk off?" Andreas asked the question and Michele's eyes went wide before his entire face flamed.

"Sorry if that was too direct," Andreas chuckled.

"No, it's fine," Michele took a deep breath. "Sometimes. But it's not...to something. It's just a release." He struggled to explain that he didn't have anyone in mind when he did it. It was more abstract than anything, and he blamed it on his teenage hormones that he did it at all.

Andreas brought his cigarette to his lips, inhaling as he studied Michele.

Suddenly, he sat down next to him on the pavement, coming dangerously close.

"Maybe you're just asexual."

"Asexual?" Michele frowned, hearing the term for the first time.

"Being just into girls or guys isn't the *only* type of sexuality there is. I consider myself bi because I'm into both. You could be asexual because you're into neither."

Michele was amazed to hear such a simple explanation. And as Andreas continued to talk to him about the different types of labels, and how no one was perfect or fit into one box, he suddenly realized something.

He wasn't alone. If there was a term for it, that meant there were more people out there like him. He wasn't...a freak.

Suddenly, the world opened up to him like never before. And the moment he got back to his room, he proceeded to consume all the information available on the spectrum of asexuality. He learned that on the extreme end some never experienced attraction or an interest in sex, while in a grayer area, some could be attracted to their partner after establishing an emotional connection. The more he read, the more he felt a sense of relief like never before. He was fine. There wasn't anything wrong with him per se. But there would be plenty wrong with him in the eyes of others if he revealed that information.

But maybe Andreas could help him with that.

Michele smiled.

He might still have a fuck ton of issues, but for the first time in too long, he felt a lightness suffuse his being.

That night, his nightmares only woke him up once—a record as far as he was concerned.

thirty

AGE SEVENTEEN

A few weeks passed, and Michele and Andreas' friendship continued to blossom. For the first time, Michele had a friend around his own age with whom he could share his worries and thoughts. It wasn't something he was used to, but it made an impact on his day to day life. More than anything, it showed him how lonely he'd been in the past.

Nicolo, seeing the change in him, continued to push him out of his comfort zone. Luckily for Michele, Andreas was there to help him. Since Nicolo thought a man required sex on a regular basis, he had weekly appointments for Michele at the same brothel. And every appointment, he brought Andreas with him to take his place.

Andreas had said it was no hardship to him since the girls were hot.

Still, Michele worried he was asking too much of his new friend. He didn't want him to end up resenting him.

But a new routine developed during that summer. Michele became more outgoing, and knowing Andreas had his back made him lower his guard and engage in more social events.

Nicolo noticed, too. He received reports on Michele,

tracking his progress and seeing a new side of him. Which is why he called him to his office one afternoon, a month before Michele's senior year was about to start.

"You wanted to see me?" Michele asked as he opened the door to Nicolo's study.

His friend was only present a couple days a week at the gym, and those were usually filled with administrative stuff that didn't allow him to leisurely meet with Michele.

"Yes, son. Come in, take a seat," Nicolo motioned to the chair in front of him.

Michele nodded, quietly seating himself in front of him. Although he'd become more open to the outside world, his own little world had remained just as...little. He still wore the same clothes, long-sleeved shirts and long pants in sweltering summer, all accompanied by his ever faithful gloves—he never left anywhere without them.

Nicolo's shrewd eyes took this all in, cataloging everything and figuring it out in his calculations. After all, he had great plans for his little friend.

"What did you want to talk about?" Michele asked, slightly nervous.

He knew his work was flawless. He took great pride in the way he worked the books of the gym, and anything else Nicolo might throw his way. It might not be something he was passionate about, but it was something he knew would pave the way for his future. Besides, he wasn't the type to do something just for the sake of it. Underneath all that calm exterior lay the seeds of a perfectionist, one who could not stand if his work was any less than perfect. And so he'd striven to do his best, learning things from zero just so he could apply himself to the tasks assigned to him—just so he could please Nicolo.

"I wanted to congratulate you," Nicolo said, popping open one drawer and taking out a bottle of champagne. "I've seen your progress, and I wanted to let you know I'm proud of you, son," he told him with a smile.

Michele blinked, slowly returning the smile as he tried to contain his excitement.

No one had been proud of him before, and to hear the words coming from his friend—the one he esteemed above all—was the most satisfying feeling in the world.

For a moment he felt a pang of guilt at his slight deceit. But aside from sleeping with those girls, he'd done everything Nicolo had asked of him. It was just a little white lie that he was telling, he thought to himself.

"Thank you. I'm glad you think so," he said with a slight blush.

"Don't thank me. It's all you, son. I know how hard it's been for you. God knows, for a little while I thought I'd lost you after what you've been through. But you went and proved me wrong. By moving on, you showed strength, and that is no little feat."

Michele nodded, his lips tipped in a smile.

"And because of that, I think you're ready for the next step."

"Next step?" Michele repeated, a frown marring his face.

Nicolo merely smiled. With a loud pop, he opened the champagne bottle, pouring the bubbly liquid into two glasses before giving one to Michele and saving one for himself.

"Can I?" Michele asked as he raised his pack of cigarettes.

Nicolo grunted.

Michele lit a cigarette up, taking a sip of his champagne and waiting for his friend to continue.

"You know the situation with my family, or at least the gist of it."

Michele nodded.

Valentino Lastra, Nicolo's nephew, was the current head of the family. And while there had always been some animosity between the two of them, all stemming from the fact that each had different visions for the future of the family, the situation had only become worse when Valentino's wife had been killed. Her death had started a conflict with her family, Agosti, and had plunged Valentino into a deep depression that had switched his focus entirely from the family business to finding his wife's killer.

It had become such an obsession that Valentino was barely aware of what went on in the family. And that finally left the business up to Nicolo—though not officially.

"I think I have the perfect way to get both our legacies back," Nicolo started, and Michele stifled a wince.

He knew where it was heading. Nicolo had always felt angry on his behalf. That he was the firstborn yet he'd always been discounted as heir.

"What do you mean?"

"I have my own issues with my family, and God knows it's been a long fight to get to where I am now. But I can't sit still anymore. Not after my brother ruined everything and then left it to his son to ruin it some more. I won't stand for that. Just like I won't stand for you being thrown aside when it's *your* legacy," he stated vehemently.

"What did you have in mind?"

"Together we can get *both*. Think about it. We could unite Guerra and Lastra. The business would boom, and *no one* would ever look down on either of us."

Nicolo seemed in his own world as he went on to explain his plan. He wanted them to work together behind the scenes and lay the foundation for a future takeover.

"This is a long-term war, son. As much as I'd love to, we can't go around killing either Benedicto or Valentino because that would raise suspicions. And you know how these people react to coups—badly. Very, very badly. Which means we'll need to do all the work from the shadows."

"Like you've been doing until now," Michele supplied.

"Exactly," Nico nodded.

Michele had heard whispers about Nicolo's obsession with Liliana's son, blaming him for her death. He did not know the particularities of what had happened, but he'd heard enough over the years to piece together some clues. Nicolo *hated* Marcello Lastra. And he aimed to kill him in the worst manner when he found him. Problem was, so far he had not been able to since Marcello had disappeared soon after his father's death.

"But for that, I'll need some help from you," Nico finally said.

"Anything," Michele assured him.

After what Nico had done for him, there wasn't anything Michele wouldn't do for him.

"No one can know that we're working on this. And that means we need to put on a front. Benedicto is still hoping Rafaelo will inherit one day, and although the best course of action would be to show him how capable you are of taking that position, we need to do the reverse."

Michele frowned.

"They already have the worst opinion of you. Think about it. What is easier? Proving them wrong, or proving them right?"

"I don't follow," Michele blinked in confusion.

"What I mean, son," Nico leaned forward, "is that we need to make them think you are not a threat. Otherwise Benedicto might get some crazy ideas and..." he trailed off, snapping his lips shut as if realizing he'd said too much.

"What do you mean? Why would they see me as a threat when I'm the legal heir?"

Michele couldn't understand what Nicolo was alluding to. More than anything, he didn't understand why he should prove people right about their prejudices against him when he needed to do the opposite to show he was capable of being a good leader.

Wasn't that why he'd been working his ass off all this time? To gain the skills to one day become the head of the family?

But while he was confused, Nicolo merely smiled, taking one of his Cuban cigars from their fancy case and lighting it up.

"Why do you think Benedicto's always been against you inheriting? Why has he *always* favored Raf while ignoring you?"

Michele blinked rapidly.

"Well... I was sickly as a child. And after, he thought I was too weak," he answered, thinking those arguments perfectly normal.

He hadn't been in the best shape growing up, and he couldn't blame his father for thinking he wouldn't do a good job. After all, he needed someone his subordinates would respect.

"You're the firstborn, Michele. Do you know what that means?"

He didn't reply.

"Let me put it another way. It shouldn't have mattered *how* sickly or weak you were. The tradition is very clear in one respect. The only possible *don* is the firstborn. Only if he dies, the next in line follows."

"But..."

"If it were that simple, do you think my brother would have chosen Valentino as his heir? He would have *never*. Not when his Marcello was much more capable, and definitely much crueler than him. Yet he didn't. Not because he didn't want to, but because he couldn't."

"I don't understand..." he frowned, more confused than ever.

"There's only one reason why Benedicto would be so adamant about Rafaelo, not you, inheriting his position. And that is..."

"If I'm not his son," Michele filled the words in as the realization dawned on him.

He was frozen in place as he saw Nico nod in satisfaction.

"You're not his son," he admitted.

"How, what... How do you know?" Michele stammered.

Suddenly, his entire life flashed before his eyes—the lie that his life had been. Because if Benedicto wasn't his father then...

He remembered the beatings, the name callings, the way he'd always ignore him and treat him as if he were the worst person on earth—or the most contemptible one.

But if Benedicto was, indeed, *not* his father, then suddenly everything made sense.

He'd never loved him.

He'd never cared for him.

He'd always...shunned him.

Because he was not his blood.

"How do you know?" he asked again, one part of himself refusing to believe it while the other rejoiced at finding an explanation for years of abuse and neglect.

"Because I know who your father is." Nico took a drag of his cigar, the smoke enveloping the room.

His eyes were on Michele, watching him carefully as he struggled to reconcile the life as he knew it with the truth.

"Who?" One word. One whispered word.

Michele downed the champagne glass in one go, pouring himself another before drinking greedily. Slamming it down the surface of the table he steeled himself.

"Who?" he repeated.

Only when his entire demeanor changed did Nicolo finally open his mouth to tell him the identity of his sire.

Though he seemed wholly intent on his friend, Michele felt his consciousness dim, his entire body trembling with the force of his emotions.

Benedicto wasn't his father. He had never been.

"Me."

One word. One word that changed everything.

They were both quiet for the longest time.

Michele did his best to hide his surprise, while Nico did his best to hide the smugness of his expression.

"I see," Michele eventually said. And he did see. Suddenly, everything was crystal clear. "I remember now. At the hospital. You saved me, didn't you?"

"I did. No one else was going to," Nico shrugged.

He'd always wondered why Nicolo would take such an interest in him. After all, Bass had been right when he'd pointed out he was only a child while Nicolo was an adult—a very busy and successful one at that. Why would he waste his time on some random child? What would he benefit from it?

"How did it happen..."

Nicolo told him. How his father had been flaunting his relationship with Cosima publicly, embarrassing Michele's mother until she'd wanted to do the same to Benedicto. And she'd chosen Nicolo for it.

"I didn't know you were mine. Not until I saw you and your eyes," Nicolo admitted.

And that was all proof Michele needed. Their eyes. They had the same eyes.

He'd often wondered about it, but he hadn't thought genetics were at work for their shared eye color.

"You look just like your mother. But you have my eyes, and hair."

Michele slowly nodded, absorbing everything in. He wasn't shocked as much as bewildered.

How had he not questioned it before?

Now, with all the facts before him, everything was clear—so much so that he felt like a fool for not wondering before. Benedicto had never been kind to him. Not once in his life. And Nico... Nico had been Michele's guardian angel since that first night when they'd met in the hospital.

"You're not upset with me, are you? I didn't tell you until now because I didn't want you to think I befriended you only for one purpose. I wanted us to have a relationship—a genuine relationship."

"I'm not upset. I'm just digesting the information," Michele replied honestly.

"And?"

"The more I think about it the more I like it," he smiled. "You know, there were times I truly wished you were my father and now... You *are* my father."

"I am," Nico chuckled. "And now you see what the problem has been, from the beginning. Benedicto couldn't admit that you weren't his or he would have embarrassed himself. In our culture, a man's infidelity is more excusable than a woman's. If he were to be revealed as a cuckold, everyone would lose respect for him."

"It makes sense now why he hated me so much."

"I'm sorry about that," Nico sighed. "And for everything that happened to you in that goddamn house."

"You couldn't have done anything. I'm aware of that. The fact that you tried to befriend me first, though, means the world to me. Thank you," he told him sincerely.

Nico had no way of knowing how much this new information impacted Michele. Slowly, happiness suffused his being at realizing he now had a father—a real father. One who loved him and cared for him. And since he'd never had that before, the feeling simply floored him.

"What do you want me to do then?" he asked, conviction shining in his voice. He was ready to do anything—as he'd been before the revelation. But now? Now he just wanted Nicolo to be proud of Michele for being his son.

"As I said, we need to pretend..."

Nicolo explained that if Michele showed himself too capable, especially in front of Benedicto's people, it might make him explode and do something extreme—like order a hit on Michele. It wasn't out of the question with how stressed Benedicto was with the succession issue, more so now that Raf was incapacitated. And one thing was for sure. He would never willingly allow Michele to inherit the family business.

"You'll need to make them think you're the prodigal son, so to speak," Nico laughed.

And the way to do it was simple.

Excess—of women, drugs, alcohol. Everything that made him look like a loser who only cared about ephemeral pleasure.

"Now you see why I've been pushing you to get out of your shell. It was all for the role of a lifetime," Nico declared with pride.

Michele nodded along, simply internalizing the information.

"And when they least expect it, we strike."

The goal, as Nicolo put it, was to get everyone to lower their guards until Nicolo and Michele could take both Guerra and Lastra.

"But why do you need both?" He suddenly asked, though he quickly realized it wasn't the right question as Nicolo scowled.

"I have the perfect business lined up. But for it to function at full capacity, I'll need the influence of *two* families, not just one. I'm slowly gaining control of Lastra, so Guerra is next. But until the time is right, you'll have to play your role."

When probed, Nico didn't say what the business was, merely implying that Michele would see for himself soon enough.

"I'll do as you say," Michele agreed.

He wasn't that keen on getting the Guerra title for himself.

Not as Nicolo seemed to be. He assumed that Michele would want revenge on everyone who'd made his life a living hell, and Michele went along with it. Th truth was that he just wanted to help Nico—with whatever it was.

If he wanted to own all of Cosa Nostra, then Michele would make it happen. Anything for him—especially now that he discovered their bond.

"I've already got my claws in Franco, and he'll be putty when the time comes," Nico suddenly said, and Michele froze.

The subject of Franco and Antonio was still a sore one for him, as evidenced by his nightly nightmares. He didn't think he'd *ever* forget everything Antonio had done to him. It was a small satisfaction that he'd gelded him and he was unlikely to ever do that to someone else, but that didn't mean he was any less uneasy about him. There were days when he regretted his decision to keep him alive. He should have killed him when he'd had the chance...

"Is that necessary?" He inquired in a forced tone.

"He's the *consigliere*. Of course it's necessary. But don't worry about it. You won't ever have to interact with him or that awful son of his again. I'll deal with everything on that side myself," Nicolo promised.

Michele sighed in relief. No matter how tough he thought himself, there was no way he could subject himself to their presence without feeling like dying—or, like killing himself.

"Good. Good," he felt a weight lifted off his chest.

They talked for a bit longer, and Nicolo explained his entire plan, but without getting too into specifics. Michele had the vague impression that he wanted to see him prove himself first, and he vowed that was exactly what he would do.

Nico's phone rang, and he was called away on business. Getting up, he gave Michele a pleasant smile as he gathered his stuff to leave.

Before he lost his courage, Michele asked a question.

"Can I call you...dad?"

Nico paused, his expression inscrutable. Suddenly, he dumped his stuff on the table and he rounded the corner to take Michele in his arms.

"Only when we're alone," he whispered gently.

Michele was stiff at first, too unaccustomed with human touch. But because it was Nicolo, he didn't reject it. Instead, he brought his own arms around his shoulders, returning the hug.

"Thank you, *dad*."

That meeting changed Michele. Whether he admitted it to himself or not, it reshaped his thinking and his plans for the future. He had already felt indebted to Nicolo for everything he'd done for him, but to find out that Nicolo was his biological father had been a game changer.

Suddenly, he wasn't so unwanted. He wasn't so lonely. Suddenly, he had a family. He had Cami, who had taken it upon herself to become a mother figure, and he had Andreas, the older brother he'd never had. For the first time in his life, he was content.

It didn't matter that Nicolo was strict in his expectations, or that he'd outlined a list for Michele to follow. It didn't matter that he was to attend weekly parties and pretend to be a druggie and an alcoholic in front of the Guerras, straining himself and pushing his limits to make sure people never saw through his disguise.

It only mattered that he now had his own people.

Months passed. Michele put on his act, receiving the expected reactions from Benedicto and Cosima. But now that he knew the big secret, he could also see the relief on Benedicto's face at not having to name Michele his heir.

Then there was Raf.

Always at home, always alone. With the exception of

Cosima, who played her role of dutiful mother to perfection, he had no one—absolutely no one.

Though Michele hated everything that had happened, a part of him rejoiced at having Raf experience on his own skin what *he* had experienced growing up.

There was alone, and there was loneliness. And he'd had plenty of each.

Not anymore.

Maybe because he felt like he truly belonged, but he couldn't find it in him to hate people. Not as he was expected to, anyway. He resented them for their behavior when he'd been a defenseless child, but now? They couldn't hurt him anymore.

His nightmares continued. His disgust with human touch persisted too. Yet his outlook on life slowly changed as he saw the future as never before—bright. Because he loved and he was loved in return.

It was one stormy night when there was a conflict at the gym that required Nicolo's attention that something changed. Michele didn't register it in time though, too drunk on those new emotions that surrounded him. He was too set in the present—in the status quo—that he could not picture a change.

In his mind, there was only one purpose—preserve that which he had. Against all odds, he'd decided that he would make his father proud; that he would revel in Cami's affection and Andreas' friendship. And so, he put on his best work.

If Nicolo demanded something of him, he did it, no questions asked. Anything to avoid seeing disappointment on his sire's face.

But that evening... That evening the seed of doubt was planted, though it would take him years and years to admit it to himself.

"There was a shooting, I can't reach doc nor Nicolo,"

Michele gritted his teeth as he spoke to Andreas in hushed tones.

There were four of Nicolo's men that were moaning in pain in the locker rooms of the gym. They'd done his best to treat them momentarily, but they needed a doctor, and quick.

"Cami said I shouldn't bother him today. But damn..."

"I'll keep trying to reach doc. You go get Nicolo. We need him," Andreas suggested, and Michele nodded.

"Michele," Cami called out as he made his way towards the exit. Her arms were full with clean towels and disinfectant.

"I'm going to get Nicolo. He needs to be here for this."

"Can't this wait?' she winced as she asked, knowing fully well that it couldn't wait. Not when they had a roomful of men on the brink of death.

"You know it can't," he pursed his lips.

"It's just... I don't know how you'll find him. It's the anniversary of Liliana's death today and he's always missing," she gave him a tight smile.

"I have to try. We don't know if the people who shot them are coming here, and if they are, we'll need Nico to call back up. You know we won't stand a chance by ourselves."

"You're right. Just...be safe, okay?"

thirty-one

AGE SEVENTEEN

Michele gave her a smile before leaving.

He had a couple locations ready to check—Nico's home, the cemetery and the old Lastra house. If this was, indeed, Liliana's death anniversary, then he should be someplace important to her.

His first stop was Nico's home. He'd rarely been there, and from what he'd heard, Nico didn't really spend too much time there. Cami, herself, had never seen the inside of his house.

It was raining heavily outside. Michele drew his hood on as he exited his car.

Nico's home was a brownstone close to Central Park. While the Lastra family kept away from the city, Nico was unbothered by such restrictions.

Shivering from head to toe from being exposed to the heavy rain, he dashed to the door, knocking and hoping someone would answer. If he had to go to the cemetery... Damn but that would take the entire night and they needed to find Nico as soon as possible.

The door creaked open, an elderly woman squinting to make out the person in front of her.

"I'm looking for Nicolo," Michele said, his hands in the pockets of his leather jacket as he sought to warm himself up.

"And who might you be?" She asked in a suspicious voice.

"Michele. If you tell him my name, he'll know."

A pause.

She studied him up and down before pulling the door wider for him to step inside.

"I've heard of you," she replied, nodding towards the stairs. "The master is upstairs, but he's asked not to be disturbed. If you wish to withstand his wrath, go right ahead," she said in a strict voice before leaving Michele in the middle of the foyer, retreating deeper in the house.

He blinked, surprised by her manner. He was, however, undeterred.

Shrugging his jacket off, he hung it up to dry before going up the stairs, rehearsing in his mind what he'd tell Nico should he find him in a foul mood.

He climbed the stairs two at a time, going to the third floor where he knew Nicolo's room was. When he reached the landing, he simply knocked, pushing the door open when no one answered.

"Nico? Dad?" He called out, looking about the bedroom but finding it empty.

His brows furrowed in confusion, he stepped back, checking the other rooms and finding them equally empty. It was when he was ready to go down to the second floor that he caught a flicker of light coming from the attic.

Without even thinking, he went to the next floor.

There was only a room there, and as he pushed the door open, it was to be bathed in light from a multitude of candles strewn around.

He stepped inside. As he reached the middle of the room, he recognized the candles had been placed around a makeshift altar.

And as he took another step forward, it was to jump back at the sight of a human skull.

Sitting within a circle of candles, the skull had been decorated prettily with a garland of flowers.

"Michele," a voice murmured from behind.

He startled, almost tripping as he turned to come face to face with Nicolo.

"Nico..." he trailed off, blinking as he took in Nicolo's disheveled appearance and the half-empty bottle of whiskey he was holding.

Nico almost never drank. To see him like this...

"What are you doing here, son?"

"There was an emergency at the gym and we couldn't get in touch."

"An emergency you say," he walked around Michele, wobbling his way deeper into the room as he sank into a plush chair. "Can't it wait?" He asked on a weary tone. And as Michele got a better look at him, he realized his father didn't look well.

"Dad," he said carefully. "Are you okay?"

Nico just sighed, turning his face towards the skull in the center of it all.

"She was so beautiful," he closed his eyes, bringing the bottle to his lips for a hefty swig. "She didn't even reach her thirty-first birthday."

"I'm sorry," Michele offered sincerely.

"He took her from me. Goddamn him!" He cried out, tears at the corners of his eyes. "Goddamn both of them!"

He was referring to his brother, Giovanni, and his son, Marcello.

Michele knew some of the story. Nicolo had been in love with Liliana and they had planned on marrying when she turned eighteen. By chance, Nicolo had been called away to Italy on some business and that had left Liliana alone and defenseless. By the time he'd returned, Giovanni had married her on account of getting her pregnant, though Nicolo had always maintained she hadn't betrayed him—that his brother had raped her to take her away from Nicolo.

"*Dio cane!* I'm going to kill him! I'm going to make that bastard wish he were never born," Nicolo continued his barrage of slurred insults.

"Let me help you," Michele offered, coming towards him.

"No!" Nico put a hand up. His face was screwed up in pain, his body hunched over. "What do you need? Tell me and begone!"

Michele bit his lip. He didn't like seeing Nicolo so anguished, but he could see he wanted to be alone.

"Can you call back-up for the gym and maybe a doctor? Doc isn't answering."

Nico nodded, taking out his phone from his pants and dialing a number.

He gave a few orders before he shut down the phone, throwing it around.

Michele saw he was no longer welcome, so he carefully took a step back.

"I'll see you soon, Nico," he said in a gentle tone.

Nicolo didn't even hear him. His gaze was arrested by the skull on the table. Before he could step out of the room, Michele witnessed his father drag himself on his knees towards the altar table, taking the skull in his hands and hugging it to his chest reverently.

"Nico..." he whispered, all to himself.

It was the first time Michele was seeing him so vulnerable and so...obsessed. Until then, he'd only heard of his obsession with Liliana from hearsay. But to witness it in person... Hell, he'd built an altar in her honor.

Shaking his head, Michele went out the door, quickly picking his coat up and getting in his car.

He hoped the back-up would arrive soon, otherwise Nico wouldn't be of much help in the state he was in.

As he drove back to the gym, he couldn't believe that the strong and stoic Nico had that kind of side to himself—a side that wasn't exactly...sane. Otherwise, he couldn't explain the presence of the skull or how taken Nicolo had seemed with it. How long had he had it with him? Was this something he did every year?

The question didn't cease to spring into his mind.

He was so focused on that matter that he almost didn't see the flash of white in front of his car. Or the men that quickly followed, the glint of metal shining even on the poorly lit street.

Michele hit the breaks, stopping just in time to witness two grown men attempting to assault a child.

He didn't think. He merely opened a compartment in his car, taking out a gun and getting out of his car.

"What the hell is going on here?" He asked, the gun behind his back.

"It does not concern you," one of the men spat at him, his hands on the squirming child.

"If you're harming him, then it concerns me," he replied, meeting their gazes head on.

He didn't know what spurred him in that moment, but he knew there was something seriously wrong with the child. He was covered in blood, his feral cries doing something to Michele.

"Let him go," he gritted out as he recognized the condition of the child. He raised his weapon, pointing it at the two men. "Let him go," he repeated.

The child looked at him with big, wide eyes. He kept struggling against the man's hold, but as his gaze connected with Michele's, he saw the clear cry for help.

In the span of a second, one man had the child in a chokehold, a knife to his throat while the other man pointed his own gun at Michele.

Though he wasn't used to such face-offs, the moment he felt himself threatened—worse, the moment he knew the *child* was threatened—there was no time for fear or hesitation.

Rain was pouring heavily—enough to obstruct someone's view. Not Michele's. Although his skills were formed at a shooting range, his aim was sharp.

He saw the man's finger on the trigger, ready to shoot. So, he shit first. One bullet to the hand, sending the gun flying, after which he aimed at the other man, catching him between the eyes.

He dropped dead before he could harm the kid.

Michele knew time was of essence, especially as the other man reached for the child. One more bullet. The man was down.

Yet the danger was far from over. Not when the noise could have alerted anyone about the shooting. Luckily, he'd been smart enough to pull his hood on, his face unrecognizable for any CCTV. His gun was untraceable, and as soon as he got to the gym, he'd replace the plates on the car.

His mind made up, he simply swooped up the shocked child and deposited him in the backseat of the car.

"Don't worry. I won't hurt you."

Michele didn't know if he understood the words or not, but one look into Michele's eyes and he seemed to become more at ease.

As soon as he got back to the gym, he took the boy in his arms, momentarily thrusting aside his distaste of touch as he ran to his room.

He spotted Cami on the way and he called her over, briefly

explaining what had happened and that the child was in a state of shock.

"You're lucky," she whispered to him after he'd laid the child on the bed. "Two doctors just came here and we have around ten armed men ready to help if anyone thinks to attack."

"Good," he sighed in relief. It seemed the men Nico had called had acted fast.

"I gather that Nico was indisposed?" Cami raised a brow, but her expression was pained.

He could only imagine what she felt knowing that the man she loved was currently grieving another woman. But she accepted her lot as it was, aware she'd never own Nicolo—not as he owned her.

"Yes," he nodded grimly. "But he got us the help," he added, pointing at the bright side.

Cami pursed her lips, straining a smile.

"Ok, let's focus on what we have here."

She went to get a doctor, while Michele studied the boy. He was about five or six judging by his size, but he also seemed malnourished, so he could easily be older.

Quick at work, he grabbed a wet towel from his bathroom and he tried to pry the white shirt from his body. There was blood—old and new. Some had crusted on his skin, one wound already infected. Aside from that, there was bruising everywhere in different stages of healing, suggesting continued abuse.

The boy flinched at the first touch, but he seemed to see that Michele meant him no harm.

"Can you tell me your name?" Michele inquired in a gentle tone.

The boy kept looking at him, his eyes fixed on Michele's. It took him a few moments to spell out his name, and even then it was a bit butchered, as if he hadn't spoken in a long time.

Solomon.

His name was Solomon.

He was a cute kid, with dark skin and hazel eyes. Michele thought he was of mixed heritage.

"The doctor is here," Cami announced, bringing in an elderly gentleman.

"Let's have a look at..."

"Solomon," Michele supplied.

Solomon looked from Michele to the newcomers, fear descending on his face as he drew himself back, flinching when the doctor tried to reach for him.

"The man here is a doctor. He wants to make sure you're fine. Is it ok if he touches you?" Michele asked, wanting to get the child's permission.

Seeing his reaction to touch, he had some suspicions as to what had happened, but he prayed to God it wasn't what he was imagining.

At least Michele had been fourteen when his abuse had started. To think of someone younger... His insides rebelled at such a thought.

Solomon pointed at Michele, then towards him.

"I think he wants you to stay, Michele," Cami mentioned.

"Will you let him examine you if I stay?" He asked, just in case.

Slowly, Solomon nodded.

The doctor proceeded then, noting the various injuries as he went along. It was only when he reached lower, to the boy's genitals and backside that he turned to Michele, a question in his eyes.

The boy looked so frightened, tears were coating his lashes.

"Leave it," Michele suddenly ordered, coming closer and kneeling in front of Solomon.

"Solomon," he started, a kind smile on his face. "We won't

touch you further. But can you tell us if anyone else touched you here?" He pointed to his crotch.

The boy nodded.

Michele asked him further, and though the boy could not verbalize his thoughts, his nods of assent gave them all the information they needed.

He'd been raped. And looking at the damage he'd suffered, brutally so.

Not wanting to upset him further, Michele gave him some food and drink and put him to sleep.

"I need someone to look into him. If it was his parents... We need to find out everything we can," Michele told Cami as he closed the door to his room.

"I'll do what I can," she nodded thoughtfully. "I can't believe that someone..." she choked out a sob. "Good God, I thought living in this life I've seen it all. But him?" she shook her head, and Michele's feelings echoed her own. He was so pissed, he wanted nothing more than to take an AK and raze to the ground everyone who'd laid a finger on the kid.

But he couldn't.

Not yet, anyway.

The following morning, Nicolo was present at the gym. He didn't bring up his encounter with the skull, or the meeting with Michele. He simply continued as before.

Michele didn't have time to care about that either, though in the back of his mind the seed of his father's instability had been sown. Still, they had more important issues to care about.

Unfortunately, only bad news was about to come their way.

Solomon turned out to be absent from the system. There was no record of his existence—anywhere. As such, the only viable conclusion was that he'd been trafficked for some sick bastards to abuse him.

Though he had no family, he slowly became quite at home

with Michele and Cami at the gym, both keen on taking care of him.

But the other bad piece of news was devastating. Solomon hadn't been only abused. He'd also been infected with HIV and was in severe liver failure.

He needed a transplant soon or he wouldn't make it.

The problems kept on piling, from his lack of identity to his seropositive status and the fact that with so little time, they would never be able to get him papers, insurance or find him a match.

It all turned into a race against the clock.

Day by day, Michele bonded more and more with Solomon, though he was still nonverbal. Cami, too, took her role seriously and tended to all his needs, setting on making at least his last weeks a positive experience.

Yet the more time passed, instead of getting used to his imminent death, everyone grew more and more attached to Solomon.

Cami cried every night. Even Michele found himself with tears in his eyes after spending some time with Solomon while knowing his end was near.

Yet it all changed when Nicolo came with a proposal.

"Remember that business I was talking about, son?" He asked one day after Michele had raged about the injustice of it all—of the fact that someone as young and innocent as Solomon would pay for the mistakes of some sexual deviants.

"What about it?"

"I think I can get Solomon a liver. But you'll have to help me," Nicolo started, giving Michele a rough outline of his plans with the transplant center.

It would be all off the books, but it would be for people's benefits—for those people that the system had failed.

Nicolo had spent enough time observing Michele to know

exactly how to frame the issue to get the young man to accept. Solomon's arrival in their lives had been rather fortuitous for his plans, and the best way to rope Michele into his projects—as he'd wanted to from the beginning.

He made it sound like a haven for the disadvantaged—for those who could *not* benefit from the system. He made it sound perfect for Solomon. And that was all he needed to get Michele on board.

Not a month later, and Solomon had a new liver. A few months after and his recovery was confirmed. He was prescribed drugs to keep the HIV under control and he was promised a normal life.

Michele was so ecstatic, he quickly agreed to help Nicolo with whatever he needed with the new transplant center. Nicolo, noting his son's affection for the boy, went one step further and facilitated Solomon's documentation and adoption papers under Cami's name.

And as he watched Michele with the boy, he knew he had his son right where he wanted—in the palm of his hand.

thirty-two

AGE TWENTY

"Mr. Guerra, I'm calling about Solomon's appointment today," the stern voice echoed in Michele's cellphone. It was the therapist's personal assistant, and that *never* bode well.

"Yes, just one moment," he said as he covered the mic, signaling Andreas he needed to step out.

He dropped the cigarette from his mouth, putting it out in the ashtray and stepped back from the room.

"Yes, please speak," he finally said when he found a quiet spot.

It was a boisterous day at the gym since one of their best fighters had just won a very important fight in Cali. They had all gathered together to celebrate the occasion. Michele knew that it would take all day, and it would likely end with all of them at some club, getting shitfaced before going to one of the brothels Nicolo had rented out specifically for this event.

"There has been an incident in therapy today," the woman on the line started. "Solomon became unusually aggressive and Dr. Hilda was hurt in a small altercation. We'd like to suggest switching therapists. It's clear that he needs much more than we are able to provide. I have a list of potential..." she droned on.

Michele's lips flattened in a thin line as he listened to the nonsense he'd been told one too many times. It always happened like that. A therapist would take care of him for a while before saying he was a much too difficult case and needed someone more specialized.

Solomon was almost nine, but his behavior was still that of a five-year-old. His language abilities, in particular, were stilted and he'd been placed in special education classes at school.

He'd been in therapy from the moment Cami and Michele had decided to keep him, all in hopes that he could one day get better and live a normal life. His problems were not from birth, though he did have a slew of health issues that had been a side effect of his untreated HIV infection. His speech impediment and child-like personality were strictly a result of his trauma.

Over the years, they'd managed to glean some information about what had happened to him. When he had nightmares, his speech reverted back to normal and he revealed some of the horrors he'd been subjected to. Other times, he would get a crazed look on his face and would print the same names on a sheet of paper—all over again. After the episode wore off, he couldn't verbalize who those people were, or why their names were important.

Michele believed them to be the names of people who'd abused him, but he only had the first names to go by and he hadn't been able to pinpoint the people Solomon was talking about.

"We've changed five therapists in the last year. How can that be good for the kid?" he refrained from adding a few swear words that would have made the question much more colorful.

"I'm sorry, Mr. Guerra. But we cannot accommodate him further. In fact, if you could come pick him up a little earlier, that would be great."

"Fine," he barked before he hung up.

He'd already been in a surly mood because of Nicolo and his crazy antics. Now with Solomon's issue he felt like punching someone in the face.

Getting back to his people, he made an excuse to take his leave, assuring Andreas he could stay behind and have fun. After all, they'd been planning that event for a long time already and Michele didn't want to be the one to ruin it for anyone.

Today it had been Cami's turn to pick Solomon up from his therapy, but she was out until a specified time which left everything up to Michele.

"Everything ok?" Andreas came out with him to get a bit of quiet from the boisterous crowd.

"Solomon. His therapist wants out," he sighed. "I'll see what can be done to find someone else. And soon. You know how he gets without therapy."

Andreas nodded grimly.

Therapy was the only thing that helped with Solomon's crises, making them more far in between rather than the daily dose from before.

"Good luck. If you want me to come with..."

"Nah, don't worry. Go have fun. I'll pick him up and we'll have a nice evening by ourselves. You know I'm not into that scene anyway," he added with a chuckle.

Three years of pretending already, and he'd never developed a taste for the party scene. He was already well known in those circles as the king of debauchery, a reputation he'd carefully built according to Nicolo's wishes. But behind closed doors, Michele was still his old, reclusive self.

He had more friends now and people he could call family. But his issues were ever present in his life.

Michele had tried therapy, too, after being called out one too many times by Cami for making Solomon do it but resisting it for himself. Yet it hadn't worked very well for him.

He was functional. That was enough. Maybe he still had issues with touch, or crowded places, or being too close to people. Maybe he still suffered from bouts of insomnia and recurring nightmares, but they were far in between now.

He'd accepted that part of himself and he'd learned to live with it. Just like he'd learned to live with the disappointment of the people in his former life.

It wasn't often that his thoughts strayed to his brother, as Michele went out of his way *not* to think about Raf and the betrayal that even after years stung. But for the sake of his image, and the animosity between them, when he did see him, he engaged in a battle of insults meant to widen the distance between them.

Though he thought himself impervious now, Michele still had a soft spot for his brother—one he'd never want to admit. Deep down, he knew it was a weakness that could get in the way of his work, and so whenever he crossed paths with Raf, he made an effort to be the worst version of himself. He called him all types of names, from retard, to stupid, to useless, to everything that came to him in the moment.

Even though he never meant any of it...

Shaking himself from those thoughts, he left the gym, getting into his car and driving to get Solomon.

When he got to the cabinet, it was to find Solomon by himself in the children's waiting room. He was playing with something in his hands, his attention thankfully distracted.

"Solomon?" Michele asked carefully when he reached his side.

The child lifted his head, his big eyes taking him in before a smile spread across his face.

"Daddy," he burst out, flinging himself to Michele.

He caught him easily, taking him in his arms and doing his best to offer him a modicum of comfort.

Though his aversion to touch was always strong, for Solomon's sake he'd learned to tamp it down.

"I hear something happened today?" he asked carefully.

Solomon drew back, regarding him with an innocent expression. He shrugged before settling back in his chair, his attention on the toy from before.

From experience, Michele knew that was the boy's cue he didn't want to speak about it, so he let him be.

"I'll go talk to Dr. Hilda, ok? I'll be out in a bit. Wait for me?"

Solomon nodded, but he didn't look at him again.

Michele sighed, getting up and proceeding towards the main office.

The assistant eventually let him inside where Dr. Hilda held a napkin to her nose—a bloodied napkin.

"Dr. Hilda," he nodded, coming inside.

The woman narrowed her eyes at him, especially as she took in his outfit and the way he looked.

His hair had grown again, and this time Michele had decided not to cut it again, keeping it shoulder length. He was dressed as he always was—in a pair of black jeans and a leather jacket. He still had his piercings and he knew the doctor was silently judging him for it.

It was why he preferred to let Cami tend to these issues. She was much better suited for them than him.

"Mr. Guerra, I presume," her snarky tone registered but Michele refrained from commenting, simply plopping himself in the seat opposite her.

"What did he do?" Michele went straight to the topic.

"We were playing a game, one of those activities, you know," she started telling him how he'd suddenly become too aggressive and had jumped out at her.

"Doctor," Michele strained a smile. "You're telling me you

want Solomon to find a new therapist because he jumped on you?"

She returned a fake smile of her own.

"Exactly."

"What triggered it?"

She blinked.

"Come on. We both know he's not the type to be aggressive with someone just because he feels like it. He reacts to triggers. So what did you do?" He asked, his tone none too patient.

"What? You're implying that I... That I did something?" she looked horrified at the accusation, but Michele didn't back down.

"I know Solomon, and I know his disposition. He's more likely to ignore you than jump on you. You must have done something to upset him, and now you're blaming it on him instead of your inadequacy as a therapist."

"How dare you?" She cried out in indignation.

"How dare I?" He rose from his chair, rounding the corner of the study and looming over her.

A shadow passed across her eyes and he knew she was afraid, her hands fidgeting under the table, probably looking for a way to call security.

Michele didn't give her the opportunity.

He had both her wrists carefully pinned in his gloved hands as he looked her dead in the eye.

"What. Did. You. Do?" he accented each word, finally getting the message across.

She looked on the verge of tears as she stammered some words out.

"He was ignoring me and moving around the room. Wouldn't listen... I just swatted his bottom a few times," she ground out eventually.

Michele's features turned black from anger.

"I leave my child with you, in a safe place, and you fucking hit him?" his voice thundered, the deadly sound making the doctor flinch.

"I... He wasn't listening..."

"And you hit him. You fucking hit him and now you're blaming *him*?"

He had the hardest time controlling his wrath. If there was something that triggered him, it was the thought of anyone doing harm to Solomon—anyone laying a hand on him.

And this woman—this woman in a position of authority—had decided that because he wasn't listening to her she could lay a hand on him.

"You should count your blessings that I'm not killing you right where you stand, Dr. However," he paused, a cruel smile on his face. "Kiss your license adieu," he said before he flung her from him.

He wasted no time in getting out of there, stopping for a second to collect Solomon before getting the hell out of the building.

Only when he was in the car he noted Solomon quietly watching him.

"Where are we going?" the boy asked in a small yet calm voice.

"Home," Michele swallowed, not wanting to show him any of the residual anger that lingered within him. "We're going to order pizza and we'll have a movie night. What do you think?"

The corners of Solomon's mouth tipped up as he nodded.

Sometimes Michele didn't know how to behave with him. He looked like a nine year old, and sometimes, he swore he could see him as a normal boy of his age. Other times, Solomon just lived in his world, ignoring everything else that went around him.

The gym was empty when they got back.

Michele noted a few unread texts on his phone, and quickly replied to Cami to let her know he had Solomon and she could take the night off—have a date or whatever she wanted to do.

Taking the boy by his hand, they went to one of the sitting rooms in the back—one that had a huge TV.

As promised, the pizza came and they both enjoyed a leisure night away from all their troubles. After making sure the boy took his medication, Michele let him choose the movie. Not surprisingly, he went for a superhero one. It was something both Michele and Solomon had in common—their love for superhero movies.

And while they watched, Michele tried to engage him with questions, reactions—anything he could to get something out of him.

The boy laughed and giggled, every now and then saying a few words that simply warmed Michele's heart.

It was towards the end of the night when Solomon's curfew was approaching that Michele took a piece of paper and drew a little something for him.

It was him—Solomon—but with a superhero suit.

"You have your own superpowers too," he told him gently. "Don't let anyone else tell you otherwise."

Solomon simply watched him, as he usually did. Only when he went to his room, ready for bed, did he turn to give Michele a small hug.

"You're my superhero, daddy," he whispered before darting inside his room.

Michele remained stunned to the spot, a silly smile on his face as happiness bloomed inside of him.

Funny how he'd always wanted to be someone's superhero. Maybe for once, he succeeded.

He didn't get to walk much further before his phone went off.

Nico.

"Dad?" he answered, knowing Nicolo needed him, otherwise he wouldn't be calling at that hour.

"We have a bit of a problem at Sacre Coeur. I need you to go check something."

"Ok, I'll be on my way."

Sacre Coeur was one of Michele's projects of the heart. As Nicolo had once told him after he'd decided to adopt Solomon, he couldn't possibly adopt every single mistreated orphan. And so he'd resolved to find them a safe place until they could be adopted by a good family.

Nicolo had given him the idea of Sacre Coeur, a secure convent in upstate New York that was known to cater to elites.

His mouth set in a grim line, he got in his car and headed to Sacre Coeur. He just had to hope the problem didn't refer to one of his kids.

thirty-three

AGE TWENTY

Rafaelo trudged his way to his dorm room, his shoulders slumped, his posture slightly less forced than before. Still, it had become such a second nature to make himself smaller, more insignificant, that even now, away from the watchful eyes of his family, he couldn't shake that off.

He was starting his third year of college, and the first time his parents had allowed him to live on campus by himself.

It had been a long battle with Cosima, who'd tried her best to keep him safe from the world, thinking that everyone was out to hurt him—and maybe they were. God knew, Raf had learned the hard way how vicious people could be during his time in high school. Up until graduation he'd been perpetually bullied for his speech impediment and his shift in personality. Everyone had gone out of their way to take a jab at him, and they especially enjoyed throwing in his face the fact that he'd fallen from the top.

Apparently, to some people it was better if you maintained your position at the bottom your whole life—keeping the status quo. The moment you changed, people changed too.

If you fell from a higher position, they were all there to laugh at you and mock you for it. If you rose to a higher position, they enviously waited in the shadows for you to fall again. No one was genuine. No one cared. That had been Raf's lesson the moment he'd changed himself. People had hated him for his previous privilege, and all that accumulated hate had burst to the surface the moment he'd become weaker.

Yet he'd survived.

It had been hard, but he'd survived. And in the process he'd seen the world through his brother's eyes, too.

Swiping his ID card at the security desk, he proceeded to the elevator before getting to his room. The moment the door closed behind him, he finally shrugged everything off, stretching himself to his full height and massaging his aching muscles.

He was the tallest in the family, but he'd actively tried to make himself look smaller, less *present*. To a degree he'd managed.

In the beginning, his father had fretted over him, trying to get him to see the best doctors and therapists. When the cause behind his condition had still remained a mystery, he'd given up —implying he'd want him dead rather than an embarrassment to the family.

Raf knew his father didn't have hope in him—not with how the famiglia regarded him, or how everyone pitied him. But Benedicto was even more horrified at the alternative of having Michele be in charge of the family. Especially after his brother had gone off the rails, drowning himself in a self-destructive lifestyle that had everyone frowning at him.

The only one who'd been by Rafaelo's side throughout the years had been Cosima. Though Raf usually ignored her, as he'd made it clear that he could never forgive what she'd done, she still spent all her time mothering him and trying to help him get better. It was to the point that Raf believed her to be delusional regarding his health.

THE PRODIGAL SON

After a quick shower, he changed into a pair of comfortable pants and a shirt and he sat down at his desk. Opening his school laptop, he started working on an assignment that was due the following day, wanting to get it out of the way before he could finally allow himself to unwind.

To everyone's dismay, he'd managed to get into college even with his special classes and unfortunate diagnosis. Though he kept his act up at all times, this was one thing he'd made some allowances for, mainly because he *needed* to escape his house.

For a while he'd been floundering, his mental health plunging into dangerous territory as he tried to keep up his act. He'd been suppressing his own self for far too long, and the effects were evident. He was having a hard time finding enjoyment in anything in his life, more often than not preferring to sit in his room, sleep, eat and play video games. He knew it wasn't a proper life, but it was his escape.

The *only* way he could find a semblance of normality was when he pretended to be yet another person in a video game. How fucked up was that?

In those games he could finally use his brain to the fullest, without downplaying his capacities or his affinity with planning.

He'd started with real time strategy games, where he would take control of a faction or an empire and see it thrive, usually going against an enemy force. It was the one area he could apply the knowledge he'd acquired while working with his father—the only time he'd enjoyed the mob business. He loved having control over everything and he'd become specialized in one of the popular games, earning his username a place on the homepage's hall of glory.

But he'd soon moved on from that when it wasn't stimulating him anymore, going for games that incorporated strategy with role playing. Due to his thirst of *being* someone, he'd managed to get himself noticed by several channels that were hosting professional games, and by the time he turned eighteen, he was already participating in small, localized competitions.

It had all changed the year before, when he'd been extended an offer to play for a bigger company. Of course, all of that involved a lot of time that he could not afford if he was at home, with his mother smothering him and following his every step.

That had been his main incentive to move to his college dorm, pursuing his studies while enjoying his rapidly advancing gaming career. While it wasn't something he saw himself doing in the long run, for the moment it was enough to keep him from actively going insane.

For his studies he'd chosen a relatively safe field—earth science and geology. All in an attempt to put on a front for everyone around him and further hide himself.

But now he wasn't just *retarded Raf*. He was *retarded Raf who talked to stones*—a moniker he'd earned curtesy of his brother.

Finishing his assignment in record time, he glanced at the clock. He had the rest of the night to relax. His earliest class the next day was in the afternoon, so he could sleep in.

Now that he'd joined the bigger gaming leagues, his focus had shifted. The moment the activity had turned into a responsibility, his enjoyment of it had flown right out of the window—or, at least, it had diminished considerably.

That didn't mean he could stop. Not when he was earning money for his playtime, which meant he could one day become independent from his family. He'd put aside every penny, dreaming of the day he could just take off.

That was his ultimate goal.

He would play, earn some money on the side until he had enough so he could leave and never look back—finally find himself. From the moment he'd seen the potential of monetizing his skills, he'd decided he could finally take control of his life in a way that wouldn't influence anyone else—in a way that wouldn't inconvenience his brother.

He'd promised Michele everything, and he was going to give it to him. In all these years, that resolve had not weakened.

What had, however, changed had been his outlook on life.

More than ever, he felt himself drifting.

He'd never had something he particularly loved, or somewhere he belonged. He'd always moved with the wind, too focused on pleasing everyone around him *but* himself.

That was going to change. He was going to put himself first.

After he finished his degree, he would leave. He already had a pretty sum of money saved up, and it would only increase in the next two years until his graduation.

Turning on his gaming computer, he logged into his game of choice—one he used strictly for relaxation purposes. It was a simple RPG that mimicked real life but against a fantastical backdrop. The goal was to make connections and alliances and complete challenges.

And if he were honest to himself, it wasn't the *game* that helped him relax. It was the friends he'd made on the other side of the screen. People who had no idea who he was or the burdens he carried—people who only knew him as his avatar, *bluebird15*.

"You're late," a digitized voice noted the moment he entered the chat.

"I had to finish my assignment," he excused himself. "The others aren't online, either," he pointed out.

There were four people in their group chat, but aside from him only another one was currently online—*curiouscat26*.

Out of everyone, his relationship with curiouscat26 was the most tense, as they often bickered about everything, from the choice of clothing of their avatars, to their interactions with other teams in the game. Somehow, they were *never* on the same page.

At times, he was sure *Curiouscat* was doing things on purpose just to get a rise out of him. Tiger and Ginny usually served as a buffer between the two of them. And now that they were the only ones present on the server, he could bet mayhem would be unleashed.

He almost groaned out loud.

Still, these were the few times in his day when he could be himself—speak like himself. He'd become so used with his stutter that now normal words posed a challenge for him, and he sometimes slipped into his role without even realizing.

He was just...lost. *There*, he admitted it to himself. He was fucking lost, and he didn't know how to find himself—if that was a possibility at all.

"Tiger is dealing with some stuff at home and Ginny has a doctor appointment. You're stuck with me today, Blue," curiouscat26 said.

"Right, just my luck," he grumbled under his breath.

"What was that?"

"Nothing. Absolutely nothing," he smiled. Curiouscat was feisty. He didn't know if she was a woman, or a man pretending to be a woman, as sometimes that happened, but she had a pretty volatile temper. Still, he couldn't deny that for all their bickering, curiouscat was entertaining. She'd made him laugh on days he hadn't thought himself capable of any levity, and she certainly always helped him immerse himself in the game and forget the outside world for a few hours.

They'd all met in the game a while back. Curiouscat had already teamed up with Tiger and Ginny, and together they'd reached out to him to complete the team. Back then he'd been a solo player, his experience enough to help him get by. But after a little back and forth and a correct solution to a tricky riddle, he'd accepted to join them. The final formation consisted of two girls and two guys, though he had no idea if any of the people on the other side of the screen were who they said they were.

He, himself, was an impostor. He couldn't discount on everyone else being one either.

"Good," a pause. "We shouldn't start without the others, right?" she asked, slight hesitation in her voice.

The game itself came with a system that allowed for easy anonymity. While they talked to each other via their headsets, their voices were changed inside the game so they wouldn't be recognizable outside of it.

Curiouscat had an annoyingly high-pitched voice that more often than not gave Raf a headache, though he didn't know if it was the effect on the voice or the fact that he just disliked the person behind it. Though, technically, dislike was too strong of a word. It was something more like...antipathy.

They only ever played in their original formation, since it was a moot point to have only half the team. Raf could see why curiouscat wouldn't want to continue without them.

"Then I'll log off. Talk to you next time," he said, his hands already on his headset to remove it.

"Wait," she burst out. "You're really leaving?"

"Well, if the others aren't around and we can't actually play, why would I stay?"

"I don't know... To talk?"

There was a hopeful quality to the tone that made Raf pause. "About what?"

Although they all got along in the game, they'd set some rules from the beginning, the most important one being *not* asking any personal questions or prying in the others' lives.

At the same time, Raf suspected they were all in the same boat. They had no one in the outside world and simply relied on digital friendships. Certainly, something about the way curiouscat said those words struck a chord in him.

"Is blue really your favorite color?" she suddenly asked, the question so inane it made him smile.

He could sense another person in need of company.

"No, my favorite color is violet," he answered cheekily.

"Violet? Why isn't your handle violetbird then?"

"It sounded too girly."

"Oh, so you wanted to make sure people knew you're a guy. Are you trying to pick up girls in the game?" she sounded scandalized, and Raf could barely hold back a grin.

"So what if I am? I'm clearly not trying to pick *you* up," he fired back.

"What if I told you I have violet eyes?"

"I'm sure you *don't* have violet eyes."

"How do you know? I very well could. Would that make you fall for me, then?"

"There is no such thing as violet eyes," he smiled. "Unless you're an anime girl."

"Maybe I am," she shot back in indignation. "But *maybe*, I really have violet eyes."

"Is it because I said it's my favorite color? Come one, curiouscat, don't tell me *you*'ve fallen for me?" he chuckled.

A pause.

"Why would I?" she replied in a *very* even tone. "I'd have to be a masochist to fall for someone who enjoys making fun of me all the time," she said with a huff.

"And now you're stalling. What's wrong, curiouscat?" Raf eventually asked, recognizing that she wouldn't engage him in conversation if there wasn't anything bothering her.

"I..." she sighed. "Just family stuff. I guess I needed a moment of normality before going back to the real world."

"What happened?" he inquired, forgetting momentarily

about their rules. She sounded so forlorn, in a way echoing his own loneliness that he couldn't help himself.

"Can't say. Rule one, remember?" her voice was soft, as if she was regretting the presence of the rule but needing to abide by it anyway.

"Circumvent it," he pushed on. "Leave out the recognizable details."

She was quiet for a moment, and Raf didn't know if she was going to say anything. Odd how they'd always been at each other's throats online yet now he wanted to be there for her—at least for a little while.

Due to its marked absence in his life, he knew what it was like to wish for someone to talk to but having no one.

He heard her intake of breath.

"Suppose your family is trying to force you to do something. Against your will. Something that benefits them but only hurts you..."

"Don't do it," Raf immediately said. He had enough experience with that and knew the repercussions of choosing to do only what other people wanted of him. "Don't sacrifice yourself for them."

"But what if there's...no way out? What if it's something that you've been told you need to do your entire life?"

Raf closed his eyes, his lips flattened into a thin line.

"I don't know what it is you're talking about, but from experience, I can tell you that doing what other people want to the detriment of what *you* want will only end badly. Don't sacrifice yourself for anyone, curiouscat. No one deserves that much. Just like *you* don't deserve to be put in that position."

He thought he heard a sniffle.

"You're not that bad, are you, Blue?" she tried to imbue some cheerfulness into her voice.

He merely smiled against his mic.

"I don't know if I can refuse. Not this. I depend on them for everything and... Agh," she cried out. "Why the hell is life so difficult?"

"What would be the fun if it was simple?" he retorted, surprising himself with the words. "I've lived with that dilemma my entire life, whether I should please my parents, or my siblings, or myself. Instead of choosing one clear path, I tried to split myself into three, change myself for every one of them so they would all be happy at the end of the day."

"And how did that end up for you?"

"Maybe they were happy, for a time. But it all imploded. And when it did, it blew in my face."

"I'm sorry," she said quietly. "How did you manage to change it?'

"I didn't. I'm still doing it, bending to everyone's whims but my own. And trust me, curiouscat, it's fucking exhausting."

"I can imagine," her voice lost some of its previous high pitch, the tone warmer, softer. If he closed his eyes, he could even feel a slight sweet taste. "I can see the road they want me to take—I can see it clearly even though I have no idea what awaits me there. All I know is that I won't be...*me*. And I happen to like myself as I am, thank you very much."

Raf chuckled. There it was, the usual curiouscat he knew.

"You must be the only one," he muttered under his breath, but it was a light teasing, and she didn't take it to heart either.

"So what? At least *I* like myself. How many people are there that can't even stand to look at themselves in the mirror? I am quite aware of my qualities and flaws, and I would say I have more qualities *than* flaws."

He felt her words like an arrow to the heart. How many times had he looked into the mirror and seen himself as the impostor he was? Hell, he barely knew himself, what was there to like if he couldn't even identify *who* he was?

"There, there, curiouscat. Aren't you going a little overboard? You should wait for someone else to sing you praises. It doesn't look good if you do it yourself," he laughed in an effort to chase away the awkwardness.

"Maybe *you* should be more comfortable in your own skin," she said it so blatantly, it wasn't meant to be an insult. Yet to Raf, that was exactly what it was.

Because he wasn't comfortable in his skin. Far from it.

He looked how he wanted people to perceive him. Nothing more, nothing less. The real tragedy was that he wouldn't even let himself dream of what he'd *wish* he looked like. He was too afraid to put that image in his head when he knew it might never come true.

Yet if he closed his eyes, he could see. He'd like to gain some pounds, maybe turn them into muscle. He'd like to straighten his posture, walk to his full height. And hell, the biggest wish was that he wanted to behave *everywhere* like he did now—without a care in the world.

"You're right," he accepted. "I'm not comfortable in my skin," he admitted his deepest secret. Why, he couldn't tell.

He was aware that his features were passable enough. He'd always been complimented on his eyes and complexion. But because of his lifestyle, he was too thin, his cheeks hollowed out, his bones sticking out and making him look entirely unappealing.

There were so many things standing in his way, he didn't see how he could one day reach his ideal—he just couldn't.

"I—I'm sorry. I didn't mean to offend you if it's something you're sensitive about," she quickly said, her tone apologetic.

A sad smile pulled at his lips.

"It's ok. It's the truth. I'm not comfortable with who I am."

"Why don't you change it then? I'm sure if you put in the effort..."

"I can't," he sighed. "Remember those family expectations of yours? I'm in the same boat. I'm just trying to please everyone," he whispered, his voice thick with emotion.

"I'm sorry," she apologized again.

He could tell she *was* sorry for bringing it up. And soon, she switched the topic, approaching lighter subjects and doing her best to make him laugh, teasing him and bickering with him in a way that would bring them back to a comfortable footing.

He appreciated that.

She'd been the one looking for advice for her issue and she'd ended up tending to *his* tender sensibilities.

"Fuck, but what type of man am I?" he muttered, frustrated, as he put his headset down. Curiouscat had gone to bed early, and he'd logged off as well.

In spite of their previous history in the game, the conversation had flowed well, and he'd felt a sense of kinship the likes he hadn't felt in a long time—maybe forever.

For the rest of the night, he simply logged into his other game, working all his frustrations and grievances in the virtual environment as he challenged everyone he could find for battle.

It wasn't a solution to his problems, but it was a damn good way of blowing some steam.

And as usual, he ended up spending the night away, sleeping in the following day and barely making it to class on time.

He hunched his shoulders as he stepped inside the classroom, taking a seat somewhere in the back and laying his stuff on his desk. Getting his glasses from their case, he pushed them over his nose as his eyes skittered to the clock on the wall. Five minutes. He'd barely made it in time.

It was odd how it was in the days he never had anything particular to do that he would waste his time and squander his sleep for absolutely no reason.

Now, after hours of having his eyes stuck to a screen, he felt worn out. He hadn't even eaten for the day, merely getting out of bed and hurrying to class.

"Rafaelo, right?" Someone asked from his side. He turned his head slowly, recognizing the guy as Steve, one of his colleagues from freshman orientation.

He nodded.

"Haven't seen you in a while, dude," he chuckled, laying his own materials on the desk.

"I-I've been busy," he said slowly.

Whenever he forced his stammer, he also had to slow his words so he wouldn't butcher his routine. It was all practice, and speed never helped.

"I can see that," he laughed as he pointed to his notebook filled with scribbles. It was mostly battle strategies for his upcoming game, but Steve probably thought he was the type to write down every single word the professor uttered.

And in a lifetime ago, maybe he'd been.

Now, it wasn't expected of him, just as it wasn't expected of him to be the best.

Due to his learning disabilities, he had extra time for assignments and during exams, everyone babying him in their own way.

He'd stopped minding it a long time ago, yet he could never shake the way some still regarded him with pity, as if people who had a harder time learning weren't people at all.

But that had been the main lesson he'd learned throughout the years. People didn't show you their true faces when you were strong. They did it when you were weak. Oh, and how they delighted in doing it.

Armed with that knowledge, he'd avoided making any friendships at college, having *some* acquaintances, but mostly keeping to himself unless it was strictly necessary to team up with someone for a class.

Class started and Steve didn't bother him further, which pleased Raf. The less people he talked to, the less he had to pretend.

Yet when the clock struck sharp and the professor ended the lesson, Steve turned to him once more.

"There's a party tonight at my frat, why don't you come, too? It's gonna be fun."

Raf blinked, taken completely unaware.

He'd been invited to parties before, mostly in his freshman year. And though he'd had some intrinsic curiosity about them since he'd only seen college parties in movies, he'd had to refuse every invite. He was still living at home back then, and Cosima would never allow him to attend anything as scandalous or that could put him in danger.

"I-I'll think a-about it," he said before he could help himself.

Steve grinned and patted him on the back before he left, leaving with Raf the instructions to get to the party if he decided to come.

Raf didn't know why he hadn't refused it. What would he be doing at a party other than embarrass himself? Maybe if he were anyone other than himself... But he could never afford to slip out of character. Should anyone find out, it would be the end of everything as he knew it.

His thoughts soured for the rest of the day, mostly because deep down, he *was* curious about the party. He wanted to be a normal teenager for once, go out and have fun. He wanted... what he couldn't have.

thirty-four

AGE TWENTY

He spent the first hour in his dorm room staring at the walls and debating what he should do. He clearly knew the answer—he should *not* go. Yet he still warred with himself because of that deep rooted desire to be normal, or as normal as he could for one night.

Though it was not the time to meet his friends in the game, he logged on.

They had a schedule that they all abided by, especially since they'd agreed on no personal details. Yet now more than ever Raf felt the need to talk to someone, to...

And there it was.

Curiouscat26 was online.

He thought about it once. Twice. The third time he just pressed her icon, opening her chat.

"What are you up to, Blue?" her suspicious tone rang out in his headset.

"I didn't realize you had no life, too, *Curiouscat*," he shot back.

She grumbled something.

"At least *you* admit you don't have one either."

"Well, as a matter of fact I'm about to have one. I was invited to a party," he retorted smugly.

"A party for clowns? Ha, ha, good try. It doesn't count."

"A frat party, you fool. Not that you'd know what that is."

"I've watched American Pie. I know exactly what that is," she said accusatorially.

Interesting. That at least told Raf she'd never been to college. He assumed she was around his age from what they had talked, but neither had ever revealed a number. That would be too personal.

"Watching and going to one are two completely different things. Nerd," he didn't know why he said that, mostly because he wanted to one up her, but the word came out teasingly, almost *too* teasingly.

"Well, if you're so busy what are you doing on the server? Go to your frat party and leave me alone," she mumbled in annoyance.

"It's a Friday night. You're really not doing anything?" He felt compelled to ask as he detected a hint of sadness in her voice.

"My family is strict," she said matter-of-factly. "I can't go out as I like."

He nodded in understanding. He knew what that was like. If he'd been living at home, his mother would have never allowed him to go anywhere.

"Well, I'll think about you at the party," he forced a laugh.

"You're not going anywhere, are you?"

"What do you mean, of course I am!"

"Come on, Blue. I rather think we're more alike than you care to admit," she added, almost chastising him.

And it was this precise reason why he thought she was around the same age as him, maybe older. She displayed a maturity and self-awareness that he hadn't encountered before. And it fascinated him.

"I was invited to one, ok?" he eventually admitted. "But I'm not sure I'm going yet. Maybe..." he mumbled under his breath.

"Why wouldn't you go? Go out and have fun for us mere mortals too. You can come back and tell me if American Pie lied or not about what goes there."

"I'm not sure," he sighed. "I don't know anyone there. I'm not...popular," he forced the words out, admitting his weakness.

"So? Does it matter what they think? You're not going there to make them happy. You're going there for yourself. So put on your big boy pants and go!"

"You're very bossy, aren't you?" he smiled.

"Damn, Blue, don't tell me you've fallen for me already," she chided playfully.

"No way. You're not my type. I happen to like shy, meek girls," he retorted, though he didn't have the vaguest idea about what he liked. And if he were honest with himself, curiouscat wasn't so bad. She was...real. As ironic as that sounded, she was more real than anyone he'd ever met, regardless that she was just a digitized voice coming out of his computer.

"Of course you would. You need someone to submit to your tyrannical will, don't you?" she asked pointedly, but somewhere along the line, their bickering had lost its edge. It was now a comfortable teasing that didn't fail to put a smile on his face.

"Are you offering?"

"In your dreams," she huffed. "Now log off and go party! I'll be waiting for your stories."

No sooner did she finish her words than her avatar went offline.

Rafaelo supposed it was her way of emphasizing he needed to go out into the world. And maybe... Maybe he did.

He spent another hour dithering before he finally decided to give it a try.

After all, how bad could it be?

Taking a shower, he chose a pair of dark jeans and a clean, white shirt. He'd heard that the polite etiquette to such parties was to bring something to drink, so before he headed to the party, he made a stop at a liquor shop that didn't card. He didn't have a fake ID, and he didn't want to go through the trouble of getting one—not when he risked being found out by his family. And that was the last thing he needed.

He bought a bottle of the more expensive vodka he could find to show his thanks for the invite before going to the frat house.

By the time he made it there, he was right on the dot.

And the house was...kind of empty.

"Rafaelo, good on you to come!" Steve greeted him, coming down the stairs and shaking his hand. "And damn, you really went for it," he whistled as he regarded the bottle of alcohol.

"T-thank you," he strained a smile, keeping up his act as he strode deeper into the house.

"It's a bit early still, but why don't you grab a drink and mingle?" Steve advised, almost absentmindedly before going somewhere else.

Raf blinked, a little confused, but he did as Steve said, going to the bar and getting himself a glass of jungle juice.

He wrinkled his nose at the red liquid, but took a sip, surprised to note the fruity taste as well as the almost nonexistent alcohol.

If he'd come so far, he might as well try to enjoy himself.

The music was blaring out loudly, and soon more people started to trickle in.

He kept to his spot on the couch, nursing the same glass of jungle juice as he observed everyone.

Considering he didn't know anyone aside from Steve, no one really minded him. Especially with how he looked, huddled in his seat, his glasses askew on his nose, his blonde locks covering most of his face.

"I haven't seen you around."

He whipped his head around, noting the presence of a girl on the couch. She was also holding a drink in her hand, sipping casually as she assessed him.

"I-it's m-my first t-time," he strained a smile.

"Really?" she intoned, her voice grating on his nerves. There was something oddly fake about the cadence of her voice, a bitter taste erupting on his tongue. "Then aren't I lucky?" she continued, coming a little closer.

Raf kept his ground, merely nodding as she started talking about some subject he'd never heard of. But he wasn't paying much attention, his eyes skittering around the room as he took in the deluge of people, all moving their bodies to the music.

The room started to fog up as more and more people came inside, and the couch was a tight fit.

"You didn't tell me your name," the girl suddenly said, her hand on his thigh. Out of pure reflex, he jumped up, spilling his glass off jungle juice all over his white shirt in the process.

"Damn," he gave a low mutter. The girl's eyes widened, and she seemed a little put off with him as she soon redirected her attention to someone else. Just as well since Raf had no interest in her. And as he walked a little around the room, he realized he had no interest in what was going on around him either. He'd witnessed enough to realize it wasn't quite his scene.

He didn't get to exit the room, though, as he came face to face with Steve, who looked a little worse for the wear than before.

"Rafaelo! My man," he yelled to be heard over the music. "Come, let's get you a drink."

Raf was about to tell him that he'd had his drink and he'd spilled it too. But before he could say anything, he found himself led to another room where there were only guys drinking and laughing and smoking.

"This is my friend Rafaelo," Steve made the introductions, saying he'd met Raf in one of his classes while adding a few embellishments to make their relationship seem closer than it was. Why, Raf couldn't tell.

He was too confused by everything going on around him, and when he was offered another glass of alcohol, he simply accepted.

The worst was yet to come. Because one glass became two, then three, and then Raf lost count.

He realized he didn't have to speak, most of the other guys doing the talking for him as they boasted about the chicks they fucked, at some point all laughing when they realized they'd fucked the *same* one.

"We have a tradition here," Steve told Raf. "If a girl fucks all the brothers in a class, she gets to make a wish," he chuckled, saying the girl they were talking about had one more guy to fuck before she'd reach that level.

Raf merely smiled, taking a big gulp of his drink.

His insides were fuzzy.

He was no stranger to alcohol, and he'd had his fair share of blackout moments in the past, most due to drinking to forget the pain of being stabbed. He'd always refused to drink with his father's men for fun, but he found the activity to be much more pleasant than he had imagined. Especially now that he was with *normal* guys his age.

And as he got drunker and drunker, his stammer gave way to a natural slur that did not take into account his made-up persona.

"Rafaelo," Steve started, but Raf held up a hand.

"Raf."

"Raf," Steve smiled. "You're not joining in?" he asked as he brought a bottle of vodka to fill Raf's already half-empty glass. He didn't even notice, bringing it to his lips for another sip as he tried to make sense of what Steve required of him.

"What do you mean?" he asked slowly, the words almost escaping him.

Only then did he notice that more people had joined in, some girls too.

"We're playing never have I ever. You know how to play, right?"

Raf nodded. He had an idea.

"Perfect!" Steve clapped. "Greg, you start," he pointed to the guy on the other side.

"Never have I ever fucked outside," he grinned as he watched everyone around.

Raf blinked, and for a split of a second, he didn't know whether to drink or not. But then, he supposed that drinking was the punishment if he had *not* done it.

So, he drank.

Everyone was quiet for a second, regarding him funnily before they moved on.

"Never have I ever..." the guy looked around, almost as if he wanted to ask something sneaky, "gotten into a knife fight."

A low sigh escaped Raf as he didn't drink this time. Maybe he'd be lucky, and he won't have to drink for all rounds.

No one else drank either, eliciting a laugh from the guy who asked the question.

The next person went.

"Never have I ever smoked weed," he laughed as he popped a joint into his mouth and lit it up.

Everyone but Raf drank. He frowned. He'd smoked with his father's men. But why was everyone drinking? Including those who were clearly smoking now.

The questions continued, all involving sex, acts of vandalism and things that seemed to be regarded as *cool* by everyone.

Raf was already so gone that even if he wanted to lie, he wouldn't have been able.

Steve's turn was up, and Raf regarded him with slight apprehension, knowing that soon it would be *him* who had to come up with a question.

"Never have I ever been in an orgy," Steve said, looking around expectantly.

Raf, who clearly hadn't, went ahead to drink, realizing too late that everyone was staring at him—including Steve.

"You've been in an orgy," he blinked, taken aback.

"Of c-course not," Raf answered, flustered.

"Then why are you drinking?"

"Oh, no, he must have thought you drank if you haven't done it."

"Wait, wait," another guy put his hand up, standing on wobbly feet. "You mean you've gotten into a knife fight?"

Raf blinked in confusion, slowly nodding. His head was already swimming in alcohol, his confidence suddenly soaring.

"No shit!" more noise.

"Did you get hit?"

"Show us!"

A chorus of voices joined in until it was hard for him to make sense of who was talking. He was vaguely aware of lifting his shirt to show some of the faded marks on his torso.

Everyone was cheering him on, and he lost count of the people who tried to talk to him. For an outsider, he was suddenly very much *in*. So much so that he was once more plied with alcohol until he could barely think coherently.

It was a few hours later that he finally excused himself and left the frat house. At the height of his euphoria, he felt very pleased with himself and how the interaction had gone. He even wagered he might have made some new friends.

Exiting the house straight onto the main road, he squinted as he tried to make sense of where exactly he was. His sight was foggy, his brain even more so.

Regardless, as he wobbled down the street, he couldn't *not* stop every five feet and pick up all the bottles and other types of trash he could find and put them back where they belonged—in trashcans and recycle bins.

At that moment, all he could think of was his civic duty to ensure the cleanliness of the city.

But that wasn't the only one.

As he waited for the light to turn green so he could cross the street, he spotted an elderly woman doing the same a few feet next to him.

He blinked twice as a bright bulb lit up in his brain—an opportunity to *excel* at his civic duty. The moment the light turned, he wasted no time in grabbing the elderly woman's arm, giving her a charming smile and proceeding to help—*drag*—her across the street.

Her protests were only muffled by Rafaelo's mumbled words as he could not even properly convey his intentions.

Instead of *let me help you*, the sound that came out of his mouth was more like.

"Lebe hell-u."

Which, of course, the elderly woman misinterpreted as a threat, especially given Rafaelo's half-smile since one side of his face was entirely numb from the excess of alcohol. Her eyes widening, she swatted him in the head with her bag, pushing him off her and running away—or as best as she could, given her age.

Raf was stumped.

He was left staring at the woman's retreating figure as his brain tried to catch up with everything.

Why had she hit him? He'd only meant to help her.

The more he pondered, the more he frowned, and he spent several minutes trying to get to the bottom of it before shrugging and deciding he needed to get home.

He was rounding the corner to his building when he heard a scream. With so much vodka in his system, he felt *almost* invincible. Which meant he thought of nothing else but diving head-first into danger. After all, someone needed help, and he was always up for offering help. It was just that he didn't know when to say no.

Raf was swaying from side to side, his eyes barely making out the shapes in the dark. Yet that didn't stop him from charging immediately when he realized it was a woman struggling against two men. They had her backed against the wall of the building, one of them with his hands on his belt while the other was hiking her skirt up.

Maybe if he'd been sober, he would have done things differently. But as it stood, his first instinct was to get involved and help the woman before he could think things out.

And so, he charged.

Ungracefully.

A little gauche.

He was, after all, barely holding himself together. Yet his inherent sense of justice dictated he should *do* something.

The girl gave a loud yelp as Raf went for the guy who was trying to undress her. He rushed with a fist to the man's jaw, all the while trying to avoid the other one laying hits on *his* body. It was a cacophony of sounds, grunts and groans as everyone hit the others.

But what was odd was the fact that the girl wasn't leaving. She wasn't running for her life. Instead, she was yelling at Raf to let them go, slapping his back and trying to intervene in the scuffle.

If he'd been sober, maybe that would have registered as a red flag. As it stood, he didn't really see it as a suspicious sign. He only believed her to be frightened, clawing her way out and trying to harm the bad men by herself too.

Admirable, in his view, but foolish.

A fist landed on his face. One in his stomach. He landed a few of his own, too. But it was all such a back and forth that no one was winning.

Until the sirens blared.

The men, aware of what that meant, were trying to disentangle themselves, but Raf wouldn't let go. In the back of his mind, he heard the police sirens and somehow honed in on that thought, knowing he couldn't let go until they showed up so the perpetrators could be punished for attempting to assault the woman.

Yet when the police car drew to a halt, the officers coming out of it, it wasn't the two men who got placed in the back of the car.

It was Raf.

In his drunken stupor, he hadn't heard the men defending themselves and pointing out Raf as the aggressor. And with how drunk he was, the police didn't even question it.

He mumbled some things in his defense, none coherent enough to be taken seriously.

And that was how Rafaelo ended up being placed in a cell for the rest night. After all, the police couldn't deal very well with someone so inebriated.

It was in the early hours of the morning that Raf woke up, startled to find himself cold and without his blanket. As he opened his eyes, he recognized he was *not* in his dorm, and that his surroundings appeared rather bleak.

His state of mind became even worse as he was told why he'd been arrested, and that his parents had been notified.

At that news, he was one step away from punching himself for what an idiot he'd been.

Especially since it wasn't long before his mother's shrill voice rang into the station, his father's low mutter following soon after.

"My poor darling. What did you do to him?" She accused the policemen, one step away from doing them bodily harm as she saw the state Raf was in.

His white shirt was still stained with red from the jungle juice. Along the way, though, he'd also collected some dirt and grime marks, making him look like he hadn't bathed in weeks. And as Cosima stepped into his cell, hurrying to hug her precious baby, it was to be hit by the nauseating smell of alcohol.

"Raf, what happened?" she drew a sharp breath, worry evident in her eyes.

Raf didn't know where to start.

Damn it, but his one night out wasn't supposed to end like that. He wanted a brief reprieve from his lonely existence, not a stint in jail for reasons he still didn't fully comprehend. And he told his mother that much too—a little more embellished, of course.

He emphasized the fact that he wanted to make friends, so he'd accepted an invite to a party and he'd drank a little more than his share—none of it untrue.

She listened attentively, nodding. He could see right away as her focus shifted, from outrage to pity.

For all the love in the world she carried him, there were moments where he could see the pity in her gaze and the disappointment that her previous son would never live a normal life. Yet she'd never told him that. She'd accepted him with his faults and all the issues that came with his *condition*.

It was a bit startling to realize that his mother, the woman who'd schemed and plotted her entire life to get him on top, would be ok with *not* fulfilling that dream.

But if there was one thing his *condition* had helped him with, it had been to see the true of his mother's affection. Yes, she was an awful person—had been awful to everyone but him. Yet no matter how much he hated her for her part in his brother's suffering, he couldn't shake the inherent love he had for her— and he probably never would.

He saw her as she was. Flawed.

That didn't make her any less his mother just like that didn't make her any less guilty for everything she'd done.

And *that* was a dilemma he warred with on a daily basis.

His mother continued to baby him while his father dealt with the logistics of his arrest. It wasn't long before he was let go, but *not* because of his family's influence. Simply because the arrest had been a fluke.

Though Raf had been drunk out of his mind, and he *had* been the one to initiate the brawl, he'd acted as he rightly believed someone was in danger. The CCTV showed why Raf might have thought the men were about to hurt the woman and he'd been given a slap on the wrist when the other participants had been called in, all confessing it had been some kind of kinky game between the three of them.

Raf had to reluctantly agree that it now made sense why the woman hadn't run, instead turning on *him*.

"My darling boy, you can't do that from now on. How can I let you live by yourself if this is what you get yourself in..." his mother continued to drone on and on, coming with him to his dorm to see him settled. Deep down in her heart, she actually wanted to get him to pack his bags and return to living at home with her.

"You know how lonely I get," she sighed, sitting on his bed and watching him with sorrowful eyes.

"B-but t-that's a t-two h-hour r-ride," he'd made the excuse, making himself smaller in his chair and hoping his mother would eventually tire of watching his pitiful self and would finally leave him alone so he could die of embarrassment.

"I know, baby boy," she pursed her lips. "I just worry about you all the time."

"I-I c-come h-home m-most wee-kends," he tried to explain.

And he did. Two or three weekends a month he was home. Was it so bad that he wanted some time to himself?

"Oh, Raf, what am I going to do with you?" Cosima lamented, taking him in her arms for a tight hug.

They talked a little more, or Cosima talked *more* as she tried to convince him to come home. When she realized it was in vain, she finally relented and left him at his dorm with the promise he wouldn't get himself into trouble again.

He happily agreed. He didn't think he'd want a repeat of the other night either, even though all the events were sort of a blur. He remembered the party, he even remembered the fight, but it was like he was a spectator in his own body.

The worst was the nausea he couldn't shake even after a hot shower and a warm meal, his head throbbing, his whole body aching from where he'd been hit.

He was lucky he'd only gotten a few bruises to his face, because if his mother had seen his torso and the many discolorations that marred it, she would have *never* allowed him to remain. Raf knew how his mother's brain worked, and if she got it in her head that her son was in danger, then there was no convincing her otherwise.

He tended to his injuries himself, taking some painkillers and finally laying down in bed to get some rest, not realizing as he slept the day *and* night away.

thirty-five
AGE TWENTY

When he next awoke, it was already Sunday, and his mood hadn't improved. On the contrary, with the alcohol completely flushed out of his system, he felt even more alienated from everyone around him.

All he could think of was that he was a farce. And he didn't know anymore how *not* to be one.

He spent the day finishing his assignments for the following week and decided to forgo going online. For some reason, he felt his inadequacy to the depth of his soul, the way he was doomed to live a life that wasn't his own—that would *never* be his own.

It wasn't even self-loathing that governed him, though he'd experienced plenty of that in the past. Now it was a simple loathing of the present and of the status quo. It was a dislike of himself and the person he showed to the world but more than anything it was a hopelessness that led to minor bouts of depression that he could barely shake himself out of.

And at that moment, he felt another one coming.

The last time he'd felt like that, Raf had stayed locked inside his room for an entire summer, his routine alternating between sleeping and his computer. He'd go through periods of not eating and almost starving himself, and then he'd switch to the other extreme, eating too much and unable to stop himself.

Now, he could feel himself plummeting again, and Friday night had only served to show him what he was missing, the friends and connection he could make but would forever be out of reach.

Yet he still had one more surprise waiting for him as he went to his classes the following Monday. People were giving him odd glances, furtively laughing at him, their eyes crinkling with unknown amusement.

He noticed, but he didn't know it was directed at him.

Squaring his shoulders, he kept his head down as he took a seat, opening his notebook and scribbling down the date.

"Did you see? I think it's him."

"It's definitely him," someone from another row laughed.

He blinked in confusion, especially as more people joined in, secretly watching something on their phones and turning to Raf to laugh about it.

It continued to his next class too, until he finally saw Steve, who decided to tell Raf the scoop.

"Here, isn't this crazy?" Steve asked with a laugh, clicking play on a video that showcased Raf's drunk ass making a fool of himself at the frat party. He didn't remember that part of the evening, but from the looks of it, some people had dared him to do silly things like dancing on the bar or waiting with his mouth open for an entire bucket of jungle juice to be shoved down his throat.

He felt ill just looking at the videos. But there was more.

Someone had filmed him getting into a fight after the party and had shared the video to the entire campus. The only issue was that no one was calling him a hero or saying he had done a great thing by trying to save a woman from being attacked.

Everyone was calling him lame, a pervert and a creep. As the story went, *he* had been the one to harass the girl and the other guys had only tried to put a stop to it.

He was being painted in the worst light, and *everyone* bought it. Suddenly, *he* was the lowlife, not the men who'd orchestrated the entire scene, and who had conveniently disappeared at this time.

Because of his usual odd manner accompanied by his stutter, the consensus was clear. Raf was the creep.

Suddenly, all the giggles and furtive glances made sense.

They were laughing at him.

Everyone was laughing at him.

The narrative was already set. He had behavioral issues so he could never get a girl, and that was the root of his frustration. The videos only showed his increased thirst for validation and the fact that he was a freak.

"Man, you shouldn't have gone that far," Steve continued. "Stacy told me you tried to pull some moves on her, too," he shook his head in disappointment. "Word of advice, learn how to read the room and when a girl's not into you," he said before he left a flabbergasted Raf standing alone in the center of the campus.

And *everyone* was laughing.

He felt ill.

He barely held it together as he hurried to his room, away from all the derisive laughter that followed him around.

Opening the door to his room, he locked himself inside, his breathing out of control, his heart pounding in his chest. He felt...disgusted with himself.

Absolutely appalled that he'd let himself fall that low and for what? For a little attention? Without the alcohol fogging his mind he could see that everyone was entertaining him, not out of some kindness or some absurd interest, but merely so they could make fun of him.

A bitter laugh escaped him. Curiouscat had been right. He'd been their clown.

Ripping at his clothes, he threw them around as he stumbled into the shower, the water pouring down on him just as he broke down, his emotions reaching the surface and making him fall to his knees with the intensity of his frustration. His arms on the cold tiles of the wall, he let the water wash over him, tears trickling down his cheeks as he let out a low howl.

In that moment, he hated everything.

He hated his life, and he hated his past.

But more than anything, he detested his own damn self. Because it was all his fault. No one had forced him to do anything.

From the very beginning, he'd done things out of his misguided sense of justice—one that always backfired on him.

He'd always held on to his ideals, thinking himself above everything because he could use cold logic in his judgment, reaching a conclusion objectively, rather than being ruled by emotion. After all, he'd been reared that way. To prioritize facts over emotions.

Yet deep down, he'd never been able to separate the two. Not when he'd had to make the biggest decision in his life and, clearly, he'd made the wrong one.

He'd hurt the one person in his life who'd trusted him unconditionally. And *that*... That still ate him up on the inside, the guilt threatening to drown him worse than the water pouring down on him, or his tears that made his eyes sting, or his screams that made his throat ache. *Nothing* could hurt him more than he'd hurt himself.

He could still remember his childhood, the time when everything had been perfect—or, retrospectively, as perfect as could be. When Gianna had still been with them. When Michele had regarded Raf as his protector—as his true brother.

It had been the most beautiful period of his life. Raf doubted he'd ever know happiness as he'd known then.

The memories of Michele drawing him personalized characters, or Gianna hugging him and telling him she was proud of him hurt just as they made him happy. They hurt so fucking bad and made the anguish he felt even more intolerable.

And who was to blame for everything he'd lost?

Him. Just...him.

"Why? Why, why, why?" he screamed as he threw his fists against the wall, hurting no one but himself. Yet he needed that —he *deserved* it.

He was on the brink, and he knew it. Though he was living daily with regret, guilt and disappointment, over the years he'd found a modicum of balance by putting it aside. After all, that was his coping mechanism. Locking stuff away and dealing with bits at a time, making sure he wasn't wholly overwhelmed.

Yet the disadvantage was that there were times like this, when everything just came crashing down. When just a little push made everything tumble down on him, unleashing a river of anguish so strong, he didn't know how to put himself together again.

He had to give it to Steve and everyone else mocking him.

Raf *was* a loser. He was a loser of his own making, and wasn't that the worst?

It didn't matter how smart, how capable, or how responsible he was?

Somewhere along the way, he'd lost the notion that he was anything but a loser. He'd lost sight of everything in his life as he'd focused only on the bad.

The incident on campus only served to emphasize the state of affairs and the fact that even something as innocuous as him going to a party could end up so disastrously.

Yet the worst wasn't that people were mocking him, or that

he'd become the laughingstock of the university. The worst was that Raf believed he deserved it.

He thought he deserved every little bad thing that happened to him. No matter how much he hoped for a normal life, or how he wished he could stop pretending, finally find his *true* self, he didn't dare try it.

He didn't deserve anything good in his life.

For that, he only had to look at his brother and the way he was actively trying to self-destruct—all a direct consequence of Raf's decisions.

He saw Michele and he knew he deserved absolutely everything that came his way.

Time passed. He found it harder and harder to get himself together. Even as cold water washed over him, he couldn't move from the spot.

His movements were sluggish, his entire body echoing the sentiments in his heart.

When he managed to get himself out of the bathroom, he pulled a robe tightly around his body, absorbing his heat and trying to calm the clattering of his teeth.

Yet did he deserve anything else but discomfort?

At first, he laid down on his bed, thinking to sleep everything off. But after twisting and turning, his mind too alert for that, he finally relented and opened his computer.

His intention wasn't to talk with anyone, though deep down that was his deepest desire. Instead, he pretended he was only checking his notifications and making sure he wasn't missing any work opportunities in the upcoming week.

No one forced him to log into his game, and definitely no one made him press on the messages icon, seeing all the missed chats.

All from curiouscat.

He blinked, a little taken aback as he scrolled through tens of messages asking if he was alright. Curiouscat actually worried about him because he hadn't been online in a few days. She...

He didn't know why that hit him so hard. Up until then he'd assumed if he disappeared off the face of the earth no one would mourn him aside from his mother. Maybe no one else would notice either because there was no one to care.

Yet it was startling to realize someone was actually checking in on him. His absence affected someone.

He was still staring at the screen when the call came, his fingers absentmindedly clicking to accept it. Yet it wasn't just that, because he also reached for his headset, putting it on.

No, he wanted this—craved this.

He wanted to know he mattered for someone. He *needed* to know that. Why, he didn't know. He had his mother, and that was more than a lot of people could say for themselves. Michele certainly had never had that...

He shook himself. He couldn't go down that road again.

"Blue? You're there?" a tentative voice asked.

"I'm here," he answered. No teasing. No jokes. Just a calm affirmation.

"Thank God," she breathed out in relief.

It struck him that for the first time her digitized voice didn't screw with his brain as much, it didn't sound so painful, or so contrived. It sounded...familiar.

And God knew he needed familiar at that point.

"You're okay? You haven't been online in a few days, and you missed the usual time yesterday..." she droned on, but he just smiled.

"I'm ok. Had a little mishap along the way but I'm ok," he chuckled, tears at the corner of his eyes.

He didn't know what that state was. He was laughing, yet tears kept poking at his eyes, wanting to be let free. It was the oddest thing.

"A mishap? Don't tell me you actually had an American Pie experience," Curiouscat exclaimed, scandalized.

"Maybe? I haven't watched the movie," he admitted.

"Blasphemy! Blue, what age are you living in? How could you? Everyone's watched American Pie!"

"I'm not that well versed in popular culture."

"Ah, I knew it. You're a nerd. Through and through, aren't you?"

"Guilty," he admitted with a low laugh.

"Ok, we can't have that. We need to remedy it. We're watching American Pie."

"We are?" he raised a brow, yet he didn't contradict her. For today, at least, he wasn't going to be his usual teasing self. He would just bask in the joy of having someone to talk to.

"Of course we are. But first, I need to know what happened to you Friday night," she said, and he heard munching noises.

"You're eating?"

"You bet I am. I'm all settled for your story. I have some Cheetos, the super spicy ones, and some Diet Coke by my side. So, I'm waiting."

"So, you like spicy food?" He couldn't help but ask.

"You're stalling. Let's hear it. What happened?"

"Well..." he chuckled to himself as he gave her a quick rundown of everything that had happened and how he'd ended up in jail—for the first time ever.

"My, it seems to me that you had quite a few firsts," she laughed. "How was jail? Damn, my brother would absolutely kill me if I ever got arrested."

"It was...cold. But I was too inebriated to feel it. I only felt the effects afterwards," he explained, though he also stored the information she shared about her brother.

"I can't believe that they think you're a creep for trying to do the right thing. The people at your college sound *very* dumb, no offense."

"None taken," he smiled. "But it was also my fault for drinking too much. I didn't realize until I saw the videos that the night wasn't quite as I remembered it," he admitted, feeling comfortable enough with her to share the fact that he'd been taken for a fool.

Maybe it was the anonymity.

Under that mask, he could be his real self.

"Those people sound awful, Blue. Why would you want to be friends with someone like that? Sorry to break it to you, but decent people don't just bully people for no reason or take advantage of clearly drunk people. That's an asshole move, and I think you know it, too."

He took a moment to answer.

"I guess I do," he sighed. "I don't know how I'm going to show my face around from now on, considering they think I'm a pervert," he tried to make light of the situation.

"Listen," she started, her tone serious. "You know that saying *in vino veritas?*"

"Yup."

"Well, I happen to think that drunk people act as their truest selves. If your first inclination, as drunk as you were, was to save someone else other than yourself, then more power to you. Don't listen to what others say when *you* know the truth, and the police records can also back that up."

"You're right," he chuckled. "You're quite the pep talker, aren't you?"

"I have to be. When no one else hypes you up you have to become your own hype man," she revealed, another piece of information that Raf carefully stored away.

"Don't tell me you have a lot of experience with getting

drunk?" he asked, not wanting to focus on something too personal, like why she had no one to hype her.

"No way," she laughed. "My experience is limited to getting the last sip from a glass left on the table before the staff takes it away. I've never had enough to get drunk, but if I did, I don't think my family would take it lightly," she laughed.

Another tidbit revealed. But then again, there could be a myriad of reasons why she wouldn't be allowed alcohol.

"Well, don't. I'll say from personal experience that it absolutely sucks the next morning."

"Note taken, Blue," she said in an amused tone. "But seriously, don't mind those people. They're just mean."

"Thank you," he eventually said. "For listening, and for having my back."

"Of course. I'll have your back every time if you let me. It can get pretty lonely here if you're not online."

"Don't tell me you waited every day for me to appear?" he genuinely laughed; the subject of his adventure dropped just as his spirits started to rise.

For all their previous enmity, curiouscat was easy to talk to—comfortable. He wasn't used to that. Just like he wasn't used to having someone to share his thoughts with. It was...disconcerting. But pleasant.

"Not *every* day," she grumbled. "I don't have that kind of time. I'm busy, you know?"

"Are you now? I thought you wasted your time playing video games."

"Hey," she exclaimed, feigning annoyance. "I'll have you know I have a *very* busy weekly schedule. You should consider yourself lucky that I make time for you."

"If you say so..."

"I'll even watch American Pie with you. See, I'm contributing to your education in pop culture. So, buckle up,

Blue. You won't be the same person once I'm through with you," she laughed, still munching on Cheetos as she pulled up a shared screen to load the movie.

"Why do I have a feeling you're right?" he mumbled, amused, as the credits rolled on the screen.

A few hours later he forgot all about his worries. Curiouscat had been right in that respect. He did feel like a new person. And it wasn't because now he had a new appreciation for American Pie. It was because he felt lighter than he had in a long time.

That movie was the first that started an almost daily routine where they would watch a movie while comment on it and have fun.

It was the best way to still keep the anonymity in place while also revealing parts of themselves they'd never shared with no one else. Because at the end of it, what did it matter if they knew the particularities of their living situations, their names, or how the other looked? They knew each other's ideals and deepest thoughts, and that was enough. At least until they switched from comedy to thriller and noir, their discussions going deeper and deeper into human morality and the implications of life-altering decisions. They shared so much of their core selves, that the person behind the screen didn't matter anymore.

Out of loneliness, a routine was born. Along with snacks and drinks of choice. Curiouscat always went for Diet Coke and Cheetos, while Raf opted for a less spicy version, choosing Pirate's Booty but sticking with Diet Coke, too.

They went through at least three or four movies a week, usually saving an hour or two afterwards for an in-depth discussion.

Suddenly, Raf wasn't so alone.

Though his guilt was always there, in the back of his mind,

he finally had someone to ground him—bring him back to earth when his demons were too loud.

It didn't take long for Curiouscat to become his best friend. And though he had no idea, it was the same for her, too.

She had her difficulties, but she always made time for Blue, her faithful friend.

thirty-six
AGE TWENTY-TWO

"That might be my favorite one," Raf mentioned as he leaned back in his seat as the ending credits rolled on.

"Really?" Curiouscat asked.

"Why? Are you surprised I liked it?" he chuckled.

"No. It's just that it's my favorite, too," she mentioned, her voice going down an octave. She'd already watched *The Mummy* before, and she'd suggested it playfully since Raf had been talking about some of his courses in college involving ancient history.

They alternated in choosing the entertainment, and since it had been her turn, she'd gone ahead and rented the movie for them to watch.

Raf just hadn't expected to like it so much, even turning a blind eye at some of the historical inaccuracies.

"Wouldn't it be so much fun to go hunt for treasures like that?" she sighed dreamily. "It sounds so…free."

"It does, doesn't it?" he smiled, imagining such an adventure for them.

"Well, if you liked it so much, don't come at me when I make you rewatch it in a few months," she giggled.

"Why not? I think we only have a short list of movies we like to rewatch. I'm definitely willing to add this to the list."

"I still can't believe this is your favorite, too," she said, almost in awe.

"Now that I think about it, doesn't it always happen this way? Last time you suggested we watched Buffy and now it's my favorite show, too."

"I was so sure you'd hate it," she laughed. "It was my favorite growing up, but the CGI is not the best."

"But the storyline is damn addictive."

"You know, I never expected you to be Team Spike," she added after a moment, sharing a funny gif with Spike from the musical episode.

His lips drew up in a smile, browsing the gifs and sending a few of his own, most of them consisting of Spike mooning after Buffy and being clueless of his feelings.

"Hey, Spike and Buffy *work*. Their feelings grew naturally, and they also had awesome teamwork. Angel was a little off from the beginning," he commented, grabbing a bottle of soda from his desk. He popped the lid off to take a sip before going into a tangent on why Spike was better than Angel in *every* way.

"I know," she gushed. "Who wouldn't want someone to be as obsessed with them as Spike was with Buffy? Even without a soul he loved her."

"Damn, Curiouscat. Don't tell me you've been a closeted romantic all this time?"

They'd been talking steadily for two years now, and in all that time she'd always tried to come across as cynical towards love and relationships, but from her commentaries on different shows, he'd seen there was more to her—a part of her *wanted* that. But for some reason she was afraid to admit it. He wondered if she thought it would make her seem weaker in front of him since he was a guy.

"I have not," she replied vehemently. "I just happen to believe real romance and fictional romance are two different things," she tried to argue in her defense. "Fictional romance is a place of comfort. Real romance? Nonexistent."

"I don't think you've met the right person," he shot back. "Maybe when you do your views will change."

Raf hadn't met the right person either, but somewhere deep in his heart, he was still hopeful. He knew the whole world was against him, his isolation becoming harder and harder to bear as the years went by.

Yet it was times like this—friendships like this—that kept him afloat. And this relationship reminded him that *everything* was possible. After all, there had been a time when he'd been so hopeless, he'd never thought he was going to have a friend, never mind someone like curiouscat. For all their differences in the beginning, she'd become his best friend over the years, helping him overcome his bouts of depression and being there for him when the rest of the world was decidedly *not*.

He'd never crossed the line, though. He might have wondered if it was possible at one point, but he'd never wanted to do anything to make her uncomfortable. He knew how vulnerable women were on the internet, and the last thing he wanted was to come across as a creep.

They'd talked about sex and romance in abstract terms, but their conversations had *never* strayed into uncomfortable territory. There might have been some jokes that could border on innuendo, but they'd both kept their interactions respectful—*fun*.

Though he could see their relationship becoming *more*, he didn't want to ruin what was already working. And by God, if she rejected him, he didn't want to make things awkward as they would undoubtedly be.

"Maybe," she answered noncommittally. "Anyway, you didn't

tell me how your meeting with your advisor went. Did you manage to get his signature?"

His face erupted in a smile.

Curiouscat could be so standoffish sometimes, but she was nothing if not attentive, not one detail escaping him. It was what he valued the most about their friendship. She knew how to listen, and she didn't merely pretend to do so. No, she took notes, making sure to ask for updates and give him her honest opinions on his issues.

He was the same with her, but the exchange was heavily skewed in his favor. She shared facts about herself, certainly more than before. But there was a reluctance to go in depth about her private life that he respected, never pushing for more.

At the same time, he didn't think he was sharing anything out of the ordinary by telling her about his scholarly projects, or the fact that he was in his last year of college and currently writing his senior dissertation.

"Yes, I did. Finally," he groaned.

It had been a battle to get all the approvals for his project, since it involved using the university's archaeological collection.

"I can't wait to read it," she told him honestly—with a hint of excitement, even.

They'd recently finished reading The Plumed Serpent by D. H. Lawrence. Though not entirely pertinent to his study, it had been a fascinating foray into the mysticism of the area. Curiouscat had been particularly taken with it, bringing it up every other day and finding new interpretations for certain passages. She was so enamored with it that Raf had once joked he would gift her a special edition with gilded pages—not that he'd *already* bought it.

"You don't even need to read it anymore," Raf chuckled. "You've heard me talk about it so much you're probably just as much of an expert as I am."

His dissertation was on the ritualistic use of precious stones and minerals in Pre-Columbian Meso-America. He'd had to do plenty of reading on the subject in order to understand the belief system in the area, the pantheon of gods and their respective purposes within the community. It had been particularly fascinating for both of them to find out more about the human sacrifices and ritualistic killings.

It had all started with an anecdote from Raf's reading, but Curiouscat had been so intrigued by the subject that she'd demanded he told her more. And so, he'd started studying with her by his side, sending her some of his reading materials and discussing a lot of the philosophical and anthropological implications with her.

It would be a lie to say his dissertation wasn't a product of *their* discussions. Curiouscat had an inquisitive mind and a great imagination, and she'd offered insights he would not have otherwise explored before.

His major focus was obsidian and its circulation across the region, looking at rituals both as standardized practices and localized ones.

Due to the amount of time he spent with his nose buried in a book on the subject, he'd become more and more narrow in his thinking, which was where Curiouscat helped him, urging him to take a step back and reconsider the wider picture when his tunnel vision was becoming too bad.

"That *is* true," she laughed. "But it's really fascinating stuff. I want to go there someday. See the temples, and the archaeological sites..." she trailed off on a dreamy sigh.

"Me too. We should go together," he threw the idea out there, more as a joke.

"You know what. We *really* should. After you graduate, you should take me on a trip to Mexico and officially introduce me to Aztec culture."

Raf was quiet for a moment. She seemed like she really meant it. He didn't know whether to continue on with a joke, or say something serious, or actually invite her...

He'd saved up enough money to afford it. That wasn't the issue. The issue was that she might not *want* to meet him—might even not like him if he wasn't behind a screen.

It wasn't the first time Raf had been plagued by thoughts like that. He wasn't bad looking by any means, but he didn't see himself as anything out of the ordinary. What if she didn't like what he looked like?

"Blue? You still there? Don't tell me I shocked you?"

"You... You'd like to meet?"

"Sure, why not?" The way she said it sounded like it was no big deal for him.

"Let me get this straight. You want to meet? *Me?*"

"Of course I want to meet *you*, Blue. Who else? But only if you want that, too. I have a family commitment later this year, but I can do it any time before that," she continued, her voice steady and sure.

It...shocked Raf.

"I'd love to," he eventually answered.

"Good. It's about time you took me on a real date," she chuckled.

Raf was still staring at his screen dumbfounded. This was real. It was happening. She actually wanted to meet him... Damn, but he really felt himself become tongue-tied.

"Where are you? I can come to you," he offered.

"You're a gentleman, aren't you?" she drawled in amusement. "I live in upstate New York. What about you?"

He blinked. He couldn't believe he was *that* lucky.

"I'm in the city."

"No shit," she blurted out. "You're serious?"

"Yep. But first, since we're actually doing this, I have to ask something," he winced, since it wasn't something entirely comfortable, but since she'd opened that gate, he needed to make sure.

"Shoot."

"Tell me you're of age. You're at least eighteen, right?" He asked, already on pins and needles as he awaited her answer. If she was younger... Until now he hadn't wanted to entertain that, but if he had confirmation of her age and she *was* a minor, then he couldn't in good conscience continue with their conversations, could he?

His heart beat wildly in his chest. He was dreading the moment to come...

"I'm twenty," she finally said, and he breathed out in relief.

"Thank God," he murmured.

"What was that?"

"Nothing. I'm happy that issue is out of the way," he tried to make light of it.

"Good. Then we could set something up soon. I'll be in the country until the end of the year, so we need to do it before that."

"Why don't you go ahead and set a date and I'll make it happen," he told her, his eyes widening when he realized how eager he sounded.

From the moment she mentioned a potential meeting he'd done his best to keep his excitement under control, but it seemed he was a little too transparent.

She didn't mind it, though.

"Next week? I can do Friday afternoon. We can meet in the city since I have a class there."

This was the first time she'd mentioned any class, but Raf didn't pay too much attention, a little too happy at the turn of events to mind the details.

"There's this café we could go to. It's pretty popular and this way you shouldn't feel uncomfortable," he gave her the details, listing the features of the café and the fact that it had glass windows. You could see everything from outside, and he would take a seat right near the window. All to make sure she was comfortable with the entire set-up.

"You're really sweet, you know that?" she said in an affectionate tone, and he felt heat creep up his cheeks.

"I'll wear a violet shirt so I'm more easily recognizable. I'm pretty tall, though, so you shouldn't miss me," he went on to describe his appearance, giving her the basic details like hair and eye color, build and anything he felt might help her find him easier.

Somehow, he was reluctant to share a picture of himself, though that would be the best option. He didn't photograph that well, and he wanted her to give him a chance in real life. For some reason, he was unusually worried about his appearance and what she'd think of it.

She gave him similar details, telling him she had dark hair and brown eyes and that she was a little shorter than average.

"But really, Blue? Violet?" she chortled. "You really wear violet shirts?"

"I'll have you know they are very nice shirts," he mumbled, though a smile pulled at his lips.

"You and your fancy violet," she laughed. "Why don't you just call it purple and be done with it? It's the same thing."

"It's not," the statement came out harsher than intended, which only made Curiouscat more amused. "There are a *lot* of differences between violet and purple," he said with a huff.

"Sorry I offended your color sensibilities, Blue. Please, enlighten me what those differences are," she made fun of him, but it was all in good humor.

"Have you heard about synesthesia?"

"Huh?"

"It's a condition where your senses are linked together. For me, all my other senses converge into taste. Sounds and colors have flavors for me."

"Wow," she breathed out. "That sounds awesome."

He proceeded to give her a rundown of his *cursed* ability, yet she seemed a little caught on the fact that he could taste sounds.

"So, music has flavors for you?"

"Yep. It depends. Sometimes the notes themselves have a certain flavor and sometimes it's the overall melody," he told her about his mother and the music she'd play for him growing up to test his abilities.

Curiouscat was quiet for a while as she digested the information. He got the distinct feeling that she wanted to ask more about that, but she eventually reined in the conversation back into the familiar zone.

"You didn't tell me the difference between fancy violet and purple."

"It's simple. Purple is man-made by mixing colors together. Violet is natural. It works the same with my tastebuds. There's a counterfeit taste to purple whereas violet has a very pleasant aroma."

"So, it all comes down to your interactions with the color and how it affects you, no?"

"Precisely. You're pretty smart, aren't you," he smiled, complimenting her.

She really got him.

"Oh, I bet I can be smarter. Watch me," she declared smugly as she opened the shared screen again, pulling up the search engine and searching for weird color names.

His eyes widened, but he couldn't help his curiosity as he leaned in, watching her brisk movements as she went from page to page.

"Are you really looking for the rarest color names?"

"Of course. If you can be fancy with your violet, then I can be fancy with my favorite color too."

He smiled, waiting.

The names started trickling in, and some of them were *really* amusing, like *mummy brown* or *dragon's blood*.

"Ok, I got it," she eventually said, moving her cursor to highlight two different colors.

Raf's eyebrows went up in surprise before he broke into a low chuckle.

"You have your fancy violet and I'll have..." she paused as she tried to pronounce the very difficult words, her breath into the mic, as well as the whispers of her failed attempts.

She cleared her throat.

"My favorite color from now on is *Cadmium Quercitron.*"

Both colors were a type of yellow. But he could admire the fact that they were both natural, though only individually, not in the combination she came up with. It was particularly amusing considering *cadmium* was a highly toxic metal. Out of all the colors she could have chosen, she went for a rare tree bark and a noxious substance.

"Good luck remembering that," he laughed.

"Oh, I will. And this is exactly how I'll introduce myself to you on Friday. I'll be Miss *Cadmium Quercitron,*" she added smugly.

"I'll hold you on to that," he challenged playfully, and they both burst out laughing.

The week passed in a blur as both Raf and Curiouscat were looking forward to their eventual meeting.

Raf, for his part, was a little wary of the meeting, scared of not meeting her expectations. He wasn't worried about her, since he didn't mind her appearance. He knew *her* and that was enough for him. Yet his anxiety wouldn't let him be. He had immersed himself into his role for so long, he'd started believing that was all he was—freak, weirdo.

As a result, he went and got a new haircut, improved his grooming, and got some skincare products to make sure he was in top shape. He even bought himself a new pair of jeans and shoes to go with his favorite violet shirt.

And by the time Friday rolled around, he was a mess of nerves and high hopes.

He didn't know what to expect out of the *date*. Though Curiouscat had never brought up romantic notions in their chat, since she used the term date, he expected their relationship to evolve to something of that nature—or, he hoped.

Unfortunately, he couldn't ask anyone for advice since he had no one aside from her. There were his parents, but they were out of discussion. He knew his father would not take him seriously and his mother would likely prohibit him from seeing her since she was just *some* girl.

Throughout the years, she'd told him numerous times her wishes. She wanted him to make an advantageous match with someone from their social circles—likely someone with a similar affiliation as that of his family.

And as she'd told him repeatedly, it didn't matter the fact that he wasn't exactly normal. Not when it was an alliance more than a marriage.

Of course, she disregarded his wishes completely, as he'd told her numerous times that he'd like to have a love match—as Cosima and his father had been fortunate to have. Yet it was a moot point.

He could read the subscript. He wasn't *whole*, he might as well be useful to the family in other ways.

As much as he could, he'd rebelled. His college degree and the fact that he lived on campus attested to that. But he didn't think anything would dissuade his mother from that.

So, he kept his date to himself.

His very first date.

He was excited like the teenager he'd never been. And though he pushed against it, he couldn't stop himself from building scenarios in his head about Curiouscat.

Maybe this was it—what he'd always hoped for. That type of partner that he would get along perfectly with, accepting him with his qualities and his flaws. He couldn't wait to hear her voice—her real voice. He was looking forward to that more than anything.

The moment Friday arrived, he woke up early, showered and put his clothes on.

He'd bought a new cologne specifically for the occasion and he dabbed it around his neck.

Maybe she'd go for a hug. He hoped she would. And then he needed to smell good.

He was worrying about the smallest things, but it was all because he wanted things to go smoothly.

Raf went to the general area where the café was an hour before the set time. He might not have been on a date before, but he knew it was proper etiquette to bring the girl flowers. So, the first thing he did was to search for a flower shop, buying her a pretty bouquet. The next stop was a convenience store where he got her some chocolate, since he knew girls liked chocolate, but he couldn't help himself from adding some hot Cheetos to his basket, since that was a sure way of putting a smile on her face.

Pleased with himself, he paid for the items before going to the café, happy to get one of the window seats as he settled himself nicely on the chair and waited.

And waited.

The hour finally came, yet there was no trace of her—or of

anyone matching her description. As a joke, she'd told him she would be wearing a yellow shirt.

Yet as he looked around, there was no one wearing a yellow shirt inside the café. Only outside did he see a girl wearing one a little further down the street, but she wasn't alone. She was with another man, seemingly arguing as he took her by the shoulder and shoved her into a waiting car. Though he couldn't get a good look at her, he was sure it wasn't curiouscat. The girl looked more like a high schooler than a twenty-year-old.

And so, he switched his attention to the other side of the street. Nothing.

In the beginning, fifteen minutes passed. He still didn't move, thinking she would eventually show up.

Another hour passed. Then another.

Raf didn't move. He was starting to worry, yet he was still hopeful.

Surely, she would come. She wouldn't stand him up, would she?

He waited until night fell and the café closed. Only then did he leave, dejected, making his way back to his dorm room.

His first thought was to log on and message her, still thinking that it was a mistake—surely something must have happened to make her miss the meeting.

But as he clicked on her username, it was to find that the account had been terminated.

What...

Suddenly, Raf realized something was, indeed, wrong. And as his insecurities poked their head to the surface, he was convinced there could only be one reason why she would do that—why she wouldn't come meet him and then delete her entire profile.

She must have seen him through the window. Maybe when he wasn't paying attention. And she must have *really* not liked what she'd seen. So sure he was of his line of thinking, that his heart shrunk in his chest, his entire being shrouded in misery and disappointment.

"Why did I have to ask her to meet me," he whispered to himself later that night.

All his hopes and dreams of normality were dashed that night, together with a deep sense of loneliness that bloomed in his chest, almost as if a piece of his heart had gone missing, vanishing into thin air.

And it had.

This wasn't *just* about someone rejecting him based on his looks. This wasn't just one date gone wrong. This was his *friend*. His *best* friend.

He feared he'd lost her forever.

Days passed. Raf kept trying to get in touch with her. Yet it was to no avail.

Curiouscat was gone. Forever.

And Raf lost his only friend.

What he didn't know, though, was that curiouscat had, indeed, showed up for the date. She'd seen him, and she'd been just as excited about meeting him, never once questioning his appearance. She'd watched him through the window when he'd not been aware, and she'd thought him *perfect*. She'd seen the flowers, the chocolate, and even the hint of Cheetos packaging and she'd smiled at his thoughtfulness, ready to kiss his cheek at the end of the night, or maybe more.

She'd wanted that date more than anything in the world. And as the time came for her to step towards the cafe, she giddily rushed forward.

But she never made it.

thirty-seven

AGE TWENTY-TWO

A month passed and Raf didn't move on.

Every day, he logged on the server to check his messages, hopeful that *maybe* curiouscat would come back.

It never happened.

If before he'd felt alone, at least his loneliness had been of his own making. He'd isolated from the world because he found it too exhausting to keep up his charade.

Yet before, he hadn't met curiouscat.

He hadn't known someone who could understand him so well without needing to know his name, his past, or how he looked like. Though, retrospectively, what he looked like must have been the thing to put an end to everything.

But now he knew what it was like to have a friend, someone he could share everything in his life with. And because it had been taken away from him so brutally, he found himself drifting in uncharted territories, his emotional stability hanging by a thread.

In fact, was it even fair to call it emotional stability when there was *nothing* stable about it, or about him?

He'd thought he had hit rock bottom before.

But now he knew the true definition of making friends with his demons for he finally let himself go. Yet it wasn't in the typical fashion.

If before he would have simply let himself languish away, burying himself deeper and deeper into himself in an attempt to forget the outside world, this time he did the opposite.

Raf tried to change himself—all within the confines of his circumstances.

He wiped his diet clean, throwing all the junk food to the side in exchange for healthy food. He finally joined his college gym and he pushed himself to his limits.

He may have done a good thing by taking a step towards change, but it wasn't with the best intentions.

Foremost in his mind was the idea that he needed to look a certain way. Maybe then his friend would come back. Maybe then...

Two weeks after Raf joined the gym he collapsed from overworking himself. His diet may have been healthy, but it was sparse and poor, his current energy levels not fit for the harsh exercises he put his body through.

He pushed himself so much, he ended up in the emergency room after fainting at the gym. Only by sheer luck did he wake up just as they loaded him into the ambulance, managing to avoid anyone calling his family.

That day, he was admitted to the hospital where he was administered fluids via IV and he was put into contact with a registered dietician to talk about his food choices.

Yet it was clear to anyone looking in that his issues ran deeper than that. So, his attending physician suggested Raf talk to a therapist, even going so far as booking a first consultation for him.

And as it dawned on him that curiouscat was, indeed, not

coming back, he realized he needed to reevaluate his life. After all, he couldn't continue living like that, could he?

So, he accepted to see the therapist, making small steps towards becoming the *right* type of person, not just a good person on paper.

Weekly, he attended the therapy sessions. He talked into depth about his past, about his parents and about his brother. He opened himself up for the first time, and he was shocked to realize that the therapist had one simple piece of advice.

Forgive yourself.

He wanted Raf to forgive himself for his role in his brother's downfall, but also forgive everyone around him. In his opinion, only then would he be at peace and ready to move on.

Raf saw the objective truth in his therapist's words. But he couldn't put that advice into practice. Not when his self-loathing was stronger than ever.

He may be putting an effort into getting better, but the demons inside his mind wouldn't rest, always whispering things to him and pushing him further into a corner.

So, though he was making progress, he was also stagnating.

Because forgiveness was too out of the question for him.

It was a few weeks later that he finally gave in, going home for the first time in months. In his short identity crisis after curiouscat had disappeared, he'd shut everyone out, refusing to meet his family for fear he wouldn't be able to keep his act up.

And how could he, when inside he felt like he was slowly dying? How could he focus his strength into a stupid act when he was using all his power to stop himself from going crazy—from effectively shutting himself from the world until he slowly withered away.

At his therapist's advice, he agreed to move home temporarily—if only to make sure he wasn't a danger to himself.

In the beginning, when he'd been told that he was exhibiting dangerous signs of self-harm, Raf had laughed that off. Yet the more he thought about it, the more he realized his therapist was right.

One way or another, he *was* self-harming—whether consciously or unconsciously. He was self-sabotaging, and he wasn't going to stop unless he made an active effort to better himself.

"My darling boy," Cosima cried out as he carried his bags inside the house, dumping them on the floor to catch her as she wrapped her arms around him.

His mother was a tall woman, but next to Raf, she looked small and fragile. So much so, in fact, that Raf felt a pang of hurt for the first time in...forever.

She'd committed an awful crime. He was aware of that and rightfully acknowledged it. But she was still his mother, and whether he wanted or not, he loved her.

He'd loved her even as he hated her.

Slowly, his arms came around her bony shoulders, returning the hug.

She'd lost weight. Most probably due to worrying about him all the time.

"I-I'm h-home," he whispered, reveling in her warmth.

It felt years since the last time he'd allowed someone to embrace him—to give him any type of affection.

His eyes misted with tears, and he barely managed to keep them at bay.

"Let's get you set up, shall we?" his mother continued, picking up one of his suitcases and leading him up the stairs.

She did all the talking. He smiled tightly at her, allowing himself one brief moment in which she was just his mother. Not someone he inherently disliked, not someone who'd ruined an innocent person's life.

For one moment, he imagined he was back in the past, when

he'd been ignorant of what happened around him, when he'd taken her love and his ability to return it for granted.

"I have so much to tell you darling. So much has changed and I never got to tell you," she droned on.

He kept an indulgent smile, yet he only internalized her words when she mentioned Antonio.

"W-what?"

"Antonio is dead. Some hussy killed him at the convent he was visiting. Can you believe that? She killed him right in the church. Good Lord, I swear I've never heard something like this before."

Raf blinked.

Antonio was...dead?

"And now Franco's in a foul mood, trying to get your father to demand retribution. She's an Agosti, you know. We've never gotten along with them, what with how their son snubbed us with the engagement, years ago. And now his sister killed Antonio? Savages, I tell you..."

Antonio was dead.

Three words and a weight was lifted off his shoulders—one that had been pinning him down to the ground, feeding his nightmares and adding to his constant worry.

He didn't bother to correct his mother when she lamented his death—didn't even try to tell her he probably deserved what he got because she would never admit it.

"So, your father promised he'd help Franco save some face. God knows, we need that after they've dirtied our name through the mud..."

She didn't get to finish her sentence, though, as she lost her balance, her hand shooting out as she caught Raf's arm.

"Mom?" he asked on a whisper.

"I'm ok, darling. Just a little spell," she strained a smile.

But it wasn't just a little spell. Not with how she was behaving, breathing harshly, getting tired every few minutes and needing to sit down.

"You'll come with us, right? To the banquet? We need to show a strong front. Especially in times like this. Beni even convinced that good for nothing of your brother to come," she grumbled under her breath.

Raf wasn't sure he was up to face his brother, not so soon after he'd taken such a powerful hit to his heart. Yet he was also worried about his mother. She didn't seem well. So, to please her, he nodded his assent, promising to join the family for the banquet at the end of the week.

Unbeknownst to him, Benedicto and Cosima had another purpose in mind for the banquet. With the famiglia adding more and more pressure on Benedicto to choose an official heir, the majority of the influential men being on Michele's side rather than Raf's, Benedicto had decided to pull the big guns.

He would use the banquet as an opportunity to show how volatile Michele was while also paving the way for an alliance for his son.

The only way Raf would be accepted as the heir would be if he brought something to the table, and a marriage to a girl from another well-regarded Italian family might just be what they needed. And the banquet was just the way to pave such a connection.

As the time for the banquet arrived, Raf tried his best to stay under the radar. His brother's presence was wreaking havoc on his peace of mind, and instinctively he tried to put himself into a worse light, making himself smaller, more insignificant.

Especially as Michele, as inebriated as always, yelled for everyone to hear what a retard he was.

Though the evening passed without incident, Raf could see that his parents planned something, especially when they approached Marcello Lastra with an offer to merge their two families.

One of his sisters had decided monastic life wasn't for her and she'd returned to civilian life. The downside was that in Benedicto's eyes, her past made her the perfect candidate.

He saw her as meek and biddable—traditional. Exactly what he needed to put Raf ahead in the running for the family legacy.

Raf, on his part, did his best to dissuade his parents from it. But it all came crashing down a few days after the banquet, when Cosima's little spell turned into a trip to the hospital.

The entire situation was grim, especially as the doctor suggested she had an onset of diabetes, likely caused by high stress.

Raf was shocked.

His mother tried to be cheerful about it, saying it was all going to be alright. Yet for Raf it was the last blow he needed at that moment.

If there was something he hadn't blamed himself until that moment, it had been his mother's health. And as he heard the dire news, he couldn't help but feel as if he'd contributed to it—that he'd been the source of that stress and the reason she was now in the hospital, getting ready to make life-altering changes for her health.

Maybe he'd realized it before, but at that point it was the first time Raf realized his self-harm tendencies were not, in fact, only directed at himself. They were making ravages all around himself, affecting every person around him.

And he wasn't sure he liked that.

"Will you do something for me, darling?" Cosima asked him a few days later, back at home. She was still weak and prone to some fainting spells, and he faithfully stayed by her side, not wanting to cause her more stress.

"W-what?"

"Will you at least meet the girl? You don't have to marry her if you don't like her. But will you? For me?"

Her features were grim, her slight body huddled against him as she released a weary sigh.

He was quiet for a moment, warring with himself. He wanted no part in their plans, yet at the same time, what could go wrong in one meeting? He would satisfy his mother and maybe then she'd stop pestering him about marriage meetings.

"F-Fine."

Not two days later and the first meeting was set. After all, the devil worked fast, but Cosima worked faster.

And so, they found themselves at the Lastra home, where Raf had the unexpected pleasure of meeting Assisi—or just Sisi.

Sisi was, simply put, unusual. She was unlike anyone he'd ever met in their circles. She lacked the artifice and the malice he was used to. And though he was still wary of sharing too much of himself during that meeting, he couldn't help but answer her inquisitive questions, doing the bare minimum to keep his façade up.

So much so, that she saw right through him.

His mouth twitched as she called him out for it, telling him she saw his telltale, that his stutter was a conscious decision and that there was a pattern for the way he paused after a syllable.

He was...stunned.

But then she smiled.

"Don't worry. Your secret is safe with me," she winked at him.

In that moment, he decided to gamble. And he gambled *right*.

"Thank you," he whispered, seeing the understanding in her eyes, but more than anything the kindness.

That meeting would only be the first as the two fell into a comfortable friendship.

"Maybe there's still a chance," he told Sisi in an effort to comfort her.

They were sitting in her drawing room. It was where they usually met since her family was pretty strict about decorum. And though they considered Raf innocuous because of his innocent manner, that didn't mean they weren't watching them closely. They were alone, but the door was wide open for anyone to walk in at any point.

"No," she declared confidently. "It's done. It's so done," she shook her head.

She'd recently been through a bad breakup that only Raf knew about, her relationship with one of her brother's friends a secret from everyone else.

"I hate that I have to pretend that everything is fine. That..." a sob escaped her lips, and she immediately looked towards the door, making sure there was no one nearby. "That my heart isn't breaking every time I think about him."

"It will get better with time. I know it will," his lips tightened into the semblance of a smile. He knew exactly what she was going through. But compared to her, his situation seemed paltry. Sisi had been with Vlad in all ways a woman could be with a man—they'd been a couple.

Raf... He'd had an internet friendship that he'd hoped would turn into something else. And he'd ended up being ghosted by his only friend. His wasn't a tragic tale. It was simply a pathetic one.

"Has it happened to you?" she blinked the tears away.

"Something like that," he shrugged, yet with a little coaxing, she managed to get out of him exactly what had happened with curiouscat and how that had affected him.

"I don't know what I did wrong," his voice trembled as he ended his story, too much emotion poured into those words.

"Raf, I'm so sorry," Sisi said. "I didn't know you'd been through something like that, too."

"Yeah, but we've never even met. It sounds so silly," he attempted a smile for her benefit.

"It's not silly at all," she drew back, her features steeped in consternation. "You clearly had feelings for this person. What does it matter if you met or not? You spent years talking. If that's not a relationship, then I don't know what is..."

"It wasn't like that," he lamely argued. And it hadn't been. They had only agreed to try to take their friendship to the next level that time.

Raf couldn't see how much curiouscat's disappearance had affected him, and that his reaction had been anything but normal. Yet in his mind, because they'd never taken that official step, it would always be *just* a friendship.

A doomed friendship.

"So what? Your feelings are still valid," she told him sternly before breaking into a smile. "Look at us. We're a pair of lovesick fools, aren't we?" Sisi breathed out.

Raf could see she was doing her best to rein in her emotions. Her eyes were watery, her nose red from holding her emotions at bay.

"I reckon we are," he agreed hopelessly.

Time passed and their friendship deepened.

It wasn't what he had with curiouscat, but it was a system of support that helped him rebuild himself from the bottom up. And with Sisi by his side, Raf started thriving again.

In a way it helped that their friendship was purely platonic, and that he didn't see her *that* way. He was simply content to have another human being by his side, someone with whom he could share his thoughts and worries.

Slowly, he sought to forget his former best friend.

Like Sisi had said about her Vlad. Maybe it wasn't meant to be.

He told himself that until he truly believed it.

His parents, seeing him hanging out at the Lastra house so much, delighted in the potential connection with Sisi's family. His mother, too, was doing better and Raf was happy he wasn't a burden to her anymore.

Yet things weren't going exactly smoothly.

Not when Sisi came to the grim conclusion that she was pregnant. Out of wedlock. With a traditional Italian family.

So Raf did what any gentleman would. He offered to marry her.

From the beginning, he didn't expect a true marriage, his previous dreams of a *great* love long dead. But he knew they could have a pleasant companionship—friendship. How many people could claim that?

In marrying her, he would both protect Sisi and get his parents off his back—this time permanently. He still had no idea that this was exactly what Benedicto and Cosima wanted, if only to get him elected for the head of the family position. Though he recognized a connection with Lastra would help Guerra, he didn't realize the full ramifications of his decision.

Even so, he was ready to face the consequences.

For the first time, he wanted to man up and be responsible, for himself and his future family. He might not love Sisi, or even feel attracted to her, but that only meant they would have a strictly platonic marriage. It didn't mean he couldn't take his role as husband and father seriously.

His decision made; he could only hope for the best.

Benedicto and Cosima insisted on a quick wedding, wanting to make sure Raf wouldn't back out of it. But both Raf and Sisi were fine with it, since that would ensure Sisi didn't start showing before the wedding.

Yet just as Raf got used to the idea of becoming a father, Sisi miscarried.

She was devastated. He didn't know how to help.

Overnight, she became a completely different person, and though he asked her if she wanted to break the engagement, she remained staunch in her answer.

They would marry.

And so, the wedding day came.

No one besides Raf's parents and Sisi's siblings was happy about it.

Even Raf became increasingly nervous as he stood in front of the altar, waiting for Sisi to walk down the aisle. He kept questioning if he was doing the right thing—if maybe, *maybe*, he was depriving himself of something vital in the future. He didn't believe in divorce. For him, marriage was forever.

He'd always wanted a love match. From the beginning, he'd dreamed of his dream girl—a faceless, formless person who would be his in all ways. He didn't know what she looked like, but when he closed his eyes, he imagined someone like curiouscat.

Funny how he hadn't thought about her in a long time. Yet as Sisi walked towards him all draped in white, a forced smile on her face, he could only think of yellow. Of *Cadmium Quercitron* to his fancy violet.

He tapped his foot restlessly against the floor, sweat beading his forehead.

"Damn it, Raf. Calm down," his father whispered from behind.

He swallowed hard.

He couldn't calm down. Especially as Sisi stopped at his side, a tremulous smile on her lips as she hooked her arm through his.

The priest began talking, the words ringing in his ears,

dimming and dimming until he couldn't follow what was being said anymore.

He couldn't do it.

He couldn't go through it. It was the most disappointing realization, because he would be breaking the trust of his dear friend. Yet he couldn't...

The priest was about to ask the crucial question. And Raf was prepared to refuse.

But the explosion came first.

Then, Sisi vanished.

And Raf had never felt more relief in his life than in that one moment.

thirty-eight

AGE TWENTY-TWO

"Got your bag, bud?" Michele asked as he saw Solomon come out the school entrance.

The boy turned around with a knowing smile, pointing at his backpack.

It was a regular occurrence for Solomon to forget his bag at school. Before, Michele had thought it was because he wanted to leave the school grounds faster, and immediately he'd worried about the worst. After all, he knew from personal experience how much he'd dreaded going to school because of his issues with bullying.

He'd studied the issue in depth, checking the security cameras at school and talking with the staff. All had assured him that there was no bullying going on, and he'd been able to breathe more relieved. Especially after he'd realized Solomon's forgetful nature didn't stem from fear or anxiety, just from a short attention span.

Solomon smiled as he reached Michele's side, extending his hand towards Michele.

"Let's go home, then. I hired a new cook and I'm told he's making your favorite pasta tonight," he winked at the boy.

Not too long ago, Michele had bought his own place, moving out of the gym. It wasn't anything fancy since he didn't require much. But it was enough for him and Solomon since he'd taken the boy to live with him.

He was too sensitive when it came to Solomon's safety, and although he knew Cami loved the boy just as much, he needed to know he was safe and by his side. Besides, Cami could come to the house whenever she wanted since he'd given her a spare key.

When they got home, Solomon went to change his clothes while Michele made a few phone calls for work.

He was Nicolo's right-hand man, and as time went by, his father had initiated him into his main businesses, too.

"I have time this weekend, yes," he told Nico. "Cami will stay with Solomon so I can head off to Philly for the meeting."

"Great, son. I'm counting on you then."

As part of his new responsibilities, he'd been asked to travel out of the city more and more, meeting with potential partners and investors. Although he'd proven himself to his father, he still wasn't allowed to make the important decisions—despite the fact that Nico knew Michele possessed a sharp mind for numbers.

"Talk to you later," Michele added as he felt Solomon's presence behind him. Hanging up, he tucked his phone into his pocket, channeling his attention on the boy.

"Can I watch TV, daddy," Solomon asked, giving him a hesitant smile.

"Of course you can, bud. But not for too long. Dinner will be ready soon," Michele said as he ruffled his hair.

Solomon giggled, running to the living room and throwing himself on the couch as he turned on the TV.

Over the years, Michele had gotten used to the idea that Solomon would likely never be normal—that he might always depend on him. But that was alright. He would care for him forever if he needed to—he was simply his.

After his brother's betrayal, he'd thought his emotions forever damaged, his humanity slipping from him and turning into dust. And it could have, had he not had his people around him. Nico, Cami, Andreas and then Solomon had taught him the meaning of love again, of family and of belonging. Even though he now knew Nico was his real father, his connections with the others showed him that you didn't have to share a drop of blood with someone to cherish and care for them.

More than anything, becoming a father to Solomon had taught him all he needed to know about Benedicto and his abysmal behavior while Michele was growing up.

It wasn't normal. It wasn't Michele's fault—it had never been.

Unconditional love did not have boundaries. It certainly didn't bank on *blood*. It simply existed. From the moment the boy had appeared in his life, Michele had become another person. He'd experienced a flood of emotions and a need to be there for someone—to be Solomon's protector.

Maybe he saw himself in the little guy. Maybe by saving Solomon he was saving himself—the him in the past. But it was undeniable that Michele loved the boy. He loved him as if he were, truly, his son. And so, everything he did, from his act to the outside world to his work with Nico, was for him. To be able to offer *him* everything.

For himself, Michele had never wanted much. Nothing more than comfort. Yet that had shifted over the years as he'd realized that only by having power could he ensure he had comfort, too. More than anything, he needed *power* to punish everyone who'd ever hurt Solomon.

He knew those men were out there. He had a list of their names. Maybe he had no other clues, but even if it took him a lifetime, he would find the bastards and he would punish them as it was fitting for the crime they had committed.

Michele checked in with their new cook who assured him dinner would be served soon. Then, he went back to the living room, plopping himself next to Solomon.

"Can I..." he turned towards Michele, a silly smile on his face. "I want to watch that show," he proceeded to do a poor job of explaining which show he wanted, so Michele simply gave him the remote, telling him to go ahead.

Solomon winked at him, immediately focusing on the TV. Michele couldn't help the chuckle that escaped him.

The boy was so easily pleased. He only needed Michele around and his favorite TV shows and he was all set.

Yet that was exactly what warmed Michele's heart. Solomon had chosen *him* as his protector. From the beginning, the boy had had an affinity for Michele. Maybe he had imprinted on him when he'd saved his life. Or, maybe, deep down he recognized that they alike—that they've been through similar things in life and were both slowly trying to overcome them.

"I have to go on a business trip this weekend, but Cami will come stay with you. That's ok, no? I'll be home next week, and I promised you I'd go to that school competition, so I'll definitely be there," Michele recounted, wanting Solomon to rest assured that he would keep his promises.

Yet the more he spoke, the less Solomon reacted. It wasn't unusual, of course, for him to simply slip in his own world, but that didn't mean Michele worried any less each time it happened.

"Bud? Are you ok?"

He turned, perusing the boy's ashen features. He was frozen to the spot, his body so eerily still, Michele knew immediately that something was wrong—something was very, very wrong.

"Solomon," he slowly reached out, placing his hand on his shoulder as he tried to get his attention.

"No!" he yelled, jumping up.

Michele blinked, worried about what had set him off. In the meanwhile, though, he could only try to assure him he was in a safe place, that no one would hurt him.

Solomon tried to run away from him, his entire body shaking so badly, Michele felt tears stab at the corners of his eyes.

"It's ok," he whispered, bringing him closer and hugging him. "It's ok. No one will hurt you, I promise," he continued to speak, hoping his voice would bring Solomon back from wherever he'd lost himself in his mind.

Solomon continued to yell and attempt to claw his way out, his voice ragged from screaming so much. The fit slowly subsided as sobs racked his body, his screams turning into cries.

Michele felt helpless. He could do nothing but wait for him to escape whatever nightmare was chasing him.

After all, he was all too familiar with the episodes Solomon was having. His manifested slightly different, and only when he was alone, on the verge of falling asleep. The memories caught him when he was most vulnerable, and they held. They grabbed on to him and they held so tightly, he didn't think he would ever be able to escape their hold.

It was why years after what had happened to him, he could barely sleep. And when he did, he was afraid of dreaming—of finding himself back there, in his hell.

"Shh, bud. It's ok. I'm here. I'm not going to let anyone hurt you," he continued to talk in gentle tones, hoping that will soothe him.

It felt like an eternity later that his cries subsided. Only the trembling of his limbs remained, his teeth clattering as the boy seemed unable to catch his breath.

"It's ok. You're safe."

Michele tightened his arms around his small body in an attempt to convey the assurance in his words. Because he *would* do anything to make sure he was safe.

Anything.

Solomon lifted one arm up, pointing towards something—the TV.

For a moment, Michele couldn't understand what he was trying to show him.

On the screen, an interview was playing with one of the most decorated generals as he was talking about military expenses the country would need in the next few years.

Solomon kept his finger up, pointing straight at the man.

It dawned on Michele that he was trying to tell him something.

As careful as possible, Michele removed his phone from his pocket, pulling up the list with the names Solomon had given him over the years.

And there it was.

Vincent. It was on the list, just as it was on TV. Vincent McBride.

"It's him, isn't it?" he asked quietly, not expecting an answer.

Solomon kept his hand up, pointing towards McBride while his expression was one of pure horror.

"Don't worry, bud. I'll make sure he rues the day he was born," he assured him gently.

After Solomon calmed down, they ate in silence. All the while, Michele's mind was quick at work.

McBride was one of the most celebrated men in the country, and due to his position, he always had top security at his beck and call. It wasn't going to be easy to get to him.

But Michele would.

He'd promised Solomon, and he would keep his promise. He

would punish McBride just as he would punish every other name on that list.

With those new developments, Michele found it hard to part with Solomon over the weekend. It was only Cami's assurance that got to him. After all, she was one of the few he trusted.

"You'll call me if anything, right?"

"Sure thing I will, darlin'. Don't you worry, Solomon and I will have the time of our lives together, isn't that so?" she turned to the boy, noting him giggle.

Some tension eased from Michele as he nodded, finally leaving and getting in his car.

As expected, the business meeting he was supposed to conduct was boring. His time was split between his hotel room and the conference room.

Yet just as he was heading into the second day of negotiations, he got a worrying text from Andreas. Putting everything on hold, he excused himself to make a phone call.

"What do you mean Antonio is in New York?" He spat the words, his throat clogged up with revulsion at the thought of his cousin.

"He's not in the city. But my sources are telling me he *is* in the state."

"Find out where he is and what he's doing. As soon as possible."

"Yes, sir."

As he hung up, he felt his limbs turn to jelly, the sensation of helplessness he'd felt in the past washing over him again.

Antonio was prohibited from ever returning to New York. Michele had seen to that, just like he'd made sure to have him under constant surveillance so he wouldn't misbehave again.

Regardless of the fact that Nicolo didn't want to strain the relations with the core Guerra leadership, Michele couldn't just let Antonio roam around freely. Not when he knew what type of predator he was.

And so, he'd had people watching him at all times. If there had been even the slightest hint that Antonio was back to old habits, Michele would have crossed the ocean and put a bullet through the bastard's skull.

What was he doing in New York?

His thoughts flooded with questions, he barely paid attention to the meeting, nodding along and taking some notes just for the sake of it. All he could do was wait for Andreas' call.

What he found out, though, made him reel.

He read Andreas' text again and again, willing for it to be a hallucination. Yet there it was. The true purpose for Antonio's return.

He took a new position at Sacre Coeur.

"Fucking hell," he burst out, not caring how people regarded him. He didn't linger to say goodbye or excuse his behavior. He left the building, jumping in his car and speeding down the street.

He didn't even bother to get his things from his hotel room.

All he could think was Sacre Coeur. The *kids* at Sacre Coeur he'd helped place over the years—kids he personally sponsored.

And now they were in the vicinity of that devil.

Dry laughter escaped him when he thought about the irony of the situation—that the worst type of devil was now on sacred grounds, ready to spread his venom at every turn.

His fingers tightened on the steering wheel, his mind honing only on getting there as fast as he could.

Sacre Coeur was in upstate New York, somewhere around Albany. It was a journey that would take him hours, and in those hours...

His breathing grew labored, his paranoia getting the best of him. Yet he couldn't stop his mind from conjuring the worst scenarios.

"Sir?" he barely realized he'd taken Andreas' call, confusion swimming in his mind.

"Sir, are you there?"

"Yes," he forced the word out of his mouth, his voice groggy.

"Are you ok?"

There was a pause.

Andreas knew some of his past, and he most definitely knew how much Michele hated Antonio for what he'd done to him. Of course he would be worried.

He released a ragged breath.

"Yes. I'm...I'm fine," he exhaled.

It felt like he'd been keeping that breath in for an eternity.

"Don't do something rash. I'm driving to Albany now, too."

"What about Solomon and Cami?"

There weren't many people Michele trusted with the two of them.

"Your father is with them. I checked."

"Did you tell him about Antonio?"

"No. I know you don't want people to know you're still keeping track of him."

"Good... Thank you, Andreas."

"I'll see you there, sir."

The phone call was godsent. It helped Michele ground himself, finding a modicum of calm. He was aware that had been Andreas' objective from the beginning, since he knew how much he would be affected by the news.

With his head a little clearer, he focused on the road, driving fast, yet safe. The impulse to say screw it all and just step on the gas pedal was overwhelming. But he wouldn't be able to help anyone if he was dead.

A few hours passed by the time Michele finally reached

Sacre Coeur. He parked his car a safe distance away before going through the back entrance.

"Signor Guerra." The nun on call recognized him.

"I'm looking for my aunt. Is she here?"

"Mother Superior should still be in her office..."

"I know the way," he raised a hand when he noted she was about to offer to take him there.

"Right, of course."

With a nod, he entered the convent, heading straight for his aunt's office.

Mother Superior was his mother's sister, and she'd taken her vows as a young woman. He'd only reconnected with her late in his teenage years when he'd started to get involved with Sacre Coeur. But it had been a fortuitous event, for having her by his side meant his dealings with the convent could go smoother. She was also the one in charge of all adoptions, Michele's main area of interest.

He just wondered how she would receive Antonio at Sacre Coeur since she'd never been overly fond of the Guerras.

Knocking on the door, he pushed it open, finding his aunt behind her desk and surrounded by a mountain of files. She'd never been one to keep up with technology and she refused to use a computer to back anything up, preferring to keep physical copies in her safe.

"Michele," she rose, a smile on her face. "What brings you here? This is...unexpected."

Not *too* unexpected considering she didn't even own a mobile phone. If he'd wanted to announce his visit beforehand, he would not have been able to, unless he called the central line of the convent.

"Aunt," he strained a brief smile, plopping himself in a chair. "Antonio Guerra. Tell me about him," he jumped straight to the point.

"Father Guerra? That's right, he's your cousin, isn't he?" she nodded pleasantly, probably thinking he was glad about the turn of events.

Oh, but she would have a rude awakening.

"Why is he here?"

"He came highly recommended," she continued. "He's been here for a while already and done a marvelous job with everyone."

He ground his teeth when he heard *a while*. Right, he'd had plenty of opportunity to prey on others.

"Who? Who recommended him?"

"Oh, someone from Italy," she waved her hand, as if it were *that* inconsequential.

"I want him out. Now!"

His tone made her frown, and she blinked in confusion.

"Michele, what's wrong? He's your cousin, isn't he?"

"He may be my cousin, but he's not fit to wear the cloth. He's not fit to be in a house of God, and he certainly isn't fit to be in the presence of children."

"That..." She seemed flabbergasted, but he could tell awareness sunk in. "Those are grave accusations, Michele," she noted sternly.

If in the beginning she'd taken a soft, familiar tone with him, now she was using her Mother Superior demeanor to show him *she* was the authority at Sacre Coeur.

"Let me be clear, aunt. I'm not asking you. I'm not suggesting that you let him go. I'm telling you that you either remove him from the premises, preferably right now, or *I* will."

"Michele!" she jumped out of her seat. "You can't do that. You'll have the whole Vatican on our heads. I told you he comes highly recommended. That's because he's *straight* from the Vatican!"

"Do I look like I give a fuck about the Vatican?" he asked with a straight face.

"M-Michele..."

"Let me put it this way, *auntie*," he smiled, but it never reached his eyes. "You take him out now, and I will leave here civilly, or you refuse, and I will go remove him with my own hands. But," his eye twitched, "it will *not* be in one piece."

"I can't do what you ask of me, Michele. It's above my pay grade. You know there's a hierarchy..."

"I see," he just nodded. "I'll return," he simply stated, standing up and going for the door. "Maybe a few days will allow you to cool your head. Think whether pleasing the Vatican or *me* is more advantageous for this institution."

And he left.

Closing the door behind him, he barely kept himself in check as he exited the premises until he stood in the main graph of the convent.

His insides were on fire as he felt the proximity to that bastard of his cousin, and though he'd put his aunt at ease by insinuating he wouldn't act now, he'd lied.

Of course, he'd lied. He couldn't afford anyone interrupting his plans when he finally reunited with his cousin.

Posing as an interested party, he inquired around for the whereabouts of *Father Guerra*, and a few nuns were nice enough to point him towards the church. Of course, he would be there, Michele smiled to himself. He had to make sure his front as a man of God was solid before putting in motion his nefarious plans.

Michele did not believe for one moment that his arrival at Sacre Coeur was fortuitous. Not when it was a haven for orphaned children—plenty for him to abuse. As soon as his thoughts strayed in that direction, he felt an unusual amount of anger come over him. Already, his hand was on his gun, feeling for the contour of the handle.

He was already familiar with the grounds at Sacre Coeur. For the past few years, he'd made regular visits to ensure the conditions of the children were met according to the funds he supplied monthly. As such, he knew well enough his way around, heading straight for the back of the church.

If Antonio was inside, he wasn't going to give him the advantage of hearing the front door open. No, Michele would go through the back, wanting the element of surprise when he finally confronted the sonofabitch after so many years.

Already, disgust churned in his gut at the thought of seeing him again. But he fought against it. He fought against everything inside of him rebelling at being in such close quarters with the source of his worst nightmares.

His features set in grim concentration, he quietly opened the back door, going towards the altar.

The church was dark, only a few candles strewn around accounted for a modicum of light. Not enough for anyone to properly see inside, and he had to wonder what his cousin was doing here at this hour. After all, it wasn't as if he was a *pious* man.

Careful not to bump into anything on his way towards the main area of the church, he suddenly stopped when he heard a voice.

"It's ok, Claudia. Like we talked before, no?"

He would recognize the vile voice *anywhere*. Hell, he'd been hearing it night after night as he fell asleep for the past eight years.

His breath on his ear, the sound of his voice echoing in his brain, the heat of a body on top of his—that was Michele's nightmare.

"Ok," a soft voice answered. *Too* soft to belong to an adult.

Immediately, he tensed.

Removing the gun from the band of his pants, he assumed his stance as he took a step forward.

He was nestled within the shadows, but soon he had enough of a clear view to be able to point his weapon.

Antonio was in the middle of the aisle next to a young girl, his hand going increasingly higher up her thigh and under her skirt.

Something snapped in Michele at that moment. His finger on the trigger, he was ready to take his aim—regardless of the uncertainty of the shot.

The mere fact that he'd come upon Antonio doing such a thing was enough to make him react. The only reason he didn't fire his shot was because another voice boomed into the church. Belatedly, he realized the doors had opened too, some outside light coming in and showing the monster of Antonio in his full grotesque glory.

"Claudia, go to the room!" The woman shouted. "Now!"

"Mamma..." the child whispered before dashing out of the church.

Michele's hand relaxed a little on the gun, but he didn't change his stance. He was still ready to blow the man's brains if the chance presented itself.

"Catalina, this isn't what it looks like," Antonio was quick to argue. "I was just fixing her dress."

"Fixing her dress? Or her underwear?"

Good, Michele thought. The woman, Catalina, recognized that *Father Guerra* was up to no good. Michele silently cheered her on, especially as she was bravely protecting her child.

Antonio tried his best to convince Catalina that he wasn't doing anything bad, yet she wasn't giving up. She didn't believe any of his excuses.

It all changed within the blink of an eye, though.

From a heated exchange of words, the conversation resorted to violence. Catalina was the first to slap Antonio when he insulted her.

Michele tensed.

He knew Antonio well enough, and he was a proud man. A woman hitting him was not only a physical blow, but one to his ego too.

Sure enough, he was on her in the next second, wrapping his hands around her throat and pushing her towards the altar table.

And as they moved, Michele lost his vantage point. Gun raised, he searched the darkness for a good place to shoot—preferably fast, before Antonio killed the woman.

Yet he might have underestimated her.

Somehow, she grabbed on to a knife from the altar, stabbing Antonio in the neck.

Michele watched, almost entranced, as Antonio stepped back, pulling the knife in an attempt to save himself but only doing more damage as blood flowed and flowed.

He was...dying.

Michele blinked. He wasn't sure of what he was seeing. In that sea of blood, he could only see himself—his young self.

In a flash, everything replayed in his mind. All the abuse and all the degradation he'd withstood at Antonio's hands.

And now? He was dead and he hadn't even suffered.

He was caught in a vortex of feeling, ranging from relief to anger to joy. He couldn't settle on one emotion, not when all of them mingled together into one sole image—Antonio laying in a pool of blood as he took his last breath.

So stunned he was that he lost track of time.

Catalina was freaking out as she tried her best to clean the blood and get rid of the body—an amusing attempt if it had been under other circumstances.

As it stood, Michele felt an overwhelming need to help her,

yet he knew he couldn't remove himself from the shadows—not without opening an even bigger can of worms.

So, he just waited, watching her struggles that were, admittedly, not half bad.

In the end, she managed to wipe all the blood from the floor —or at least to the best of her ability. Then, she had the wonderful idea to stuff Antonio's body in the confessional booth.

A smile played at Michele's mouth at the irony.

There he was, the model of piety, now crucified for his sins.

thirty-nine

AGE TWENTY-TWO

He waited until she left the church before he left his spot, moving carefully towards the confessional.

Michele didn't know why he felt a need to see Antonio's lifeless body with his own eyes. Maybe, deep down, he imagined that was the answer to his debilitating nightmares. Maybe, just maybe, seeing the proof that his tormentor was now forever dead would help him truly move on.

He hoped, even as he knew the truth. Antonio had damaged him beyond repair.

Opening the door, he took in the man's crowded body and the way blood still poured out of his wound.

At the same time, he noted something else.

It was faint, but it was there. A pulse. And the lightest breath.

"Of course," Michele let out a dry laugh. "There's nothing that can kill the devil, is there? Even in the Lord's house."

A pained groan escaped Antonio before his eyes fluttered open. He was barely conscious and would likely not be alive for much longer.

Yet it was enough for Michele to make sure that *he* was the last thing his cousin saw before he went back to the hell he belonged to.

"Miss me, dear cousin?" he leaned closer, murmuring the words so Antonio could hear him. "Don't worry. I'm just here to send you where you belong," he said with a smug smile.

A low hiss erupted in the air as Antonio tried to say something.

Michele didn't mind it, removing a small blade from his pocket and bringing it to Antonio's neck. The first stab wound had nipped the artery, but it hadn't been enough to make him bleed dry. Michele merely facilitated that by enlarging the stab wound.

More blood pooled.

And not a few seconds later, Antonio was dead.

For good.

Yet Michele still didn't leave. An odd melancholy gripped him, and later, as Catalina returned with another girl and a suitcase, he couldn't help but watch the show before him—how two nuns buried the dead body.

He kept to the shadows, yet he took in every detail.

He didn't know why he was so reluctant to leave Antonio even though he'd seen the evidence of his death. Deep down, he wasn't satisfied with how things had played out because he knew how it would all be painted.

Antonio's disappearance wouldn't be taken lightly, and eventually, the two women would be found out. When that happened, they would sanctify Antonio while vilifying the nuns.

He was sure about that, just as he was sure he couldn't let it happen.

Yes, Antonio might be dead. But even in death justice could be served—or, in this case, *more* justice.

He watched the women until they finished burying the suitcase, lighting a cigarette and planning his next move. A low smirk pulled at his mouth.

Oh, he had the perfect plan.

When he exited the convent, Andreas was outside waiting for him.

"You didn't do anything bad, did you?" he asked, his eyes zoning in on the blood on Michele's sleeves.

"Nah," Michele answered dismissively. "But I'm about to do something worse," he smiled.

"Do I want to know?" Andreas winced.

"Probably not. But you'll help me do it anyway."

"Ok, let's hear it then," he sighed, following Michele to his car.

"I need a sweep of Antonio's computer, phone, and any other device he might own."

"A sweep? But..."

"I want anything that might be incriminatory in the slightest."

"But..."

"It seems he was sent to Sacre Coeur by someone high up in the Vatican," Michele explained. "That means he managed to slither his way to the top, or at least had the connections to do so. I need to show the entire world that saintly Antonio wasn't so...saintly."

"Wasn't?" Andreas blinked.

"Oh, I didn't tell you? He's dead."

Andreas opened his mouth to speak but Michele held a hand up.

"And I didn't do it. Believe it or not, a nun was behind everything. I just happened to be around to enjoy the spectacle."

He proceeded to explain to Andreas everything he'd witnessed as well as the plan he'd concocted while the nuns were burying his body.

"That's... Wow. I do believe that will ruin his reputation forever," Andreas nodded, promising to help when the time came.

And so, a day or so later, they found themselves back in the cemetery, digging up the suitcase and absconding with it in the graveyard keeper's shed.

While Andreas stood guard, Michele got creative with what he thought would be a fitting display of Antonio's false piety.

Though the smell was already ghastly, he wasn't deterred. Not even the worms and maggots that had already made their home inside his body could stop him. He just put on a pair of industrial gloves, and he proceeded to cut through the body, rearranging his organs and making sure everything pointed to the rot of his soul.

He might have drawn some inspiration from medieval pictograms he'd studied, but by the end, the finished product exceeded all his expectations.

Especially as he set about decorating the copy of Michelangelo's Pieta that graced the convent's graph with Antonio's remains.

It took some effort, but he managed to arrange the body and its organs in the perfect position—Antonio's corpse in Mary's arms in the ultimate defilement. Or, the ultimate fake idol. Wasn't he one, after all? Hiding behind his cloth and putting on a saintly appearance just to defile the innocent behind closed doors.

Some parts of the body were in worse stages of decompositions than others. His head, in particular, was barely hanging from the neck. The tissue had been eaten away, starting with the puncture wound that had caused his death before moving all around the circumference of the neck. There was only wasting muscle and strained vertebrae that were holding it together.

To a degree, Michele supposed the rest of the tissue would be gone just in time for the show.

"That looks..." Andreas grimaced as he took in their handiwork.

"I know. Just what we needed," Michel said, finally satisfied. Or, he was, once he painted five words on the statue.

I KNOW WHAT YOU DID.

Taking a step back, he nodded appreciatively at the masterpiece he'd put together before pulling his cellphone and snapping a few pictures—capturing *all* angles.

"Do you think that would help?" Andreas inquired as they left the convent.

"Not really. But it will enrage everyone," Michele smirked.

And it did.

Michele made sure to send the pictures to every high official from the Vatican, presenting them with the evidence of Antonio's sins—in the format of a hidden hard drive of child pornography—and as such *their* sins for overlooking what was right under their noses.

By the time the nuns discovered the body, the Vatican was already in uproar.

But the episode didn't end there for Michele. Not when his aunt, suspecting he might have had something to do with it, called Nicolo to let him know of the situation that had arisen at Sacre Coeur.

In turn, Nicolo demanded a meeting with Michele.

As he went to meet his father, Michele was sure there wouldn't be any issue. He'd exacted revenge *his* way, and he was rather proud of what he'd done. Why, his sleep had been so much better. He'd finally managed to keep his eyes closed for almost five hours—in itself, a miracle.

And so, he never expected the slap that landed on his cheek —the second time Nicolo had *ever* laid a hand on him.

"What the hell did you do, Michele?"

"What do you mean?" he drew back, eyes wide with surprise.

"It *was* you," Nicolo spat. "I should have known that chit would have never been capable of it," he said, turning towards his office and rubbing at his temples.

"That chit? Who are you talking about?" Michele narrowed his eyes, stepping fully inside the room.

Nico knew more than he was saying, and Michele's senses were prickling with aggressive awareness. Had he known about Antonio?

"That Agosti woman. Damn it all," Nico swore, kicking at a chair.

"Agosti?"

"Catalina Agosti," he clarified.

"She *did* kill him," Michele explained. "I just finished the job."

Shrugging, he moved aside, leaning against the wall and watching his father closely.

"You shouldn't have gotten involved, son. You should have stayed in your lane."

"And what? Let Antonio take advantage of someone else? You *know* what he was like."

"And that's exactly what I needed," Nico said, once more *not* making sense.

"What you needed? For what?"

"Sit down, will you?" Nico invited him, taking his own seat across from him.

"She's my main asset in drawing out my nephew," Nico started, explaining in depth his plan—for the first time.

Catalina Agosti was Marcello Lastra's weakness. She was also the mother of his child.

"Dad, I don't care *who* that child's father is. She's a child! Innocent!" He couldn't help the way his voice rose as he spoke out.

"Innocent? None of them are innocent," Nico spat, looking more deranged than Michele had ever seen him.

Over the years he'd suspected that his obsession with Marcello Lastra was getting out of hand. Nico blamed him for Liliana's death, and he'd sworn to make him pay for it. It didn't matter that, from what Michele had gathered, Marcello had been only thirteen when she'd died—by suicide. Nico had it in his head that it was Marcello who'd killed her and wanted to return the favor.

"You have to understand, son. I didn't mean for the child to get hurt," he immediately amended. "Antonio was just a pawn to drive a wedge between the two families. And while they are at each other's throats I can jump in," Nico smiled smugly.

Michele kept his quiet. He didn't agree with Nico's actions, and he resented the fact that his father hadn't deigned to tell him Antonio was back in New York—especially when he knew what his cousin meant for Michele.

For a short moment he wondered if he hadn't brought him himself. Yet he didn't dwell on that much. He *couldn't*. He trusted Nico too much to doubt him like that. More than anything, he *knew* him and how thoughtful he was to those around him. Michele didn't think he was capable of putting a child—children—in danger just to advance his obsessive revenge plans.

But Michele also saw only what he *wanted* to see—what he needed for the sake of his own sanity. For too long he'd put Nicolo on a pedestal where he could do no wrong that it was hard for him to regard his father as anything but perfect.

It was a logical flow he wasn't aware of, no matter how much he tried to keep himself objective. He had such deep appreciation and gratitude for everything Nicolo had done for him that he was unable to think negatively about him.

In spite of that, he'd noticed a slight decline in Nicolo's mental health, his obsession growing worse and worse with each passing year.

If Michele were honest with himself, he was scared for his father. He was afraid he was going to do something drastic and then Michele would lose him.

And that... Michele wasn't sure he could withstand that.

The meeting ended up with somewhat of an agreement. Michele agreed not to pursue the Antonio matter further while Nicolo managed to get Michele to agree to help him get Marcello Lastra.

At that time, Michele had no clue what he was signing up for.

It was weeks later that Nicolo called him over again, having a specific mission for him.

"You want me to do what?" Michele blinked, unable to believe his ears.

He'd guessed Nicolo was losing it, but not like *that*.

"Come on, son, it's not that hard."

"I may be putting on an act for everyone, but even *I* don't go there, dad," Michele tried to explain.

He was flabbergasted that his father would ask something like that of him when he knew his past. Hell, Michele was the last person on earth who'd even think of doing something like that.

"I'm not saying to *do* it. Just rip her dress, scare her a little. I need a good show at the banquet and a way to further cause conflict between their family and yours," Nico rolled his eyes, as if *that* wasn't bad at all.

Nicolo had instructed Michele to corner Catalina Agosti, the new wife of Marcello Lastra, and pretend to assault her.

"You just need to play your role as you've done until now. Make a bit of a scandal and pretend you've had too much to drink. You're already an expert at that."

"Yes, but I didn't have to hurt anyone before, least of all someone *innocent*!"

Michele still remembered Catalina from that night at Sacre Coeur and he'd admired her courage and the way she'd defended her child from Antonio. If anything, that alone had earned her his respect. And because of that, he found himself unable to agree with Nico's plan.

"Son, you won't hurt her. You'll just scare her a little. Enough so there can be a show. I've already prepared Franco and he can't wait for his opportunity to publicly accuse her of the murder of his son."

And therein lay another issue. Nico had taken Franco under his wing—how he'd done it, Michele could not understand. But his uncle had been very susceptible to Nico's words and had immediately believed Catalina guilty of murder. Never mind the fact that with Antonio's reputation and *inclinations* anyone could have killed him.

"Dad..." Michele groaned, taking a seat and scrubbing his face.

He hated moments like this. When he was caught between his feelings for his father and his own—albeit barely standing—morals.

He'd never denied Nico anything. But this... He had issues with it.

"Then I'll just have to see that someone else do it. But..." Nico regarded him furtively, knowing just how to spin the tale so Michele would agree, "I can't be sure he'll stop at *just* a scare."

The implication was clear. Either Michele did it himself and stopped at a certain point, or someone else could do it and simply...not stop.

"Just scare her?" he lifted his head, watching his father warily.

"Just scare her."

"Fine," he sighed. "I'll do it."

And he *did* do it. He pretended to be his usual drunkard self, accosting the woman in bathroom, and he did it with his usual façade—emotionless and remorseless.

He didn't linger afterwards.

It didn't matter what the outside world saw. Michele couldn't help but be disgusted with himself for inflicting such damage on an innocent woman.

And so, he returned home.

Cami was in the living room with Solomon, and upon entering the apartment, Michele gave her a quick nod as he hurried to the bathroom to wash himself and remove the stench of alcohol from his body. Yet that wasn't the only thing he sought to remove as he clawed at his skin to erase the memory of Catalina's touch on his skin.

Only after did he return, spending some time with Solomon and Cami and calming down for the first time that evening.

He'd known it would be hard for him to do it given his convictions, but it had been even harder to withstand someone's touch for such a prolonged period.

That night, for the first time in too long, Michele couldn't sleep, his nightmares at their peak.

And he had to wonder just how far he'd go for Nico's sake.

forty

AGE TWENTY-TWO

The more time passed, the more Michele became worried about Nicolo.

His obsession with Marcello Lastra knew no bounds, and Michele could see that his father was heading down the path of no return.

From the beginning he'd taunted the man and tried to attack his family and he feared that Marcello would snap at some point.

He'd tried to approach the subject with Nico, but it had fallen on deaf ears. Even Cami had tried her best to make him see reason.

"It's Liliana," she'd told Michele one day. "It's all because of her."

"But he was just a kid," Michele had argued. Marcello had only been thirteen when his mother had died and unlikely to have had anything to do with her death.

"I think it goes beyond that. He sees Marcello as the starting point. It was because of him that he lost Liliana. Deep down, I think he always wanted him to be his son..."

Michele had nodded, though the statement had hurt him, too. Yet he'd tried not to take it too much to heart. Nico was suffering, it wasn't fair for Michele to add his hurt feelings to the equation.

"Mr. Guerra. Thank you for coming," the guidance counselor said, startling Michele from his thoughts.

"No problem. I told you. Anytime Solomon needs something, you can contact me," he strained a smile.

Solomon was fidgeting by his side, his gaze on the floor.

He was shy with strangers, and he'd only met the guidance counselor a few times before, at registration and at school events.

"I gather Solomon didn't tell you yet, but there's a fundraising event at the school at the end of the month, and we've asked the kids to provide signatures from their parents that they are allowed to attend and participate in the events. They also need to be accompanied by a guardian."

"Solomon hasn't mentioned it," Michele frowned, glancing down at his son.

Solomon was more bashful than usual, which told Michele he felt guilty about not bringing it up.

"He's the only one who hasn't provided a signature and we wanted to inquire if everything is okay and if he wants to participate," the woman explained.

"What do you say, bud? Do you want to go?" Michele asked as he went down on one knee to be on eye level with Solomon.

The boy bit his lip, looking slightly apprehensive.

"Could you excuse us for a moment?"

"Sure, go ahead," the woman nodded, leaving the room and to give them a little privacy.

"Talk to me bud, what's the issue?"

It wasn't the first time Solomon had refused to go to a school event. Michele had never pressured him with anything, always leaving everything up to the boy. But this time he hadn't even mentioned it, and that made Michele think there was more to the story than *just* a signature.

"Do you want to go?"

Solomon shrugged.

He didn't say no, though, and that told Michele everything he needed to know. Solomon *wanted* to go, but there was something holding him back.

"I'll make time and we can go together."

"No," he shook his head. "I..." he trailed off, his big eyes watery.

"What is it?"

"I don't want us to go," he said in a small voice. "The kids... they say you're not my real dad and they'll make fun of me," he whispered, ashamed.

"Solomon," Michele drew back. "You know I *am* your father. It doesn't matter what anyone says. You're my son and I have the papers to prove it."

And he had. After he'd turned eighteen, he'd done everything in his power to make the boy his official son and heir. He would settle for nothing else. Otherwise, why was Michele working so hard to please everyone if not for Solomon?

"But..."

Raising one hand, Solomon touched Michele's face, his little fingers brushing against his pale skin before he pointed to his own, darker one.

"They'll know," he said dejectedly.

"Bud, has anyone said something to you?"

He shrugged again.

"Listen to me. I am your dad, no question about that. If anyone says otherwise, you can just tell them I'm a vampire and can't stay out in the sun," Michele winked at him.

Solomon watched him intently before a wide grin spread across his face.

"Okay, daddy," he let out a low giggle.

"Does that mean we're going?"

He nodded.

"Good, then let's sign those forms and I promise you we'll make a great team."

After they took care of the forms, Michele promised Solomon to get him ice cream. Andreas was already waiting for them at the car and Michele instructed him to take them to a gelato near them.

As the car drew to a halt, Michele's phone rang. Seeing it was one of his father's men, he gave Andreas a nod, urging him to go on with Solomon while he took the call.

"Yes, what is it?"

"Sir," the man swallowed uncomfortably.

"Talk, Luigi. What happened?"

"It's Nicolo. He..."

A deafening sound exploded in his ears.

Dead.

Nicolo was dead.

Luigi continued talking, but Michele only caught a few words here and there. Nico had been trying to lay a trap for Marcello, but he'd been the one to die, instead. Luigi had been on stand-by, waiting for Nico's orders when he'd seen someone carry his dead body to a car before an ambulance had come to get Marcello. Luigi had confirmed Nicolo had been dead when he'd seen him, his body already mangled and destroyed.

"He killed him, sir. He killed him and everyone associated with him," Luigi cried out, grief evident in his voice.

All of Nico's men loved and respected him. All.

And all had died alongside him.

But none had loved him like Michele.

"I see. Thank you for the call," he said before he hung up.

His gaze was distant, his mind blank.

Minutes passed yet he couldn't seem to get a grip on himself. There was a dull ache in his heart, but it was numb—most likely because he couldn't yet believe it was true. He couldn't...

He needed out.

Getting out of the car, he told Andreas to take Solomon home before he took a cab to the gym. He didn't want Cami to hear the news from anyone else.

All the while, he felt he was living in an alternate reality.

Nicolo couldn't be dead. He couldn't...

But he was.

He'd chased his obsession until the very end, and it had gotten him killed.

Michele was in shock. In the back of his cab, images flashed through his head. He remembered how Nico had looked the last time he'd seen him, just the day before.

He'd been fine, and now...he wasn't.

Michele wasn't sure how to feel anymore.

This had never happened before to him. He'd never loved someone only for them to turn up dead, and because of that, he didn't know how to cope.

He didn't know how to deal with the prospect of never seeing him again—not for decades to come, or however much Michele had left until his life ran out. That one thought haunted him like no other.

When he'd opened his heart for other people, he had known the risk of getting hurt. But he hadn't imagined *this* type of hurt. Not for many, many years to come.

For all his faults, Nico was his father—and he'd been a wonderful father at that, too. He'd always cared about Michele, helping him with his trauma and giving him a home to call his own.

Nico hadn't just fathered Michele, he'd *molded* him into who he was today. And it was because of him that he still lived.

Otherwise, he would have long taken his own life. That hit him the hardest, and he felt his throat clog up with so much emotion, his eyes misted with tears.

"Are you okay, sir?" the cab driver asked.

"Yes," he nodded, though his voice came out dry and rough.

He brought his hands to his face, massaging his temples in an attempt to alleviate the pain building there.

Yet he couldn't escape the images. He saw Nico, he saw their times together, all those moments they'd spent bonding and having a good time. He saw those times and he didn't know how he held back his tears.

It took Herculean effort for him to keep himself from breaking down.

Bringing a hand up, he wiped an errant tear from the corner of his eye, steeling himself.

He had to be strong. Now more than ever. He needed to be a man and break the news to Cami. Already, he knew she would take it the worst.

Whereas Michele had known Nico for a little over a decade, Cami had been with him for far longer, dedicating her life to him even though he regarded her only as a friend.

He'd had plenty of conversations with Cami over the years, and he knew exactly how she felt about Nico. She idolized him, yet it wasn't a selfish type of love. It was a constant that only grew stronger with time. She'd never been jealous of any of Nico's flings, knowing that he always returned to her. In turn, Nico had given her his confidence.

Though they'd never been exclusive, Michele didn't think Nico had held another woman in such a high esteem as he had Cami. She wasn't just his lover and friend. She was his partner. Their relationship ran so deep that Michele was afraid to even tell her, knowing she wouldn't take it well.

Hell, *he* wasn't taking it well. But he also didn't know how to cope. His experience with feelings—with *deeper* feelings—was feeble at best. Although he knew how to differentiate them, and he knew he did have them, he had a hard time handling them when they were too strong for him—when they threatened to overwhelm him.

Nico had helped him ground himself when he'd felt his own humanity slipping—that sensitive part of himself that had always sought to look for the best in everyone. And he'd managed. He'd saved Michele and *some* of his former self by teaching him how to detach himself and take everything in stride.

He'd taken those lessons to heart, and he'd thrived. He'd closed his heart to his family and his brother, and he'd managed to move on. But some things just weren't meant to stay closed. As exemplified by the love he bore to the people around him. From *them*, he'd never been able to detach himself.

With Solomon's arrival in his life, he'd had an even harder time *staying* detached. And so, he'd let himself feel. He'd let himself love and he'd let himself care.

And now... It was backfiring.

Because he was feeling everything *too* strongly. So strongly he didn't know if he could deal with what was happening around him.

The cab pulled to a stop in front of the gym, and handing the driver a few notes, Michele got out.

He didn't know how he was going to break the news to Cami, but he had to do it.

Taking a deep breath, he closed his eyes, willing himself *not* to freak out. He'd have time to grieve later. Now, he needed to take care of his responsibilities.

"Michele, what's up," one of Nico's men nodded at him as he entered the gym.

"Cami? Is she here?"

"She should be in Nicolo's office. I think I saw her go there a while back."

"Good. Thanks," he said before heading straight there.

Turning the knob, he was surprised to find the door locked.

"Cami?" He called out, but no one answered.

In that split second he had a gut feeling that something was wrong. He didn't linger in hopes she *would* answer. He simply kicked at the door, time after time until it finally opened.

"Cami?" He asked again, going deeper inside the office but not seeing her.

He breathed out relieved.

She wasn't there. Nothing was wrong.

But that relief was short-lived as he turned, spotting her in the corner—spotting her *lifeless* body in the corner.

A scarf connected from the doorknob was tied around her neck, cutting into her circulation. She was already purple from the lack of oxygen, and Michele wasted no time in getting to his knees and tearing it from her neck—everything in hope he was *not* too late.

But he knew. Deep down, he knew it was too late.

"Cami, don't you dare do this to me," he spoke fast, his voice clogged with emotion.

Gathering her in his arms, he quickly threw his gloves to the ground before placing his bare hands on the column for her neck, brushing them gently over her skin as he looked for a pulse.

Nothing. No pulse. Just...nothing.

Michele blinked, a turmoil unlike any other settling deep into his being as he stared into the face of the woman he'd loved like a mother. A woman who'd taken him in and given him affection when no one else had.

"Cami..." he croaked, opening his mouth to say something else just as his tears fell. Not one, or two, but a deluge of tears that fogged his sight just as his mind was fogged by the veil of despair that had fallen over him.

"Why? Why? Why?" he called out, the tears rolling down his cheeks just as he cradled her body to his chest, hugging her one last time.

He cried and cried, and suddenly, he couldn't keep it all in anymore.

He couldn't stop himself from feeling. Not when he just lost not one, but both his parents.

God, but Michele could still remember the first time he'd met Cami, how she'd made him hot chocolate and tended to his wounds. She'd seen him, and she'd cared for him.

And he...

He didn't know what to do anymore.

Not when his heart—or what was left of it—was breaking into pieces, melting away never to be recovered.

He still waited for it all to be just a bad joke. For Cami to wake up and chastise him gently, as only she could.

"Darlin', stop that."

He could hear her voice. The way she always called him darlin' when no one had ever called him anything other than monster. But to her, he'd been more. So much more. Just like she'd been to him.

No one dared approach the office.

They heard the wails of pain and the cries for mercy, and they knew.

They knew something must have happened.

And so, Michele was left alone with Cami, crying his heart out and mourning the only parents he'd ever known.

He'd thought he could be strong for Nico. He thought he could man up and put a leash on his emotions.

But her? Her, too?

"Why, Cami," he cried out, his voice barely audible from too much screaming. "Why did you leave me, too?"

Even as he asked the question, he knew. She must have found out.

This was exactly what he'd feared when he'd set out to break the news gently to her. He knew how much she'd loved his father. But for her to go this far? *Too* far?

It felt like an eternity until he could move from that spot, and it was only when he spotted an envelope on the table.

Laying Cami gently on the floor, he plodded to the table, lifting the envelope up.

He recognized her cursive immediately, and his eyes flooded with more tears as he carefully opened it, studying its contents.

It was a goodbye letter.

And an apology.

Cami was sorry that she had to leave that way but there was no life for her without Nico. She'd known that at twenty, she knew it at almost fifty. Nico was her whole world, and she wanted to be where he was—regardless of the fact that he was likely going to Liliana.

More emotion burst through the surface as Michele read her words.

How could someone be capable of so much love yet never expect *anything* in return? Because that had been Cami. She'd loved Nico with everything in her, and she'd loved Michele as Nico's son, and later, as her dear friend.

He mourned her loss and wanted to yell at her for leaving him, but as he read her last thoughts before she killed herself, he realized that he could have never stopped her.

Where Nico went, she followed.

She only asked for forgiveness and wished him all the best.

Take care of Solomon for me. I hope he won't

miss me too much, and if he does, tell him I'm sorry. I'm truly, truly sorry Michele. Yet no matter how sorry I am, or how my heart breaks at the thought of leaving you alone, I would never be able to live on knowing he's gone.

He's always been my weakness, and I accept the blame. I am weak. So, so weak. But I've loved one man my entire life. And without him, there is no life.

I know you'll hate me for this. I know you'll blame me and resent me for leaving you alone. You won't understand now, but one day you will.

One day, you'll find someone like that, too. And that day you'll forgive me.

With love,
Cami...

Next to her name, there was another word. One that was scribbled with uncertainty, the many indentations of the pen on paper revealing indecision.

Michele could see why. Because that one word encapsulated everything.

Mom.

She'd signed herself *mom*.

A chasm opened in Michele's heart. There it was. The proof. He *had* lost a mother.

And he'd never be the same again.

forty-one
AGE TWENTY-TWO

The funeral was a few days later. They buried Cami in a beautiful mausoleum. Michele would have liked to place Nico there, too, but they hadn't been able to recover his body. Instead, he'd added a few of his favorite things in Cami's coffin. At least that way she should have something of his even in the afterlife.

All throughout, Michele had been like a zombie. Andreas had been the one to arrange everything, making sure things were perfect for the funeral.

The first couple of days after the funeral Michele was in complete denial, neglecting himself and Solomon, closing himself to the outside world and spending far too much time staring at his bedroom walls.

He only snapped out of it when he heard Solomon's cry of help, darting out of his room only to find the child on the floor, having tripped on a small toy. Michele quickly scooped him up, laying him on the couch to treat his bruise when Solomon asked the inevitable question.

"Is Cami coming?"

"She's not coming. She took a long vacation, and she won't come to see us anymore."

"Why?"

Michele's heart beat in his chest at the speed of a thousand beats per second. He didn't have it in him to tell Solomon the truth. Not when it would break the boy's heart. Solomon loved Cami just as Michele had. But then, who hadn't loved Cami? She'd been the epitome of kindness, always there to help,

"Remember how she used to tell you she wanted to see the Mediterranean?"

Solomon nodded.

Cami had always dreamed of going on a cruise with Nico on the Mediterranean and would often talk about the places she wanted to visit in Italy—Nico's homeland.

"She finally saved up enough money to go there. So, she's taking a very, very long vacation."

"She really wanted to go there," Solomon agreed. "I'm glad she managed it," he finally said, and Michele exhaled in relief.

Maybe at some point he would tell him the truth. But if he were honest with himself, he could barely face it himself. He didn't know how the boy would react. And considering Michele wasn't at his fullest, he didn't trust himself to care for Solomon if the boy also succumbed to grief.

"Great. Then it will be just us for a while. And Andreas."

"Nico?"

"He's with Cami," Michele lied.

Solomon nodded thoughtfully.

"It was time he took her out," he blushed. "Even I could see they liked each other."

"Damn, bud," Michele chuckled. "Good observation skills you have there," he added as he ruffled his hair.

"Bad word, daddy," he giggled.

"Good thing you know so you won't repeat it, right?" Michele winked.

The interaction was enough to add some levity to his mood, and in an effort to forget about everything, he simply dedicated himself to Solomon and his activities.

But that wasn't the only thing that occupied his thoughts.

Soon, as grief morphed into anger, he decided he would do everything in his power to avenge his parents. He'd long promised himself that he would get revenge in Solomon's name. Now he just added a few more people to the list.

Marcello Lastra would pay. He would pay with cash and blood and everything he held dear for daring to take away Michele's father, and as a direct consequence, his adoptive mother.

His conviction only strengthened when he managed to chase away the pain that fogged his mind. He couldn't bring Nico or Cami back. But he would make damn well sure that Lastra would experience the same pain he did.

Nico's teachings were finally getting to him as he saw the world in a whole different cadence. No longer was he concerned with right or wrong. Only with win or lose. And he intended to be *only* on the winning side.

Though in the beginning his first instinct had been to go to Lastra and kill him in cold blood, he couldn't do that. No, death was an easy way out for all the pain Michele was feeling. He needed to return that pain tenfold. Only then would he be satisfied.

And so, he started observing, studying Marcello and his habits, likes and dislikes. He aimed to become an expert in the man so he could thoroughly destroy him—annihilate everything he cared about until he was just a shell of a person ready to pull the trigger on his own damn life.

But he couldn't do that without backing. So, the first order of business was to make sure he had the resources to achieve his plans.

As such, when he wasn't spending time with Solomon, helping him with his schoolwork or just playing, he was concocting ways to take power from Guerra. Now, more than ever it was imperative to do so in order to get some support.

He had Nico's men, but they weren't nearly enough for what he had in mind.

So, he applied himself like never before. While he was scheming to get the Guerra title for himself, he made sure to use his skills with numbers to make the right investments. All in an effort to build an initial capital that he could use to kickstart everything.

It didn't take him long to do that. More than anything, as he busied himself with work, he started to forget his pain, burying it deep within himself. After all, wasn't it better to ignore it than deal with it?

Michele knew that giving in to his anguish would mean the beginning of the end.

His ruthlessness in the business world soon became unparalleled, his only purpose to build capital. His name became synonymous with winning. And a lot of people didn't like that.

But Michele couldn't care less.

His only purpose was to build his fortune, infiltrate the Italian businesses and end Lastra once and for all.

"You're tense," Andreas noted.

Michele sat by his side, tapping his foot restlessly as he stared at the soccer field ahead.

They were both present at Solomon's end of month festivities, cheering on the boy as he got involved in some of the more physically demanding activities—like the friendly game of soccer they were playing now.

"I'm waiting for confirmation from the P.I. I hired."

"You could have asked any one of our men."

"No," Michele shook his head. "I need this as quiet as possible. I'm only using the men for family business, nothing else."

"Are you sure you can trust him, though? McBride is a powerful man."

"I told him what happens if he betrays me," Michele added bitterly.

He'd been juggling too many things at once—Nico's leftover business, his new investments, the investigation into Lastra and now the one into McBride. When he'd decided he was going to make everyone pay, he wasn't kidding. He was going all out.

Yet that also meant he was stretching himself thin.

The moment he'd gotten his hands on Nico's businesses, he'd started the process of revamping everything, finally putting into practice advice Nico had never wanted to hear from him.

While Nico had dedicated himself solely to profit and influence, Michele wanted to do things *slightly* different. He was still gunning for profit and influence, but he also wanted to build a haven for people like him and like Solomon. For *his* people.

"I'm worried about you," Andreas breathed out. "Have you slept more than a couple hours in the last month?"

"You know I can't sleep," was the only thing Michele said as he popped a cigarette in his mouth, taking a deep drag.

"You're going to send yourself to an early grave, sir. I know you're hurting, but you need to take more care of yourself."

"I know, Andreas. I know. I just can't afford it right now. We finally managed to buy the center in the Bronx and that will need remodeling and state-of-the-art technology. There's too much to be done," he stated staunchly. "After this is over, I'll need you to go over the offshore accounts, make sure nothing is a liability."

Andreas nodded.

One of his main objectives had been to build his own clinics and research laboratories. Solomon's condition was foremost in his mind, and though the HIV medication he was taking kept the virus at low levels so it wouldn't be transmissible, thus allowing him to lead a normal life, that wasn't enough for Michele.

He still remembered those days when he'd thought Solomon was going to die because no hospital would admit him due to his lack of documentation. Or the fact that to them he was nothing but another statistic. He was going to take everything in his own hands to ensure that Solomon would never have to face that again—by financing his own health centers.

Though the idea had come to him years before, he'd never been able to implement it—not when Nicolo had been more concerned about the financial side of the transplant ring.

Michele had come up with the best idea to funnel money into the business—medical fraud and stealing from big pharma. But he had never been allowed to transform his *own* idea into reality. Nico hadn't outright rejected it; he'd just said later. Then, years passed and later remained...later.

Now, he'd suspended all operations to the transplant center and had instead focused on his new hospital.

In his mind, he was simply paving the way for his son to have a full and healthy life.

"I have to say how impressed I am, sir," Andreas mentioned. "In such a short time, you've tripled Nicolo's money, and the projection is only going up," he praised quietly.

Andreas been by Michele's side for years now, yet he'd never seen him so focused—so unyielding.

But Nicolo and Cami's deaths had done a number on him.

One moment he was fine, and the next, it was like something had died inside of him, too. There was a harshness to the way he dealt with his business interests and in the short time since he'd gotten involved in that, he'd already gained a hell of a reputation for being ruthless.

He stripped companies of everything in horrendous take-overs.

In Michele's words, business wasn't for the saints.

He spared no one as his tunnel vision dimmed and dimmed, his only purpose destruction.

Though he used an alias in his financial dealings, that name was already synonymous with ruin.

Andreas couldn't help but worry. He knew Michele, for they've always been good friends, sometimes as close as brothers. And he knew exactly how kind and thoughtful he could be. To see him do a one-eighty so suddenly? It was concerning. Too concerning.

"We have the money for the clinic. Lastra and McBride are next," Michele added grimly. "But we can't rush the last two. No matter how much I'd like to. Planning involves time. And I won't make a single mistake. I'll make them pay until they *beg* me to spare them. And I won't," he said with a cruel smile.

Andreas' lips trembled as he returned a feeble smile of his own.

Michele had men currently doing minute reports on both Lastra and McBride, and if he was so cruel with business owners he didn't know, then Andreas had no clue how he would behave with people he loathed.

At the same time, he couldn't begrudge Michele his hate. Not when one man had killed his father while the other had abused his son. He was entitled to his revenge, and Andreas wanted to see justice be served. He just worried that Michele might lose himself along the way.

"We'll need far more than that, Andreas. McBride is a rich and influential man. I doubt I'll be able to get to him unless I mingle in the same circles," his lips flattened in a thin line. "But that's for later. First, money and information. The *next* step is action."

There it was, the rationality of madness. Though the taste of revenge had poisoned Michele, he was still smart enough to act cautiously.

His first instinct was to go for blood, but he'd managed to quell that thirst—for now.

Utter destruction was more than just blood on walls, so much more. It was suffering, anguish, despair. He wanted them to feel everything *he* had felt when he'd heard about his father or when he'd found Cami's still warm body.

He was going to damage them beyond repair, and only then would he kill them—after they begged him to because they couldn't withstand the weight of their sins anymore.

"That's wise. What about the rest of the names?"

Michele grimaced.

"I have a list of alternatives. People from McBride's circle or adjacent to him in any way. But I'm not sure yet, and I don't want to show their faces to Solomon. Not after how he reacted to McBride."

"Maybe the P.I. will have more answers."

"I hope so. If my hunch is right, we're talking about a pedophile ring. And if McBride, a decorated general, is involved, I imagine the rest are equally as influential."

"You can do this, sir. I know you can," Andreas gave him his vote of approval—ever the supportive friend.

"*We* will do this, Andreas. Together," Michele finally smiled, the type of smile that lit his entire face and Andreas found himself blinking, his cheeks heating up.

"Daddy, did you see? I scored," Solomon ran towards them, all flushed and sweaty from the exertion.

"You did, bud! Good job," Michele ruffled his hair. "Are you happy we came, now?"

Solomon nodded fervently.

"It's so much fun. I love it!"

"I didn't know you had such an affinity for soccer," Michele chuckled. "Maybe we can schedule some private lessons for you? Would you like that?"

"Really? Yes, please!" Solomon jumped up and down.

"I'm glad you found something you like doing," Michele said as he took one towel from his bag, beckoning Solomon to him to wipe him down.

"Can we go get ice cream after this?" The boy blinked innocently at Michele.

"Hmm, can we?" Michele asked with a knowing smile as he winked to Andreas.

"Please daddy, please Andreas! Can we?"

"Sure we can, bud. But first, I'll need you to go and say goodbye to your teachers. It's the polite thing to do."

Thinking on that for a second, Solomon nodded, dashing out from his grasp and heading to the field where his teachers were.

"He's gotten so much better in the last few years," Andreas noted quietly. "Sometimes it's hard to imagine he's the same kid you brought home six years ago."

"He has, hasn't he?" Michele nodded. "There's so much more I want to do for him, but I don't know if I can..." he sighed.

"You're doing enough. I'm serious. Biological fathers don't love their kids the way you love Solomon. And he knows it, too. It's why he's blossomed like this. It's *all* because of you."

Michele's gaze was distant.

"He's the reason for which I'm doing *everything*," he finally said.

forty-two

AGE TWENTY-TWO

"I've managed to get a hit on some of McBride's finances. I'm sending you a copy right now. Everything is hush hush with the guy. I may need some more time," Gregory, the P.I. Michele had hired, recounted.

"I'll take a look at that. Continue with your work," Michele told him before hanging up.

Opening his computer, he pulled up the file Gregory had sent.

Just as he was about to read through it, though, the power went out in the entire apartment.

"Damn it," he cursed, getting up and rummaging through his things for his tablet—hopefully that would be charged.

"Daddy," Solomon's voice cut through his focus. "What's wrong?"

"Nothing's wrong, bud. It's just a small blackout, the power should be back soon," he explained, using his phone to light up the hallway as Solomon carefully made his way towards him.

"I don't like the dark."

"You're not alone in that," Michele chuckled. "I'm not particularly fond of it, either."

It was around eight in the afternoon, and Solomon still had time until his curfew. Without power, though, he quickly grew restless.

"Here's what we're going to do. I'll bring some flashlights and we can play a game of chess. What do you think?"

Solomon debated his options, finally relenting. He wasn't the biggest chess fan, but he did love playing with Michele, especially since lately his father had been busier than before. Any opportunity to play with his dad was a golden one for Solomon.

"You take these to the living room and prepare the game. I'll be with you in a second," he instructed as he placed a few flashlights in his arms.

When Solomon was out of earshot, Michele dialed Andreas.

"There's a blackout at the apartment," he started, his voice grave. "I'm looking out the window right now and none of the other buildings seem to be affected. I need you to investigate it and send a few men here, just in case," he said succinctly.

Michele wasn't one to take chances just as he wasn't one to believe in flukes or coincidences. Already, he had a bad feeling in his gut, but he didn't want to worry Solomon too much.

"Yes, sir. I'll do that. I'm downtown so it won't take me too long to get there, either."

"Good. I'll see you in a bit. In the meanwhile, see if you can access any of the lobby feeds. I want to know if someone messed with the wires or something."

"On it."

Once that was taken care of, he painted a smile on his face as he went to Solomon's side. Though he hoped the blackout had no outside interference, he couldn't discount that when he'd made a *lot* of enemies in a very short period.

Already, his brain was quick at work in case something was up. He had a built-in steel vault as a mini panic room for Solomon, and at the slightest indication that danger was looming, he'd take the boy and lock him inside. The vault could only be opened from the inside so Michele was sure no one could penetrate it.

When he stepped inside the room, Solomon had already laid out the pieces for the game and he was excitedly waiting for Michele.

"Let's see what we have here, bud," Michele smiled while taking a seat.

His phone by his side, he kept his eye out for Andreas' messages in case he found something.

They started playing. Solomon's attention was momentarily distracted from the blackout while Michele put on a jovial mask while he continued to be on alert.

> Nothing on cameras.

The text from Andreas was meant to alleviate some of his worries. Instead, his panic increased even more as he heard a sudden sound.

Not one to risk *anything*, particularly Solomon's safety, he put his hands on top of the boy's.

"Listen. I want you to go into the vault, the one I showed you before. I need to check something and make sure it's safe. Do you understand what I'm saying?"

They'd done simulations in the past and Solomon knew not to question him on such issues.

His big brown eyes regarded Michele warily for a second before he nodded.

"Is everything alright, daddy?"

"It will be," Michele assured him, ready to face the world if he had to in order to keep the boy safe.

Placing the flashlight and one of his spare phones in the boy's hands, he opened the vault and ushered him inside.

"You know the drill. You don't open it until I tell you it's safe, ok?"

Solomon nodded.

"I love you, daddy," he said in a small voice.

Michele hated that he had to worry him so much, but he'd take the chance if it meant keeping him safe.

"I love you, too, bud. Hang tight, ok?"

Closing the door to the vault, he waited until he heard a light snap, sign that the vault was sealed.

His expression changed immediately as determination swept over his features. He wasted no time in gathering a few guns and plenty of ammo as well as a bulletproof vest. After so long with Nicolo, he knew how to take care of himself. And considering the shit he'd gotten himself in, he couldn't discount anyone coming for his neck.

Holding tightly on to his gun, he stepped towards the door, placing his ear on its cold surface as he simply listened.

At first there was silence. To the *untrained* ear it was silence. But as he closed his eyes, zoning in on those pertinent noises, he knew instinctively that someone was moving about the stairwell. Based on the pattern of certain sounds, he was sure it was a rehearsed formation.

Professionals.

He knew instinctively he was the target, and if he managed to hold on until his own men arrived, everything should be fine. More than that, knowing Solomon was safe in the vault gave Michele all the confidence he needed.

He wouldn't let some mercenaries come for his life. Not today, and not if he had something to live for.

Quickly shooting a text to Andreas to let him know the situation, he continued to observe.

Holding his breath, he focused once more on the sounds, detecting an increase in frequency. Almost as if his body knew before his mind, he jumped back just in time to get out of the way as the door was bombed to pieces.

Michele rolled on the floor, assuming his stance and aiming his gun at the men quickly entering the apartment.

He gave them no time to act. Though they were all armed up and armored from head to toe, he had the advantage of his slightly hidden spot as he aimed for the first man's head.

One down.

He did the same with the second. And only when he aimed for the third did they realize where he was hiding, a storm of bullets coming his way.

He dodged, throwing himself on the other side of the sofa while he reloaded his gun.

Damn it, but how many were there?

Raising his head, he saw three more men come inside, and he aimed his gun, pulling the trigger for one of them just as *he* pulled the trigger on Michele.

It happened so fast he didn't get to dodge the bullet, nabbing him in his right side.

He winced in pain but didn't let it stop him.

Throwing his empty pistol to the side, he grabbed two automatic guns, both fingers on the triggers as he unleashed a destructive force on the unwelcome visitors.

He didn't care who they were or who had sent them. They were in *his* home and threatening *his* family. That alone ensured them all a swift visit to the grave.

All fell to the ground as he continued to fire. Despite the adrenaline rush, Michele managed to keep his wits about him and notice the red light moving about the room.

"Fuck," he muttered as he flew in the air, the bullet from the sniper hitting him in the shoulder where his vest didn't cover his body. He didn't get to get up as another bullet hit him in the chest—yet again in an area that wasn't covered by the vest.

His breathing grew harsh as blood oozed from his wounds, his movements sluggish, his entire being filled with pain. He coughed some blood, his throat clogged and barely working.

Just a bit more.

He had to withstand it until the others came. Until...

He dragged himself on the floor towards his phone. His mind was growing foggy, his sight even more so. Immediately he knew they must have nicked an artery, or some major vein and he was bleeding profusely. He didn't have long. Maybe a few minutes, tops.

His bloody fingers reached for the phone right as more steps resounded in the hallway.

Before he could do anything, three more men entered the room. Two were wearing full gear while the other was dressed in civilian clothes.

The man barely spared Michele a glance as he headed straight for the back of the apartment.

Michele's eyes grew wide as sudden realization descended upon him.

They... They weren't there for him?

But that wasn't all, was it? They knew exactly where to go—where the vault was.

He opened his mouth to say something—what, he didn't know. But the man's voice resounded first.

"Solomon? I know you're there. Your daddy is hurt and is asking for you," the man said.

All at once, despite the pain—despite *everything*—Michele knew this wasn't random. This was a localized attack with a clear purpose. They must have been on to him for a long time if they had that much information on him and Solomon.

At that moment, Michele could only pray that Solomon wouldn't open the door—that he'd listen to Michele and not open the door to anyone other than him.

He couldn't hear what Solomon replied—if he did at all. But the man did something else that surprised Michele. He used *his* voice.

"It's okay, bud. You can come out."

His mouth trembled as he dragged himself on the ground. Nothing else mattered but getting to his son and making sure he was ok.

"No, no, no," he mumbled, barely able to get the words out.

He dragged his heavy body to the hallway until he had a full view of the vault.

A click sound, and the door opened.

"Where is my daddy?" Solomon asked, sneaking his head out.

The men were by the door, waiting.

"He's right there, why don't you come see him?"

Something wasn't right...

"No," Michele called out, this time the sound a bit louder.

They weren't attacking him. They were just waiting...

Solomon opened the door wider, coming out of the vault.

His gaze was searching about the apartment, ultimately meeting Michele's on the floor.

He tried to shake his head. He tried to move. But he was in too much pain to be able to do either. Michele could only stare at Solomon, watching his precious expression turn sad as he saw his father bleeding on the ground.

Yet it was too late.

The red light, the same one that had hit Michele, was now flickering towards Solomon, moving around his body until one dot settled on his forehead.

"No, bud, no," Michele spoke fervently, yet the words were mere whispers. His eyes watered, his mind rebelling at what he was seeing. He felt the helplessness to his core, the way he could only watch his son but unable to warn him—protect him.

He was his father, damn it. And yet, the most he could do was crawl one more inch, bleed one more drop—all in an attempt to save him.

But it wasn't enough.

"Daddy," Solomon called out that sweet word, taking one step forward before the dot became one hole and he fell.

"NOOOOOOOOOOOOO!"

The sound was wrenched from him, erupting in the air as he witnessed the life go out of Solomon's eyes, his body unmoving on the ground.

It happened in a split of a second.

A second in which his entire world ended.

"Kill him," the man ordered, giving Michele an indifferent look before striding out of the apartment. Yet it was in that moment that his features were forever ingrained in Michele's mind.

There was enemy, and there was foe. There was death and there was inferno. There was a promise, and there was a vow. For Michele, unconsciously, it was all the latter.

One last shot, and Michele's eyes fluttered closed.

The men were out of the building by the time Andreas made it to the apartment, finding a dead Solomon and a Michele that wasn't far behind.

Tears, anguish and a vow of vengeance.

Andreas did everything in his power to ensure that his friend survived.

He didn't.

That night Michele died a second time.

And yet again, he was still alive.

But the world... The world would never be the same.

forty-three

AGE TWENTY-THREE

"The doctor said you can go home at the end of the week," Andreas spoke as he strode into the private salon, dropping the bag of food he'd gotten for Michele on the table.

His boss didn't acknowledge him.

Sitting upright in his bed, he was merely staring at the window, his expression devoid of any feeling.

It had been two months since they'd laid Solomon to the ground. The funeral had been simple, and only a few trusted people had been in attendance.

Fresh after two surgeries, Michele had been brought to the site in a wheelchair, his condition too bad for him to move by himself. Still, that hadn't stopped him from going crazy with grief, rupturing his stitches and requiring an additional surgery to fix the damage.

He'd been inconsolable.

Andreas had never seen a man so stricken by grief before.

Michele had cried and raged, his entire body shaking with the power of his emotions.

Yet that had been the last time he'd displayed *any*.

After Solomon had been buried, Michele had simply...ceased to exist.

He was still alive, thanks to the prompt intervention from the doctors. But his recovery had been a long and hard road since his morale had fallen to the ground.

If he were honest with himself, Andreas had to admit that he didn't know *how* Michele had survived. Not with how his soul seemed to have died with his son.

And now there he was. Quiet. Unfeeling.

His heart ached for him, just like it did for the poor child who'd been killed in cold blood.

But for Michele to be the one to witness it? To see his son murdered and unable to do anything? He knew that must hurt more than anything else.

And so he hadn't pressured Michele. He'd gone at his pace with him, only hoping that someday he'd return to the person he was—though deep down he was aware that was a silly dream.

Michele as he knew him—as *anyone* had known him—was simply gone. In his place now remained someone—*something*—not quite human. At least, devoid of any human feelings.

"I won the bid for the place you wanted. The penthouse," Andreas added, stepping deeper into the room.

Michele grunted.

"Is there anything else I can do?"

"No." The clipped word didn't surprise Andreas. What followed, did. "I'll take care of everything myself."

Michele turned, facing him for the first time.

There was an eerie emptiness inside his eyes, so light and hollow.

"Understood," Andreas nodded.

He could sense that Michele did not care for company, so he quickly reported everything that had happened since the last time they'd spoken before excusing himself.

As Andreas left, closing the door behind him, Michele found himself alone once more.

With slow yet exact movements, he retrieved his wallet from a drawer, opening it and staring at the items inside.

There was a picture. One he'd taken with Solomon on his last birthday when they'd gone to Disneyland. They were both making funny faces for the camera and playing with some of the props available.

Bringing his fingers to the picture, he lightly traced Solomon's features.

Gone. He was gone... His boy was gone.

He stared at the picture for an eternity, as he usually did on most days.

A choked sound escaped him as a lone tear fell down his cheek. Even crying was out of reach for him. He'd cried so much his tears had dried up.

Tragedy after tragedy and he'd cried and cried. Yet now, faced with the biggest hit in his entire life, he found himself strangely empty.

"I'm sorry I couldn't protect you, bud," he whispered. "But I promise you." He took a deep breath. "At the end of the day, no one will be left standing. No one."

Including him.

He was still living not because he *wanted* to, but because in those last few moments when he'd looked into Solomon's eyes, watching him draw his last breath in the world, he'd promised himself and his son that no one would get away unpunished.

As he'd closed his eyes, losing consciousness in the face of his many injuries, his mind had honed in on one thing —vengeance.

He wouldn't die. He *couldn't* die. Not when he had an entire list of people to destroy.

It had been extremely hard to push through his grief and

guilt. And in a way, he hadn't really moved past them. He'd only buried them so deep inside of him they wouldn't be able to affect him—not until he fulfilled his purpose.

He shut down absolutely all types of emotions except for hate. That, he nurtured daily by staring at the picture of his son and by remembering his family—all dead.

Spending so many days in the hospital allowed him some mental clarity, and his next steps were carefully planned.

He would get rid of everyone in his life, assume his position as the Guerra head and hunt down every single bastard who had a hand in the tragedy that was his life.

But he also knew that for him to do that he needed absolutely no distraction—no attachment.

And so, the first step was cutting all ties.

The end of the week came and he got discharged from the hospital. His condition was still precarious, but he couldn't afford to die, so he didn't strain himself.

Instead, he focused on the *passive* ways he could accomplish his plans.

He spent the following weeks building his own trusted network of people before delving deeper in the stock market and hostile take-overs. For what he had in mind he needed capital. He'd already seen he was good at manipulating the stock market and at playing mental games with boards of directors which ultimately brought him immeasurable wealth. So he kept at it, filling his off-shore accounts and setting the foundation of what was to come.

The first step in removing himself as far as he could from his old life came when he summoned his brother for a meeting.

Over the years their meetings had been sparse. Every time Michele saw Rafaelo he was cruelly reminded of his old life—of the him he'd used to be and the abuse he'd withstood. He was reminded of the fact that everyone had failed and abandoned him.

And his brother wasn't any better.

Once upon a time, he'd been the only one Michele had trusted. And that trust had earned him the biggest betrayal of all.

"Why call me here, Michele?" Raf asked as he came inside. He didn't even bother to keep up his act.

"It's time to put everything to rest, Raf," Michele said, bringing a cigarette to his lips and inhaling deeply. His eyes were dead, just like his countenance.

"I don't understand. I did everything so you could have what you wanted. What more do you want?"

Michele avoided meeting his brother's eyes. Despite everything, he still *felt* something for him—to his great shame. But because he still felt something for him, the hurt was much more potent. Suddenly, every bit of pain resurfaced—the way he'd never been able to have one bit of happiness without tragedy getting in the way.

He regarded his brother and he saw everything he wished he could have been or had—love, a family...happiness. The loss of everything was more marked by what he knew his brother had done to him. And yet... Michele had never actively tried to punish him for it.

Why was that?

Why had he turned a blind eye all this time?

He regarded Rafaelo and he suddenly understood.

To be dead was to be liberated. Finally his mind was at peace with everything—with knowing what he must do.

"No. You did *nothing*, Raf," Michele strained a smile. "Here, have a glass. I think it's time we had a long conversation."

Raf looked at him askance—a little hesitant. He was well

within his right to be suspicious, but Rafaelo amazed him as he took a seat, accepting Michele's offering of a glass of whiskey.

"What conversation?" Raf asked in a weary tone.

"You'll see," Michele drawled, bringing his glass up before taking a big gulp.

Raf did the same.

In no time, his eyes became droopy before he slumped in the seat, the drugs in the alcohol having their intended effect. Not a while later, Andreas arrived with a few men to carry an unconscious Raf out of the building and towards his next destination—an auction block.

Michele simply watched, a small voice inside of him rebelling at his actions. But he killed it. Just like he killed any subsequent thought he might have about mercy.

There was no mercy. Not anymore.

"Armand sends his regards," Andreas said a couple days later as he entered Michele's study. He placed a box of limited edition whiskey on the desk.

"Good," Michele nodded. Armand had some influence in Chicago, and Michele wanted to expand his scope as much as he could.

"He wants something," Andreas continued, an unlikely hesitation on his face.

"What?"

"Your brother. He wants the first buy opportunity."

"Why?" Michele frowned.

"I think this is why," Andreas took out his phone, showing Michele a picture of Armand and his wife—his deceased wife who bore a striking similarity to Rafaelo.

"No," Michele said dismissively. "I asked him to be placed on the market for labor—strictly labor."

If Rafaelo looked so much alike Armand's dead wife, then he

only wanted him for one thing and one thing only. Michele might be a monster, but he drew the line at one thing.

He'd lived through that hell and he wouldn't put another through it.

"I want him out of the picture—indefinitely detained," he felt the need to clarify his reasons for sending Raf to the auction block.

"I see. I'll relay the message."

"Make sure he doesn't get him through trickery either." Michele added as Andreas made to leave.

"Of course."

The evening of the auction came and Rafaelo was sold to a factory in the south. Pleased with the outcome, Michele started plotting his next move. One that required a little more effort, and the vetting of his doctor first.

"You're as good as new," the doctor told him after the consultation. "Your injuries have healed unusually well, even the scarring is minimal," he praised as he regarded Michele.

He shrugged his shirt back on, barely hiding his expression of disgust at having foreign hands on his person. Still, it was a necessary step.

"That means I can resume strenuous exercise?" Michele asked, just in case.

"Of course, go ahead."

And that was all the encouragement he needed.

"I have their location. Texted you the details," Andreas told him over the phone.

"Good. Have some people on standby in case things get out of control," Michele instructed before hanging up.

Strapped from head to toe with guns and knives, Michele donned on a black mask before entering the apartment building. Benedicto and Cosima had relocated to the city for a time, and they'd rented an apartment on the Upper West Side. Perfect for

Michele to pay them a visit and then disappear into the night as if he'd never been there in the first place.

As he got to the door of the apartment, Michele knocked.

Benedicto was the one to answer, his eyes bulging in his head as he took on Michele's scary appearance. Before he could give a cry of alarm, though, Michele withdrew a machete, cutting his throat. One hand in his hair, he severed the head, removing it from the body and watching how the blood poured from it.

Nothing. He felt absolutely nothing.

Kicking the body aside, he kept the head in his hand as he stepped deeper in the apartment.

"My love," Cosima called out, coming out of the bedroom wearing just a negligee. The moment she saw Benedicto's head in Michele's hand, she started screaming.

Letting out a tired sigh, Michele pursed his lips before he threw the head at her, hitting her hard in the chest and making her reel back before falling on her ass.

"Wha-what... Beni..." her eyes wide, she regarded the severed head in disbelief. "No... This can't be..."

Michele lifted his mask, wanting her to see it was *him* before he dispatched her, too. But he didn't think he would make it as easy on her as on Benedicto. After all, at least his *father* had been mostly hands off while Michele was growing up, preferring to ignore him. Cosima, on the other hand, had spared no opportunity to make his life a living hell.

"You..." she spat at him, though he could note the terror getting hold of her. Still, he had to give it to her. She was handling this much better than he'd expected.

"Raf... It was you, wasn't it? Did you... did you kill him?" she asked in a low, hurt whisper.

"And if I did?" Michele smiled—the smile of a sick man.

"You're a monster," she choked out.

"Ah, but that's already old news. We established that a long time ago."

"You're here to kill me," she whispered.

"Bingo. Although, I still haven't decided how. You see, I've dreamed about this for so long, I've made up thousands of scenarios. Now? I'm a bit conflicted."

She tried to move away, but he was quick to secure her hands before her back, tying her to the couch as he rose, looking around the place and debating what her death should be.

"Just do it," she cried out. "Just... do it."

"Now, you're awfully impatient, Cosima. Let. Me. Think," he enunciated as if he were speaking with a child.

She scowled at him, throwing a barrage of insults his way that did absolutely nothing but make him laugh.

Just at that moment, a sharp sound erupted in the air. Michele's brows rose in curiosity as he rounded the corner to the kitchen, noticing a pot of water boiling on the stove.

If that wasn't a divine sign, he didn't know what was.

Smiling to himself, he went back to where Cosima was, pulling her to her feet before taking her to the kitchen.

"Before I do the honors," he spoke in her hair. "I want you to die knowing this was *all* your fault. Raf, Benedicto, *everyone*. It was *your* fault."

"I-I... No. I-I didn't..."

"Shh, I don't really care what you have to say in your defense," Michele murmured in her ear. "I only care about the fact that soon you'll be dead, and I will be the last one standing. The last *Guerra* standing. So let that sink in. All your efforts, all that scheming. It was for *nothing*."

He smiled as he felt her panic rise. But it was too late. Her fate was decided, and it was just a matter of seconds now before she met with her husband on the other side.

His fingers buried deep in her scalp, he grabbed her hair at the same time as he pushed her head into the boiling pot of water. She opened her mouth to scream, but that was a big mistake as the steaming water made its way up her sinuses and down her throat.

Her entire face became a mottled mess of red, the skin melting off the bone and clinging to the pot as he pulled her back.

"Damn," he muttered. He'd hoped for a more drawn out death.

He pursed his lips. At least he now knew that boiling someone alive wasn't that good of a method.

There was still a faint pulse, but he suspected she didn't have long—not with the agony he knew she must be feeling at having her entire face burned so badly.

Her mouth was wide open as she tried to inhale some air into her lungs. Unfortunately, her airways were so badly damaged that she was already living on borrowed time.

A sick smile spread over Michele's face as he lowered her to the ground. Using a smaller knife, he made a small incision at the base of her throat, perforating her trachea. Air filled her lungs, buying her a little more time.

But he wasn't satisfied.

Bringing the knife to her front he simply continued cutting into her flesh, making cuts everywhere and enjoying the ways she couldn't even scream in pain. He used her as a canvas for his madness, and the results were far too gratifying.

He didn't know how much time passed before she finally drew her last breath, depriving him of his fun. But alas, he'd accomplished what he'd set out to do and Cosima had met her rather gruesome end—just as he'd wanted.

Humming a soft melody, he rose, gathering Benedicto and Cosima's bodies in one place before throwing some gasoline on top of them and lighting them up like a Christmas tree.

He knew time was of essence now, but he couldn't help lingering a few more moments to enjoy his masterpiece. He even took out his phone, snapping a picture of their burning bodies to save as memento.

Then, he walked out and never looked back, finally putting to rest some of his childhood demons.

Months passed. Michele succumbed to his madness more and more until hardly anything was left of his old persona. Andreas was the only one left to bear witness to the change, and mourn the friend he'd lost.

There was nothing remotely salvageable about the new Michele.

He killed indiscriminately when the mood struck. He ruined businesses on whims. From the outside, he exuded only chaotic energy, his moods dictating how he acted, his paranoia seemingly his *only* quality.

Only Andreas had access to the inside, knowing fully well that despite the unrestrained frenzy that seemed to rule Michele, there was pure genius and unaffected rationality behind it.

But more than anything, there was no more humanity.

That was the most dire consequence of Solomon's passing. He'd died and he'd taken any bit of compassion Michele had felt before.

Andreas hated the way his friend had turned out, but he couldn't blame him. He'd tried to put himself in his position, and he'd had to agree that he might have done the same.

But as Andreas thought Michele had reached the point of no return, he was proven wrong one day.

"It's Armand, sir. He's been calling all day about the restrictions you put on his business."

"Tell him to be thankful he got away with his life intact,"

Michele grumbled from his seat, his eyes on his tablet as he monitored the stock exchange.

"Sure, sir."

Andreas did as ordered, giving Armand one last piece of advice to *not* get on Michele's bad side for that would ultimately end bad for him.

Yet the man didn't listen.

Not an hour after their conversation, Andreas noted Michele's eyes grow wide as he checked his latest email.

"Armand," Michele croaked. "I want his location. Now."

Andreas blinked, unaware of what Michele had seen to prompt such a command. Still, he did as ordered.

As soon as Michele had the confirmed location, he instructed Andreas to join him in his private jet as they went to Chicago on a short business trip.

Andreas didn't know what had happened, but he wagered something had gone terribly wrong in the negotiation stages. Armand was known as a dare-devil, but this time the devil he'd offended was not just a regular one. And Andreas knew Michele had a special type of plan for Armand, otherwise he wouldn't be going to such extremes to see him.

A while later they landed in Chicago, a car waiting to take them straight to Armand's place.

"What are we doing there, sir?" Andreas finally voiced his question.

"I seem to have a score to settle with our friend Armand. One I didn't even know about," Michele narrowed his eyes, his expression thunderous.

Andreas nodded along, afraid to ask more. He could read Michele's moods and this one typically ended up in a massacre.

When they reached Armand's home, they were cleared before going inside.

"Michele! What a pleasant surprise. Are you here to meet

my nice little whore?" Armand chuckled as he came down the stairs to greet them.

There were guards everywhere, stationed at every single entrance.

"Of course, old friend," Michele exclaimed, a fake smile on his face. "I wanted to congratulate you on your wit. You got me there," he laughed as he opened his arms to receive Armand for a hug.

That was the first sign something was wrong. Michele never invited *any* type of touch. To do so meant he had an ulterior purpose and...

They hugged, the steel of a blade glinting ever so slightly in the sun. Andreas immediately blocked the view from Armand's guards.

Head bent low, Michele murmured something inaudible in Armand's ear before twisting the blade, ensuring a quick death. Throwing the body to the ground, both Michele and Andreas withdrew their weapons, firing at the stationed guards and taking everyone out before they could attack them.

When it was all done, Michele popped a cigarette in his mouth, blood staining his pale features as he stared out the window of the massacre.

"Andreas," he finally spoke, and Andreas' ears perked up.

"Yes, sir."

"My brother," Michele started, causing Andreas to frown. "Make sure he ends up with the right buyer this time," he said, simply turning and leaving.

Andreas stared at his retreating back for a moment before everything dawned on him.

Except, this was both his greatest hope and his worst nightmare. He couldn't understand Michele anymore.

Had he done this for his brother? Or had he done this simply because Armand had overstepped his boundaries, ignoring Michele's orders?

The old Michele would have done it for the former. The new Michele? He had killed for less. A blow to his ego of this magnitude was enough to trigger a sea of blood.

Andreas sighed.

His boss was a complicated man. Yet the seed of doubt was already sown. If there was even a sliver of the old Michele buried somewhere under all that unfeeling façade, then maybe not all was lost.

Maybe, just maybe, there was hope.

Or so he thought.

That hope died, too, when Michele callously used and discarded Venezia.

Because that was the moment Michele killed the *last* bit of humanity he had left.

TO BE CONTINUED

Read The Counterfeit Lover here!

Printed in Great Britain
by Amazon